Fake

DRAGONS OF THE CROSSROADS BOOK 1

LORI SALTIS

VAGABOND TALES

Copyright © 2016 by Lori Saltis
ISBN: 9781967542017

Cover art by DAZED Designs

Published by Vagabond Tales.
All Rights Are Reserved.

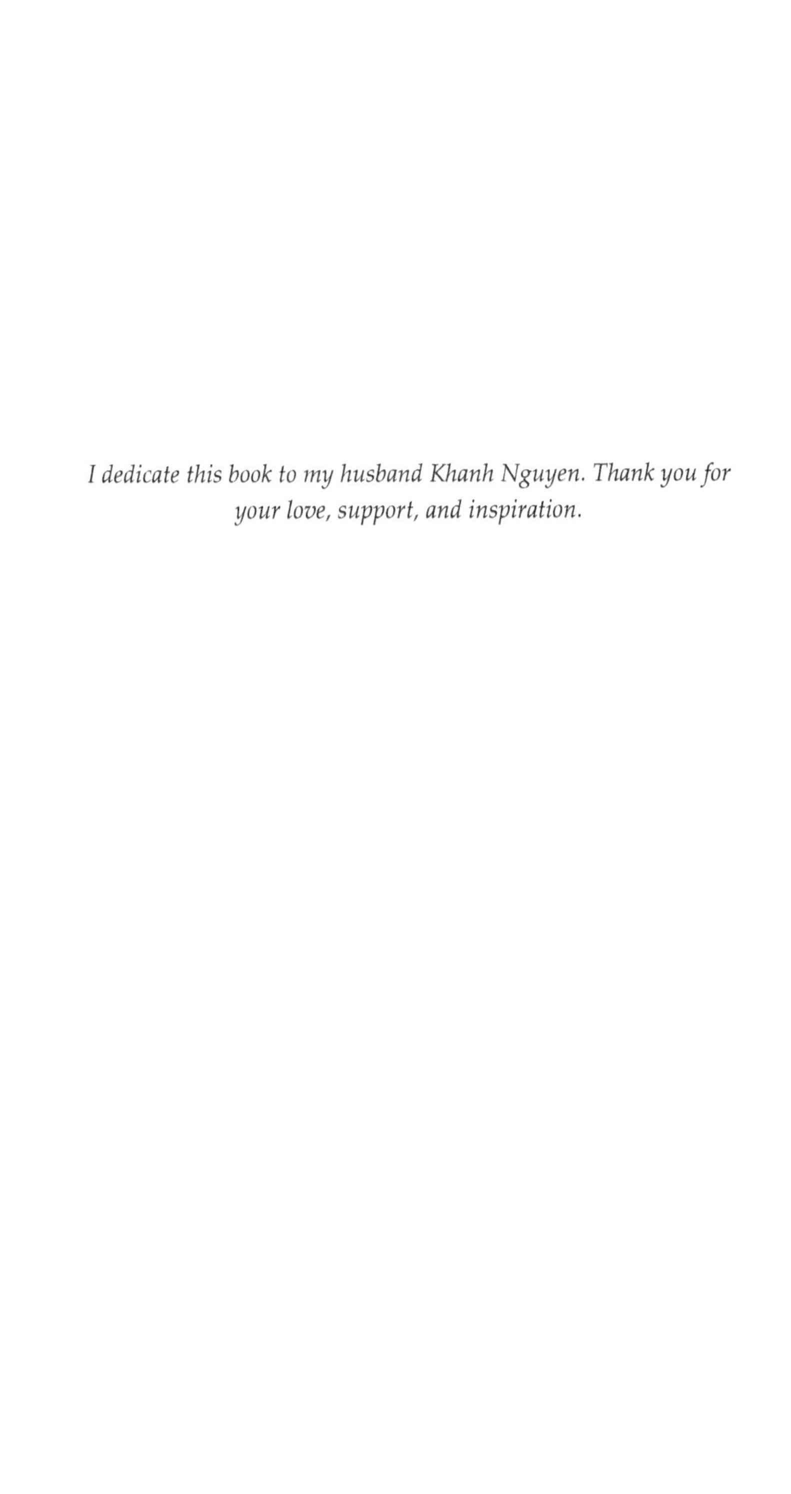

I dedicate this book to my husband Khanh Nguyen. Thank you for your love, support, and inspiration.

Penny

I get to school this morning and there's a pink sticky note on my locker. It reads: *dumbass.*

I rip off the note and stick it to the multicolored wall of insults inside.

retard

drink bleach

go die

You're probably wondering how I got to be so popular. It's because I'm fake.

No, really. I am fake, and it makes me sick and angry enough to punch a hole in the wall, but I don't. I can't, because too much depends on me being a big fat phony. Since I can't be real, I keep to myself. I've tried acting shy, but come off as stuck up. Maybe I am. I don't want to be here and I can't fake that. I didn't try making friends and wound up with none. How can you have friends when you're silent, have attitude, and are considered to be a

fuckin ugly ass ho

That's the first note. It appeared on my locker the day after

Kevin Anderson came up to me during lunch, which went like this:

Me: (munching sandwich and minding my own business).

Arsehole named Kevin Anderson: (waving a tiny liquor bottle in front of my face like he's offering a dog a biscuit) "Hey, Penny. Penny, right? C'mon, let's go to the park."

Me: "Piss off."

Arsehole: "Do you know who I am?"

Me: "Piss off."

Arsehole: (throwing gang signs that look more like spasms) "Bitch. I play football. You're lucky I'm talking to you, bitch."

At first, I thought the notes were from him. Then I traced the giggles and sneers to the Daisy Chain, a crew of girls who are all on the same diet and shop at the same three clothing stores. Apparently, turning down booze being offered by Kevin Anderson is a crime punishable by cowardly acts of malice. There's so little honor in this place. None of them has the mettle to have a go at me alone.

I pull out a binder and see the sticky yellow note at the center of them all:

no one likes you

I know. And that's how I want things. I'm reminded every time I open my locker to keep up my guard and trust no one.

Sitting through class is pure torture, but not because no one likes me. Up until now, I've never been to school. Homework, notes, tests were completely alien to me. I had to figure it out on my own, which made me look a right gom. Letters were sent home stating that, "Parkside Academy is a Center for Educational Excellence!" There are no remedial classes and I needed to catch up or flunk out. My stepfather threatened me with a tutor, which lit a fire under me like nothing else. My grades are somewhat less sucky now.

First period is English Lit with Ms. Chang, who doesn't like me. I don't take it personally because she doesn't like anyone, including herself. She hates to lecture, so we do a lot of in-class reading, which is fine by me. I'm doing well in this class.

Until today.

We finish reading a chapter from *Roots* by Alex Haley, whose ancestors had been slaves. Instead of "surprising" us with the usual pop quiz, she announces, "We all have family. Tell me about yours. You can write about your nationality, ancestors or your family unit. I want a minimum of one page. Two pages for extra credit."

I stare at the blank paper for a long time. If I could, I'd walk out of this place and never come back. Instead, I put pen to paper and write the fake story of my life. Each stroke is like a needle scratching my skin.

My name is Penny Sparrow and I was born in Ireland. I have a younger brother, Kai, who is twelve years old. I don't know much about my father because he left my mother before I was born. The same thing happened with Kai's father. We lived with our mother, Bridie, on our grandparents' farm outside of Dublin. My mother is a singer and musician. She taught guitar and violin lessons to local kids. She met my stepfather, Bill, in a pub. He is an American from San Francisco. They got married and we moved here.

All. Lies.

Well, almost all. The parts that really matter.

The rest of the day is one big slice of misery pie. I don't stick around for after school activities because a) they're shite; b) I'll get picked on and c) I can't fight back.

The reason I can't fight back comes home after work and browbeats my mother over his least favorite subject: me.

"Do you know how much her tuition is setting me back? She needs to knuckle down and stop wasting my money."

Not their money. His money. I'm sixteen years old and I know how bad that sounds.

"She is doing better, darling. She's already finished her homework." Bridie's voice quivers against Bill's bluster.

"Finishing her homework is the bare minimum. She should be studying instead of sewing." He raises his voice on the last word to make sure I can hear him over the whirr of my sewing machine. They're in the hall outside my room. How could I not hear him? "And what about Kai? He can barely read."

"He can read." Bridie's voice falters. "He... he doesn't like to."

"He's flunked all his reading tests."

"I told you, darling, they were homeschooled. They're not used to tests."

"Homeschooled." Bill snorts. "Is that another word for running circles around you and doing what they want?"

I grip the fabric too tight and my sewing machine makes a chewing sound. Bollocks. I'm not going to ruin my new skirt over a bottle-head like Bill. I loosen my hold and straighten the seam to keep the stitches from going crooked.

Kai slips into my room as I come to the end of the hem. He's wearing a plaid flannel shirt and the denim waistcoat I'd made for him, with little pockets for his guitar picks. He plops onto my bed and whispers, "I can read."

"I know," I whisper back.

"Not that Bleater stuff in school. It's too boring."

"I know."

He glances out the door. "Think he'll let us go?"

"I'm going whether he likes it or not."

"Yeah?"

I shrug as if my stomach isn't in knots.

"I need them with me, darling." Bridie's voice sweetens and takes on a subtle, persuasive tone. "It's supposed to be a family show. It'd be nice if you'd come along."

Kai and I exchange grins. Mum is turning on the Charm.

"I don't like bars," Bill grumps.

"It's not a bar. It's a pub. They serve some lovely meals. Remember, you had their chicken pot pie and thought it was delicious."

"I don't know why you have to go at all. You're not even getting paid."

Our grins fade. Bill's pushback has been getting more insistent lately.

Bridie's voice remains cheery. "The tips are good."

"If the INS finds out about those tips…"

"They won't. I'll be getting my green card soon and it won't even matter." I can almost see her teasing tap on his arm. Then she weaves her Charm with honey. "There's a nice beef stew on the stove, cooked up special just for you, and a Newcastle in the fridge. We'll have pudding when I get home."

Bill's chuckle makes me puke in my throat.

"Why don't you come with? Wouldn't you like to watch us perform?"

I hold my breath.

"Of course, but not tonight, I'm tired."

I exhale. You know the Charm is working when the mark believes he's in charge, making the decisions.

Bridie coos, "Long day at work? My poor darling. How about a shoulder rub?"

Bill sighs. "That'd be nice."

Their footsteps echo in the stairwell.

"We're on." Kai bounces off the bed and scampers out of my room.

I close the door, though I want to slam it shut. Slam away the rage I feel at having a mother who won't stand up for herself and insists we live this horrid, fake life. I yank my notebook out of my satchel and write what's real.

My name is Penny Sparrow and I am a Strowler. Strowlers are traveling people. Some call us Gypsies. Others call us worse things, like gyppos and pikeys. We don't have nationalities. If you mean legally, I'm a citizen of Ireland, but I haven't lived there much. We stick to our own kind and don't deal much with Bleaters. That's what we call ordinary people.

Strowlers live on the Crossroads, which is sort of like a secret society of underground clans. On the Crossroads, there are two paths you can take: the Glory Road of righteousness or the Wayward Way of freedom. Things like divorce and being gay are forbidden on the Glory Road, which leads to my family.

My mother, Bridie Sparrow, is thirty-three years old and has been married three times. My father, Gerry Kestrel, was her first husband. Strowlers marry young and they were no exception. She was sixteen. He was seventeen. They ran off to London to make a living as musicians. They woulda-coulda-shoulda — except for one thing: Gerry was gay. He told Bridie right after I was born. Nice timing, Da.

Then they met Matthew Wong, a roving minstrel on the lam from the Two Dragon Clan. Gerry and Matthew became best mates. Bridie and Matthew became something more. They married right before Kai was born.

We all lived in the same caravan, and survived by our music and our wits. It made for a glorious life, forsaking the laws and protection of clan to walk the Wayward Way, until Gerry and Matthew were murdered.

Bridie became a toadeater with all the disgrace shoved down her throat. We lived on the edge of her parents' mercy in the Nest they run outside Dublin. Strowler women shunned her, turning their backs rather than speak or even look at her. At night, their husbands would scratch at the door of our tiny caravan and promise money for services she refused to render. They'd curse her for a whore, regardless.

Bridie wanted a ticket out, something that would restore her dignity. If that meant becoming the trophy wife of a visiting American businessman, so be it.

So be it.

Three horrid words that set in motion our fake lives. I'm not my mother. I won't live a lie for the rest of my life. Somehow, I'm going to get us out of here and back to a place where we can be real.

Paul

"Does it still hurt?" asks Tony.

"No." It itches like crazy, but I can't say that, so I scratch my leg to keep from scratching my chest.

Tony gives a single nod, barely moving his head. Anything more would be unmanly.

Old Fong leans over me, his face hovering just below my chin. Close enough to catch a whiff of stale cigarette breath mixed with dentures. Rank. I want to squirm back in the chair. The vinyl surface sticks to my sweaty skin. Old Fong is too old school to use AC.

He runs his calloused, nicotine-stained fingertips along the edges of the blue dragon tattooed over my heart. "Good. Completely healed. No scabs or scarring."

"When can he begin training again?"

I roll my eyes. Not that I expect Tony to cut me an inch of slack.

"Today." Old Fong bows. "You are the last Dragon Son I shall tattoo."

"I'm not the Dragon Son yet," I mutter.

He speaks over me, "The one who replaces me shall have

the honor of tattooing your son."

Son? I don't even want to think about that. My skin peels off the chair as I slide forward. Neither Tony nor Nicotine Breath moves out of the way. Oh, yeah. I have to give face. I nod my head, just once. "I am honored by this distinction."

Old Fong grunts.

Tony tosses my T-shirt into my lap. "Let's go."

"Where?" I ask before tugging the shirt over my head.

"Head Elder wants to see you."

My shoulders tense up. "What for?"

My cousin frowns down on me. "Head Elder requires you go to him. You don't question his commands."

"Okay, okay." I slide off the chair and follow him outside.

The tattoo studio is located on the second level of the front building in the Two Dragon Clan's compound. There are five buildings altogether, each three-stories high and constructed almost 500 years ago with thick, mud-colored brick walls and black, ceramic-tiled roofs. A massive outer wall connects each structure, making the compound impenetrable for as long as it's been in existence.

The only entrance into the compound is through a gate leading to the interior courtyard of the front building. Back in the day, archers on the second and third levels would've mowed down enemies who breached that gate. Nowadays, the courtyard is used as a parking lot.

My dad's dark blue Mercedes is in its usual spot. This morning, he got a phone call during breakfast and was out the door in half an hour. From what I overheard, he went to Kowloon. No explanation why and I know better than to ask.

"Hurry up," Tony hollers from the stairwell.

I trot after him like a good boy. We go downstairs and across the courtyard. The mid-afternoon sun bakes this part of the compound and the humid air needles my skin, making the tattoo sting. I can't wait to get back to cold, foggy San Francisco, except I'm going to have to find a way to explain why I'm returning from summer vacation a month late and with a dragon tattoo. Maybe I'll say I ran away to Amsterdam and got inked during a rave while floating on a cloud of ecstasy. It's less crazy than the actual reason:

Tradition.

When you live on the Crossroads and walk the Glory Road, tradition is the be-all and end-all of existence. I'm not supposed to question any of it, not even the wacky stuff. Like the tattoo? Five hundred years ago, my ancestor discovered he was a dragon when he turned fifteen.

For. Real.

I guess.

Anyway, that's why all the Two Dragon Clan men get tattooed, but not the women. At this point, I'm not entirely sure if that's unfair or not. I poke at my itchy flesh. "When can I scratch my tattoo?"

"Never," says Tony.

"You never scratch your tattoo?"

He shakes his head.

Ain't he the shit? Always so damn perfect. Always the role model. As my paternal first cousin, he's been the boss of me since I was born, my Big Brother. Hard to believe that will ever change, even after I become the Dragon Son.

Tony stares straight ahead like a guy who kicks ass and takes names. I'm still growing and seriously hope to gain a couple of inches on Big Brother, but I'll never have that square chin or high forehead and deep-set eyes. Tony is the one who got the Lau family looks. I wound up with my mom's wide-set eyes, high-cheekbones and round chin. It makes me look soft, which I hate, but at least Mom doesn't look like her father, Head Elder.

My stomach twists. I whisper, "What do you think Head Elder wants?"

"He probably wants to see your tattoo. See that it was done properly."

See that it was done properly? Kidding? Sometimes, Tony talks like he's ninety instead of nineteen.

"No way. Head Elder knows Old Fong doesn't make mistakes." We reach the archway at the end of the courtyard. Above us loom the rusting spikes of the old Iron Gate, which was meant to drop down and trap the intruders. "Something's going on... maybe something to do with my dad going to Kowloon this morning."

Tony stops and turns to face me. His chest rises and falls before he whispers, "My father."

I suck in air so I don't speak, since talking about his father, my Uncle George, is forbidden.

Something brushes my mind, another consciousness. It feels like a push, not physical, but mental, sort of like the beginning of a headache. I drop my guard, allowing Tony to communicate with me using the Silent Speech.

My father has asked to be reinstated in the clan.

My eyes widen. *No way. That won't happen.*

He's spoken to Head Elder and he might be allowed into the compound for the Summoning Ceremony.

I hesitate. *Do you want to see him?*

No. Pain glints off the steel in his eyes as he looks away. Uncle George is Tony's weak spot. You punch it and he flinches. Something I'll never do, though I can't show sympathy, either. That would hurt even more.

If Head Elder says something, I'll let you know.

Emotion drains from Tony's face as he gives that single nod.

We start walking again, heading across the main courtyard. Where had Tony heard that rumor? Does it matter? I don't believe it. Uncle George has zero chance of rejoining the clan. Head Elder doesn't forgive anybody for anything.

We stop in front of the round moon gate built into the stone wall surrounding the Ancestral Courtyard. Two sentries, one male and one female stand on either side of the gate. Both, like Tony and me, wear the loose black pants and white T-shirts that are standard issue around the compound. I spread my arms and legs wide so the male sentry can pat me down. This time last year, there weren't any guards. Now, everyone gets searched before entering, from the cleaning crew to the Dragon Son, all because of Uncle George. I glance back at my cousin.

Tony's face is a wall of stone. "When Head Elder is done with you, come find me in the west exercise yard."

I stifle a groan. I hate sparring with the sun in my eyes, though I'd rather spend two hours doing that than two minutes with Head Elder. "Change places with me?"

The stone doesn't crack.

"I know what to get you for your next birthday."

An eyebrow lifts. "What?"

"A sense of humor."

Tony's lips twitch before pressing into a line. Sometimes, I can get him to grin, but not today. He juts his chin toward the moon gate.

On the other side, I stop in front of the spirit wall and tuck my shirt into my pants. Head Elder won't notice if I look neat, but he'll sure as shit notice if I look like a slob. The giant dragon carved into the greenish-gray stone surface glowers down at me. When I was a kid, it sorta spooked me. Spirit walls are meant to block the evil dead, who for some reason can't figure out how to move around corners. The kids who lived on the compound had told me this particular wall stays frozen cold, even on the hottest days and touching it means four years' bad luck. Kids tell each other crap like that all the time. I don't believe it anymore, but I still walk a wide path around it. Just in case.

I head across the courtyard toward the original clan

compound, carved into the caverns of Chisel Knife Mountain. Vegetation creeps down the side of the mountain and hangs in tendrils over archways carved into the rock. Colorful, ceramic tile dragons coil up the pillars on either side of the main entrance, symbolically guarding the Ancestral Hall of the Two Dragon Clan. Another, smaller entryway leads to clan head-quarters and the offices of the Elders.

There's no place on Earth like this. At least, no place I know of. My fingers practically itch to draw it, but if I do, I'll be toast. Clan rules forbid anyone, even the Dragon Son, from documenting its existence. As our clan grew, the compound spread out into the walled fortress it became. Bribes to government officials have kept our compound off paper and out of the Hong Kong tour books. The remote location in the northwest border of the New Territories also helps.

If outsiders find out about the caverns, it will ruin every-thing. We'll get tourists and archaeologists clamoring at our gate. That can't be allowed. The secrets of the Two Dragon Clan must never be compromised. Uncle George learned that the hard way.

Inside clan headquarters, I stop and let the cold air chill my damp skin. The caverns maintain a year-round temperature of about sixty degrees. The overhead lights flicker off the white-washed walls as the corridor darkens before brightening again. Electricity and plumbing were installed years ago in this cavern, but has been difficult to maintain. The Elders could have moved their offices into the main compound, but tradi-tion keeps them in place.

As I head down the corridor, I start sweating again. What the hell does Head Elder want with me now? I stop in front of the Dragon Son's office. Maybe I should see Dad first.

"You will obey me."

That sounds like Dad. His loud, muffled voice comes from the office across the hall. Head Elder's office.

Another angry voice speaks. It sounds like Head Elder, but I can't make out what he's saying. Are he and Dad arguing about Uncle George? I lean closer to the door, but their words remain muffled. I step back. Snooping on clan elders is not the action of a *Xia*, a righteous warrior.

"I am the Dragon Son." Dad's shout penetrates the thick wood. "I lead this clan, not you."

I can be righteous some other time. I breathe deep, channeling my internal energy. *Chi* spreads like warm fire through my body. I focus on the voices, listening as they become clearer despite the barrier.

"I will not allow your sin, your dishonor to ruin us," says Head Elder. "I don't care what arrangements you have made with your brother. You will stay silent. Starting tomorrow, you will train Wai Kit to produce the Dragon Shout."

My mouth drops open. What the hell? The Dragon Shout? No way. That training isn't supposed to start until next year.

"No," Dad states. "He's too young."

"He is not too young and you will train him. He must be capable of producing the Dragon Shout by the time of the Summoning Ceremony."

"That's not enough time."

"A week is plenty of time. More than enough."

"Wai Kit is still recovering from his tattoo. The Dragon Shout requires absolute control over one's *chi*. He won't have that by tomorrow."

"No more excuses." There's a pounding sound, like a fist on a table. "You will train Wai Kit to be the next Dragon Son."

"My brother–" Dad starts.

"Your brother will keep silent or pay the price." Head Elder's voice lowers. "I want my grandson fully capable of taking over as Dragon Son by the time of the Summoning Ceremony. During the ceremony, you will present Wai Kit to Jade Dragon as his heir. After that, you can say whatever you want, but I warn you, your sin will condemn the innocent and the guilty. You will be ousted as Dragon Son and replaced by Wai Kit."

My mouth goes bone dry. Replace Dad as the Dragon Son? What is going on? What sin could he have committed? It must be Uncle George. He's done something, committed some new crime, and once again, Dad is trying to save him.

The doorknob twists. Shit! I scurry back as far as I can before the door swings open.

Dad strides into the hall. His face is red and his eyes dark with rage.

I freeze. Do I look as guilty as I feel?

He stares at me for a moment. "Son, what are you doing here?"

I blink a few times before finding my voice. "Um, Head Elder wants to see me."

The anger drains from his face, though his expression remains grim. "Old Fong is finished with you?"

I nod.

"Let's show Head Elder."

I follow Dad into the office. Our feet make no noise on the plush, dark carpet. Head Elder sits behind a large wood desk. There's no clutter on the surface or anything personal, like a framed family photo. No computer, either. I don't think he knows how to use one. He's wearing a suit and tie, like always, even on the hottest days.

My face goes blank. All personality drains out of me so I look like the obedient sprout he expects. Back home in San Francisco, my friends had talked about their grandfathers being great guys or old grumps. I never say anything about Head Elder. "Great guy" doesn't work and "old grump" doesn't begin to cover it. It must have been rough on Mom, growing up with a father like him.

Head Elder stands. Behind his thick-lens glasses, his eyes

narrow in on me like a specimen under a microscope. "Grandson, you are fifteen years old, a man now. Show me the proof."

As I raise my shirt, a chill prickles my skin. Head Elder's lair is probably the coldest room in the whole of the caverns.

He walks around the desk and leans over so I can see the age spots dotting his scalp through his sparse gray hair. I know he's examining the pearl. One of the fringe benefits of being the Dragon Son and his heir is having a different tattoo than the rest of the clan. Our dragon has a pearl inked at its throat. All dragons have pearls containing the essence of their power, which grow in size and strength according to their wisdom and experience. Since Dad and I are Jade Dragon's direct descendants through his first born son, we have access to that pearl. Or so I'm told.

A dry smile cracks Head Elder's lips. "You lack one skill before you can become Jade Dragon's heir."

Jade Dragon. Not my father's heir. Does he think I don't notice? Since I'm that stupid, I'm not going to say shit.

His eyes narrow with annoyance. "The Dragon Shout. You will begin training tomorrow."

I turn to Dad, my mouth gaping open like, *what?* Personally, I think I'm a terrible actor, but they're too busy being pissed off at each other to notice.

Dad's hand moves to my shoulder. "Let's go, Son."

Head Elder frowns, but doesn't try stopping us as we ditch his office. I breathe a little easier once we're outside. I chew my lip to keep from blurting out everything I'd heard.

Dad is silent until we're crossing the courtyard toward the spirit wall. "Tomorrow is a big day. You need to rest."

"I can't. Tony's waiting for me in the west exercise yard."

Dad's face seems to freeze for a moment. "The west?" He gives a strained chuckle. "Your Big Brother isn't easy on you."

I shrug. "No one's easy on me."

"A *Xia's* life is never easy. And the Glory Road is a difficult path to follow. I wish I could spare you."

"Spare me from what?"

Dad glances back at the entrance to the Ancestral Hall and whispers what sounds like, "Everything."

"What?"

He shakes his head. "No exercise for you today. You'll need all your energy for tomorrow."

"Um, okay. I'll go tell Tony."

"I'll come with you." His shoulder brushes the spirit wall.

My stomach lurches. Dad continues on through the moon gate as if nothing has happened. Doesn't he realize? Four years bad luck. But you only believe that if you're a boy, not a man. After all, how can you get bad luck from touching something? Sucking in my breath, I walk past the wall, brushing my hand against the rough surface. Rather than icy, the stone is on the cool side of warm. I exhale. If there's any bad luck, I'll share it with Dad. Then maybe it won't be so bad.

As we stroll across the main courtyard, everyone we pass, men, women and even little kids, bow their heads in respect. They look at Dad with veiled curiosity, probably because he's in a business suit instead of the standard issue workout pants and T-shirt he wears around the compound. He nods back, a lot like Tony's single, manly nod, though not as stiff. His gaze seems calm, but I can tell he's tense by the pinch between his eyes. Maybe I should say something. What? If I admit to snooping, will he tell me what's going on? Hell no. My back will have a date with a bamboo cane. I need to find another way to bring things up.

"Dad?"

"Yes, Son?"

"How come I have to learn the Dragon Shout now instead of next year?"

"Head Elder and I decided to complete your training early."

"But, why?"

The pinch between Dad's eyes deepens. "You don't question our decisions. You obey."

"Yes, sir." I take a hesitant breath. "Can I ask you one more question?"

Dad nods.

"So, Jade Dragon and the first Head Elder, they were cousins, just like me and Tony. Um, so does that mean Head Elder has authority over the Dragon Son, the same way Tony gets to tell me what to do?"

The pinch becomes a ravine. His voice rises, "No. Absolutely not." He takes a breath and speaks in a quieter tone, "Jade Dragon founded the Two Dragon Clan and devised our martial skills. He honored his older cousin by making him Head Elder and allowing the position to be hereditary, but Head Elder does not rule over the Dragon Son."

We continue on in silence, my unspoken question like a wedge between us: why does Head Elder tell you what to do?

Sunlight fills the west exercise yard, reflecting off the brick surface, making me squint. Tony stands in the center. He shifts into a cat stance, bending his knees, sliding his right foot in front of him and lifting the heel. Raising his broadsword above his head, he twists his wrist. A beam of light sparks off the blade. He runs to the east wall, slicing his sword through the air in rapid succession.

Using the Climbing Skill, he bounds up the wall until he reaches the top. He spins around and, sword thrust before him, launches off the edge and flies across the courtyard to the west wall. He lands, balancing on the thick, uneven ledge and jabs his sword at potential enemies on either side of him. Then he leaps off the ledge and spins midair, landing in the center of the courtyard in a drop stance, his left knee bent and his right leg slid to the side, the sword held above his head.

Damn. I've been practicing the Flying Dragon form for months, but I don't have Tony's finesse. No one expects me to, not yet. Not until today. Why does Head Elder want me to be fully trained? Maybe it would be worth being punished to ask. I turn my head.

The tension in Dad's face has disappeared. Pride fills his eyes. He whispers, "Perfect."

I swallow hard. Whenever Dad looks at me, there's always this hint of worry in his eyes, like he's not sure I'll make the grade. Will he ever look at me like he does at Tony, like I'm the pride of the clan instead of a potential loser?

With a big smile, Dad walks across the courtyard. "Well done, Son."

Tony stands and swipes a forearm across his sweaty brow. "Thank you, Uncle."

Gratitude shines in Tony's eyes as Dad pats his shoulder. I dig my toe into a crevice between the stones. If I was nineteen, I'd be that good. Maybe even better.

Standing side-by-side, Dad and Tony look almost identical, like twins born twenty years apart. Which is funny because Dad and Uncle George actually are twins, but fraternal, so they don't look a whole lot alike.

Is that Uncle George's problem? Being the younger brother by two years would be one thing, but by two minutes? Do those minutes torment him, keep him awake at night, thinking about how close he came to being the Dragon Son? I barely know my uncle. The Two Dragon Clan is divided between warriors, craftsmen, and scholars, and Uncle George went the scholar route. As such, he traveled a lot, gathering information, sort of like a noncombatant spy. Whenever he and Dad were together, they'd act all friendly and back-pounding, as if they were best buds. Then Dad would turn away and Uncle

George's face would lock into this narrow, hateful glare. Only for a moment. Not long enough for me to say anything, but enough to send a chill through me, even now.

Dad turns to me. I run to join them. His other hand settles on my shoulder. "I couldn't be prouder of the two of you. I know there have been difficulties." His voice trails off for a moment. I hold my breath. Will he say something about Uncle George? "But we have remained a family, united together. I need the two of you to be loyal to each other, always."

Tony replies immediately, using my Chinese name, "Yes, Uncle. I'll always be loyal to Wai Kit."

"I'll always be loyal to Wai Yi," I reply.

Dad's eyes remain troubled. His hands drop from our shoulders. "Let's go home."

Home, at least for the summer, is the large building on the east side of the compound. Like the west and central buildings, it has an interior courtyard. The ground floor had once been used for storage and livestock. It's been renovated so it's now sort of like a hostel, reserved for visiting clan members. Only families have private rooms and everyone has to share the bathrooms and kitchens. With the Summoning Ceremony only a week away, space is filling up fast. Several families are having their evening meal in the courtyard instead of the gloomy interior. I feel their eyes on us as we head upstairs.

It seems unfair that the entire third level is the living quarters of the Dragon Son and his family, but that's how it's always been. Of course, back in the day, the Dragon Son could have more than one wife. I smirk. Then I think about Dad having another wife and family. That would suck.

Inside, I slip off my sneakers and head down the hall toward the frantic sound of trolls being massacred in the living room. My cousin, Aaron, sits cross-legged on the floor in front of the TV, his thumbs jabbing at the controller buttons as he slaughters his way through a dungeon. Little Brother – that's what I call him. I don't want that to change; don't want him and Tony to get in trouble because their father is causing trouble again. They would have shared in Uncle George's disgrace if Dad hadn't intervened.

Mom sits on the couch with a magazine on her lap. It's kind of funny. She always dresses casual and almost never wears make-up, but she loves reading fashion magazines. I guess they're her guilty pleasure. Maybe she learns stuff from them because on the rare occasions she does dress up, she looks amazing. Better than all the models in those magazines combined.

Her name is Michelle and Dad's name is Michael. I think it's kinda cute. Everyone close to them calls them Chelle and Mike. Well, everyone in San Francisco. They have Chinese names, like we all do, but here in the compound, they're mainly referred to as Dragon Son and Dragon Son's Wife. And, yeah, I'm called Dragon Son's Son. It sounds better in Cantonese.

Mom's wearing workout clothes, so she must have just come from teaching a class on the Swift Step. I frown. She's one of the masters of the art and because of her I'm pretty good at it, too. Thing is, she looks too pale and has got those dark circles under her eyes. She's turning the pages of the magazine too quickly, like she's not really seeing what's on the page.

She nearly died when I was born. Later, she was diagnosed with some kind of heart disease that kept her from having any more kids. She isn't supposed to exert herself too much, but she hates sitting around and loves teaching. Stress is what can really make her ill. I'm sure she knows what's going on between Dad and Head Elder. Is it making her sick? If it is, why don't the two of them cut their shit out?

Aaron glances up at me. He looks like a middle school version of Tony, right down to the critical frown. "Why are you standing there like that?"

Mom jumps up, the magazine falling to the floor. "Have you seen your father?"

I nod toward the hall. "Yeah, he's right behind me."

Dad walks in. "We met in Head Elder's office."

Tony picks up the remote and turns off the TV.

"Hey!" Aaron cries out. Tony's frown silences him.

Mom wipes her hands down her pants. "You saw your grandfather?"

"Yeah. He wanted to see my tattoo." The patch of skin over my heart tingles. I scratch my leg. "He wants Dad to teach me the Dragon Shout, starting tomorrow."

"What?" She turns to Dad, stuttering out her words. "But, but, I thought…"

Dad shakes his head.

Mom gives a short gasp. "No. There's not enough time. He's already missed too much school. I'll tell my father." She brushes past Dad, but before she reaches the doorway, she stops and turns.

My parents stare at each other without talking, not out loud, anyway. In Silent Speech, they're probably shouting.

Tony herds Aaron and me out. We give each other wary glances before heading to our rooms. After closing the door, I flop on my bed and stare at the ceiling. A gecko stares back. It blinks once and goes back to searching for mosquitoes.

I wish I could confide in one of my cousins, but Aaron's only twelve-years-old, and Tony… I heave a long sigh. If I admit to snooping, Big Brother will see it as his duty to report my misconduct. It's weird how Tony, who's such a cop, wound up with a father like Uncle George.

I reach under my pillow and slide out my drawing pad. Uncle George isn't the only one with guilty secrets. This summer, I reread my favorite novel, *Return of the Condor Heroes*. At night, with the door closed, I've been drawing the characters.

I flip through the pages, quickly passing the bad starts and crappy stuff, and lingering on the decent drawings like the one of the giant eagle. I did okay with the feathers, but his beak and claws turned out pretty good. I keep flipping until I get to the hero of the novel, Yang Guo. I drew him with long, scraggly hair, dressed in patches and rags because he's an outcast. He had it rough. Always misunderstood. Never good enough. Never what his elders want him to be. I know how that feels.

I turn the page. A girl dressed in a flowing white robe flies across the paper, a sword in her hand. Little Dragon Girl. Pretty, smart and brave. Just the kind of girl I'd like to date. I snort. Date. Yeah, right. I can only hope my parents keep their word and don't arrange a marriage for me. Though their marriage had been arranged and they turned out okay. They seem to love each other.

Someone knocks. I slam the pad shut and shove it under the pillow. "Yeah?"

Mom leans in. "Your grandfather was pleased with your tattoo?"

"Yeah, I guess." I pause. "Are you okay, Mom?

"Of course." Her brow furrows. "Why?"

I shrug. "Just making sure. You take your medicine every day?"

Her strained smile softens. "Dinner will be ready soon." She closes the door.

I reopen the pad to Little Dragon Girl. If only I can meet someone like her, someone who understands, someone whose family is as messed up and full of secrets as mine. Then I won't feel so alone.

Penny

I take off my jeans and tug on a pair of black bike shorts. Then I slip into my new skirt and twirl, watching the black and green satin shimmer in the bright beam of the study lamp hooked over the top of the desk. Nice lift without showing the goods beneath. I button up a matching satin blouse with gold flowers appliquéd down the front and finish off my costume with white ribbed socks that cover my calves.

There's a tap at the door. Bridie enters. She's wearing a cap-sleeved dress with a fall-colored floral pattern that sets off her curly red hair and bright green eyes. People used to mistake us for sisters. Not anymore. She looks her age and maybe even older. It makes me sad. Does it make her sad? Her smile holds little joy. "Are you ready, darling?"

Darling. I hate it when she calls me that. She never did before we left the Crossroads to plant ourselves among the Bleaters. It reminds me of how fake my life has become.

Anger clutches my throat and I can't answer. Bridie must see it snapping from my eyes because she steps away without a word.

I tug on my clogs and clomp around the room, shoving my

gillies and penny whistles into a gym bag. As I snatch the D whistle off the dresser, I come face-to-face with the photograph taped to the mirror.

Two men stand together, arms around each other's shoulders, both with spiky black hair, multiple piercings and leather biker jackets, as alike as twins, except one is Irish and the other Chinese. Gerry had blue eyes, though he didn't pass them on to me — mine are as green as Bridie's. Matthew's eyes were brown and Kai's have turned out hazel.

Both Kai and I have pale skin and thick, reddish-brown hair, but that's where our resemblance ends. I have Gerry's round chin and pointy nose and Bridie's rosebud mouth. Kai got Matthew's blunt nose and chin, high cheekbones and full lips.

When Bridie met Bleater Bill, she told him a fake tale of being abandoned by her baby daddies. My mouth twists into a bitter curl. The truth is staring right at Bill if he ever takes a good look at the photo. Bridie wants me to take it down, but I refuse. Instead, I promised to fake if he asked who they were, to lie about the two men who'd been my fathers and her husbands.

My throat aches. I swallow hard.

Bridie and Kai walk past my room, carrying their instruments. I sling the gym bag over my shoulder and follow them downstairs. It's the only house we've ever lived in and it's enormous. Upstairs has two bedrooms, an office and a bathroom. The downstairs has a kitchen, a living room, the master bedroom and two bathrooms. Why so many bathrooms? There was only one in our caravan for five people and we made it work.

As we head toward the garage, we pass Bill, who's settled on the couch in front of the TV. He holds a beer in one hand and clutches the remote in the other. He's in his fifties, I think, since he's both graying and balding, and has a gut spilling over his belt. He's a partner at an accounting firm, whatever that means, and doesn't like to exercise or go places, though he does like watching sport.

He'd been married before to a lady who'd died in a car crash. They didn't have kids. Bill doesn't seem to have changed anything since she died, not the aging furniture, the discolored drapes or the fading wedding photos hanging above the mantel. It feels like we're guests and if the dead wife returns, we'll be asked to leave.

Too bad the dead can't come back to life.

Bill mutes the baseball game and twists toward us. He ignores me and Kai, and eyes Bridie's dress from demure scoop neckline to ankle hem before he speaks. "What time will you be home?"

Bridie kisses his forehead. "By eleven, darling. Enjoy your game."

"I'll be waiting." Bill turns back to the TV.

We load the instruments into the boot of Bridie's car. I don't fight when Kai insists on the passenger seat. The back suits me. I don't want to talk.

As we pull out of the driveway, Bridie announces, "We'll open with 'Raggle Taggle Gypsy'."

Kai groans. "We always open with 'Raggle Taggle Gypsy'."

"It's a good opener. You have to learn that, Son. Start with a song that has some excitement, but not all the excitement. You need to build your list. Ebb and flow." We come to a stoplight. Bridie glances back at me. "What sounds good for your first dance? 'Boys of Ballisodare'?"

"Okay."

"Your skirt looks lovely, by the way."

"Thanks." I gnaw my lip. "Why don't you wear the skirt I made you?"

"Well, you know, darling, Bill doesn't like me wearing something so short."

"It's not that short."

"Bill thinks it is."

I clutch my elbows. Bridie always wore miniskirts before—my chest tightens—before everything went to hell. Now, pleasing Bill is everything. She can't waste her Charm on things like skirt length. It's a precise tool, to be used at the right moment and with the right amount of pressure. Any enjoyment we get out of life now depends on that delicate silver thread.

Strowlers believe we're descended from a coupling between the great dragon, Master Stoorworm, and Leannán Sidhe, daughter of Maeve, queen of the fairies. It's from that union we received Charm to persuade, Fake to deceive, second sight to tell fortunes, and the power to bless and curse. Yet here we are at the mercy of a nob like Bill. How is that right?

When we reach Clement Street, Bridie pulls into the loading zone in front of the Auld Sod. It's an Irish pub with two Republic flags hanging on either side of the front door in case the name isn't obvious enough. We've performed here almost every Thursday since we arrived in the U.S. We could have performed more if Bill would let us.

Inside, the usual punters line the bar, mostly Sharpers of the traveling variety. The Auld Sod is a Crossroads crib, and good thing, too, or it'd be out of business like a lot of the local shops. The Crossroads has its own economy and ways of earning gelt. The ups and downs of the Bleater world don't affect us much. Which is another reason Bridie shouldn't have married Bill. Even skilled Bleaters can't find work lately. How does she think she's going to make any money outside tips?

A cheer rises as we enter. Bridie's face lights up and she calls out greetings to the Strowlers she knows by name. A whole family of Wrens has shown up, along with a Snipe, a Tern and a couple of Warblers. She looks so alive, so much like her old self. The crack in my heart becomes more jagged.

She stops, full on, causing me to bump into her.

At the other end of the bar stands a man wearing a bulky black and silver Raiders jacket over a pair of faded jeans a size too small. His meaty hands grasp the backs of two barstools as he stares at the bartender pulling down a tap to fill a pitcher.

I grit my teeth at the sight of his shaved head and ruddy, weathered face. Why does he have to be here?

Bridie continues walking at a normal pace. As we approach the man, he turns out, blocking our way. His flint eyes fix on Bridie and he tilts his head. "Well, well. Look who we have here."

The sound of his voice with its long southern drawl makes me want to kick something.

"Good evening, Mr. Kingfisher," says Bridie.

"Now, Bridie, how many times do I have to tell you? Everyone calls me Kingfisher."

"Kingfisher, then. Good evening."

If only we could tell him to bugger off, but he's the Upright Man, head of the Strowlers in San Francisco, and like it or not, we have to acknowledge him and be polite.

We head for the refuge of the stage at the back of the bar, little more than a raised platform against an exposed brick wall that's hung with a green and gold banner proclaiming, "It's the *Craic!*" Except it's minus *craic* with Kingfisher here. He's like Bill: he sucks the fun out of the room.

While Bridie and Kai tune their instruments, I sit on the top stair and lace up my soft-soled gillies. In front of the stage, there's a small wooden dance floor surrounded by tables. As usual, Kingfisher settles himself front and center with a pitcher of beer. While he slurps through the suds, he keeps his beady eyes fixed on Bridie, like he's in stalker heaven. If Gerry or Matthew were here, they would dump that pitcher over his head and toss him out the door, Upright Man or no. It's a good thing Bill isn't here. Kingfisher would show even less respect to a Bleater than a Sharper and chat up Bridie right in front of him. And then Bill would forbid us from performing ever again.

The thin, leather lace snaps as I tug it too tight. "Bugger," I mutter. I yank it out and reach for a new one in my bag. If only I could dump that pitcher over Kingfisher's ugly pate, but it would only make things worse. Bridie would have to apologize, making her obliged to Kingfisher. Who knows what he would ask of her. No, scratch that. I know exactly what he would demand. The new lace almost snaps between my fingers.

The tables and standing room around the stage fill up, though Kingfisher remains solitary. Other Sharpers walk over to him and shake his hand or linger to talk, but none sit with him. None dare, not without invitation, and Kingfisher isn't inviting.

At eight o'clock, Bridie and Kai strap on their guitars and I pick the high D penny whistle from my bag.

"Thank you all for coming tonight," Bridie says into the microphone at center stage. Then she strums the opening chords to 'Raggle Taggle Gypsy'.

The crowd, especially the Strowlers, breaks into applause. Kingfisher whistles and pounds the table. The pitcher shivers and the beer sloshes.

Bridie stops strumming and sings the first verse a cappella, her high, clear voice sweet, though with a sly edge that suits the lyrics.

> *"There were three gypsies a come to my door,*
> *And downstairs ran this lady, O!*
> *One sang high and another sang low,*
> *And the other sang bonny, bonny, Biscay, O!"*

At the chorus, her fingers move to the guitar strings. Kai

and I step forward to join in. Dancers step onto the wooden floor, blocking Kingfisher from view.

I tap my foot to the beat as I play the penny whistle. It feels so right, how things should be: my family on stage, surrounded by an audience. All that's missing… my throat tightens. I lower the penny whistle and cough. I have to stop thinking about my fathers. They're dead. This is my life now, a shadow of what it had been. Is a shadow worse than nothing at all?

I swallow to moisten my mouth and put the whistle to my lips. Bridie finishes the final chorus and strums to the end of the song.

Applause and cheers fill the pub. Bridie bows her head. "Thank you. If you'll be so kind as to clear the floor, we'll play a jig and my daughter, Penny, will show you some real Irish dancing."

I step off the stage and onto the floor. As the crowd moves aside, I find myself facing Kingfisher. Foam drips down his shirt as he swigs his beer. I wish I'd worn my hard shoes so I could somehow "accidentally" kick him in the bollocks. I close my eyes and take a deep breath. He isn't worth the consequences. I have to forget about him and focus on the music or my timing will be off. I look over my shoulder. Bridie tucks her fiddle to her chin and Kai holds the bodhrán. I nod. They nod back and begin playing 'The Boys of Ballisodare'.

Arms at my sides, I step to the beat of the jig, lifting my legs into high kicks that bring cheers from the crowd. Dancing in front of an audience is the best because I forget myself and become another person: the dancer, an otherworldly girl who knows a fairy secret shared by few others.

As the jig finishes, I bow. Applause dances across my skin, making me smile. My hands brush down my skirt. It must have looked nice as it swung along in time to the music. I should make another using the same pattern. I return to the stage without a glance at Kingfisher, willing his vile presence to blend in with the rest of the crowd.

We perform for another thirty minutes. Bridie alternates between guitar, fiddle and mandolin while Kai plays the guitar or the bodhrán. I play penny whistle or the bodhrán and dance two more jigs. When we finish our last song, Bridie leans into the microphone and says, "Thank you. We'll be taking a short break and be back to play another set."

I follow my mother into the ladies' room. Bridie goes straight to the mirror, sets her purse on the counter and takes out her compact. As she powders her face, she says, "Darling, your skirt is gorgeous. I should wear that one you made me. It would look marvelous with my suede boots."

I almost agree, until I think of Kingfisher's eyes on her. My arms cross as I lean against the counter. "Why does he have to be here every time?"

"Who?"

"You know who."

She applies a fresh red coat of lipstick and smacks her lips. "He's the Upright Man. We can't get on his bad side. Just smile, regardless of what he says." She avoids making eye contact in the mirror.

I shrug. No way would I smile at that bounce.

We re-enter the bar and Kai is sitting at Kingfisher's table. Fear spreads across my chest. Has he done something to offend the Upright Man? I suck in my breath and turn to my mother. The tight line of her mouth curls upward.

"Here come the ladies." Kingfisher's jovial drawl doesn't match his hard gaze. "Thought I'd buy the boy a pop."

Kai sits on the edge of his chair, straw in his mouth. He looks up at me and rolls his eyes.

"How sweet," Bridie exclaims. "Son, did you thank Mr. Kingfisher?"

"Just Kingfisher. Have a seat." He pushes out the chair next to him with his foot. "What can I get you ladies?"

Bridie perches. "Just water. I have to save my voice."

"Nothing," I say as I sit between my mother and brother.

Kingfisher turns toward the bar. "Two waters over here."

My shoulders tighten. I don't want to be obliged to him, not even for water.

Kingfisher reaches over and rubs the top of Kai's head. Kai pulls back and glares. "Quite a little spark plug you have here, Bridie. How much does that Bleater husband of yours know about these kids and their dads?"

Fear returns, only this time it burrows into my gut. After we arrived in San Francisco, Kingfisher showed up at our first gig at the Auld Sod and already seemed to know everything about us. Our "shame" is common cackle among the Dublin Strowlers. All I can figure is one of the rakes Bridie turned away had leaked to Kingfisher out of spite.

The waitress places our glasses on the table. Bridie takes a sip before she answers, "Enough."

"How do you explain the one being an Irish girl and the other being a half-breed?"

Kai makes a loud noise through his straw. I glare daggers at Kingfisher and wish so hard for my hard shoes. Bridie sets down her glass. "That's none of your business."

"I make it my business." Kingfisher takes a swig of beer and belches. "Sooner or later, that hob's going to figure out he's being Charmed."

She meets his gaze. "I'm not Charming my husband."

"Have you told him yet that you're Strowlers and that you bedded both men in your canting crew?"

Bridie's chest rises and falls.

Kingfisher leans back in his chair and drains his glass. "You and them kids are Sharpers. It's in your blood. Sooner or later, you'll get snapped. Best stash your game while things are plummy."

Bridie stands. "It's time for our next set. Let's go, children."

I push my untouched water toward the middle of the table. Kai takes another noisy pull on his straw before he jumps up.

Onstage, Bridie's hands shake as she reaches for her guitar. After Gerry and Matthew died, she faced down so many rake-hells. I hate seeing her rattled by this one. I lean close and whisper, "Don't let him get to you."

Bridie snorts. "Him? Hardly." She adjusts the strap.

"What's the next song?" asks Kai.

Our mother bows her head. Her hand covers her eyes for a moment before it becomes a fist. She looks up and gives a brisk nod. "Black is the Color."

Kai's mouth drops open. I blink and stutter, "But… but… really?"

Bridie touches the pendant under her dress, a silver and gold trinity knot given to her by Matthew for her thirtieth birthday. "Solo, I think. You two take a seat."

"Mum…" I begin.

Bridie turns abruptly. The stage lights make her green eyes hard and bright. "Sit."

A million things come to mind, but I can't say any of them. I turn to my brother. "Come on, Kai."

He doesn't budge. I tug his arm until he drags after me toward the stools at the side of the stage.

Bridie steps up to the microphone. "And we're back for our next set."

Applause and whistles greet her. Across the dance floor, Kingfisher pours a glass from a fresh pitcher.

"Has anyone here ever been in love?" she asks. The crowd laughs and applauds. "More than once?" More laughter. "I thought so. Well, I confess, I've been in love twice and both of them black-haired lads." She strums the guitar. "This song is for my true love, my only love."

> *"Black is the color of my true love's hair*
> *His lips are like some rose so fair*
> *He's got the sweetest face, He's got the gentlest hands*
> *I love the ground whereon he stands."*

Why is Bridie singing the one song she swore never to sing again? Kai clutches his guitar – Matthew's guitar – to his chest while my knuckles whiten around the penny whistle Gerry gave me.

> *"I love my love and well he knows*
> *I love the ground whereon he goes*
> *I have a wish the day would come*
> *When he and I could be as one."*

Does Bridie care what happens to her children? She claims she does, claims she married Bill and moved to America for our sake, to give us a better life, but that isn't true. She faked herself into believing it. The truth is right here; it's followed her onto the stage. She wants to fade away, but can't. The pain is too deep.

> *"I'll go to the Clyde, I'll mourn and weep*
> *For satisfied I can never be."*

Kingfisher is right. Our fake can't last. Bridie can't Charm Bill forever. I have to find a way to convince her to return to the Crossroads. Until then, I won't be satisfied either.

Paul

"Son." Dad's voice sounds far away, like the tail end of a dream.

My room is cool and dark. I close my eyes and burrow deeper under the bedcovers.

"Son. Wake up."

A bright light fills the room with jagged edges. I want to throw my pillow at the offender until I roll onto my back and blink up at my father. My stomach twists. That's right, the Dragon Shout. We start training this morning.

"Get dressed, and meet me in the kitchen."

Dad leaves. I stare at the ceiling. No geckos. They must still be asleep. Lucky bastards. I know I should haul ass out of bed, but what I really want to do is tell Dad and Head Elder to settle their fight without me in the middle. Fat lot of good that would do, except to unite them in their desire to punish me, and I'd still be expected to learn the Dragon Shout.

When I get to the kitchen, Mom and Dad are standing at the sink. Their hushed voices fade into silence. Steam seeps from the lid of the tall metal steamer on the stove. Tony sits at the table, arms folded and face solemn. He isn't usually awake this early. He could be up to say goodbye until next week, but that would be weird. Plus, why is he dressed in workout clothes instead of in pajamas like Mom? He isn't coming with us. Is he?

Mom's face looks tight and pale, as if she'd spent the night cooking instead of sleeping. I hope that isn't true. It's bad for her heart to not get enough sleep. She lifts the lid off the steamer. The sweet flour scent of steamed buns fills the air.

My mouth waters before I ask, "Vegetarian?" I don't like the meat ones.

Mom nods with a smile that doesn't reach her eyes. She uses tongs to lift out three large buns, placing each on separate plates.

Tony gets up and sets the plates on the table. Dad joins us and Mom brings over a pot of tea and cups. Then she goes back to the counter and takes out three more buns, placing them into a cooler.

I blow on my fingers before lifting the bun to my mouth. Then I blow on the white dough surface before taking a bite. The combination of mushrooms, onions and bamboo shoots coated in a thick, rich sauce burns my tongue, but still tastes so good. While I fan my mouth, I stare at the steamer, willing more buns to be inside. Maybe some lotus seed ones. Those are my second favorite.

Dad reads my mind. "Just one. Too much food will affect the flow of our *chi*."

Our *chi*. Just Dad and me? "Is Big Brother coming with us?"

Dad nods. "The Dragon Shout training is always guarded by a trusted and honored *Xia*. I chose your Big Brother."

Metal clatters on the kitchen floor. Mom picks up the tongs, tosses them in the sink and walks away.

Tony ducks his head and picks at the bun on his plate.

I reach out using the Silent Speech. *What's going on?*

He doesn't look up. *Choosing me for the honor will make Head Elder angry.*

No shit. Why is Dad aggravating Head Elder and using Tony to add fuel to the fire? Isn't it enough that Big Brother has to suffer from his father's disgrace? I can't ask those questions any more than I can refuse to go along with the training. I used to think the payout for all my obedience would be freedom as an adult. I'm starting to wonder if the exact opposite is true. Dad doesn't seem free. He seems trapped and Mom right along with him. I don't want to sign up for that, but I don't have a choice. That thought makes the bun sit in my stomach like a rock.

When we're ready to leave, Mom stands at the front entrance. She kisses me on the cheek, squeezes Tony's arm and hands Dad the cooler before closing the door behind us. Is she still mad? Maybe I should have told her what I'd overheard. Or would that make things worse? I grit my teeth. It's my own fault for being a snoop, though blissful ignorance wouldn't have made this situation any better.

It's after sunrise and the mountain casts deep shadows across the compound. As we approach the Ancestral Court-yard, I don't see the sentries until they step out of the shade of the moon gate. Dad motions them aside. After exchanging glances, they move back into place. I don't think anyone is exempt from being searched, not even the Dragon Son. This is going to get back to Head Elder.

We follow Dad around the spirit wall and toward the Ancestral Hall, where two sentries stand guard at the entrance. Dad doesn't seem surprised. Maybe they're extra security, along with Tony, to keep anyone from learning the forbidden skills. Neither guard makes any move to stop us.

I hesitate at the entrance. The Ancestral Hall is forbidden to children, even me. My tattoo tingles. The edges burn. I'm not a child anymore. I step across the threshold and breathe in the heavy scent of candle wax mingled with incense.

We walk across the smooth brick floor, our footsteps echoing off the rough, unadorned rock walls. I trail behind, turning from side to side. The cavern is larger than I thought, though I know it has to fit at least 200 people during the Summoning Ceremony. Flickering candles set in crevices carved into the walls provide most of the light. The Elders haven't allowed electricity to be installed, saying it will disturb our ancestors. Thing is, our ancestors were warriors. How could something like electricity spook them, so to speak?

The altar to Jade Dragon stands against the back wall. A huge copper lantern suspended from the ceiling illuminates the dark cherry wood panels and the red and gold tapestries draped over the surface. Above the altar in a carved alcove stands a statue of Guan Yu, the patron god of the Crossroads. Way back in the day, about 2000 years ago, he was a general, so he wears battle armor and carries a halberd in his right hand, the Glory Road side. If we were a Wayward Way clan, he'd be holding the halberd in his left hand.

For the record, I'm left-handed, something else Head Elder blames my parents for.

At the center of the altar on a jade pedestal sits an oblong wood plaque. Inscribed in gold on its surface are the words: *Spirit tablet of the illustrious Jade Dragon Lau Hong Dao, defender of the Hakka and founder of the Two Dragon Clan. Respectfully set up by his pious son, Dragon Son Lau Chao Zong.*

Is it true? Is our ancestor really a dragon who descended to Earth and took the form of a man to protect the Hakka people? When he died, his body supposedly dissolved into smoke and blew into the sky where he regained his dragon form. Then, he broke off pieces of his pearl and formed them into smaller pearls, which he left for his descendants. One of those pearls is embedded into the top of Jade Dragon's spirit tablet.

I grew up on stories of Jade Dragon's heroics, but they always seemed just that: stories. Sort of like the Monkey King in *Journey to the West*. Thing is, if it's only a story, how does Jade Dragon manifest his presence during the Summoning Ceremony?

Dad sets the cooler on the floor and reaches past the porcelain cups of tea and gold plates piled with fruit to open a small drawer beneath a copper plaque. He takes out six sticks of incense and holds the ends to a lit candle until they smolder. Lifting the sticks above his head, he bows three times. Then he stares at the spirit tablet with this weird look in his eyes, like he wants to cry. My mouth goes dry. It's my fault. I don't know how or why, but it is. He turns a stern face to us without a trace of tears. The candlelight tricked my eyes. Why would Dad be crying and how could it be my fault? I exhale and want to smile, but can't, not in this solemn place.

He divides the sticks evenly between Tony and me. "In my presence and the presence of our ancestor, Jade Dragon, I want you to swear the Oath of Fraternity."

What the hell? My mouth drops open. So does Tony's, which at any other time would be hilarious. "Uncle, Paul and I already are brothers."

"Brothers can betray each other," Dad pauses. He looks down for a moment. His voice becomes tight, "Betray the blood that binds them. I want you to be brothers by unbreakable oath." Steel returns to his eyes. "Repeat after me. We two, Tony Lau Wai Yi and Paul Lau Wai Kit…"

Tony lifts his three sticks of incense above his head. I do the same. I swallow to moisten my throat and repeat my father's words.

"… Swear brotherhood, and promise mutual help to one end. We will rescue each other in difficulty; we will aid each other in danger. We ask not the same day of birth, but we seek to die together. May Heaven, the all-ruling, and Earth, the all-producing, read our hearts. If we turn aside from righteousness or forget kindliness, may Heaven and Earth destroy us."

We place the incense sticks in the same brazier.

Dad's eyes glitter in the candlelight. "Hold this oath in your hearts. It binds you for life. Paul, you are my heir, but Tony is your older brother and that will never change. You must obey him as you would obey me. Bow to your older brother."

When taking the Oath of Fraternity, a symbolic older brother is chosen. Of course, it's Tony. I turn to Big Brother and bow at the waist.

"Stop this at once." Head Elder's voice echoes through the chamber as he strides toward us, flanked by the two guards from the entrance. My heart starts pounding. I move forward to stand between him and Dad, but Dad grabs my arm and yanks me back.

Head Elder's jowls quiver in his reddened face. He speaks in a tight whisper, "What have you done?"

Dad gazes down on him. "You are not to question the actions of the Dragon Son."

"You gave the son of a traitor authority over the future Dragon Son."

"My nephew isn't a traitor."

"Your actions are traitorous to our clan."

"I am the Two Dragon Clan."

"And I enforce the laws and discipline of the Two Dragon Clan." Head Elder turns to Tony. "Lau Wai Yi, in the presence of Jade Dragon and our ancestors, kowtow before the future Dragon Son and declare him your master."

"No." Dad's voice rose. "Son, Nephew, follow me."

Head Elder motions the guards, who move to stand in Dad's path.

Dad pins them in place with his gaze. "You dare stand in the way of the Dragon Son?"

The guards look from Dad to Head Elder.

"Stand your ground," orders Head Elder.

"Out of my way," counters Dad. "I am the Dragon Son and you will obey me."

"Disobedience to me will cause your expulsion from the Two Dragon Clan," says Head Elder.

The guards freeze. The whole clan could splinter depending on their next move. How much does it suck to be them? From their panicked expressions, a whole hell of a lot.

Thing is, I want it to happen. No more fake bullshit or pretending we're all united. Everyone chooses sides and then… I don't know. Maybe Head Elder and his followers can walk out the front gate and start their own clan. Or maybe there will be some kind of war. That doesn't scare me because most people will choose Dad's side and we'll win… unless Head Elder really does have some kind of huge secret that will ruin everything. Sweat dampens my forehead. All right then. Facing the truth is better than living some big fat lie, right?

Tony drops to the stone floor and bends over, pressing his forehead to the ground at my feet. Heat rushes to my face. If running away was an option, I'd be so gone.

"Son, no!" Dad calls out.

Does he mean Tony or me? It doesn't matter. I reach out to Tony. *Big Brother, this is stupid. Don't do it.*

Tony rises to a kneeling position. His gaze remains calm and cold. *Little Brother, I will do whatever is necessary to keep our clan united.* He bends again, pressing his forehead to the floor twice more. Then he takes a breath and speaks in a loud, clear voice that echoes off the walls, "I, Lau Wai Yi acknowledge Lau Wai Kit as the future Dragon Son and my master. I will serve and obey him and, if necessary, give my life to protect him and the Two Dragon Clan."

My stomach trembles and in a weird way, I want to laugh. Why is everyone making such a big deal out of this? I obey

Tony. Everyone knows that. And someday, I will be the Dragon Son and Tony's master. Like that would ever stop him from bossing me around.

A tight smile splits Head Elder's scowl. He motions the guards to follow him out the front entrance.

Dad stretches out his arm, palm forward. His chest rises. His mouth opens wide, as if to shout, but the sound that comes out is more like a whisper, "Kaah."

A vibration, like a small earthquake, moves through the cavern. Above the entrance, the stone shelf cracks and splinters. Shattered pieces fall to the ground. A copper brazier tumbles and rolls, spilling incense sticks and ash.

The Dragon Shout.

My first thought is, I'm supposed to be able to do that? My second thought is, way to piss off Head Elder.

And he is pissed. Even as he backs away from the destruction, he throws Dad a look of pure hatred. And I finally get it. Head Elder hates Dad because he can never be as powerful as him, not without the Dragon Shout. That's why Head Elder wants me to learn the Dragon Shout, so he can use me against Dad. I give a little snort. So not going to happen.

Head Elder turns to the guards. "Clean this mess." He steps over the rubble and out the entrance without looking back.

Dad swipes his hand across his brow. A sheen of sweat coats his cheeks and glistens off his forearms. He motions Tony and me to follow him into the small chamber behind the altar. Out of sight of the guards, he leans against the wall and closes his eyes. I always picture Dad as being almighty, but at that moment he looks drained. I take a step toward him. Tony catches my arm and shakes his head.

Dad whispers, "Learn from my bad example. I used the Dragon Shout in anger, allowing toxic *chi* to spread through my body. Whatever the situation, do not attempt the Dragon Shout unless you are calm and in control." He takes a deep breath. Color returns to his face. His eyelids flutter open. "Son, go get the cooler."

Tony and I exchange looks. Then he shrugs and leaves the chamber.

Dad pulls away from the wall and straightens up. "We're going into the caverns."

The caverns? Well, hell yeah. Finally. All my life, since I've been old enough to walk, I've wanted to explore the caverns, which are forbidden to children and most of the clan. Only the Dragon Son and the Elders know the extent of the tunnels and caves carved into our mountain. I try sounding casual as I ask, "Is that part of my training?"

Dad nods.

I manage not to do a fist pump.

Tony rejoins us. Dad reaches for a lantern set in an alcove. He twists the wick to brighten the flame. "Follow directly behind me. The caves go for miles and it's easy to get lost." He lifts the lantern, illuminating a narrow opening at the back of the chamber.

I almost step on Dad's heels, I'm so eager to get inside. When we reach the opening Dad stops and turns. Tony remains in place, his arms folded tight.

"Son," Dad's voice is gentle. "Come with us."

Tony shifts the cooler to his other shoulder. Is Big Brother actually fidgeting? Today is full of firsts.

"Your father's actions have nothing to do with you," Dad continues. "It was his disgrace not yours. Now, come. We need you with us."

Tony ducks his head and hurries to join us. I keep my face blank. I know the last thing he wants is sympathy. We walk through a narrow passageway to another small chamber. The lantern's light flickers off the stone surface. I squint. Is there some sort of pattern on one of the walls?

Dad twists the wick again, revealing not a pattern, but

series of drawings. I take a few steps closer. It's a man demonstrating the different stances of a martial form. He has long hair and a mustache, and wears loose trousers, a short tunic and a pair of boots. There's writing beneath the drawings, but it's difficult to read without getting closer. Dad lifts the lantern to better illuminate the wall. "Do you recognize the form?"

I examine the position of the man's feet and the angle of his body, how he propels himself forward. "It's the Swift Step."

"All of our clan's martial forms are drawn on the walls of these caverns. That's why it's forbidden for anyone but a chosen few to enter past the altar."

I scratch my leg to keep from glancing back at Tony. It must feel like crap having to view the scene of his father's crime. I don't know the whole story. Only that Second Elder had caught Uncle George in the caverns, taking pictures with his phone. Why did he do it? The rumor is he'd stacked up major gambling debts. Rival clans would pay top dollar to learn the Two Dragon Clan's secret martial skills. Uncle George knew the penalty for such a betrayal. He has no place in our clan anymore.

"Come." Dad turns from the wall and heads for a passage leading to a rough stone stairway.

We follow Dad through a series of tunnels and chambers, stopping often so he can point out the drawings on the walls. As we walk, our footsteps echo around us. After a while, I hear another sound, faint at first before becoming distinct, the sound of rushing water. A cool breeze blows through the passageway. I suck in the fresh air and look up. I can make out the rock formations above. The farther we go, the lighter it becomes until Dad no longer needs the lantern. The passageway gets wider until we enter a large chamber filled with light coming from gaps in the rocks above. Greenery creeps around the edges of a passageway that looks to lead to the outside world.

Dad takes me to a wall with a drawing of a life-sized man, the same man as in the other drawings. He stands with his legs parted, knees slightly bent, one hand balled into a fist at his side, the other thrust palm outward. The Dragon Shout. There are two smaller depictions beside him. In one, he stands in the same stance before a large boulder. In the second drawing, the boulder is reduced to rubble.

"The guy in the drawings, is he Jade Dragon?" I ask.

He shakes his head. "It's the first Dragon Son, Lau Chao Zong. He posed while Jade Dragon drew the forms."

My mouth drops open. "Jade Dragon was an artist?"

"Jade Dragon had many abilities." Dad's tone makes it clear the conversation is over.

I started drawing when I was a kid and everyone thought it was cute. After I became a teen, it stopped being cute and became a waste of time, according to them. That's why I have to hide my sketchbook from almost everyone. They don't want to hear that drawing isn't just a hobby for me or that it's something I need to do.

I climb a pile of rocks that form a crude platform to get closer to the main drawing. Had Jade Dragon knelt here when he sketched his son's face? Although the lines had faded, Lau Chao Zong's stern mouth and determined gaze still show his personality. Jade Dragon had used his artistic abilities to aid the clan. I could do the same. Is this the right time to say something to Dad? Would there be a better time? I take a breath and shift around.

Dad is looking at Tony. "Son, come closer. He's your ancestor as much as ours."

Tony hesitates before joining him, his head bowed as if he can't look our ancestor in the eye.

Dad grips Tony's shoulder. "You must stop carrying this burden. Your father is responsible." He pauses and closes his eyes. His next words are a whisper. "The guilt is his."

All right, already. Can everyone please get past Uncle George and his epic fail? I sigh and face the first Dragon Son. No, they can't. It's the kind of failure that will be talked about for generations. For a moment, I almost feel sorry for my uncle. He got married before Dad. Had a son before Dad, but nothing is going to change the fact that Dad is the Dragon Son and he isn't.

I hoist myself up another level and crane my neck. Is there some kind of shelf behind the drawing of the Dragon Shout? I squeeze between two boulders and peer into the dark enclosure. Cool. Maybe Jade Dragon or his son hid some secret scrolls in there. I wriggle my way inside, groping around the tight enclosure, but all I come up with is dust.

"Son, what are you doing up there?"

I cough. "Nothing." I squirm back out and climb down to join him and Tony. "Are we going back to the Ancestral Hall?"

"No. We're staying here for the week."

"The whole week?"

Dad points at a tarp covering a heap of stuff against the wall. Tony pulls away the tarp like a magician, revealing cots, sleeping bags, lanterns and plastic containers that hopefully hold more food. If it weren't for all the bullshit with Head Elder, I'd think this whole thing was pretty damn cool.

"There's a pool in the next cavern," Dad says. "We'll use that to bathe and the stream running into it for water." I open my mouth. "We'll relieve ourselves outside." I close my mouth. "During the week, you will learn the Dragon Shout, how to find your way through the caverns, and-" he reaches under his T-shirt and pulls a gold chain from around his neck, "-how to wield the Yang Pearl."

A coiled dragon pendant dangles from the chain, its center set with a shimmering pearl, the largest piece from Jade Dragon's great pearl.

I hold my breath while Dad drapes the chain around my

neck. As the amulet lies against my chest, I feel a surge of power, like an electric shock. With careful fingers, I lift the amulet and stare into the depths of the Yang Pearl. Something brushes my mind, like the Silent Speech, but it's not Dad or Tony. It's something huge with glistening scales that coil as it moves through air and water.

I gasp. The connection breaks. My heart pounds. I look at my father with wide eyes.

Dad nods. "Jade Dragon."

Penny

This morning's sticky note reads: *Penny Sparrow gives lousy head* and includes a crude drawing of a cock and balls. On the Crossroads, this would be the same as challenging me to a duel. Whoever did this would step forward and we'd settle things with our fists. I don't know what Bleaters are supposed to do. Cry? Not bloody likely. Peach? Sharpers don't snitch. Sucking it up seems to be the only alternative and it's making me hate myself, almost as much as I hate whoever is doing this.

As I walk down the hall, I hear whispers.

"Slut."

"Whore."

I spin around.

Three of the Daisy Chain stroll by, their arms linked and their mouths pursed into mean little smiles.

I stand my ground. "Say that to my face."

They look at me like I'm dipped in shit and continue on in snotty silence. With their backs to me, they burst into high-pitched giggles and one says, "She's so weird."

Kids passing in the hall stare at me, some with pity, while

others look quickly away as if what I have is contagious. What do I have? Why do these girls hate me? Is it about Kevin Anderson? I haven't done anything with him, or any other boy for that matter. The warning bell rings, jangling my nerves.

I'm still seething when I drop into my desk in English Lit. Ms. Chang starts out with a pop quiz on *Macbeth*, which I ace. My mouth twists as I think of Bill's words about my education. He doesn't know shite. I've been reading Shakespeare for years. Matthew and I would act out the scenes for our family.

While Ms. Chang grades papers, she tells us to read *Twelfth Night*. I open my notebook and start drawing costumes for Viola and her twin brother, Sebastian. The whole play revolves around everyone getting those two confused for each other because back in the day, a woman would never dress like a man. I start with a basic sketch of both characters in leggings, thigh high boots, and short, belted tunics. My lip curls. Too boring. I draw fitted biker jackets over the tunics and give the twins spiky Mohawks with long, braided tails. Much better.

A shadow falls across the page. I look up. Ms. Chang smiles as she hands me the graded quiz, until she glances down at the notebook. She huffs before she speaks. "I said read, Penny, not draw."

"I'm drawing Viola and Sebastian." Matthew would have loved that answer. Ms. Chang looks at me like I'm speaking a foreign language. "I've already read *Twelfth Night*."

Ms. Chang huffs again. Then she clicks her pen, scratches out the 'A' on the quiz and replaces it with a 'B.'

Typical Bleater. No idea of fair play. The quiz crumples in my fist. It would feel so good to hurl it at her stiff back. With any luck, I'd get expelled. Then I think of Bill's reaction. He wouldn't shut up about it for weeks – no, months. I shred the quiz in my lap. After the bell rings, I toss the pieces into the trash on my way out the door.

This is all Bridie's fault. She went to primary school in

Ireland for a couple years and told us how she'd been called a dirty gyppo, and that the teachers expected her to be stupid. Did she think it would be any different for me? How could she dump me into this hateful place, all for the sake of an easy life?

For Strowlers, education of the Bleater variety comes last. Working and fighting come first and we start learning both at an early age. Work includes anything from manual labor to parting Bleaters from their gelt with a bit of shammery. Musical talent is encouraged if you can earn a living from it. We learn these skills from our elders, not from people like Ms. Chang, who are paid to act like they give a toss when they don't.

Other Crossroads clans have different policies on education, like the Two Dragon Clan. Matthew caused a huge stink when he dropped out of Oxford to be a wide boy, living by his wits on the Wayward Way. With all his smarts, it seemed a waste for him not to teach Kai and me a thing or two. Bridie and Gerry sat in on some of the lessons since it's difficult to write lyrics when you're basically illiterate. Everything we learned applied to our lives and it was such a good life. At night, we'd perform on stage as Wild Sky, playing a fusion of Celtic folk, rock and punk. During the day, the adults would work odd jobs or shams while I sewed and took care of Kai. We never had much money, but so what? Who needs money when you have happiness? Has Bridie forgotten all about that?

I can't stand another minute in this hellhole. Unfortunately, my next class is U.S. History and Mr. Cole always takes attendance. I'll have to wait for gym to cut class. The P.E. instructors are too lazy to do anything except pretend to pay attention while we muck about on the field. I haven't been caught yet. All I have to do is slip out of the dressing room, through the parking lot, across the street and I'm in Golden Gate Park, easy as you like.

There's no note when I get to my locker. The Daisy Chain needs to rub all their brain cells together for an entire day before they can come up with the next insult. Whoever is doing the dirty work seems to know my schedule since I haven't been able to catch her. Yet. When I do, there'll be hell to pay and I'm the devil.

"Hey, Penny." Kayla Hipp comes up beside me and turns the combination at the next locker.

Kayla is all right. She's not a friend, but she talks to me when we're at the lockers. I glance at the sticky note at the center of the wall of insults: *no one likes you.* Maybe I need to try harder. I smile. "Hey."

"I love your outfit," she says as she pulls out her U.S. History book.

"Thanks." It's important for Strowlers to look flash when going out among the Bleaters. No one knows my blouse was rescued from a thrift store pile for ninety-nine cents. I'd cut off the sleeves and the collar, and those ridiculous shoulder pads, but left the frilly material down the front. I made the skirt from a gorgeous paisley print I'd found in a fabric store remnant bin. Ankle-length, it suits me just fine and looked rum with the blouse. I finished the outfit with a black, fringed scarf.

"Did you make it?"

"Most of it."

"I love the scarf. Did you make that, too?"

I finger the beaded fringe as I nod. I knew it'd turned out rum.

Kayla stares at the small mirror attached to her locker door. Her index finger smears the thick black eyeliner rimming her lids. She likes dressing different, too – sort of Goth. Today, she's wearing black leggings and a huge, black baggy T-shirt printed with a red cartoon skull. "I wish I could sew."

"You can. Anyone can. You should take sewing with me

next semester. Ms. Gagliardi is a really good teacher. You can do any kind of project you like, even knitting."

She gives a wistful sigh. "I'd love to know how to knit."

"It's easy. I can teach you." I gnaw my lip. The next step would be to invite her home, but I can't. When we first moved in, Bill stated there would be no friends allowed in his house. He doesn't want the mess. His words. Teenagers, to him, mean mess. He's such a bellend.

"Hey, Penny." Speaking of bellends. I don't turn, but that doesn't stop Kevin Anderson. "Hanging out with Hippo?"

Kayla's shoulders hunch. Her cheeks redden. Hurt fills her eyes.

"Penny. Hey. Why you hanging with fat-ass Hippo?"

"Ignore him. He's a knob." I pull out my American History book and shove it in my bag. "Did Mr. Cole give us homework yesterday? I couldn't tell."

Kayla clears her throat. Her voice shakes. "He wanted us to watch that show about George Washington on KQED last night."

"I know. I mean, besides that."

"My buddies want you to meet them in the park," Kevin calls out.

Now, that I can't ignore. I start to turn.

Kayla catches my arm. "Kevin's been telling everyone you met him in the park."

"I didn't meet him. I ran into him when I was cutting gym yesterday." He'd waved a handful of his endless supply of tiny liquor bottles. One of his parents must work for an airline. "He told me to come over and I told him to fuck off."

"He told everyone you went down on him."

Penny Sparrow gives lousy head.

I drop my book bag and spin around.

Kevin stands in the midst of his usual crew of toadies. I've overheard girls talk about how cute he is. All I can see is a face too red, hair too blond and a mind too small. His mouth is fixed in a smirk and his eyes glint blue cruelty.

Gerry taught me never to reveal my hand in a card game or a fight, so I show a poker face and speak cold. "You said I went down on you?"

He shrugs.

"Say it's a lie."

"Why should I?"

I stride up to Kevin and look him in the eye as I enunciate each word, "Say. It's. A. Lie."

He makes a sucking sound followed by a gulp.

My fist connects with his jaw. His head snaps back. I punch him in the gut and he falls backward, landing on his arse with a hard bounce. Pain shoots through my hand. I haven't hit anyone in a long time and it never felt so good before. My heart beats faster and I have to restrain myself from kicking him while he's down.

Silence falls over the hall. Kevin's crew stares down at him with gaping mouths.

I return to my locker and a wide-eyed Kayla. "Yeah, I watched that show." I reach for my bag. "It was kind of boring."

"Come back here, bitch. I'm gonna kick your ass!" Kevin uses his toadies to claw his way back to his feet.

I sigh. Bad day to wear a long skirt. I'll have to fight my way around it. I tug up my skirt, tucking it into the waistband.

Alarm shows in his eyes, chased by relief as the bell rings. He calls out over his shoulder as he scurries down the hall. "In the parking lot. After school."

"I'll be there," I shout after him. I slam my locker shut. "Shite. Now I can't cut gym."

Kayla blinks. "You're not going to fight him, are you?"

"Of course I am. I accepted his challenge. I can't back down now."

"Where did you learn to hit like that?"

I bite my lip. Time to fake and work the sham that keeps me from saying I'd been raised to fight. "I took a boxing class in Ireland."

Kayla's eyes narrow skeptically. "They teach boxing at school in Ireland?"

"No, at a gym."

"Oh."

As we head down the hall toward history class, other students stare and whisper. News travels fast. Kayla gazes at the other kids before casting a quick, guilty glance at me. Then she speeds up so we no longer walk together.

No one likes you.

My throat tightens. Why did I even try? Am I that lonely? I don't want to think about the answer, so I walk even faster, bypassing Kayla to get to class first.

I take my usual seat in the back. Kayla sits beside another Goth girl in the middle row. People are eyeing me as they cackle to each other. My cheeks burn, but I hold my head up proud. I've done what none of them dared and stood up to a common footpad. If my bravery in the face of their bleating cowardice makes me a pariah, so be it.

Mr. Cole comes in and everyone shuts up. While he drones on about George Washington, Father of Our Country, blah, blah, blah, I think about how to fight around my clothes. The skirt will hamper my movements and give Kevin an advantage. I have P.E. for fifth period. I can stay in my gym clothes and hide in the girls' loo until after sixth period. That will work.

The classroom door opens and Vice Principal Ikeda steps inside. She glances around the classroom, looks at me and says, "Penny Sparrow, come with me. Bring your things."

Everyone watches me shove my book into my bag and walk out the door. My fingers itch to flip them the bird. I follow Vice Principal Ikeda at a glum distance as we head toward the administrative office. It looks like Bridie and Bill will be fighting over me again.

Paul

Sweat trickles down my cheeks and drips off my jaw. I want to swipe my forehead, but my bare arms are just as slick. I wipe my wet palms down my pants and squint at the midmorning sun filling the Ancestral Courtyard with light and heat. Not a cloud in the sky. Is this how an egg feels sitting in the middle of a frying pan?

"Is he ready?" Head Elder glares at me from the shade of the red awning set up in front of the Ancestral Hall for the Summoning Ceremony. Dad and Tony stand beside him, expectation clear in their eyes.

An egg has it easy. All it has to do is fry.

Dad walks up to me. "Are you ready?"

I nod. My tattoo, which hasn't bothered me all week, now itches and burns.

Dad hangs the Yang Pearl around my neck.

As the smooth side of the amulet rests against my skin, I feel the now-familiar thrum of power. I close my eyes as that power spreads through my body and tingles at my fingertips. I raise my left arm.

"What is he doing?" demands Head Elder.

My eyes pop open.

"Silence," commands Dad.

I grit my teeth. Dad knew Head Elder wouldn't approve of me using my left hand for the Dragon Shout, but he insisted the use of the dominant hand is more powerful. It's also another way of showing Head Elder who's in charge. I'm all for that, but not the bullshit that comes with it at this particular moment. If I can't concentrate, I won't be able to do what they want, and then I really will be a fried egg.

I shut my eyes and once again focus as the power of the Yang Pearl flows through me.

Jade Dragon plunges through the ocean, causing rogue waves to appear on the surface. He remains invisible, moving through water and sky, gaining the wisdom and power necessary to – slowly, so slowly – fill the holes in his great pearl. He seems to pause as he notices my presence. Such a speck of a boy, yet still his descendent.

I open my eyes. The Yang Pearl glows. I hold out my palm in the direction of a man-sized, straw-filled dummy hitched to a stand across the courtyard. As I open my mouth, I use my voice to focus the power surging through my body out through my palm.

I breathe out the power sound, "Kaah."

Both dummy and stand propel backward, smashing into the wall and crumpling to the ground. A nearby tree trembles as leaves and twigs fall from its branches.

My legs wobble. I suck in my breath and the tremors worsen. A dark pattern veils my sight and a loud buzzing sound fills my ears. The Yang Pearl tingles against my skin. I take another breath – slower this time – and concentrate on the pearl, allowing its energy to spread through my limbs. My vision clears.

Dad and Head Elder look at each other instead of me, their faces red and angry.

The buzzing fades.

Head Elder pounds his fist into his palm. "He must be able to achieve the Dragon Shout without the aid of the Yang Pearl."

"He can," Dad's speaks over Head Elder, "But not without difficulty. He's been practicing all morning for this demonstration. I'm not going to exhaust him. He needs more time to regain his strength and replenish his *chi*."

"This is your failure – your unwillingness to train your son properly."

My heart hammers, making me dizzy again. It's not Dad's fault. Without the Yang Pearl and the faraway power of Jade Dragon, I'd struggled to achieve the Dragon Shout. Dad had been patient and Tony encouraging, but it had knocked me on my ass until yesterday, when I was able to shift a boulder without the aid of the pearl. I lick my lips. They feel like sandpaper. I could try again, but I need water.

"Head Elder, my heir has proven his ability to succeed me. This demonstration is over." My father strides across the courtyard toward me. His hard expression softens as he speaks. "Are you all right, son?"

Honest answer?

No.

Correct answer?

"Yes." I take off the Yang Pearl and hand it to him. The thrum of power evaporates as Jade Dragon disappears into a cloud bank. I swallow, trying to moisten my throat. "I'm thirsty."

Dad looks over his shoulder. "Son, go get your brother some water."

Tony heads for the entrance to clan headquarters. Third and Fifth Elder brush past him as they enter the courtyard. Both are men, with their yang numbering, while Second and Fourth Elder are female with even, yin numbers. Despite this, there isn't a true balance, not with Head Elder included. Why isn't there a Sixth Elder? Is it intentional, to keep the women outnumbered? I frown. That's not fair. Maybe when I'm Dragon Son, I can change that. Who would I make Sixth Elder? Auntie Cat. Definitely. She'd kick ass as an Elder. She's Dad's younger sister, so she'll probably still be alive after he dies…

Dad. Dead. What am I thinking? The sun must have fried my brain.

Third Elder approaches Dad. I call him the Vampire because he's got this creepy, pointy smile like a grinning corpse. "Dragon Son, the delegations from the other clans are gathered in the grand pavilion, but there's a problem. The Beggar Chief insists on smoking a cigar. It has an offensive odor. The other clans have protested. The chief of the Iron Fan Sisterhood is threatening to walk out."

"Brother Ash likes to make trouble." Dad shakes his head. "My son and I need to prepare for the Summoning Ceremony. Can't someone else take care of this nonsense?"

"I have the delegations on a conference call in my office. Perhaps if you spoke to them." The Vampire shows his yellow fangs as he motions toward the entrance to headquarters.

Hesitation crosses Dad's features. He looks at Head Elder, now deep in conversation with Uncle Tool. That's what I call Fifth Elder. He's Head Elder's oldest son and struts around the compound like he's the boss and everyone else is bullshit, and he talks to Mom like she's still a child. Good news is he's older than Dad, so hopefully I won't have to put up with him as Head Elder when I'm the Dragon Son.

Tony reenters the courtyard and Dad's expression clears. He turns to me. "Stay here with your Big Brother."

I nod. I want to wait in the shade, but I don't want to get any closer to Head Elder and his tool of a son. Tony tosses me a sweaty plastic bottle. The cold water tastes like sweet relief and

I already feel a hundred times better. I wish I could drain it dry, but excess of anything would be bad for my *chi*.

"You did good," Tony whispers. "Don't let Head Elder tell you different."

I smile before taking another gulp. I don't give a damn what anyone else thinks, as long as Dad and Big Brother are happy.

After Dad and the Vampire leave the courtyard, Head Elder hollers, "Wai Yi. Go to the end of the courtyard."

What the hell is he up to? Nothing good. I turn to Tony, whose face has gone blank. *Don't go.*

Tony inhales through his nose. *I have to. I can't disobey him.* He walks across the courtyard until he gets to the designated spot. Then he turns and faces me. *Whatever happens, don't be afraid. I can take it.*

Head Elder lifts his head at an imperious angle, as if he thinks he's looking down on me even though I'm taller than him. "Wai Kit, you will demonstrate the Dragon Shout using Wai Yi."

The slick bottle slips from my fingers. Water sprays my legs. I reach out to my father. I can't sense him, but I cry out anyway. *Dad. Help. Head Elder. He's trying to get me to hurt Tony.*

No answer. That's why the Vampire insisted on a conference call. He's making sure Dad is too distracted for me to reach.

"Now," shouts Uncle Tool. He's standing there with his arms folded and legs apart, like he's a thug in a third-rate movie.

I shout back, "No."

Head Elder's mouth twists in an ugly sneer. "So, it's true. Your father didn't teach you to use the Dragon Shout on a man."

He's twisting things around again. Trying to make it Dad's

fault. "He did, but not without the Yang Pearl. There wasn't time. I…"

"You will do as I command."

Little Brother. Tony's voice brushes my mind. *You did it before. You can do it again.*

No. Not without the Yang Pearl.

Remember, you were able to push me.

I need the Yang Pearl. Without it, I might use too much power. I could hurt you. I could kill you.

You won't. I have faith in you. Have faith in yourself.

I take a deep breath to steady my pounding heart. Tony believes in me. I can do this.

"Grandson," Head Elder snaps his fingers. "The Dragon Shout. Now."

A cold breeze gusts through the courtyard. Leaves and twigs skitter across the cobblestones. Where did that come from? Jade Dragon! Is he somewhere overhead, awaiting the Summoning Ceremony? Or is he waiting for his descendent to prove himself worthy and take command?

Head Elder snaps his fingers again.

Who the hell is that old man, a mere human, to order me around? Maybe I should demonstrate the Dragon Shout, but not on Big Brother. Head Elder's baleful glare makes my left palm itch. I lift my hand, but instead of blowing the old man into the wall, I snap my fingers.

Head Elder's jaw drops.

"I am the Dragon Son's heir. I obey no one but him and Jade Dragon."

I stride across the courtyard toward the entrance to head-quarters. Head Elder and Uncle Tool recover enough to block my way. I veer and enter the Ancestral Hall instead.

Inside, I halt before turning in a slow circle. What the hell? Last night, when we finally headed home, the Ancestral Hall looked identical to when we first entered. Since then, the main cavern has been swept clean and additional lanterns lit to provide twice as much light. Fresh coils of incense hang from the overhead beams. Benches line the walls and straw mats have been rolled onto the floor.

Everyone will be arriving soon for the Summoning Ceremony, which means Head Elder is running out of time. He'll be after me any moment now, trying to use me as a weapon against my father. I shiver, the cold air chilling the sweat on my skin. The old creep has to find me first. I grin. All I need is a good hiding place. Not a problem.

I run around the altar, grab a lantern and head into the caverns. I turn the wick as low as possible to find my way along the path.

The past week hadn't been so bad. During the day, I had practiced wielding the Yang Pearl and performing the Dragon Shout. At night, Dad had led Tony and me through the caves, into different chambers with even more drawings. It would have been fun, like a camping trip, if it hadn't been for all the expectations dumped on my shoulders.

"Wai Kit," Head Elder's voice echoes from behind. "Come back at once."

Anger burns in my throat. I bite my lip to keep from yelling, 'Like hell!' so I don't give him anything to hone in on. I pick up my pace. Soon, they'll see my light and be able to follow me. In case they're already on my tail, I wind around several bends, taking the alternate routes Dad taught me.

"Wai Kit."

That sounds too damn close. Head Elder can sure move fast for an old man. I turn off the lantern. Darkness envelops me, but I know I'm not far from the end of the path. I press my back to the wall and keep going, quick and silent. The cold, gritty stones scrape my skin, but that's okay. I'll take a lot more punishment to ruin Head Elder's game.

I stumble over a jutting rock and grasp at the wall to keep

from falling. The lantern flies from my hand. The sound of its crash echoes through the caverns. The smell of kerosene fills the air.

"Wai Kit. Stop where you are."

Damn! I press against the wall and hurry forward. As my eyes adjust to the dark, I can make out the shapes of the rock formations. I round a tight corner and the walls of the cavern become wider and more visible. They'll never catch me now. I run toward the sound of water, breathing in the fresh air that blows through the passage.

When I get to the Dragon Shout Chamber, I turn from side to side. What should I do? I can run outside and hide in the forest, but maybe that's what they expect. Maybe there are already guards outside waiting for me to appear. And what about Dad and Tony? They're going to come looking for me. Dad is going to be so pissed. I rub my forehead. Aw, shit. Maybe I shouldn't have run off.

Footsteps sound behind me. I'm out of time. Where can I hide? I twist around and come face-to-face with the drawing of Lau Chao Zong. It's almost like he's beckoning me into the cubbyhole. Quick and silent, I clamber up the rocks and squeeze into the crawl space behind the drawing. My temples pound and my breath sounds like shouting. I jam my fist to my lips and breathe through my nose.

Head Elder's voice comes from outside the chamber, "Did he come this far?"

"We don't know," replies an unfamiliar male voice. "He dropped his lantern. He might have gotten lost in the dark."

More footsteps sound, followed by an angry voice, "What have you done with my son?"

Dad. I exhale through my fingers. I start to wiggle out and stop. Would my sudden appearance make things better or worse? I squirm further in.

"Your son ran away," replies Head Elder.

"Why?"

"Because he is disobedient."

"Wai Yi told me what you ordered him to do, against my command, and now he's lost."

"Your son is lost because he lacks discipline and ran like a child instead of obeying orders like a man."

Mean old liar! My knuckles scrape against the sandy stone. The cubbyhole is starting to get uncomfortable, but if it makes Head Elder sweat to think he lost me, I can stay here for hours. Still, I don't want Dad to worry. I close my eyes and reach out to him.

Dad, it's okay. I'm all right.

Son! Where are you?

I'm hiding in the Dragon Shout chamber. Do you want me to come out?

Dad hesitates a few moments before replying. *No. I don't want Head Elder having any further access to you. Wait for your Big Brother. He'll come get you.*

Okay. I also hesitate. *Dad, I'm sorry…*

Don't be. None of this is your fault. Stay put.

"The guards will fan out through the tunnels," Dad says aloud, his voice crisp with authority. "I want my son found in time for the Summoning Ceremony."

I sigh as footsteps become fainter, moving in multiple directions away from the chamber. How long will I have to stay in here? It's getting stuffy, not to mention really cramped. Good thing I don't have claustrophobia. I close my eyes. Maybe I can pretend I'm lying in bed. Yeah, right, on the world's most uncomfortable mattress.

"Are they gone?"

My eyes pop open. That sounds like Uncle Tool.

"Quiet, you fool." That's definitely Head Elder. It sounds like they're in the chamber, right below me. "Our plans have changed. Inform Third Elder. Use the Silent Speech. I want none of this spoken aloud."

Then why is he talking out loud? Maybe Head Elder can't practice the Silent Speech. It requires absolute trust between two people. He obviously doesn't trust anybody, not even his own son. How sad is that?

"What are we to do?" whispers Uncle Tool.

"We must find my grandson and keep him away from his father."

"But the ceremony… the blessing from Jade Dragon…"

"After we disgrace and banish the Dragon Son – former Dragon Son – I will take possession of the Yang Pearl and commune with Jade Dragon."

My mouth gapes open. What the fuck? Is he serious?

Even his son gasps. "Will Jade Dragon allow this?"

"He will, once he learns of his descendant's transgressions," Head Elder speaks with complete certainty, as if he knows the mind of Jade Dragon. As if!

"What about the other clans. Should we dismiss them?"

"No. I want them present to witness the Dragon Son's disgrace."

"What about Wai Kit? Will he cooperate during all this?"

"He will in exchange for his father's life and the safety of his cousins, and his mother."

Fifth Elder doesn't say a single word to protest or defend his sister. He really is a tool.

The silence stretches into minutes. I stretch my neck, straining to listen, but don't hear a thing, not even footsteps. Had they left the chamber as silently as they entered? Or are they still lurking? I don't dare move.

Dad? I reach out. No answer.

Every passing minute feels more like ten. I shift a little so my tattoo isn't pressing against the coarse stone. Some symbol of manhood. Maybe five hundred years ago, a fifteen-year-old was considered an adult in the Two Dragon Clan, but not anymore. Even if I do replace Dad, I won't be allowed to rule until I'm eighteen years old, the standard age of adulthood on the Crossroads.

I get that light-bulb-above-the-head feeling. That's why Head Elder wants to overthrow my father. It will give him three years of complete control over the Two Dragon Clan. This can't wait. I have to warn Dad right now.

I squirm out of the cubbyhole, sit on the ledge and listen. All I can hear is water gurgling in the next cavern. I climb down the rock pile and though I tiptoe, I can still hear my movement. I want to use the Silent Step, but that takes a lot of *chi* energy and I'm already running short.

Tony's mind brushes mine. *Little Brother?*

My shoulders sag. I exhale before answering. *I'm here, in the Dragon Shout chamber.*

As soon as I see Tony, I want to hug him, even though he's staring at me with that critical grimace.

"You look like crap."

He's right. My black pants are dusty gray, and my arms and upper body are streaked with cold sweat and cave dirt.

"Come on. You can get cleaned up before we go back through the caverns." Tony nods toward the water chamber.

I don't budge. "Are you kidding?"

"The other clans are already assembling in the Ancestral Hall. You are the Dragon Son's heir. You must look presentable…"

Big Brother, listen to me. Head Elder is plotting against Dad.

What do you mean?

I repeat the conversation between Head Elder and Uncle Tool. Tony's grim face goes blank. Then he rubs his forehead, as if trying to reconcile what I said with what he wants to believe.

You're sure that's what you heard?

I want to yell, 'Dude, Head Elder shits all over you and your dad. What makes you think he won't do the same to my dad and me?' I already know the answer. Tony thinks his dad deserves it, and by extension, so does he. Appealing to emotions doesn't work with Tony. Only logic.

That's exactly what I heard. Don't you see? Head Elder wants to use me to take over the clan.

But how is he planning to disgrace your father?

I don't know. Does it matter? He'll make some shit up.

He can't do that. Jade Dragon will see through any lies. It must be something to do with my father.

I didn't want to say it, but it doesn't feel any better letting Tony be the one to figure that out. I can see it in his eyes, how it makes him despise his father a little more. He gestures with his head toward the path. *Let's go.*

We go as far as we can without the aid of Tony's lantern, until the darkness becomes impenetrable. He turns up the flame to the barest flicker. I have to follow close behind or lose him in the gloom.

Voices and footsteps vibrate throughout the caverns, but it's impossible to tell how close or far. My throat aches and my bare skin feels clammy. All I can think about is getting to Dad before Head Elder tries anything.

A light shines off the wall further down the path. Tony turns off his lantern and hands it to me. *Stay here. Don't move.* Then he's gone.

I clutch the lantern and gnaw my lip. I feel like a little kid and I hate it.

The progression of the light stops. A voice calls out, "Have you found him?"

The light wavers. There's a crashing sound followed by scuffling noises. Then silence.

I hold my breath.

The light moves upward and becomes steady.

Little Brother.

I exhale as I run toward the light. Rounding the corner, I find Tony standing over two unconscious men. He sets a lantern down between them, takes my lantern and we move forward.

I glance back at the fallen men. Could I have done that? Training and actual combat are two entirely different things, which must be why Head Elder wants to take over now, while I'm still a newb. I stare at my cousin's straight back. Maybe after we return to San Francisco, Dad will let me go with Tony on his missions so I can get some real life experience. First we have to get through the caverns, which are starting to feel like the beginning and end of all existence.

Tony stops abruptly. He cocks his head.

Son. Dad's mind brushes mine. *Hang on. We're almost there.*

I get a case of the shakes, now of all times. I'm not sick or scared, at least, not any more. Maybe it's relief.

Distant footsteps come closer. A dim light brightens as it approaches. Dad appears, surrounded by a troupe of guards. I run to him. He grips my forearms and starts to speak.

I interrupt with the Silent Speech. *Dad, Head Elder is plotting against you.*

Dad's relieved expression scrunches. *What do you mean?*

I repeat what I overheard.

Dad's grip tightens before he lets go. *Don't say anything. I can't trust everyone here.* Then he says aloud, "We must hurry. The Summoning Ceremony is about to begin."

Paul

We hustle along a path that winds around to the back of clan headquarters. My stomach flutters against the fear that Head Elder has already put his plans in motion, though what can he do now that Dad knows? He and his goons are probably still schlepping through the caverns, trying to find me. What a laugh. Maybe he'll get lost and miss the Summoning Ceremony. That would be sweet.

We head straight for Second Elder's office and barge in without knocking. Dad orders the guards to stay in the hall before closing the door behind us.

Second Elder shows no emotion as she rises from behind her desk. She's dressed for the ceremony in the flowing, dark blue robes of an elder. Her square black hat calls attention to the thin, puckered scar that slashes across her forehead, leaving a pale line through her left eyebrow. She's the clan's top swordsman and earned the title the hard way. I don't have a nickname for her since she's pretty cool.

"It's worse than we thought," Dad tells her. "He plans to overthrow me during the ceremony."

Second Elder sucks in her breath. "Head Elder would

divide our clan while the other clans watch? That cannot happen."

"It won't happen, thanks to my son." Dad turns to me with a proud smile. My chest swells. Finally, he's looking at me the same way he looks at Tony. Then he nods toward the back of the room. "There's a bathroom to the left. Go wash up."

I've gone from hero to grimy kid in five seconds flat. Story of my life.

The mirror above the sink shows how grimy I really am. I reach for a bar of soap shaped like a seashell, but it doesn't smell like the ocean or even soap. More like a rosebush in full bloom. I hate the smell of roses, so I use plain water to scrub off the worst of the dirt, leaving the sink and the embroidered pink and white hand towels caked with muck. Second Elder isn't going to be happy. Maybe when this is over, I can buy her some new towels at the night market in Kowloon.

There's a knock at the door. I crack it open.

Tony stands outside looking clean and sharp in black trousers and a white dress shirt. He hands me a similar outfit. "Hurry up. It's time to go."

I tug on the clothes and rake my fingers through my wet hair before rubbing a dark smudge off my nose. I almost look presentable except for one thing. Tony didn't bring me different shoes. I glance down at my workout boots. The black cloth has turned gray with cave dust and the battered leather tips look weird with my pants. Maybe no one will notice. Yeah, right.

Mom stands beside Dad in the center of the office. Both are wearing scarlet silk robes with long sleeves that drape to the floor. The robes are bound with dangling gold cords and embroidered with gold dragons chasing each other's tails. It's like they've put on superhero outfits because they look confident and serene, like a powerful *Xia* couple that kick ass without blinking an eye. Then I notice the Yang Pearl draped around Dad's neck. Jade Dragon must be sending out his power vibes. I could sure use some.

Mom unfurls an identical robe and beckons me over. I'm about to become a super *Xia*, too. I stand still, arms spread, as my parents drape and bind me. My stomach starts to tremble. I take a slow breath to allow my flow of *chi* to calm me. I want to be like my parents. I want to make them proud.

Tony stands nearby, wearing a simple gray and black robe draped over his clothes. It's weird to think that if Uncle George had come out first, we'd be changing places. Does Tony ever think about that? I'll bet Uncle George does. All. The. Time. He'd be a crap Dragon Son. Though would he have turned out different if he'd been first born? I can't imagine Dad being any different, so, no.

Fourth Elder enters. She's shorter than Second Elder and the sleeves of her ceremonial garment drag on the ground. She has grayer hair and kinder eyes, and no cool scar, probably because her specialty is Chinese medicine. No nickname, too, because she takes good care of Mom. When she speaks, she tends to draw out her words with long tones.

"Dragon Son, all those attending the Summoning Ceremony have assembled. We await you and your family. Head Elder knows you are aware of his plans. He's been warned that any attempt to speak his lies will result in his expulsion from the ceremony and our clan."

Dad glances at Tony before he says, "Good."

I don't need any further proof this all has to do with Dad's loser twin. Poor Tony.

Fourth Elder turns to Mom with a grave expression. "Dragon Son's Wife, are you well enough to attend the ceremony?"

Mom continues straightening the folds of my robe. "I'm fine."

I twist around to look at her more closely. Are the circles under her eyes darker than usual? "Mom?"

She gives a final tug and takes a step back, her stern expression reminding me, for a moment, of Head Elder. "You are the Dragon Son's heir. Make us proud."

Dad presses his fingers to her wrist and tilts his head as if listening. "Your pulse is uneven."

Mom tugs her hand away. "I'm fine. My father must see us united as a family."

Dad nods, though worry remains in his eyes.

The ceremonial robe weighs heavy on my shoulders. I've looked forward to this day my entire life and Head Elder had to go and ruin everything. He's even made Mom, his own daughter, sick. I can't let that old man think he's done us any damage. I shift so the robe rests more comfortably on my frame and announce, "I'm ready."

My parents' tense frowns become smiles as they look at me before turning again to each other. If they're using Silent Speech, I hope they're saying, 'I love you.'

Guards accompany us from Second Elder's office to the Ancestral Hall. It's sad to think they're not protecting us from outsiders, but from our own people, our own family. When this is over, Dad's going to have to do something about Head Elder, but what? Maybe Jade Dragon knows what's going on and can provide some wisdom. Despite the heat, I get the chills realizing I'm about to meet a dragon.

Dad and Mom enter the hall first, followed by me, Tony, and Second Elder and Fourth Elder. Clan members handpicked for this honor fill the cavern in precise rows, all facing the altar. Candlelight flickers off their expectant faces. My family goes to the front of the altar and turns to face the crowd, while Second Elder and Fourth Elder take their places in the front row with the rest of the elders. Head Elder fixes his reptile eyes on me, like he's Godzilla and I'm Tokyo. He looks me up and down and doesn't seem to notice my dirty boots, which is not normal. My spine tingles. Did he guess I'm the one who ratted him out? I hope so. I want him to know he can't make me his stooge.

A gong sounds. Mom and Tony take several steps back and kneel, along with the rest of the clan. I turn with Dad to face the altar. A man dressed in the flowing, dark robes of a Taoist priest holds six sticks of lit incense, which he divides evenly between us. Then he steps back and strikes the gong again.

Everyone goes silent, though the walls echo with a hum of anticipation. I almost forgot about this part of the ceremony. Jade Dragon first manifested as a dragon at the age of fifteen. Before his earthly death, he prophesied that one of his descendants would also manifest as a dragon. Since then, each heir of the Dragon Son has stood before the altar at the age of fifteen. Now, it's my turn. Is it really supposed to happen right at this moment? Wouldn't I have felt something before this?

If I do become a dragon, Head Elder will shit his pants. Who's Godzilla now, old man? I force myself not to grin. Despite how great that would be, I don't want to be a dragon. Being the future Dragon Son is hard enough.

Minutes pass. I chew my lip, checking myself internally for something… anything? Nope. No dragon mojo. How long is this supposed to take? Is there a time limit for manifestation?

The gong sounds again, and I exhale. Okay, I'm not a dragon. Cool. As my shoulders relax, I hear a hissing sound behind me. It's Head Elder. Is he relieved or disappointed? Who cares?

Dad kneels in front of Jade Dragon's spirit tablet. I drop to my knees beside him. Following Dad's lead, I hold the incense sticks above my head and kowtow three times, my forehead touching the stone floor. Then Dad speaks.

"Jade Dragon, your firstborn son is before you. I am the pearl at your throat, the instrument of your will. I seek the wisdom and righteousness that are my inheritance through you. Come forth now. We humbly beseech your presence."

"Jade Dragon, we beseech your presence," intones the clan.

The gong sounds three times and after each toll, everyone kowtows in unison. After the third bow, the priest takes the sticks of incense from Dad and me, and places them in the main brazier on the altar. Then he backs away.

Dad closes his eyes and takes a deep breath. Silence fills the room and something more: that kind of heaviness and crackle of energy that hangs in the air right before a huge thunderstorm. My stomach quivers. If only I was outside. Maybe I could catch a glimpse of our ancestor above the compound. But no, it's better to be at the altar, in the actual presence of Jade Dragon.

The Yang Pearl begins to glow, softly at first, growing brighter until its glare dazzles my eyes. I blink hard. Spots dance. A cold breeze blows from the back of the altar, stirring incense smoke and candle flames. It picks up strength, rustling my hair and chilling my skin through the robe. The pearl embedded in the spirit tablet glows as well. A beam of light emanates from its depths. A similar beam radiates from the Yang Pearl. The two rays join to become a single shaft of light.

I gasp as a golden glow envelops my father. He closes his eyes and bows his head. Is that part of the ceremony? I follow his example, just in case. After a few moments, I feel this weird sensation, like electricity, is crackling all around me. I slit open my eyes. The glow surrounds me as well. I can feel its thrum in my chest. I want to reach out and touch it, but my fingers are digging into my knees.

Dad's eyes open as he lifts his head. "Jade Dragon, behold your heir, my son." He stops and takes another deep breath. "Lau Wai Kit. He is the pearl at your throat, the instrument of your will. He seeks the wisdom and righteousness that are his inheritance through you."

Dad lays his hand on my collarbone. Power flows through his palm and rolls down my spine. I jerk. It's like a powerful electric shock without the pain. The power surge intensifies. Cold fire pulses through my veins. The Yang Pearl is nothing compared to this. I feel like I can destroy the Ancestral Hall if I want to.

Jade Dragon swirls through the sky overhead, diving in and out of clouds, impatient to return to the sea. Then he turns his gaze to me. His eyes glow red.

Stand. Jade Dragon's voice, ancient and cold, echoes distantly as if from the bottom of a well.

The energy surging through me lifts me to my feet. My breath comes in spurts as I realize I don't have control of my movements.

"Son?" Dad's whisper sounds far away.

Turn.

I spin around, lifting my left arm and thrusting my palm out toward Head Elder. Power coils in my belly, demanding to be released.

Kill the traitor.

Breath trembles in my chest. The pressure makes my nose feel like it's going to start bleeding.

"Son?" Dad's voice becomes more urgent.

Your father cannot – will not – kill his wife's father. You must. Jade Dragon's voice trails off in a hiss.

I wait, but nothing happens. Then I realize. Jade Dragon has pointed me at Head Elder, but he's not going to shoot the gun. I am a weapon with a conscience and I have to make the decision.

To be honest, for a split second, I consider it. Then I remember my mother. *I can't. He's my grandfather.*

His treachery will not cease until he dies. Another hiss.

I can't. I won't.

Then you must live with the consequences, hatchling. The time will come when you have no choice. Jade Dragon's voice fades away.

The power drains from me, making my knees wobble. I blink hard and shake my head. Then I realize I'm still standing in front of the crowd with my palm aimed at Head Elder, whose reptile eyes finally show some emotion: fear. Ah crap. What should I do?

I clear my throat. "Um, Jade Dragon spoke to me and," I pause, my mind blank. "And… he… uh…" I make a wide awkward sweep with my hand to include everybody. "He wants us all to work together and not plot against each other. Um, that's all."

Okay, that was lame. I swivel around and kneel beside Dad. It takes all my remaining strength not to pitch face first onto the floor. Neither the spirit tablet's pearl nor the Yang Pearl has any radiance. Ah crap. Have I ruined the ceremony?

Dad's mind brushes mine. *Son, what happened?*

Jade Dragon. He spoke to me. He really did. But – but it was bad.

Be calm. We'll talk later.

Dad stands and gestures for me to stand and face the crowd with him. My knees still shake and my limbs tremble. All that's keeping me upright is the thought of fainting in front of all these people. Then Tony's eyes catch mine and hold me in place.

You can do this, he says.

Dude, you don't know. It was bad.

Doesn't matter if it was good or bad. You can do it.

Tony's right, like always. If he says I can stand, then I can. Somehow, that thought calms me. Strength returns to my limbs.

Dad's voice fills the hall, "Jade Dragon has spoken through my heir. We must heed his virtuous commands. We are the invisible *Xia* that protects our people from criminals and injustice. We must act righteously with one another as well."

Wow, Dad really knows how to spin some bullshit. Is that another skill I'll need to learn to be an effective Dragon Son?

Everyone rises and applauds, except Head Elder, who stands with his arms folded. Wait until he finds out Jade Dragon wants him dead. He owes us his life.

Dad gestures Mom and Tony to join us in front the altar. As the hubbub dies down, the Crossroads clan leaders are led into the hall and queued up for their oaths of fealty.

Traditionally, during September, the clans of the Crossroads pay tribute to the ruling clan of their district on a day of that clan's choosing. The Two Dragon Clan always chooses the day of the Summoning Ceremony. In cities all over the world, similar ceremonies will be taking place, except San Francisco. That ceremony will happen when Dad returns.

Brother Ash, the Beggar Chief, swaggers down the corridor, his long staff thudding the ground before him. He wears a frayed orange tank top over a bright yellow one, both tucked into a pair of baggy, stained pants bound at the waist with colorful, ragged strips of cloth. His flip-flops reveal dirty feet beneath the tattered cuffs of his pants. His thick black hair lay atop his head in an untidy pile with uneven strands coiling past his shoulders. A sparse mustache and beard surround his mouth, and between his lips is clenched an unlit, half-smoked cigar.

He comes to a halt in front of Dad. A tense silence fills the room, all eyes on his staff, the symbol of a Beggar Chief's authority. If he raises it above his head, he will be challenging Dad. They would then head out to the courtyard where they would fight, not just for victory over each other, but also for the supremacy of one clan over the other.

Dad and Brother Ash stare at each other without blinking. I hold my breath. The Beggar Chief lifts his staff, taking the other end in his hand. He holds it before him with outstretched arms and bows.

I exhale. Then I crane my neck to examine the staff. It looks old and worn, though the carving of a man wrestling a giant snake is still visible. It must be a worthy weapon. How many Beggar Chiefs have held it before him?

Brother Ash lowers the staff and leans against it at a relaxed angle. He removes his cigar and grins, smoothing the deep lines between his eyes. "Walk in peace, Dragon Son."

"Walk in peace, Beggar Chief," Dad replies.

"Dragon Son, it seems the wealthy dislike the stench of the poor."

At the other end of the corridor, the Iron Fan Sisterhood's Chief stands with her arms folded tight and her glare fixed onto the back of the Beggar Chief.

Dad's lips twitch, but he doesn't smile. "Beggar Chief, you are mistaken. Sister Seventeen objected to the stench of your cigar. The other clan leaders complained as well."

"Ah, they misunderstood. The cigar was meant as a courtesy, to cover the stench of my poverty."

"Perhaps you'll allow me to give you a more expensive cigar next time."

Brother Ash sniffs his cigar and a look of disgust twists his face. "You're right. This one stinks worse than poverty." He shoves it into his pocket.

I grin. Brother Ash winks at me. He's cool, like John Walks Long, the Beggar Chief of San Francisco.

"Beggar Chief," calls out Head Elder, always the buzzkill. "The other clans are waiting."

Brother Ash smirks over his shoulder. "Forgive me. Beggars have no refinement." He cups his right fist with his left palm and bows. "Dragon Son, the Beggar Clan of Hong Kong offers the Two Dragon Clan their fealty for the coming year. A thousand years of prosperity to you."

Dad returns his salute. "Our two paths shall be as one."

The Beggar Chief strides back down the aisle. Sister Seventeen ignores him as they pass each other. She wears a white silk uniform with billowing sleeves and a dark red sash. I know from her name that she's the seventeenth chief of the local Iron Fan Sisterhood, with a direct lineage of leadership passed down from *sifu* to disciple. I can tell from her no-nonsense expression there will be no hijinks.

She halts in front of Dad and bows, covering her right fist with her left palm. "Dragon Son, the Iron Fan Sisterhood of Hong Kong offers the Two Dragon Clan their fealty for the coming year. A thousand years of prosperity to you."

So it goes, through at least ten clans and maybe more. I lose count. I'd be bored if I wasn't so aware of Head Elder standing a few feet away.

After the last clan makes their oath, Dad and I, along Mom and Tony, salute the crowd and bow. Dad speaks in a confident tone. "The descendants of Jade Dragon are honored by your presence. Although a Dragon Son has never been successfully challenged, we don't doubt the prowess of the Crossroads clans. We are determined to be worthy of the honor of leading those who walk the Glory Road for another year." He gestures toward the front entrance. "We invite you to join us now for a banquet to honor our commitment to one another."

The crowd begins filing out, quietly murmuring among themselves. They'll head for the pavilion in the central courtyard. All week, while training in the caverns, I'd looked forward to finally being able to attend the grand feast at the end of the Summoning Ceremony. Now, all I want is to go home and go to bed. Well, maybe take a shower first, and if Mom has some leftover vegetable dumplings in the fridge, that would be great, too.

Head Elder approaches us. The tight stretch of his lips could be mistaken for a smile if it weren't for the hatred in his eyes. He leans forward and whispers as if conferring with Dad. "You think you can hide your transgression. No matter what you do, it remains. If your family knew, they would despise and reject you."

Mom gazes on her father with cold eyes. "That's not true."

Head Elder looks her up and down. "You are a weak woman who gave birth to a weak son. You have chosen to stay at the side of a weak man. You are worthless. From this time forward, you are no longer my daughter."

All color drains from Mom's face. Her eyelids flutter. She swallows hard and takes a deep breath before saying, "So be it." Then she turns and, head held high, strides down the corridor.

Dad glares at him. "You are a power hungry fool and you'll die alone."

Head Elder's left cheek ticks.

Dad turns and follows Mom, Tony on his heels.

I don't budge. Head Elder knows Mom has a bad heart. Why is he messing with her like that? Someone needs to mess back. "What transgression?"

Head Elder sneers, "I'm not going to compound your father's cowardice by telling you."

Frustration boils my blood. He caused all this trouble for what, some evil lie or half-truth blown out of proportion? "Jade Dragon knows you and the other elders are plotting against my father. He ordered me to kill you, but I refused because you're my grandfather. I guess that doesn't count anymore."

Now he's the one who turns pale. Satisfaction spreads through my chest as that lizard gaze becomes fearful. "Your father told you to say that."

I shrug. "You'll never know."

"Little Brother," Tony calls out from front entrance.

I stroll past Head Elder like I'm a boss and he's bullshit.

Tony frowns as I approach him. "What did he say to you?"

I bite my lip. Maybe I shouldn't have told Head Elder about

Jade Dragon. Tension balls up in my stomach. "Um, he said Dad's a coward."

"Don't listen to him."

"Of course not."

My feet falter as I follow Tony into Second Elder's office. Mom sits backwards on a chair, her head resting on her folded arms. Dad stands behind her, his hands pressed into her back. I want to go to them, but Fourth Elder grabs hold of my arm. "Your mother is ill. Your father is healing her."

My nails bite into my palms. So, Head Elder managed to get to Mom after all. Is that why he said all those terrible things, to make her sick? My regret over what I said to him vanishes. I wish I'd said worse.

Mom lifts her head. Color has returned to her cheeks. She takes a deep breath and nods her head.

Dad's hands slip away. He looks drained after expending his *chi* on healing. His eyes close and he rubs his forehead.

I tug away from Fourth Elder and hurry to my mother's side. "Are you okay, Mom?"

She manages a smile. "I'm fine. It was nothing. Your father took care of it."

I turn to my father. "Dad?"

His eyes open. He gives his head a shake. Then he beckons me to follow him to the far corner of the room. Despite the distance from the others, he uses the Silent Speech. *What did Jade Dragon say to you?*

I duck my head as I repeat Jade Dragon's words. Then, after a moment's hesitation, confess. *After you and Mom left, Head Elder called you a coward. I got mad. I told him what Jade Dragon said.*

Dad sucks in his breath. I knew I blew it. His reply is like a soft whisper. *It's all right. It's probably for the best. He won't dare try to seize the Yang Pearl now.*

I exhale with relief. Then I look up. Dad doesn't seem

angry, more like determined and something else. He seems sad. My stomach clenches again. I hesitate, not wanting to make things worse, but I need to know. *Why did Jade Dragon want us to kill Head Elder? Why didn't he do it himself?*

Dad's gaze becomes distant. *He's a dragon. He no longer lives in the Earthly realm. We either do as he bids or live with the consequences. Jade Dragon won't do our work for us.*

But will he help us if we're in trouble?

Dad shrugs. *Dragons are capricious beings. It's impossible to predict their actions. We can't expect Jade Dragon's aid. It's likely he's already gone.*

That isn't the answer I want. I trail behind my father as we rejoin the others.

"This cannot continue," says Second Elder. "The power struggle between you and Head Elder will tear our clan apart."

"I agree," Dad says. "I must confront Head Elder, but not while my family is here. He'll continue using them as weapons against me. That's why I want you," he glances at Tony, "all of you, to return to San Francisco immediately. You'll fly home tomorrow."

My insides go hollow. I feel like I'm back in the cavern, hiding in the crevice, helpless. Mom and Tony's voices sound like static as they attempt to reason with Dad. I remain silent. I know that look on his face.

Dad waits until they're finished. He turns to Tony first. "I am the Dragon Son. You will obey me."

Tony's resolute expression becomes unsure. He bows his head. "Yes, Uncle."

Dad and Mom withdraw to the back of the room. They stand with their heads tilted close, almost touching. Neither speaks aloud. Mom's arms are folded tight, but after a few minutes, the tense expression on her face softens and she wraps her arms around his neck.

I turn away and head for the door.

"Where are you going?" asks Tony.

Big Brother is not going to stop me. "I want to see Jade Dragon one more time before we go."

"I'll come with you."

"Fine." Whatever. I scratch my tattoo. I hate being treated like a kid.

The Ancestral Hall is darker now with the candles burning low. No one else seems to be around, but Tony checks around to be sure. I stand before Jade Dragon's tablet. The embedded pearl gleams in the candlelight, but holds none of its previous supernatural glow. Still, Jade Dragon can't be too far away.

I reach out using the Silent Speech. *Ancestor.*

Waves crash and foam boils on the surface of the South China Sea as Jade Dragon swims toward a forest of kelp.

I shiver as a chill washes over my flesh. *Ancestor, please protect your son, my father.*

Green and brown fronds sway with the current, like thick, hairy arms beckoning Jade Dragon into their depths. He doesn't look back.

Penny

"Is she doing her homework?" As usual, Bill talks like I'm not sitting right there. He's on his way to work and acting almighty in his fine business suit, like he's the Man and we're his worthless dependents.

Bridie looks up from the sink where she's washing his breakfast dishes. "Of course, darling. Every night, I check and make sure it's done."

I share a quick smirk across the kitchen table with Kai. Bridie doesn't check shite. Our homework is beyond her ken.

"This is her last day of suspension. I want her to be prepared to go back to school." He spares me a glare. "Are you?"

I take a bite of toast and chew as I answer, "Yeah."

"No more brawling. No more cutting class. On Monday, there better be a much better attitude."

I drop my toast. "He told the whole school I gave him a blow job. Wouldn't you have punched him, too?"

His face reddens and he won't look me in the eye. "I know that boy insulted you, but hitting him wasn't the answer. Besides, his parents could have sued us if you'd hurt him."

All about money. All the time. And, of course, my reputation isn't worth a brass farthing.

"He's been warned to stay away from you. If he gives you any more trouble, you're to go to a teacher and ask for help."

Not a single bloody clue. Most of the teachers at Parkside Academy think Kevin walks on water. The only reason he got in trouble this time is because a teacher's assistant saw the whole thing and told Vice Principal Ikeda. Even so, Kevin only got suspended for two days, while I got a whole week. He probably spent the time stealing liquor from his parents and slagging me off online, him and the Daisy Chain. Too bad for them I don't give a tinker's damn about social media.

Bill turns to Bridie. "I'll look at her homework tonight."

She flutters her lashes. "Please do, darling. I'm afraid it's a bit complicated for me."

Bill sighs and pats Bridie on the bum before heading out the kitchen door to the garage.

My throat burns. I want to vomit. "You can't keep him Charmed forever."

Bridie glances nervously at the closed door before hissing, "Shush."

I whisper loudly, "Charms fade."

Bridie turns from the sink, soapsuds flying as her hands go to her hips. Still, she waits for the sound of his car rolling down the driveway before she speaks. "I'm not Charming Bill. Not anymore."

Kai gives a little snort. I cross my arms and meet her gaze without blinking.

Bridie looks down. "Well, maybe just a little. Just enough to, you know, keep him hooked. You're right. Charms fade. They're only meant for short term deals." Her green eyes flash as she looks up. "But this isn't short term. I want my marriage to work and I'm willing to do what it takes."

"Do you even like him?"

"He's not bad. There's worse out there than Bill."

"You didn't answer my question."

She picks up her coffee mug and leans against the counter. "Look, we could have a nice ride here if you," she looks from me to Kai, "both of you, would cooperate."

Why should I cooperate if she won't answer my question? Not that she needs to. The answer is obvious. I want her to face it, face what we gave up to be here. "Do you think Gerry and Matthew would have told me to have a better attitude," my fingers make quotation marks, "after being scumbered by some knob? No. They'd have expected me to thrash him."

"And then they would have hunted him down and given him a basting." Kai punches the air.

Bridie looks into her cup. "That's over with now."

I hate it when she acts defeated, as if Gerry and Matthew's deaths had killed her spirit. It still has to be in there somewhere. I pound the table. "It's not over with. Not for me or Kai, or for you. We're Strowlers, Bridie. We weren't born for this." I gesture widely with my hands. "Staying in one place, pretending to be normal. We're not normal. We're not Bleaters."

"We are now." Bridie takes a grim sip of coffee before turning to Kai. "Are you ready for school?"

"No." Kai drops his spoon. Milk splashes out of his cereal bowl. "Penny's right. I hate this. I want to go home."

"This is our home."

"No, it's not. The road is our home." His hazel eyes storm over and his voice rises with accusation. "It was our home, until you sold our caravan."

My heart lifts at finally getting some backup from my quiet brother. I know he feels the same way I do, but he's never been one to speak until necessary. Our definition of "necessary" is pretty different. Sometimes I think I should be like him, but I'm not. There's too much of Gerry in me.

Bridie gives a tight shrug. "I had to. We can't eat air."

"Let's go back to London and buy a new one."

"Son, we can't go back. You know that. It's too dangerous."

"Let's go back to Ireland," I say. "We don't have to stay at the Nest. We can live in Dublin."

Bridie shakes her head. She grips her coffee mug with both hands. "I don't want to go back. Not to London, Dublin, any of it."

Kai shoves back his chair. "What about us? What about what we want?"

"I'm doing this for you. You think I wanted to marry Bill? You think I want to be his little wife? That I want to spend all my time and energy keeping him happy? I did it to give you children a better life, a life away from the Crossroads."

I hate it when she uses us as her excuse. "We belong on the Crossroads and so do you."

"Really? You want to give up this rum house with all its riggings." Bridie sets down her mug and starts counting each item on her fingers. "Good food, proper medical care, proper schooling, nice clothes, new computers, your own rooms – all to go back on the road and live in a trailer."

"Yes."

Kai nods vigorously.

Bridie purses her lips. After a few moments, she gives a resolute nod. "Right. You want to be Sharpers and live by your wits, so let's do it."

I don't trust this obvious change of tactics. I meet her mocking gaze. "Do what?"

"Be Strowlers. Go busk for spare change on Market Street and see how far it gets us."

"You're serious?"

"Of course."

"Today? Right now?"

Bridie nods.

"Ah, yeah." Kai gives a fist pump before jumping out of his chair and launching himself upstairs.

I follow slowly. Bridie isn't well educated, school-wise, but she has plenty of street smarts. She's obviously hoping some lesson will be learned that will turn Kai and me into happy, grateful little Bleaters.

So not going to happen.

My dance costume, while flash, is all wrong for busking. If the busk goes wrong - say, the *gardaí* chases you off, you have to be able to blend in with the crowd. I put on jeans and a black t-shirt. Concrete will wear down the soft soles of my gillies, so I place my hard dance shoes in the gym bag, along with the penny whistles.

Downstairs, Bridie waits with Kai. She's wearing an orange peasant blouse over a denim miniskirt and moccasin boots. Her legs are pale from lack of sun. Kai has on his treasured Pogues t-shirt; the one Matthew gave him. He sways with impatience, knocking his guitar case against his knees.

Bridie tosses me a tambourine. It jingles as I catch it. "Bring your transit pass, but no money. I don't have any money, either. If we want lunch, we'll have to earn it."

"What about Bill?"

"We'll be home before he is, though if I had my way, we'd be gone until tomorrow. That way, we'd have to busk until we earn enough for dinner and a hotel for the night. I want you two to remember how hard that life was."

Bridie obviously thinks her children have grown soft in confinement. She's about to learn different. I lift my chin. "Let's go."

We walk a couple of blocks and catch the light rail downtown. At Powell Street station, another busker has already taken the primo spot in the atrium outside the turnstiles. He's strumming his guitar like it's a weapon and singing "Like a Rolling Stone" at the top of his lungs, his long dark hair swishing around his shoulders as he sways back and forth. The punters hurry past him since they don't like being hollered at.

"Someone beat us here," Bridie remarks. "We'll have to play in the street."

I nod toward 'Bob Dylan's' empty guitar case. "He won't be here long. No one's tossing him any gelt."

"We can't afford to wait around. Time is money." Bridie's know-it-all expression makes me grit my teeth.

We go up the escalator. Tag-rags cluster around the metro entrance, begging money off the Bleaters who, for the most part, ignore them. My nose crinkles as we pass one with a strong urine stench. Sharpers look down on tag-rags – junkies, pushers, pimps and prostitutes. Substance abuse and vice aren't tolerated on the Crossroads, but is living off of Bill much different than prostitution? Can't Bridie see that?

This part of Market Street is one big tourist trap, packed with malls, fast food restaurants and chain stores. Biggest trap of all is the cable car turnaround. A queue of tourists snakes around the block as they wait to board the antique trolleys, which must slowly turn around on the tracks before making the journey up and down the steep hills to Ghiradelli Square. We made the trip once. It would have been fun if Bill hadn't ruined it by complaining about the cost.

Other buskers have taken over this prime spot as well, so we head down the street toward the bay, though we don't go too far. There's nothing to be gained by venturing into the area known as Boomlandia. After the tech bust, businesses failed and thousands of jobs evaporated almost overnight, according to Bill. He told us, smug as you please, that tourism and the financial institutions are all that's holding the city together. Whatever the truth is, a lot of buildings are empty or occupied by tag-rags, so there's no point in going near them.

After walking about two blocks, Kai says, "I'm thirsty."

Bridie shrugs. "We don't have money to buy a bottle of water."

I glare at her. She's deliberately making this harder than it is. There's a large drugstore on the corner. Without a word, I lead the way inside to the water fountain.

As Kai drinks, Bridie remarks, "Not too much, son." She nods at a sign saying the toilets are for customer use only. Does she want him to pee in the gutter? Even in London, we never did that.

We cross the street to a small plaza next to a mall. Bridie takes out her violin and sets the open case on the sidewalk in front of us. She and Kai tune their instruments and I do some quick stretches before replacing my clogs with my hard dance shoes. They're designed for jigs and inlaid with resin to make a tapping noise as I dance. The mid-sole is flexible and the tip reinforced so I can dance on my toes.

People hurry by, ignoring us. No one wants to be bothered, not until we prove we're worth their time.

"Let's start with the Beatles," Bridie says. "Everyone loves the Beatles." She tucks her violin under her chin and plays the melancholy opening chords of "Nowhere Man". Some people turn their heads, but no one stops. Kai joins in on guitar and vocals while I play the tambourine and sing along.

"Nowhere Man" gets us nowhere. Not even a dime is tossed into Bridie's case the entire song.

She shrugs. "Well, we're only getting started. Let's give the Beatles another try. Something more upbeat."

"Here Comes the Sun" earns us some smiles as well as spare gelt, including a couple of dollars. Bridie looks at the money and gnaws down a smile. "We can't play the Fab Four all day. I think it's time for Penny to earn her keep."

I meet the challenge in my mother's eyes. "It'll have to be a jig. How about 'Penny's Prance'?"

Bridie's face goes blank. I wipe my palms on my thighs. Suggesting that song is risky, but she's the one trying to relive the old days like it's some kind of punishment. She's forgotten the joy of playing our own music. "Penny's Prance" was written for me and I haven't danced it since Gerry and Matthew died.

"I... I doubt your brother remembers that one."

"Yeah, I do." Kai sets his guitar in its case, takes out a penny whistle and plays the opening bars.

Bridie closes her eyes and sucks in her breath. There's no joy in her face when she looks at me again. Her bow attacks the violin strings as she strikes up the tune.

Maybe I pushed her too far, but I need Bridie to know... to understand that no matter what, I don't want our songs to be forgotten. I miss the first beat and shake my head to clear my thoughts. I have to concentrate or I'll trip and sprawl all over the bricks.

Arms pressed to my sides, I pick up the tempo, the tips of my shoes tapping out the rhythm. When my legs kick up, people slow down. Some stop. Some stay to the end of the song. Applause surrounds us as I bow again. Dollar bills fly into the case. Bridie's eyes widen. My smile hurts my face. I can't let the punters see I really want to cry.

As the crowd disperses, one man remains. He's well over six feet tall, with an impressive girth made grander by the long, patchwork coat he wears like a robe of state. His baggy gray trousers, faded and streaked with dirt, are tucked into a pair of knee-high, fringed leather boots. His long brown hair and full, chest-length beard, both shot with gray, sprout from his round, red face like a lion's mane. In one hand he holds a knobby staff, almost as tall as he.

He drops a five dollar bill in the case and smiles through his beard, revealing yellow, uneven teeth. "Very nice." His voice has a gentle rumble.

"Thank you." Bridie's lips remain parted, as if she wants to say more. Then she simply nods.

He nods back and continues on his way, striding down Market Street, his staff thudding the ground before him, a king on progress through his realm.

"The Beggar Chief," I whisper.

"No…" Bridie's voice trails off as she stares after him.

"He's got the staff," Kai says.

"That doesn't mean he's the Beggar Chief." Bridie scratches her knee with her bow. "Though I suppose there must be a Beggar Clan in San Francisco."

Of course there's a Beggar Clan. How can there not be? San Francisco is a fulcrum on the Crossroads, just like London and Dublin. All kinds of Sharpers live or pass through here, including the Dragon Son, the head of the Crossroads. I swallow those words, not wanting to spook Bridie. I clear my throat. "Mind if I buy a bottle of water?"

Bridie frowns. "Just one. And all three of us share." She reaches into the case and hands me just enough change for the one bottle.

Kai gags. "Gross."

I sigh. Bridie really wants to push her point, doesn't she? I shove the coins in my pocket and head for a drug store across the street. I feel a little guilty when, as a paying customer, I use the loo.

When I reach the crosswalk, I hear Bridie and Kai playing Cat Stevens' "Where Do the Children Play." Even from across the street, I can see the light of joy in my mother's eyes. Real joy, not that happiness she fakes to keep Bill Charmed.

"Please, please remember who you were," I whisper before I rejoin them.

"Ready for another dance?" she asks.

I nod.

"How about 'The Strowler Girl's Jig'?"

Now I go blank. That's another Wild Sky song written for me. Is Bridie really getting into the spirit or is this payback for dropping "Penny's Prance" on her? Does it matter? As long as Bridie is playing our music, she's being reminded of what we'd once had and can have again.

It's been more than a year since I last danced or even practiced this jig. It involves intricate heel/toe tap combinations and I mess up a couple of times before I get back in the rhythm. My frown of concentration turns into a smile as I relax and let my body feel the beat. A growing crowd gathers and by the time I take my final bow, Bridie's violin case is overflowing with dollar bills.

Not everyone in the audience is smiling. A woman dressed like a prison guard on holiday looks us over with disapproving eyes. "Shouldn't these two be in school?"

"Not today," Bridie replies with a bright smile. The woman gives us a long stare as she walks away. I wonder if she's related to Vice Principal Ikeda. Bridie mutters, "Mind your own business, you gobby cow," before turning to Kai and me. "We better move on. Don't want the *gardaí* asking what you're doing out here. Besides, we have enough for lunch."

A scabby tag-rag lurches toward us. He grabs hold of Bridie's case, clutches it to his chest and skitters through the crowd. I freeze. I don't care about the money. I care about this day, the first good day in a long time, being ruined by some cracked-out swill tub.

"Oi!" Kai takes off after him.

I'm on his heels.

Bridie grabs my arm. My shoes clack against the bricks as I flail backwards. I try tugging away, but her fingers dig into my flesh as she hollers, "Kai! Son, no. Get back here right now."

Kai halts, probably because he's wearing Matthew's guitar and doesn't want it ruined in a brawl. Still, he glares at Bridie as he stomps back. "He's getting away."

"Let him. I swear, the two of you…" She lets go and presses her hand to her heart. There's fear behind the anger in her eyes. "You catch up with him, he'll hurt you."

"Or we'll hurt him."

"We can't just stand here," I say. "We have to stop him."

"Stop him how? You brawl with him, these Bleaters will call the *gardaí*, who'll want to know who we are and what we're doing out here, trying to earn money without green cards." She takes a deep breath. "Well, I hate saying I told you so and I really hate losing my violin case, but I suppose it's worth the lesson. The Crossroads are dangerous. Without the protection of the law or our clan, we're helpless. We can't go back to our old life; don't you see? I'm sorry, darlings, but that's the way it is."

The bearded man comes striding toward us, staff in one hand and Bridie's violin case in the other. He holds it out to her with a courtly bow. "I believe this belongs to you."

Bridie gapes before she speaks. "Why, yes, thank you. Thank you so much."

"My pleasure." His eyes twinkle as he speaks. Then he turns away to leave.

Bridie bites her lip. If she doesn't say something, I will. Then she bursts out, "Walk in peace, Beggar Chief."

I smile. I can't help myself. She nudges me. I nudge her back.

The man turns back around. His gaze becomes shrewd. "Well, now. Who do we have here?"

"We're Strowlers," I say.

"Ah, I see. Kingfisher's people?"

"No," we all say at once.

The Beggar Chief raises his bushy eyebrows.

"We're not American Strowlers. We're from Ireland," Bridie explains.

"Well, that explains the accents." He bows again. "John Walks Long, at your service."

She gives a little bob. "Bridie Sparrow."

"Walk in peace, Bridie Sparrow."

"These are my children, Penny and Kai."

"Walk in peace, Beggar Chief," I say and Kai echoes.

He nods. "Walk in peace, children." He turns to Bridie. "Are you out here from necessity?"

"No. Well, not exactly. I want the children to remember their roots."

"I see." He gives a gentle nod.

"Is there any way I can repay you?"

"I ask nothing in return. The pleasure of such song and dance is payment enough. I'll have my people keep an eye on you when you next perform. Will you return soon?"

"Um, no."

My heart sinks. For a moment, I want to ask John Walks Long if I can come with him. A short, stupid thought. Even if he agrees to take me, I can't abandon Bridie and Kai, no matter what.

Kai's head drops and he stares at his shoes. I'm pretty sure he's having a similar thought.

"I mean, not with the children." Bridie's sounds hesitant. Then she picks up steam. "When I perform with them, the weekends are more likely. By myself, yes, soon."

"Then perhaps I shall see you soon." John Walks Long gives a sweeping bow, his long coat swooshing about his legs before he strides away.

I chew my cheek to keep from talking and ruining things. Kai plucks at his guitar strings as if tuning them.

"Well," Bridie gives a breathy sigh. "What a fine man. One certainly feels safer on the streets with him and the Beggar Clan about."

"Sort of like Mad Maud." I hope I sound casual.

Bridie smiles at the mention of the Beggar Chief of London. Her gaze becomes distant. "Dear Maud. She was a real friend. I… I…" She clears her throat. "I think we're done for the day."

"Are we really coming back this weekend?" Kai asks.

Bridie blinks a few times before looking at him. "What was that, darling? This weekend?" She rubs her chin. "Bill watches sport all weekend long. He won't care if we nip out to rehearse where we won't bother him. I'll tell him we're going to the park. This is sort of a park, isn't it?"

A little squeal escapes my throat. Bridie pretends not to notice. She hands the case to Kai. "Count it up, darling. Probably enough for lunch in Chinatown." Her gaze becomes distant again. "Same as in London. Funny, how that is."

Funny, yeah, but no one is laughing. I suck in my breath to keep tears from my eyes. I know I shouldn't get my hopes up, but it's too late. Hope soars and I fly with it, all the way back to London.

Paul

It's lonely at the top, and by 'the top', I mean 39,000 feet above Japan.

For the past few hours, I've been trying to think of a bogus emergency that will convince the pilot to turn the plane around and head back to Hong Kong. Nothing comes to mind that won't get me arrested, and that won't help Dad one bit.

We're in business class, and Tony and Aaron already have their chairs stretched out into beds. I don't get how they can sleep, even if we did leave for the airport at 3:00 a.m., and by leave, I mean snuck out with no goodbyes to family or friends. I thought Dad was going to drive us, but a guard got behind the wheel of his car. As we drove away, Mom looked back at Dad until the gate closed behind him. The tears in her eyes didn't fall.

She looks more stoic now as she stares at her video screen, watching some dumb comedy movie that doesn't make her laugh or even smile. My chest tightens. Maybe I should confess and tell her what I overheard, but what's the point? I'm sure she already knows whatever dark secret Head Elder is threatening Dad with. If she wanted me to know, she would have told me by now. That's why Tony and Aaron can sleep, because they don't know there's something more to what's happening besides Head Elder being power hungry. Ignorance really is bliss.

Mom turns off her screen and closes her eyes. After a few minutes, her breath becomes even. I peer at my cousins to make sure they really are asleep. Then I reach into my backpack and slide out my drawing pad and pencil. I sketch Mom's profile. Her mouth looks tense rather than slack and her eyes are closed tight. The harder I try, the worse it looks, almost like she's dead. A chill shivers through me. I turn to a blank page. My mind goes blank, too. What do I want to draw? I can't think of a single thing.

I slide open the window cover, but there's nothing to look at, not even Japan, just clouds. Is Jade Dragon anywhere nearby? No, he can't be. He would knock the plane out of the sky in his wake. How do dragons avoid airplanes? Maybe they fly far enough above to avoid collision. I draw the curve of the earth across the bottom of the page. Then I draw a plane bursting through a cloud bank, and above that, a dragon streaking through the upper atmosphere. Maybe dragons are what cause turbulence…

The plane shakes and lurches. I look out the window, half expecting to see Jade Dragon's scaly, coiling length flying alongside us. No sign of him. Good. I don't want him following us. He needs to stay in Hong Kong and watch over Dad. My teeth clench. That isn't going to happen. Our ancestor made it clear he's not going to stick around and help his descendants. I shove the pad into my backpack. What good is Jade Dragon if all he does is show up once a year and toss around some blessings? So what? Anybody can do that. With a huff of disgust, I close my eyes. I don't sleep.

I force a few bites of breakfast down my throat, plus two cups of coffee with plenty of sugar. It doesn't help. I shamble alongside Mom as we go through customs at San Francisco International Airport. There's a van waiting for us and I climb into the very back, hoping I can stretch out. Nope. Aaron ignores my glare and settles beside me. He takes out his violin and checks its polished wooden surface for damage. Then, for whatever damn reason, he starts tuning the strings, each pluck emitting a grating, monotonous tone. What the hell? Is he going to perform with an orchestra in the next ten minutes? I elbow him. He scoots over a little and continues plucking the strings and winding the pegs. I nudge him harder. He sticks out his tongue the smallest amount so it's barely noticeable and glances at Mom. Little shit. Isn't that racket bothering her and Tony? Nope. They're each staring out the window, alone with their thoughts.

The driver exits the freeway and navigates the canyons created by the skyscrapers of the financial district. He turns left on California Street and heads uphill into Chinatown. We get stuck behind a slow-moving cable car. Its driver is clanging the bell with a crazed urgency, like the zombie apocalypse is upon us. At least it shuts down Aaron and he puts away his instrument of torture.

The van winds through the congested streets, passing sidewalks packed with shoppers ducking in and out of the vegetable stands, fish stalls and butcher shops, until the driver turns into a narrow, dead-end street officially known as Joseph Alley. Though for more than a century the Chinese have called it Dragon Alley. We come to a stop at the end of the alley in front of a three-story building with dark green ceramic awnings that resemble bamboo. Above the entrance is a white marble plaque inlaid with gold characters proclaiming this to be the location of the Two Dragon Clan *Kongsi*. A *kongsi* is a clan meeting hall for overseas Chinese.

Our clan bought the building while it was being constructed, right after the 1906 earthquake. They made sure the top floor had an unobstructed view of the San Francisco Bay, since facing water is supposed to be super good luck. Dad's father made it his permanent residence back in the seventies when he moved in with his second wife, Auntie Cat's mother. It caused some big scandal I'm not supposed to know about. Whatever. I'm glad. Spending every summer at the compound is enough. Living there year-round with Head Elder would be a real pain.

The front door opens and a guard hurries down the stairs to help the driver with our luggage. The lobby is dimly lit and empty, except for the reception area where the guards monitor the alley using video surveillance. My parents supposedly run a *kwoon*, a martial arts studio, in the building, though anyone interested in taking classes will be told they're not accepting new students at this time. Plenty of training takes place in the huge gym in the basement, but the students are all members of the Two Dragon Clan. The *kongsi's* banquet hall occupies the ground floor and is members only, of course.

Back when the place was built, the Hong Kong style of floor numbering had been used, meaning the ground floor is what Americans call the first floor. Our first floor is what Americans call the second floor, and so on. This is only important because the Dragon Son's family always occupies the third floor. For Chinese, three is a lucky number, but four is super bad luck. So, according to the American system, we live on the unlucky floor. Once that was realized, there was talk of moving to the second floor, but that would mean sacrificing the good *feng shui* and great view on the top floor. It was finally decided that anything Chinese overrules anything American, so the Dragon Son's family remained on the "third" floor.

The first floor has offices and guest rooms. The second floor is where the Dragon Son's adult heir is supposed to live, but after Dad became Dragon Son, his brother's family settled there. I guess I'm supposed to kick them out when I get married. I wouldn't mind if Tony and Aaron stayed, except for one thing.

Right on cue, the elevator makes a dinging sound. The door slides open and out steps that one thing: Uncle George's wife, Auntie Sylvia. She's wearing a dress, same as always. Well, sometimes she wears a skirt. I've never seen her in pants or a pair of shorts. I guess she's supposed to be fashionable with her poofy, reddish-brown hair, manicured nails, high heels and piles of expensive clothes, but who is she trying to impress? I don't know what she does all day. She doesn't teach martial arts like Mom or have any kind of job. A maid does all the cleaning and dinner is delivered every night. She doesn't even check Aaron's homework. I'm the one who does that.

Auntie Sylvia's diamond hard eyes soften as they fix on Tony. She dashes out of the elevator and wraps her arms around his neck. "Son. At last you're home. You don't know how much I missed you." She kisses his cheek, leaving a red lipstick mark.

"Hello, Mother." Tony looks embarrassed.

I don't blame him. Hey, lady, he's your son, not your husband. Also, Auntie Sylvia has this smell, like she's been hit by a florist's truck carrying a million roses. It gags me. I'm glad Mom smells like Mom, all normal and wholesome.

Auntie Sylvia makes a high-pitched miffed sound. "Is that all you have to say after three months? 'Hello, Mother'? I want to hear everything, all about your time at the compound." She takes his arm and starts leading him into the elevator.

Tony tugs away. "Don't you want to say hello to everyone else?"

Another miffed sound. The diamond hardness returns to her eyes as she looks at me. "Nephew."

"Auntie." The word tastes like sand.

She holds out an arm for Aaron. "Welcome home, son. Did you miss me?"

Aaron blinks, as if he forgot she's his mother. He goes to her and doesn't reciprocate her one-armed hug.

"Look at you. You're so skinny. Didn't anyone feed you?" She herds her sons into the elevator without a backward glance.

Mom crosses her arms and shakes her head. I don't know what the bad blood is between her and Auntie Sylvia because, of course, no one will tell me. I don't remember a time when they've ever been friendly beyond having to exchange a few necessary words. Auntie Sylvia has always avoided Mom, but lately she's been ignoring her, like she doesn't exist. Mom acts like she doesn't care, but it steams the hell out of me.

"What a bitch," I mutter.

"What was that?" asks Mom.

I shrug. I don't care if I'm in trouble for speaking the truth.

After a moment, Mom sighs and shrugs, too. Must be the jet lag. And the fact she agrees with me.

The guards arrive in the lobby, carrying our luggage. Mom presses the up button on the wall and turns to them with a smile. "Please, take the elevator. Drop off my nephews' luggage first. We'll take the stairs. We need to stretch our legs after that long flight." She waves away their protests.

This is why everyone loves my mom. She's Head Elder's daughter and the Dragon Son's wife, but she treats everyone the same. The elevator is small, about the size of a coat closet. With the luggage, we can't all fit in. Auntie Sylvia would've made those guys haul our crap up the stairs while she took the elevator. She'll probably see red when they arrive, thinking Mom did it to make her look bad. Actually, maybe Mom had. Her smile stays on her lips as we head upstairs.

When I get to the second landing, I notice Mom is lagging behind, so I wait for her to catch up. It's not like her to get winded climbing stairs. Is her heart bothering her? She doesn't look pale or unwell. Just tired.

As we continue up to the third floor, I ask, "Are you going to call Dad?"

"Of course."

"When?"

"He's expecting me to call at midnight, Hong Kong time." Mom pulls out her phone and glances at the screen. "In about half an hour."

"Shouldn't you call him now?"

She doesn't answer.

"Why wait?"

Mom gives me a look, the one that says I'm not getting anywhere so I might as well shut up. But this is important. We need to call Dad now. Can't she see that? I stomp up the rest of the stairs and lean against the wall with my arms crossed. I gnaw my lip, but can't hold back a huge yawn.

Mom brushes my bangs off my forehead. I jerk away. She sighs. "Your father is in a meeting right now and can't be disturbed."

"A meeting? With who?" Uncle George? Head Elder? Both?

"I can't talk about it."

"Not even with me?"

"Go to your room and get some rest. I need to talk to your father in private first. After that, you can talk to him all you want. I promise."

I know I'm acting like a kid, but she's treating me like one. "Okay, whatever."

I tug off my sneakers and place them on the shoe rack before heading down the hall. Then I stop and look back. Mom holds her shoes in one hand, but instead of placing them on the shelf, she stands there, watching me. Though her face is pinched and weary, love radiates from her dark brown eyes. A tiny ache stabs my chest. If I was eight-years-old, I'd run to her for a hug. Instead, I shrug and manage a goofy grin. Her smile brightens her face before she turns away to set down her shoes.

Right after I get to my room, the guards arrive with two suitcases full of crap that needs to be unpacked. Instead, I flop back on my bed. It feels weird being in my room again. There aren't any geckos on the ceiling. It's cold and dry compared to the heat and humidity of Hong Kong. In a couple of days, I'll be back in school, back to being a normal kid. I still have a ton of schoolwork to catch up with. Ugh. I don't want to think about that. My head feels fuzzy and sticky, like it's full of cotton candy. My eyelids droop, flutter and shut. Just for a few moments…

When I open my eyes, my cheek is sticky with drool. I wipe the slime from my mouth and glance at the clock on the nightstand. Ah, crap. I've been out for more than an hour. I don't feel any better for it. I want to turn over my pillow and go back to sleep, but I get this panicky feeling in my stomach. What if Mom came in and saw I was asleep, and decided not to wake me so I could talk to Dad? No, she wouldn't do that. I perch on the edge of the bed. They must still be talking. It wouldn't hurt to find out and if I'm quiet, I might overhear something.

Yeah, you'd think I'd know better now. Thing is, if I don't snoop, I stay ignorant and frustrated, and I'm sick of that.

With Silent Steps, I head for my parents' room. The door is cracked open, which is weird. I thought their conversation would be private. You can't do Silent Speech over the phone. I stand at the doorway and listen. Mom isn't talking. Is she even in there? I smell a familiar stench. Roses. I peer through the crack.

What the hell?

I can see Mom's legs on the bed, twisted at a weird angle. Did she fall asleep, like me? I open the door a bit more. Auntie Sylvia is leaning over Mom, her back blocking my view. Then she twists aside and tosses away a pillow covering Mom's face. She leans over again and seems to put her hands around Mom's neck.

"What are you doing?" I yell.

Auntie Sylvia jumps up, her pale face now bright red. Her hands go behind her back as if concealing a guilty secret. "Paul – your mother. There seems to be something wrong with her. I just tried to wake her up."

I shove her aside and lean over my mother. Mom stares at the ceiling with blank eyes. She isn't breathing – No! She has to be breathing.

I give her a shake. "Mom. Mom, wake up."

She doesn't move. I put my hand to her mouth. No breath. My fingers slide to her neck. No pulse.

No. No! I turn to my aunt. "Call 911!"

Aunt Sylvia's diamond eyes become slits. "We can't allow outsiders into the *kongsi*."

I stare at her for an incredulous moment. Then I look around and see Mom's phone on the bed near her hand. I grab it and punch in 911.

Auntie Sylvia runs from the room.

"911," says a calm, female voice. "What is your emergency?"

My mouth goes bone dry. I swallow hard and the words tumble out. "My mom – my mom. She's sick. She's not breathing. She needs help. We live at 88 Joseph Alley."

The dispatcher says something as I drop the phone. My heart is beating so fast, I'm getting dizzy. I take a deep breath. I have to calm down. I have to do this. Whatever it was I did to that stupid doll in CPR class.

I tilt back Mom's head and breathe into her mouth, twice. Her chest rises and falls. That's a good sign, right? I pump Mom's chest, 30 times. I press my ear to her mouth to listen for breath, but I can't hear anything over all the noise in the hall.

Tony bursts into the room. "Is she breathing?"

I shake my head.

He pushes me aside. Then he closes his eyes and inhales.

As he exhales, he lays his hand over Mom's heart, infusing her with his *chi*. Moments pass. Drops trickle down his cheeks, but it isn't sweat. His hair is wet. He grows paler. Mom doesn't move.

"Shit," he whispers.

Tony never swears.

He breathes into Mom's mouth. Again, her chest rises and falls, but she's obviously not breathing on her own.

A tinny voice comes from the phone. I snatch it up. "Are they coming?"

"Yes," says the dispatcher. "Please stay on the line."

"Tell them to hurry. She's not breathing."

"What is your name?"

"Paul. Paul Lau."

"All right, Paul. Paramedics are on their way and should be there any moment." She pauses. "How old are you, Paul?"

What the hell does that matter? "Fifteen."

"Has your mother been sick before?"

God. Please. No. I swallow. "She has a heart condition."

"All right. I'll let the paramedics know. Are you alone, Paul?"

"No, my cousin is here. He's doing CPR."

"Is your mother responding?"

Tony draws away. The look on his face…

"No." The word comes out like a croak. I lean against the wall to keep from falling. My hand drops to my side. The wail of a siren comes through an open window.

Footsteps pound on the stairs. In the hallway, I hear Auntie Sylvia's voice calling out, "In here, in here!"

Paramedics come rushing in. They brush Tony aside and lean over Mom. One begins administering CPR. Tony leans beside me. He looks at me. His mouth opens and closes. He looks away.

A numbing veil drops over me. Through it, I watch two

firemen enter the room, carrying some kind of machine. One of them says something to Tony and me. Tony puts his arm around my shoulders and leads me out of the room.

The hallway feels like the bottom of a well. Above, a voice repeats several times, "Clear." A buzzing noise follows. I realize I'm still clutching the phone and shove it in my pocket.

At some point, the firemen carry the machine out of the room. They don't look at me. One of the paramedics gestures Tony over and says something. Both look at me. I pull myself from the wall and go to them. The paramedic takes a few steps back.

Tony speaks in a soft voice, "They couldn't save her. I'm sorry."

I blink. I know that means Mom is dead, but it doesn't make sense. Mom can't be dead.

"You should say goodbye before they take her away."

"Away?" Why would they take Mom away? I go into the room. Mom's suitcases had been pushed into a corner. The stuff on her nightstand had been shoved aside. I straighten a tilted lampshade before I sit beside her.

Her eyes are closed. I touch her hand. She feels cold. I reach for a blanket to cover her. Then I notice the pillow. Auntie Sylvia had been holding that pillow. I squeeze my eyes shut, trying to remember what I saw: Auntie Sylvia lifting the pillow and tossing it aside. Lifting it off of Mom's face…

What had Auntie Sylvia done?

My stomach churns. Nausea clutches my throat. I grasp Mom's hand. I go over in my mind what I'd seen, over and over again.

A paramedic comes in and speaks to me, but I can't hear what he says. Tony comes and goes. I ignore him.

Auntie Cat appears beside me like a ghost, wearing a white, silk martial arts uniform, with baggy pants and flowing sleeves. Strands of black hair escape from her bun and drift around a feminine version of Dad's face. She must have been teaching a Tai Chi class when she heard about… I take a breath that hurts my throat.

"Oh, God. Chelle. It's all too much," she mutters. She wipes the tears from her cheeks and red-rimmed eyes. Then she reaches down and squeezes Mom's hand. The tears return. She wipes her face again. After taking a deep breath, she turns to me, laying a gentle hand on my shoulder. "We have to go now, Paul."

I stand. I've been as tall her since I turned fifteen, but I feel like a small child beside her. I allow her to lead me out of the room.

In the hall, the paramedics wait with a stretcher. On its surface is a long black bag with a zipper down the middle. I gasp. No. No, they aren't going to put Mom in that. I stumble backward. Auntie Cat tightens her grip to keep me from falling. I shake her off and run to my room.

Auntie Cat follows me. She closes the door, but through it I can still hear the shuffling sounds as the paramedics move my mother's body. My knees give way and I sink onto the bed. Auntie Cat sits beside me. She wraps her arm around me and rubs my forearm. A long, sharp zipping sound scratches my nerves.

Auntie Cat bites her lip. She blinks and tears roll down her cheeks. I've never seen her cry before, had never even imagined that she would. She always seems so calm and in control.

The veil slides off me. This is real. Mom is dead. I can't just sit here. I have to let Dad know. My stomach twists at the thought. How are we going to live without her? I reach into my pocket and pull out Mom's phone. My eyes narrow at the recent calls list on her screen: one to Dad, but it had lasted less than a minute. Then Head Elder had called her immediately after that. Had Mom even talked to Dad? Or had they started talking, and then Mom ended their conversation to take her father's call? What had Head Elder said to Mom? Something to upset her? I press Dad's number and put the phone to my ear.

"Who are you calling?" asks Auntie Cat.

"My dad." I frown as the call goes directly to voicemail.

"Michael Lau," Dad's voice is followed by a mechanized female voice, "is not available to take your call."

Auntie Cat takes a breath. Her voice shakes as she speaks, "Paul, your father is dead."

Paul

Dad. Dead. How?

I try saying those words aloud, but can't. Auntie Cat hugs me. I sit stiff and still. She says something I don't understand. At some point, she leaves the room. I don't move. If only I could turn into a statue and not move, or think, or even breathe, then I wouldn't have to feel the searing pain that lies beneath the surface of my skin.

Tony stands in front of me. He says something about shock and needing family. What family? I have no family, not anymore. He places his hands on my shoulders and gives me a gentle shake. I blink. His face comes into focus. His usually rigid features are smeared with misery and his eyes awash with unshed tears. He loves Dad, and loves Mom, too, maybe more than his own parents. His parents... Auntie Sylvia... what has she done?

"Come with me," Tony speaks quietly.

I need to be alone. I need to think.

Tony's hand slides to my forearm and tugs. I don't budge. Tony's grip tightens and his voice, though still hushed, becomes firmer, "Little Brother."

Little Brother. I still have family, a brother. We'd sworn an oath. And after that oath, Dad gave instructions. *You must obey him as you would obey me.*

I allow Tony to lead me from the room. As we head down the hall, we pass my parents' bedroom. I can see the now-empty bed and that pillow, the one Auntie Sylvia held over Mom's face.

We go to the living room. Everything looks the same: the brown leather couch we bought last year to replace the worn-out cloth one, the magazines carelessly tossed on the coffee table right before we left for Hong Kong in June, and on the mantelpiece above the fireplace, the large, framed photo of Mom and Dad on their wedding day.

I take my place on the couch, at the end closest to the TV. Tony sits beside me in Mom's spot. He knows that's Mom's spot. What is he thinking?

Auntie Cat enters the room and sinks into the brown leather armchair. Dad's armchair. She looks at me and asks softly, "Do you want some water?"

I swallow. My mouth feels dry, my lips cracked. I shake my head. I don't fucking want water. I want answers. "What happened?"

Auntie Cat grips the armrests. "This is what I heard from Head Elder. Mike went to Kowloon to see our brother. While they spoke, an assassin appeared. He was after George. There was a struggle and your father was killed."

Pain stabs my gut. Not just dead. Murdered. I cough to clear the ache in my throat. "The killer was after Uncle George?"

"According to Head Elder."

"Why? What'd he do?"

Tony stares at his lap as he answers, "Head Elder said my father owes gambling debts which he refused to pay, so a killer was sent after him."

That sounds possible, but something isn't right. It's too convenient that Dad happened to be there. And why wasn't he able to defend himself? "What kind of killer?"

"Shinobi."

Shinobi have skills similar to the Two Dragon Clan. A powerful one would have a chance at killing Dad, but he wasn't the target. Why would they send such a warrior after Uncle George? "Who saw the Shinobi, besides my father and Uncle George?"

Auntie Cat answers, "No one."

"How did he kill Dad?"

"We don't know. No one has told us yet."

Shinobi are the ultimate assassins of the Crossroads. They don't make mistakes and they don't leave behind witnesses. "Why didn't he kill Uncle George after he killed Dad?"

Tony's brow wrinkles. Good. He gets it. This is all bullshit. Then our aunt answers, "George was armed. By the time he pulled out his weapon, the Shinobi had killed Mike. George shot at him, but he got away."

My chest tightens. Breath comes hard and fast. Am I really expected to swallow some bullshit story about a Shinobi? I look from Auntie Cat to Tony. Can't they see it? Do they really think it's a coincidence that Uncle George was with Dad and Auntie Sylvia was with Mom, and now they're both dead?

"Paul?" Tony touches my shoulder.

I jerk away. I jump up and dart behind the armchair, gripping the frame for support.

Tony's expression is bewildered. Is he faking it? Is he in on it, too? No, he can't be. He can't, because if he is... nausea burns my throat.

Auntie Cat turns and stares at me. "Paul?"

Auntie Sylvia appears in the doorway, her eyes pinched red and face masked with sorrow. "The paramedics are gone. They said the coroner will call…" Her voice falters as I stab her with a look that I wish could kill.

"You did it. I saw you."

Auntie Sylvia seems to grow even paler. She takes a step back. Words stumble out of her. "Nephew, I'm… I'm so sorry. I… I didn't know what to do. I… I…"

"You killed her. I saw you."

No one speaks. Tony and Auntie Cat stare at me like I'm crazy. Auntie Sylvia looks scared. She looks guilty.

Tony stands. "Little Brother…"

Hold this oath in your hearts. It binds you for life.

No. None of that. No more blind obedience. "Listen to me. I saw her. She killed my mother."

Auntie Cat comes around the chair to stand beside me. She speaks in a calm voice, "How did she kill her?"

I exhale. She's Dad's sister. She'll listen to me, even if no one else will. "I came into my parent's bedroom. I was quiet, in case Mom was still on the phone with Dad. I saw her," I jab my finger at Auntie Sylvia, "sitting on the bed, leaning over Mom, holding a pillow over her face. She pushed it away and then put her hands around Mom's neck. She killed her!"

"No," Auntie Sylvia gasps. "That's not true."

"It is true," I shout. "You murdered her." I start for her, but Auntie Cat catches hold and yanks me back. I spin around. For a moment, I almost shove her into the wall, but the small part of me that isn't batshit crazy manages to hold back. My heart slams against my chest and I suck in air to slow it down.

Auntie Cat's consciousness touches mine. Despite her pain-pinched face, her inner voice is coldly rational. *Paul, you have to calm down. Anger and threats won't lead to the truth.*

I know she's right, but it's so hard. I take a shaky breath that barely softens the ragged edge of my anger.

Auntie Sylvia takes another step back and looks as if she

wants to run. Then she glances at Tony. She licks her lips. "No, that's not what happened. He's confused."

"What happened?" asks Auntie Cat.

Auntie Sylvia wipes her hands down her thighs. She swallows and her face becomes more composed. "My husband called to tell me his brother had been murdered."

Tony looks at his mother, incredulous. "Dad called you?"

"I was surprised, too. He must have been in shock." She takes a deep breath as a tear trickles down her cheek. She wipes it away quickly. "I came upstairs to find Chelle and see if she had heard – to see if I could help. I found her on the bed, not moving. I thought she was asleep. I tried to wake her. A pillow was against her face, almost covering it. I moved it away. It didn't seem like she was breathing, so I checked her neck pulse. That's when Paul walked in."

Tony exhales and wipes his brow. He looks at me sympathetically. "Little Brother, you're in shock. It's natural to want to blame someone."

My mouth gapes open. How can anyone believe that crock of shit?

Auntie Cat says, "Paul, I came over because your grandfather called me. He had called your mother to tell her what happened to your father. He said she didn't respond. She didn't hang up and he couldn't hear anything. He asked me to check on her, to make sure she was all right."

"Why did he call you? Why didn't he call her?" I jut my chin at Auntie Sylvia. "She lives here."

Auntie Sylvia replies, "Head Elder called and left a message while I was talking to my husband. He must have called Cat when he couldn't get a hold of me."

"Head Elder also called me," says Tony. "I was taking a shower and I didn't hear my phone ring."

Why didn't Head Elder call me? My phone. I played games on the plane until the battery went dead. I was supposed to charge it when I got home and forgot. If I had, maybe I could have gotten to Mom in time. My breath starts to hitch again.

Auntie Cat slides her arm across my shoulders. "You know she had a weak heart. The shock must have been too much for her."

"No," I shout. I lower my tone and my voice trembles. "She wouldn't do that. She wouldn't die and leave me alone." I thrust a finger at Auntie Sylvia. "You killed her. And Uncle George killed my father. You murdered my parents. Why?"

"Paul, stop it." Tony's eyes reflect anguish and anger. He loved Dad, but Auntie Sylvia is his mother. He'll never believe me. "You don't know what you're saying. You should go to your room and lie down."

I shake my head. "I'm not staying here. I won't stay in the same building with her."

"I'll take him home with me," says Auntie Cat. "Help him calm down."

Why won't anyone listen to me? I shake off Auntie Cat and run down the hall and into my parents' room, slamming the door shut. My knees buckle as I collapse onto the mattress.

My fingers brush the pillow, still indented from my mother's head. I reach for the other pillow: the one Auntie Sylvia used to smother her, and turn it all around looking for evidence. Nothing. But what can I tell from a pillow? I shouldn't touch it. I should leave it for the police.

I punch the mattress. There will be no police. How can I get justice?

The door opens. Auntie Cat steps inside and closes it softly behind her.

I glare at her. "Uncle George was with Dad. Auntie Sylvia was with Mom. Now, they're both dead. They're working together. It's so obvious. Why don't you believe me?"

"Because George and Sylvia hate each other. You have no

idea how much hatred there is between them. They would never work together."

They wouldn't. I know they wouldn't. Which is why it's the perfect crime. If I hadn't caught Auntie Sylvia red-handed, they might have gotten away with it.

Who am I kidding? They did get away with it. Head Elder used their hatred for my parents to do his dirty work. No one will believe me because no one wants to believe a crime as awful as this.

"Do you want to come home with me?" asks Auntie Cat.

I can't stay here and have nowhere else to go, so I nod. She pulls out her phone and starts tapping.

I go to the dresser. On top is that muddy brown mug I'd made in 7th Grade ceramic class. It was my first attempt and I thought it'd turned out pretty crappy, but Dad had said he liked it, and he'd used it to hold his spare change. Next to it is the two-sided mirror I'd bought for Mother's Day. Looking back, it was a stupid gift since Mom doesn't use make-up, but she'd said she loved it.

I'll never buy her another gift. I blink. Tears run down my cheeks. I wipe them away with the back of my hand. The mirror is hanging off the edge of the dresser. Mom wouldn't leave it like that.

I tilt the mirror and see a hairline crack across its surface. How the hell did that happen? Maybe the paramedics had knocked it over when they rushed in. Now they'll have seven years bad luck.

Bad luck. Dad and I had both touched the spirit wall. Had that bad luck somehow transferred to Mom? Is that why she and Dad are dead? I shove away the mirror like it's made of fire. It teeters before falling over on top of the dresser.

My eyes sting and snot dribbles from my nose. Who said crying is supposed to make you feel better? It makes me feel worse, like I'm a helpless child. I swipe my face with my sleeve. Then I turn to Auntie Cat. "Let's go."

We go to my room to get my suitcases before taking the elevator to the ground floor. When we reach the front entrance, Tony and Aaron block the way. My heart pounds so hard it hurts. Why can't they let me go?

Aaron's shoulders are hunched, his eyes wide and expression confused. "I'm sorry about your mom and dad. They were… they were…" He rubs his nose with the back of his hand. Tears fill his eyes. "I loved them, too, you know."

My words come out hoarse, "I know."

Tony tries to stare me down, but it doesn't work. Pain blurs the edge of his imperious attitude. His whisper is also hoarse. "Little Brother, don't leave. Stay with us. We're your family."

My chest quivers. Big Brother and Little Brother, they're my family, but they're also Auntie Sylvia and Uncle George's sons. They'll never believe me and I can't stay, knowing that. I roll my suitcase forward, determined to push past them if they won't move.

After a moment's hesitation, my cousins step aside.

I wait on the sidewalk while Auntie Cat exchanges a few final words with Tony. Headlights shine in the fog as a car rolls into the alley.

Auntie Cat comes out and we climb into the back of the rideshare. As it drives away, I look back and see Tony standing in the street, staring after us. He raises his hand. I turn away.

Penny

"Class, I want you to form teams for our next project," announces Ms. Gagliardi.

I know how this is going to play out, so I stay in my seat and sketch a pattern while the rest of the class buddies up. I don't have any buddies. Even Kayla goes out of her way to avoid the lockers when I'm there. My chest tightens, but I don't know why. I don't care.

After the hubbub dies down, Ms. G. calls out, "Penny, do you have a team?"

I shake my head.

"All right, let's see." She glances around the room. "I'll have you join Sarah and Dani."

That's right. Put me with two members of the Daisy Chain, even though they openly and loudly gag.

Yay team.

Why are teachers, even cool ones like Ms. G., so clueless?

My team settles into a corner and badmouths me while tossing some fabric around as if they're working on something. I finish my pattern, cut the fabric and start sewing while half the class is still trying to figure out how to thread the bobbin. I'll have my pinafore finished before the rest of them have even started their projects. It's really flash, too, with ruffled shoulder straps and buttoned flaps over the pockets. Everyone is going to be jealous, which, of course, will make everything so much better. The tightness in my chest squeezes my heart.

If only I could shove my backpack into my locker and head for the park, but I can't cut class anymore. The teachers have been ordered to keep a close eye on me, which is to say they monitor me for bad behavior, but turn a blind eye when I'm being bullied. The Daisy Chain circle me like sharks, openly insulting me since I can't retaliate. I feel like I'm walking through life with my hands tied behind my back.

I don't give a fig about getting kicked out of this joke of a school, but if I'm expelled, I won't be allowed to perform anymore. Bill and Bridie made that clear. If it were just the Auld Sod, I would have thumped each of those bints twice over by now, but it also includes our "rehearsals" on Market Street. Dancing for the applause of the Beggar Chief and his crew makes me feel like I'm on the Crossroads again. I can't give that up or I'll be dead inside.

As I stitch the last bit of ruffle to the left strap, I see Ms. G. talking to Sarah and Dani. Sarah's smile bares her too-white teeth while Dani's oily brown eyes slide off our teacher and ooze a warning at me.

Ms. G. comes up to my table. She's a heavyset, gray haired woman with hazel eyes and a kind smile. She favors bright, batik print dresses and woven shawls tied around her shoulders. "Penny, are you working alone or with Sarah and Dani?"

Do they really expect me to give them credit for my work? "Alone."

"Why?"

I shrug. "It's better this way."

Ms. G. lets loose a deep sigh, rustling the fringe on her shawl. "See me after class." She walks away.

Nothing I do here is fucking right. This school is a microcosm of the larger world where the Bleater elite set their minions on the Gypsies and outcasts. Is dancing in the streets, even for the Beggar Chief, worth this? I think not.

The bell rings. I keep sewing while the other kids file out. As Sarah and Dani pass me, Dani asks in her breathless whine, "Don't you ever go online?"

Rarely. Not that it's any of her business.

"Because there's a ChatBack page all about what a whore you are."

I stick out my foot and hook her ankle. I feel the satisfying tug of her weight as she sprawls into her crony. Sarah shoves Dani back. Giggles erupt all around them.

Dani points at me. "It was her, she tripped me."

I smirk. "Oops."

Sarah glares at me through the thick mascara caking her lashes. Then her lips twist. "You know what it says on ChatBack? That you've sucked off half the guys at this school."

Everyone looks at me. I stand, slowly, the chair squealing as it slides behind me. I flex my fingers. Getting expelled will be so worth smearing that sneer off her face. Both girls try to back away, but the other kids won't budge. Interesting. Maybe they're sick of Daisy Chain bullshit, too.

"What's going on?" Ms. G.'s voice booms above the hum of tension. The crowd reluctantly parts as she shoulders her way in.

Damn. I don't want to get expelled for tripping. I want to do a lot more damage than that.

Dani puts on her victim face. It's an ill fit due to the malice snapping in her eyes. "Penny tripped me."

Ms. G. turns to me. "Did you trip her?"

I shake my head. "No. I was just sitting here."

"I saw her do it." Sarah talks through her nose, in that high-pitched mean girl accent they all have. "She stuck out her foot and tripped Dani."

Ms. G. raises an eyebrow. "And I heard what you said to Penny, you and Dani. You know this school has zero tolerance for bullying."

I snort. That's rich.

Dani's cheeks puff like a child on the verge of a tantrum. "She tripped me on purpose. Are you saying that's my fault?"

"I'm saying I can report all of you to Vice Principal Ikeda or you can call it even and walk away."

Their mouths gape open, making them look like stunned carp. As they push through the crowd, Dani shouts, "I'm dropping this class."

Ms. G. rolls her eyes and sighs out, "Good." She closes the door behind the last student before beckoning me to her desk.

I stop a few feet away, waiting for the other shoe to drop.

"I'm sorry, Penny. I should have known better. Those two are doing so badly in class. I thought you could help them." She reaches into a desk drawer. "Truth is, you don't belong here, and neither do I. This is my last year at Parkside Academy." She hands me a pamphlet titled *San Francisco High School of Art and Design*. "I'll be teaching here next year."

Not the shoe I expected. I stare at photos of students draping muslin onto sewing mannequins. Is there really such a wonderful place? It seems too good to be true.

"Show that to your parents. Maybe you can join me there next year."

"I want to go this year." I tuck it into my book bag. I want to say more because she's the only person to stick up for me since I don't know when, but I get a tickle in my throat that makes me feel like I'll cry. All I can do is murmur, "Thank you," as I leave.

In the hall, it takes all of my willpower not to pull out the pamphlet. I don't want anyone to see what I'm looking at and report to the Daisy Chain. A sharp whistle makes me look toward an open classroom door. Kevin Anderson leans out, makes a V with his index and middle finger and thrusts his tongue in and out between them. A knee to the groin would make him bite that tongue, but I have to content myself with flipping him off.

"You know you want it," he calls after me.

I make a mental note to spit in Kevin Anderson's face on my last day in this hellhole.

When I get home, I go straight to my room, close the door, pull out the pamphlet and pour over the details. The school promises to prepare students for a career in fashion design. Strowlers don't have careers, but I like the idea of making money selling the clothes I design. The students look like a bunch of creative misfits, laughing and working together. Longing clogs my throat. Maybe I could even make friends there. Best of all, it's a charter school, so tuition is free. That will definitely fetch Bill. He might even let me go next semester if he can get a refund from Parkside Academy.

Wait a minute.

What am I doing? I don't want to go to school, any school, even one as rum as this one. Right? I chew my knuckle while I read the class descriptions again. If I'm stuck faking a Bleater life, I might as well get some use out of it.

There's a tap at the door. I shove the pamphlet into a drawer and say, "Yeah?"

Kai's head pops in. "Mum's not back yet."

"So?"

"So, Bill will be home soon."

Oh, bother. If Bridie would grow a backbone, she could go where she pleases, when she pleases without worrying about His Nibs. "I'll be right down."

I gather my homework and settle at the kitchen table with a

cup of tea and some biscuits. I can't concentrate on any of it because I keep glancing at the clock. She should have been home an hour ago. What's keeping her?

"He's here," Kai calls out from his position at the kitchen window.

"Sit, sit!" I hiss.

He slides off the counter and skids across the floor to the table. Grabbing his pencil, he leans over his maths homework. The garage door rumbles. I take a deep breath and bury my nose in an American History textbook.

Bill walks in. His suit looks rumpled and his face weary from the workday. He stops when he sees us and heaves a put-upon sigh. "Hi, kids."

"Hi," we chorus back.

"Doing your homework?"

"Uh-huh," Kai holds up his paper. "Algebra."

Bill turn to me. "Penny?"

"Thomas Jefferson. He wrote the Declaration of Independence. He also owned slaves. What a hypocrite."

His chuckle seems sincere. "I won't argue with that." He glances around. "Where's your mother?"

I shrug. "Shopping."

He frowns. "Her car is still in the garage."

"She took the light rail."

"What about dinner?"

"I think we're having leftovers from last night."

He grunts and heads out the kitchen door to the main part of the house. I exchange worried glances with my brother.

"There you are," Bill's muffled voice comes from the hallway.

Bridie must have come in through the front entrance. We jump up and press our ears to the door.

"Hello, darling." Her voice sounds too high.

"Where have you been?"

"Oh, just nipped out for a bit."

"What were you doing?"

"I went to the post office. Remember, you asked me to pick up some stamps."

"Penny said you went shopping."

I hold my breath. Kai nudges me. I nudge him back.

"That, too."

"Didn't you buy anything?"

"No. I was so disappointed." The flow of her voice becomes easy and soothing as she turns on the Charm. "I went to Cozy Teas. You know, the little shop near Union Square that sells British products, the one that carries those biscuits I love so much," she gives a sad little sigh, "and they were out."

I exhale. Kai nudges me again. This time, I shove him back.

"You should have called the shop before going all that way," says Bill.

"Oh, darling," Bridie's tone becomes teasing. "It was just an excuse to get out and do a little window shopping."

"What about dinner?"

Leftovers! I want to shout.

"I thought I'd make a bubble and squeak, if you don't mind leftovers."

I wipe my brow.

"Leftovers are fine." Bill pauses. "Should you leave them alone like that?"

"The children? Of course, darling. Penny is old enough to watch her brother for a bit."

"I don't know that she's up to the responsibility."

Kai's hand covers his snicker. I grit my teeth.

"She's doing much better this week."

"This week has been fine," Bill admits grudgingly. "But what about next week?"

"Even better, I should think."

"You always think the best of people."

There's a scuffling sound. Bridie's voice becomes breathless. "Not now, darling. I need to get dinner started."

Kai and I exchange looks of disgust. How can she stand him touching her? We go back to the table. I stare at my book without picking it up. I've seen Bridie kissing Matthew and getting a bit – um – frisky, and it never bothered me, but the sight of Bill touching her makes me want to puke.

The kitchen door opens and she scoots inside.

"What took you so long?" I whisper.

Bridie presses her hand to her heart. "Bloody Muni. The train broke down and we had to wait for another one. It took forever." She turns to Kai. "Darling, go out to the porch and get my guitar. Be snug about it."

Kai cracks open the door and peers down the hall before venturing out.

She collapses into a chair. "That was too close. I'm going to have to stop."

I bite my lip to hold back a bitter retort. She wasn't always like this. She used to be as daring as her husbands. That right there. Two husbands and cheeky enough to live with both. It won't help to point that out. I need to prod her on. I try sounding patient. "You love busking. Why stop now?"

"If Bill finds out…"

Nope. Can't be patient. "So, what? Mum, Bill doesn't own you. You shouldn't have to hide this from him. If you want to busk, you should be able to. You don't need his permission."

Bridie heaves a grim sigh. "So young. So much to learn."

"You or me?"

Her eyebrows arch. So do mine. I'm not about to back down. I'm tired of having a doormat for a mother.

The door opens and Kai slides in carrying Bridie's guitar case. She smiles like he's her golden child. "Thank you, son."

I roll my eyes. This isn't a conversation I want to have in front of him and she knows it.

She opens the case and pulls out a white square envelope addressed to Bridie Sparrow and Family. The handwriting has a grand, old-fashioned kind of scrawl. "The Beggar Chief handed me this today."

"What is it?"

Bridie shrugs elaborately and makes a show of reaching for a knife to slice open the envelope. She pulls out a card. Her brow knits as she silently reads.

I'm almost bouncing in my chair after a few moments. "What's it say?"

"Well," she breathes out the word. "It's an invitation to the Beggars' Banquet."

My jaw drops. I exchange wide-eyed looks with Kai. "We're invited to the Beggars' Banquet?" I whisper. How is that even possible?

"Not as guests. The Beggar Chief has asked us to perform."

"Kidding?" All my desire for confrontation has flown out the window. We need to do this. I need to treat it as a done deal. "This is so awesome. I'll make a new costume for me and a new dress for you."

Bridie licks her lips. Hesitation colors her words into pale things. "Well, I don't know. After all, today was such a close call."

I want to hurl my textbook against the wall, except that would seal the deal. I swallow my ire. I'm a Sharper. I need to think sharp. "Mum, how can we turn down such an honor?"

"Yeah," says Kai. His glare is so fierce, I'm afraid he might lose his shit before I have a chance to reason with her.

"Well, there's that." Bridie's lip twists as she kneads the invitation.

The door swings open. She shoves the invitation under the guitar case as Bill walks in. His frown darkens the room. "What's going on? I thought you were making dinner."

Bridie flutters a smile. "Oh, nothing, really."

"Look, I've been working all day to support you and these kids. My dinner is your top priority right now, not teaching them a new song or whatever the hell you're doing."

Her face goes blank. The old Bridie would have told him to stuff it. The new Bridie is about to cower and wheedle. Bile clogs my throat. I can't sit through this. I close my book and am about to stand when Bridie's easy smile returns. "Actually, darling, the PTA is putting on a talent show in a couple of weeks. They want Penny to perform an Irish jig and they asked if Kai and I could play along. I thought I'd say yes."

I try not looking as surprised as I feel. Is she really…?

"It would be good for the children to perform at a family friendly function, don't you think?"

She is. She's working a sham. I manage to keep my face neutral, even though I want to shout for joy.

Bill harrumphs. "I don't know if we should reward her after all the bad behavior."

"Well, the PTA is the one who's asking, not her."

"True." He looks at me. "Do you want to do this?"

I need to show Bridie I'm on her side, working the sham with her, so I toss Bill a proper load of shite. "I know I haven't been the best student and I've gotten into trouble. Maybe if I do this, I can show how much I appreciate everyone trying to help me. What do you think?"

He rubs his chin, a sure sign that a mark is taking the idea as his own. "I agree. When you're given an opportunity to redeem yourself, you should take it." He turns to Bridie. "All right, she can do it, but I want to see her grades improve in the meantime."

"Oh, they will, darling. Certainly they will." Her voice sweetens. "You'll come along with us, won't you?"

I suck in my breath. Here we go, the persuasion part that seals the deal.

Bill's eyes become dazed. "I suppose… I don't know…"

"I know you're busy, but it would be lovely to have you there. Hopefully, we won't be going on last. Even so, there will be lots of other children performing. It'll be a treat."

"Jesus, Bridie, I don't want to sit through a talent show with a bunch of other people's brats."

She pouts prettily. "Suit yourself, but no grouching when we come home late."

Bill chuckles and pats her cheek.

Her pout becomes a seductive smile. "Can I pour you a brandy?"

"No, I've got some work to finish before dinner. Maybe later, after the kids have gone to bed."

Bridie's smile fades as the door closes behind him. "Pay the piper," she whispers.

Not for long. Not if we can get the hell out of here. Performing at the banquet is huge. We can make our mark on the Crossroads there. Having the endorsement of the Beggar Clan will help us to work shams and make our own gelt, enough to escape from this house.

"Well done, Mum," says Kai with a gleeful grin.

She shakes her head. "What have I done?"

Second thoughts so soon? I can't let her go there. "Got us the biggest gig of our lives, that's what."

"We're playing for honor, not gelt."

"It can lead to gelt."

"Maybe. If we were still on the Crossroads."

"I'd rather be a poor Strowler than a rich Bleater."

She drums her fingers on the table while she stews that over. "You're a self-involved little madam, you know that?" My mouth drops open. How can she say that? She's the self-involved one. "Always prating on about going back to Ireland without a thought for the rest of us." She turns to Kai. "Your sister wants to go back to Ireland. What about you, son? Do you want to go back?"

He looks at me like I'm a stupid cow. "No."

"Why not?"

His shoulders lift in a tight shrug. "I don't fit in."

Bridie's eyes shoot fire at me. "They treated him like a by-blow and half-breed, or have you conveniently forgotten that?"

Heat rushes to my face. People had said those very words and worse to Bridie right in front of Kai and me. I don't want my brother living with that poison again. "No. I mean I don't want us to go back to the Nest."

"I should think not." Her lips press tight. Then she gives a nod. "Right. I didn't want to tell you, but you should know. While we were there, your grandparents were making plans to marry you off."

For a moment, it feels like my heart stops beating. I whisper, "What?"

"You're sixteen years old. High time you were married, according to them. They were going through a list of likely lads. The ones traveling the farthest topped the list, so you'd be out of my evil sphere of influence."

My lips move, but I don't speak. How could my grandparents do that to me?

Bridie gives an exasperated sigh. "Darling, what did you think the life of a Strowler woman is? We marry young and have lots of children. We keep the caravan clean and cater to our husbands' needs. That's our Glory Road. If that's not what you want, you walk the Wayward Way or become a Bleater."

"What about guys?" asks Kai. "If we'd stayed in Ireland, would I have gotten married when I'm, like, sixteen or something?"

"Strowler lads get married a little later, more like nineteen or twenty. You'd be expected to have your own caravan and earn your living prize fighting, working shams and doing manual labor."

"No way. I want to be a musician, like my dads."

"That's fine, as long as you can provide for a wife and family. An unmarried Strowler is a disgrace, at least, on the Glory Road."

I rub my forehead. Everything has gotten turned around and upside down. Bridie is only capable of seeing the negative these days. I need to remind her of the good things, our good life. "So, you and Gerry said bugger all that, right? And walked the Wayward Way."

Bridie folds her arms and leans back. "We did, and took Matthew along for the ride. And look where it got us. I want more for you two. That's why I left the Nest and married Bill." She looks down. "Maybe I better send the Beggar Chief our regrets."

"No," Kai and I both say. We look at each other. We both know she's done with me. It's his turn to take up the cause.

"Mum," he says with an earnest face. "What do you think Gerry and Matthew would want us to do?"

She raises her head. "They'd want us to play at the banquet, the tomfool pair of them."

"Why don't we do that, sort of like a tribute to them?"

Bridie and I both blink. Look at who else is learning how to Charm. Will she take the bait? By the way she's chewing her lip, she's on the cusp.

"That's daft," I say. "How will that be any kind of tribute?"

"Penny." Bridie glares at me. "Don't be snide." She turns to Kai. "That's a lovely thought, son. I've already started working the Charm on Bill. No point in going back now."

Under the table, Kai and I bump fists. I keep a blank face, though my knees are still shaking. Wow. I thought my grandparents loved me, but they schemed to have me spirited away in an arranged marriage. Dublin is out. I don't want to be anywhere near them. That leaves London, a tougher proposition since we have nowhere to live. What about ditching Bill, but staying in San Francisco? Then I could go to that school.

It'll take gelt we don't yet have, so I'll need to be patient, which feels almost impossible after the day I had at Hellhole High.

"It will be our last hurrah before settling into the Bleater life," Bridie announces as she stands.

The hell it will. It will be the beginning of our new life. All I have to figure out is how.

Paul

My neck itches. I tug at the collar of the shirt Auntie Cat has just ironed. She holds out a tie. I shake my head.

"I suppose it doesn't matter if you wear one or not." She pauses, waiting for a response, but I have nothing to say. "Can you change into your dress shoes?"

I shake my head again. I'm not taking off my Vans. Mom bought them for me the last time we went shopping at the Ocean Plaza Mall in Kowloon.

Her fingers pluck at the skirt of her plain, black dress. The she lays her hand on my shoulder. "You don't have to go."

"Is that bitch really going to be there?"

"It would look bad if she wasn't."

So, she is going to be there, crying fake tears and convincing everyone she isn't a murderer. Good. I want her there so I can look her in the eye and remind her of her guilt and eventual punishment.

I'm the fucking Dragon Son and your day will come.

I yank away and go downstairs to wait in the studio. If it was a normal Friday morning, Auntie Cat would be teaching Tai Chi, but she'd cancelled all her classes this week. I stare at my reflection in the mirrored wall. I didn't brush my hair and it's sticking up on either side of my head, making me look like a startled rabbit. Easy prey. No fucking way. I rake my fingers through my hair, adjusting my expression until cold, sullen eyes stare back. Good.

Through the storefront window, I see a rideshare waiting for us. I pat my pocket, making sure I'd grabbed my transit pass. If it gets too weird or crappy, I'll bail. Should I go back and grab my phone? No. It's been ringing and buzzing all week, full of messages from Tony, Head Elder, and a whole bunch of people I don't want to talk to. I finally turned it off and haven't looked at it in a few days.

I stare out the window as we drive through the foggy gloom of the Sunset District and head east, toward the sunnier side of the city. Auntie Cat takes out her rosary and starts fingering the polished black beads. I can't tell if she's praying or nervous, or both. I stare at the silver crucifix at the end. I want to grab it from her and demand to know why God let my parents die.

"Do you think Mom and Dad are in hell?" That just came out. I don't know why I asked.

Auntie Cat puts on her 'proceed with caution' face. "No, of course not."

"Do you think they've been reincarnated?"

"Catholics don't believe in reincarnation."

"Yeah, but you're a Chinese Catholic. Do you believe in Jade Dragon?"

"Of course," she answers without hesitation.

"A lot of people don't believe in dragons, especially Christians."

"As you pointed out, I'm a Chinese Catholic." A small smile lifts her lips.

If things were different, I would have smiled, too. Instead, renewed anger boils up from my stomach. "Maybe Jade Dragon isn't real. Why didn't he save my parents?"

She shakes her head sadly. "I don't know." Then she switches to Silent Speech. *I told Head Elder what you said about Sylvia and your mother.*

So you do believe me!

I believe your father was murdered by either George or Head Elder. As for Sylvia, she's so hateful, I can believe almost anything of her. Head Elder would never sanction the murder of his daughter, even if he disowned her. If Sylvia killed her, she acted on her own.

But why?

She doesn't reply. Maybe she doesn't think hatred is reason enough to kill, but I do.

The car heads into the Broadway tunnel. My chest tightens. We're almost there. Auntie Cat presses her rosary into my hand. "It can help having something to hold onto."

I shove the beads into my pocket. I'm not religious and I'm not going to start now. Mom and Dad hadn't been religious either. A little Buddhism here, a little Taoism there: that was it. The only thing that mattered was venerating Jade Dragon.

God and Jade Dragon, they play on the same team. Distant. Uncaring. Basically useless. I'm done with both of them.

My stomach shrinks into a tight, hard ball as the car pulls up in front of the Pacific Avenue Mortuary. I want to ask the driver to take me back to Auntie Cat's, but if I do, I won't see Mom.

The mortuary's double doors swing open. Tony and Aaron come out and stand under the green awning. They're wearing identical black suits and matching ties, which, at any other time, would be hilarious. I would've smirked before asking which one of them is taking my order. Now, I turn away and wish they'd disappear.

Auntie Cat opens the door and climbs out. I don't move. I can't.

She bends over and peers in at me. "Paul?"

I shake my head.

After a few moments, she steps aside.

Tony grips the roof as he leans inside. His cold expression has softened with concern. I stiffen and look straight ahead. He's concerned because I've accused his mother of murder.

"Little Brother," he speaks gently.

I gnaw my lip and blink back tears. I don't want to miss Tony or long for his company. If only we could talk, but what good would it do?

"Hey, Paul?" That voice belongs to Aaron.

I sigh and turn. Aaron stands beside his brother, his eyes bewildered and face forlorn. It's not their fault their parents are murderers. I don't want to punish them.

"You guys look like waiters in those suits," I mutter as I slide out of the car.

"Yeah, well, you look like a monkey in your suit," Aaron replies.

"Hush," Tony says.

For a single moment, everything feels normal. Then I have to make my legs move forward, into the mortuary. My cousins walk on either side of me while Auntie Cat goes ahead. Inside the lobby, the hum of chatter mutes to silence as we enter. Everyone stares at me. Who are these people? I mean I recognize them. It's the usual crowd of distant relatives and clan members who show up at the banquets. I've gone to their weddings and red egg parties, and hung out with their kids, but I don't know any of them. I can't tell who would've sided with Dad and who with Head Elder. It makes me suspicious of them all. A sad face can mask an evil heart. Speaking of which, I don't see Auntie Sylvia. Maybe she made some lame excuse to stay home. I hope not. I want to see her. I want to throw the rosary in her face and call her a murderer in front of everyone.

Auntie Cat leads the way up a wide, marble stairway to a

chapel on the second floor. Huge wreathes surround the altar, their pedestals overflowing with cascades of flowers and ribbons. If this was the actual funeral instead of a viewing, I'd already be at the front, dressed in white rags and bowing as each visitor comes forward to pay respect.

The altar has been set up with candles and more flowers, and offerings of fruit and incense. In the center sits a large, framed photograph. That picture... I recognize it from my parents' wedding album. It's a headshot of Mom with flowers wound through her hair. Her smile is so girlish and her eyes full of hope. As we get closer, I see the coffin behind the altar. My mother – she's inside that box. My feet falter. I stop. A tremor rattles through my body. My hand covers my eyes as I choke back a sob.

Tony's arm slides across my shoulders. "It's all right, Little Brother. I'll go with you."

Leaning against Big Brother, I stumble forward. When we reach the casket, my knees shake. It takes several deep breaths before I can look down.

Mom lays nestled in a blue velvet cocoon. I almost don't recognize her with all that makeup and her hair styled in puffy curls. Her eyes are closed tight and her mouth pulled down, as if she's trapped in an uneasy dream. Someone has dressed her in a white silk blouse with a Mandarin collar, something she wouldn't have worn in a million years.

I pull away from Tony and reach into the casket. Her hair feels sticky from too much hair spray. With trembling fingers, I gently tug out those stupid curls into natural-looking waves, until she looks more like my mother.

My throat aches, making it harder to swallow back tears. I whisper the last words that I should have said, that had been robbed from me. "I love you. Goodbye."

My hands clutch the edge of the coffin, my fingers digging into the plush lining. Tomorrow, Mom will be flown to Hong

Kong. I'm supposed to follow the next day, supposed to be the chief mourner at my parents' funeral on Chisel Knife Mountain. Everyone will expect me to play nice and not point the finger at the real murderer, Head Elder, a man who killed his own daughter.

The rustling noises behind me grow louder as people enter the chapel and slide into the pews. I turn around. A sea of faces stares at me, sympathy in their eyes, but do any of them really care how my parents died? None of them will listen to me. All they care about is keeping the status quo. Anger burns through my chest. I should shout the truth and make them listen.

"Little Brother?" Tony stares at me with cautious eyes. Do I look weird? My face feels too hot.

"I… I need to use the bathroom. By myself, okay?" I hurry down the aisle, dodging concerned glances and sympathetic murmurs. Out in the foyer, I shoulder past the people making their way into the chapel and head downstairs.

When I reach the bottom step, I look back. No one followed me. Good. I'm shaking so bad I don't know how my legs are holding me up. I look around. There are folding screens in almost every corner. I almost duck behind one until I spot the bathroom sign. I push open the men's room door so hard it hits the wall, and head straight to the faucet. Cold water takes the flush from my cheeks, but does nothing to cool the rage in my heart, the anger I feel toward the murderers and myself.

I raise my head and stare at my dripping reflection. "The truth," I whisper. "You have to face the truth."

Jade Dragon had warned us. He had ordered Dad and me to kill Head Elder or face the consequences. We made it worse by touching the spirit wall.

My hands slams down on the sink. I grip the edge to keep from throwing punches at the mirror. After a few moments and a few deep breaths, I grab a handful of paper towels and wipe my face. Dad and I failed. He and Mom paid the price. What should I do now? Return to Chisel Knife Mountain and finish the job?

How will I do that? I'm supposed to be the almighty Dragon Son, but the Dragon Shout is a wobbly toy in my hands. I'd need to somehow get hold of the Yang Pearl. Let's say I do. Then what? Wait until all three murderers are standing in one place and blast them? Not going to happen. The best I can hope for is killing Head Elder before I'm taken down.

Wait. If I die, Uncle George becomes the Dragon Son. Is that why he and Auntie Sylvia murdered my parents, so they could seize power? I know Auntie Sylvia would love to see Tony become the heir. I rub my chin. Okay, that works for them, but Head Elder won't be on board with that. Is there some kind of power play going on between the three of them?

Maybe Head Elder didn't order them to murder my parents. But if they did it on their own, Head Elder would've walloped them by now, unless things had happened as they said, which I don't believe for one second.

Shit. I can't kill them all in a rage of vengeance. I need to know the truth and I don't have a damn clue how to get it. The damp towels have wadded into a ball in my fist. I hurl it at the trashcan and leave the bathroom.

As I head down the corridor, I hear a familiar voice coming from the stairway. Auntie Sylvia. So, she dared show up after all. Should I confront her now or wait until she's standing in front of Mom, acting like there isn't blood on her hands? I duck behind a folding screen.

Heels click across the marble floor. Auntie Sylvia's voice rises above the sound. "I'd love to go out for lunch afterward. Let me send my sons home first." She heaves a dramatic sigh. "They're so young. They don't understand the need to eat and relax after such a trying experience."

"Trying?" repeats another woman.

"Well, sad. Tragic. You know what I mean."

The sound of their heels comes closer. They're heading toward the bathroom. Through a gap between the panels, I see *her* walk by, all dressed up as if she's going to a dinner party, as if she's not guilty of murder. The reek of roses curls around the screen.

"Will you take custody of him, Sylvia?" asks the other woman.

"I suppose so." Her voice sounds evasive. "Head Elder has ordered that I take custody. Of course, I'll comply."

The hell you will! The words almost burst from me. It'll be a cold day in hell when she gets custody of me and I'm going to fucking tell her to her fucking face.

I open the bathroom door silently, hoping to startle her. Then I step inside with a frown. The women's bathroom is different. It has an extra room with couches and mirrors, and boxes of tissues.

Auntie Sylvia's voice echoes from the stalls in the next room. "Can I tell you something? You have to promise not to tell anyone else."

"Of course," says her friend.

"Paul won't be returning from Chisel Knife Mountain. I mean, I'll take legal custody, but he'll be staying with his grandfather from now on."

I freeze. What?

"He doesn't know?"

"No. I've been so upset. He'll throw a fit and I don't want to deal with that."

"What about Catherine? You know she won't care about Head Elder's orders."

"That's not my problem. The clan can deal with Cat and him, not me. I'm not up to it."

My heart pounds so hard, I barely hear their continued

chatter. Head Elder is planning to kidnap me. I have to get out. I have to get away.

I spin around and see two purses on the counter. I hesitate. An honorable man, a *Xia* on the Glory Road, doesn't steal.

Fuck that. I need cash. And who better to take it from?

I reach into the first purse and open the wallet. The driver's license shows the photo of a vaguely familiar woman. I shove it back in and reach for the other purse. I don't bother looking at the license. I don't want to see Auntie Sylvia's face. I grasp all the paper money and leave the change so she won't notice her purse is lighter.

A toilet flushes.

I shove the money into my pocket and creep out of the bathroom. After glancing up and down the corridor, I move with Silent Steps to the back exit, covering the distance without sound. I reach for the door handle and stop. What about Auntie Cat? She'll be so worried. I don't have my phone, but I have to leave some kind of message that I've run away. I take out the rosary and drape it on the handle. No one else will recognize it. Hopefully, she won't see it until I'm long gone. I wince as the door creaks open. Then I slide through the smallest possible crack before easing it shut.

The exit door leads into an alley that doubles as a parking lot for the hearses. I squeeze past them and find myself on Pacific Avenue. In the middle of the day, on a busy street, I can't use any of my stealth skills, like the Swift Step or the Climbing Skill. A couple of blocks away, I spot a bus heading to the stop on the corner of Pacific and Powell. My stomach trembles while I wait for the light to turn green. I don't want to draw attention by jaywalking. A bunch of old people cluster around the stop, most of them hauling handcarts full of fruit and vegetables. They make for lousy camouflage since I'm taller than most of them.

I cast nervous glances at the mortuary, but so far no one has come outside. The approaching bus is a 12, which means it's heading for the Mission District. I've snuck over there a few times to check out the murals and cool graffiti. Members of the Two Dragon Clan hardly ever leave Chinatown, except to go to other Chinese neighborhoods, like where Auntie Cat lives. Which makes the Mission District the perfect place to head for. I swallow hard as the bus pulls into the stop. This is it. No going back. I pull out my transit pass and climb aboard. After a quick glance around, I sit beside a large guy who provides ample cover against anyone peering in the window. The bus turns right onto Powell. I hold my breath until it turns right again, onto Broadway and out of sight of the mortuary.

Getting off on 24th and Mission is like entering a different city. It's sunny and warm, and the bums bask in the sunlight instead of huddling in doorways against the cold bay breeze. Latino music pours out of the windows and doors of the shops and restaurants. Vendors line the sidewalk, selling tamales, horchata, and sizzling sausages grilled in their carts. Anyone my age is probably in school and I stand out like a sore thumb in this damn suit. I gotta ditch these clothes. I look up and down the street and spot a thrift store half a block away.

Inside, I wander up and down the aisles. How should I dress? I glance at other shoppers. Most are parents with kids. A few punks root through the racks, digging for '80s treasure. They're pierced and Mohawk-ed, and their clothes are ripped and frayed in the right spots. If I looked like them, the clan could never find me...

A lightbulb flickers above my head.

I trail the punks, trying to look casual as I gather their discards. Inside a dressing room, I count the money I stole. Eighty-eight dollars. Double eights. Some people would say that's lucky. Yeah, I am one lucky guy.

I have eighty-two dollars after trading in my suit as part of the payment for a pair of frayed jeans, a black t-shirt with a faded Metallica logo, and a thick, hooded army jacket with patched elbows and lots of pockets.

Outside, I pull up the hood, but still feel exposed. I don't have a clue how to cut and dye my hair, or change my face. I continue down the street until I come to one of those stores that sells cheap, trendy shit to teenagers. Inside, I find a red and black striped beanie and a pair of round, John Lennon-style glasses with tinted lenses. After putting them on, I study my reflection. I look more wannabe than punk. Then I spot some fake septum rings in the display case. I stick a plain metal one in my nose and, damn, it's amazing how something so small can change how you look.

Now I'm less visible, but I still gotta figure out where to go. A lot of homeless people are squatting in the abandoned buildings off Market Street, which means that's the first place Tony will look. I need to find someplace less obvious, where I can blend in. Above the counter are old posters from the hippie days. One of them has big, groovy letters that read, 'Haight-Ashbury.' I tug the beanie so it covers my hair and head out the door.

Paul

I get off the bus at the corner of Haight and Ashbury. Now what? I don't want to stand here looking stupid, so I start walking. I need to find a place where I can sit and think, but I've never been in this neighborhood and don't have a clue where to go. The storefronts are bright and colorful, trying to lure in customers with hippie nostalgia.

I don't see any hippies. There are a lot of homeless people. Some of them hold up cardboard signs pleading for help, while others rattle paper cups full of change. A group of street kids ambles past me carrying McDonald's bags and cups. My stomach rumbles. I haven't eaten anything today. I've barely eaten all week. It's weird that I'm hungry now, but a burger couldn't hurt. I follow a trail of discarded wrappers to a McDonald's across the street from Golden Gate Park. If I cut through the park, I can be at Auntie Cat's house in about twenty minutes. She'll be pissed as all hell at me for running off and selling my suit, but she'll get over it after I tell her everything. The trip to Hong Kong will be cancelled. She'll stand up to Head Elder and fight Auntie Sylvia for custody of me.

Then what? I stop and lean against the wall of a liquor store. Head Elder will stop at nothing to get his claws on me. He murdered his own daughter. Do I want Auntie Cat to be his next victim? My fists pound the brick wall before I push away and continue down the street.

Inside McDonald's, I order a Happy Meal and take the only remaining seat, next to a shabby, scabby guy who smells worse than he looks. Luckily, he gets up and leaves before killing what remains of my appetite. As I chew on my burger, I try to think above the din of the street kids shouting across the tables at each other. Most of them look like runaways. A *Xia* holds himself aloof from outsiders, especially outcasts like these kids. I stop chewing. Yang Guo in *Return of the Condor Heroes* was an orphan and an outcast. He disappeared and everyone wrote him off until he returned for revenge.

That's what I should do. Head Elder wants to rule the clan through me, but he can't do shit without me. He'll probably try to bluff his way through until the next Summoning Ceremony. If I'm not there, the clan will lose face and they'll blame him. The longer I stay away, the worse it will get. The other clans will get suspicious and probably try to take over leadership of the Crossroads. Head Elder won't have time to work his evil schemes when the clan is struggling for survival. On my eighteenth birthday, I'll return to Chisel Knife Mountain and deliver justice. That's what Yang Guo would do.

I feel buzzed. I don't know if it's from the caffeine in my soda or from having a plan of action. I've spent the past week wishing I were dead. Now, I'm glad I'm alive.

The street kids carry their cups out of the restaurant, so I do, too. Outside, the fog is rolling in, making the air damp and cold. Where should I spend the night? People with backpacks are crossing the street, heading into the park. Should I follow them and see where they sleep? All of them have sleeping bags. I should get one, but how much is that going to set me back?

I wander down Haight Street. Kids huddle in the doorways of closed shops, asking for spare change. Should I join them? Would that be weird? I settle in a doorway by myself. Across the street, people shout. A fight breaks out and ends just as quickly. As it gets dark, other people start showing up, adults heading for the bars and nightclubs. The street kids start drifting away in different directions. I drift, too. I hike up a steep hill lined with large Victorian houses. Spotting a hose next to a driveway, I turn it on low and refill my cup. After taking a drink, I look around guiltily. Peeing is a bad way to say thanks, but I don't have much choice if I want to keep walking. I move away from the faucet and whiz in a drain.

After walking a few blocks, I come to a house with dark windows. I slink onto the porch and huddle behind a wooden rail hung thick with trailing ivy. Despite this shelter, cold air settles around me, seeping through my jeans. I take off the glasses and rub the indents in the skin behind my ears. Then I rub my nose and almost tear the ring out. I put it and the glasses into a pocket and pull up my hood, tightening the drawstrings under my chin. I've done this before. Well, not this exactly. On Chisel Knife Mountain, I'd been sent into the forest with nothing and been expected to get through the night in one piece. In Kowloon, I'd spent nights on the rooftops of high-rise buildings during my training. This isn't so different.

Who am I kidding? This is completely different. Dad or Tony had always been somewhere nearby. Here, for the first time, I'm alone. The word brings a dull ache to my chest. No parents, no family, no friends. Alone.

I sleep in fitful spurts with uneasy dreams. A blaring car alarm startles me awake and I huddle in the corner, heart pounding, until I realize it has nothing to do with me. Still, the sun is up and anyone walking by can see me. I creep off the porch and stretch my stiff limbs. Despite the cold, my armpits are humid. My mouth tastes like sand. It hits me that I can't brush my teeth. I have to buy a toothbrush and toothpaste, and even then I need running water and a sink. Being homeless is more complicated than I thought. I need some guidance and there's only one place to get that. I make sure my glasses, beanie and nose ring are in place before heading downhill.

More money is gone after buying coffee and a breakfast burrito. I doubt I can last a week with what I have left. I eat without tasting and wipe my hands on my pants. Haight Street is a busy place on a Saturday morning. There are lines out the doors of some restaurants. The people waiting talk in loud, excited voices about what they did last night. I watch a bum approach a group with his hand out. They turn away, faces pinched, like he smells bad. How do the homeless survive? I spot a group of kids my own age, but keep walking when I see them passing around a bottle of Jack Daniels.

I slow down when I see another group lounging under the awning of a hippie souvenir store. Three guys and two girls sit in a circle and pass around a couple of huge muffins and a large Styrofoam cup. They're all wearing the uniform of the street kids: ripped jeans, black leather jackets and boots. Something about them feels different. They look cleaner than the others. I lean against the wall and wait.

The tallest guy, who has a short red Mohawk, calls out, "Hey, Lennon."

It takes a moment to realize he means me. "Yeah?"

"What's up?"

I shrug.

"You just run away?"

I nod.

He looks me up and down and shakes his head. "Go home."

"Can't."

"You can't stay out here."

"Yeah, I can."

"What about your family?"

"Don't have one."

Our eyes meet. He's sizing me up. He runs his index finger along the row of small, silver hoops that ridge his ear. Then he nods for me to join them.

"What's your name?" he asks as I sit.

I open my mouth and shut it again. He cocks his head. "Think fast. Something easy. I'm JJ." He turns to the others. "What do you think?"

"Too pretty and too soft," scoffs a dark-haired, brown-eyed guy. "He'll make good money, but they'll eat him alive."

My eyes widen. "I'm not gonna do that."

"Yeah? How you gonna eat?"

"I'll get a job."

"You got I.D.?"

I shake my head.

The third guy says, "You can try selling Molly, but you gotta find a supplier and there's lots of competition."

I stare. Those are my choices? Being a hooker or a pusher?

JJ folds his arms. "Look, we gotta eat, so we hustle. If you hang with us, you gotta contribute. That's gonna mean selling your scrawny ass, whether you like it or not. You don't gotta do butt sex. Blow jobs earn decent bread."

My jaw drops. He's trying to shock me and doing a damn fine job. As I get to my feet, I mumble, "K. Thanks."

"JJ, cut your shit out," says one of the girls. Then she calls out, "Hey, you can spange."

I turn. "Spange?"

"Yeah, spange. You know, ask for spare change."

"He won't earn enough," says dark-haired guy.

"Give him a chance."

JJ sighs. "Dude, you should go home."

"I don't have a home."

"What's your name?"

"Lennon works," I reply.

The other girl smiles and says, "Lennon. That's cool."

"Look, Lennon," JJ's eyebrows raise as he says the name, "You can hang with us for a couple of days, 'til you figure out what you're gonna do."

I nod and rejoin them. They introduce themselves. The smiling girl is Nix. A blue bandana covers her curly red hair, making her freckles stand out against her pale skin. The other girl, Amethyst, has a head full of tiny braids and a pierced eyebrow and upper lip. The dark-haired guy is Sway. The third guy is Good Dog Carl, but everyone calls him just Carl. He's shorter than me and has blond hair with dark roots.

"Let's bounce." JJ makes a gesture with his shoulder and we head out to the street.

For the next couple hours, at JJ's instruction, I work the bus stops, approaching the older passengers and claiming I've lost my transit pass. On the first try, I must have looked as ashamed as I felt, because the woman gave me a dollar. After that, it became a little easier, until by noon, I've panhandled almost ten dollars.

"Not bad," JJ comments when I show him the take. "We'll work this angle while you're still a fresh face."

That night, I return to the hippie store and perch on the stoop with Nix and Amethyst. The guys take off down the street toward the park. My stomach churns. There's no way I'm going to do that. I'd rather sleep in a ditch and dig in the trash for food.

"Spare change?"

The girls sound like a stereo on either side of me. Amethyst lifts up a McDonald's cup while Nix holds out a piece of cardboard that reads, 'Homeless and Hungry! Please Help!'

A man reaches into his pocket and drops some change into

the cup. Nix turns to me. "Only use a cup from, like, McDonald's or Burger King. If you use a Starbucks cup or some kind of coffee place, people will think you're spending their money on lattes."

"Spending it on McDonald's is better?"

She shrugs.

A group of adults pass by, chugging down coffee like it's liquid gold. Do they think their precious brew is too good for us? What a bunch of hypocrites.

Amethyst looks at me with sympathetic eyes. "I don't like turning tricks, either. It's…" She grimaces and shudders, "gross. Thing is, it's easier for us," She nods at Nix, "to spange. People prefer giving money to girls. Check it out." She hands me the cup. "Go stand on the corner."

Ten minutes pass and no one drops even a penny into the cup. My stomach twists as I hand it back to Amethyst. I barely made fifteen dollars working the bus stops all day. I can't survive on that, not for the next two years.

"If you're a guy, you gotta have a gimmick," explains Nix. "Like a dog or a broken leg."

I don't want either, so that's not going to work. Even at the bus stop, most of the people I approached knew it was a scam.

A woman wearing yoga pants and a tank top approaches, grimacing as she tugs along a screaming toddler with snot dripping from his nose. Amethyst rests the cup on her knee and Nix flattens the sign. The woman stops in front of us, her face nearly as red as the kid's. The toddler's screams increase, one small hand groping toward the plastic bag she's carrying.

"All right! All right!" The woman reaches into the bag, pulls out a small, colorful cardboard box and gives it to him.

The kid slams the box to the sidewalk with a shriek that breaks my eardrums. The woman lifts the squirming bundle into her arms and continues on. The kid howls over her shoulder, hands straining toward the fallen box.

Amethyst crawls over to the box, opens it and peers inside. She shakes her head and starts to toss it away.

"Hey," Nix calls out. "What is it?"

"Chalk." Amethyst looks inside again. "Excuse me. Broken chalk."

"Yeah?" I hold out my hand and she tosses me the box. I look inside. A treasure trove appears before my eyes. "It's colored."

Both girls giggle.

I kneel on the sidewalk in front of them and sweep away the cigarette butts and other trash. Then I stare at the girls, taking in the shapes of their faces, the curves of their necks, and the color and texture of their hair. Both girls stare back with pinched brows. I dig around in the box until I find half a stick of blue chalk. Hunching over the square of pavement, I start sketching an outline.

After a few moments, Nix asks, "Um, Lennon. Are you drawing us?"

I nod. They shriek. What the hell? I look up. They're running their fingers through their hair and wiping their faces on their sleeves. When done, they smile and sit completely still. I don't have much experience with girls outside the clan. Well, even inside the clan. I don't know if this is normal behavior. It's kind of cute, though, like them. Now, I feel nervous, wondering if I can even pull it off. A man jogs past, not even looking at us, his foot barely missing my hand. His running shoes smeared the outline of their faces. Amethyst flips the bird while Nix swears a blue streak at him. I use my fingertips to repair the damage and continue drawing. I'm going to show jerks like him that we're people, not scum you can shit all over.

Nix starts warning off the foot traffic, while Amethyst holds up her cup and calls out, "Support the arts."

Some people are annoyed as they step around me. Part of me wants to stop. My family would expect me to stop. I keep drawing and manage to capture Nix's wide, appealing eyes and Amethyst's crooked smile.

A guy with gray hair and a brown leather jacket stops and watches for a moment. Then he reaches into his pocket. "That's pretty good." He drops a dollar into Amethyst's cup and walks away.

I stare at my hands, coated with colorful, grainy powder. I knew I wasn't wasting my time learning to draw. I wish I could tell my parents. More people stop to look and contribute. Some make comments, mostly one or two words.

"Good."

"Not bad."

"What the hell?"

JJ is standing over me. "So, you got talent, huh?"

"Look, look!" Amethyst thrusts out her cup, heavy with spange.

JJ fingers through our take. "Chump change compared to what we just made, but it'll do for now."

I shrug, trying not to show the relief coursing through me. I carefully pick up each piece of chalk, no matter how small, and put them back in the box. The spange is used to buy dinner at McDonald's. As I wolf down my cheeseburger, I think about the delicious meal Mom would have made tonight, like sesame chicken with mushrooms and water chestnuts. That's my favorite. I usually helped in the kitchen, cleaning and slicing the vegetables while we talked about stuff. My eyes start to sting. The burger sticks in my throat. I wash it down with a long slurp of Coke.

I figured we'd be sleeping in the park, so I'm surprised when we hop a bus heading downtown. No one pays, so I don't, either.

"Do you guys crash in one of those buildings?" I ask, because if that's where we're heading, I'm going to have to bail.

"You mean Boomlandia?" JJ shakes his head. "Nah. You had to get in there, like, right after the crash. Hobos there are territorial as hell."

"Not all the buildings," argues Nix. "Some are full of families. Some are really scary, though. Full of users who would slit your throat for a dime bag. Most of them don't have water or electricity. Don't worry. We got better digs than that."

We get off on Market Street and JJ leads the way to a hotel beneath the freeway. He pays cash to a sketchy guy at the front desk, who barely looks up from the porno on his laptop, except to leer at the girls. It makes me want to punch him in the face.

The room smells like mold and old cheese. The only furnishings are a rickety double bed, a metal chair and a chipped desk covered with pizza boxes. Clothes lay in meager piles all over the floor. Sway points out the bathroom like it's a great luxury.

JJ plops down on the chair. "Here's the deal. We got this place cuz none of us are tweakers. We hustle 'til we make the rent. If you wanna party with what's left of your cut, that's cool. Booze, weed, 'shrooms, you're golden. We catch you with meth or crack, you're out."

"I don't do drugs," I say.

Sway rolls his eyes. "Just come up with your end and you can stay."

I sit on the floor and wait while the others take their turns in the bathroom. By the time I get in, there's no hot water and the threadbare towels are wet. I wash quickly and go back out to the room, dark now, except for the glow of a streetlight shining through the frayed curtains. Prone forms occupy the bed. From their hair, I can tell it's the girls.

"Lennon," Carl calls out from under the window.

I step around JJ and Sway, who lay on the floor in nests made from sleeping bags and blankets. Carl scoots closer to the window and flips open his blanket. My chest tightens. I don't want to sleep next to some random guy, but is there a choice? I take off my jacket and bundle it up for a pillow before lying down next to him.

Carl spreads a blanket over both of us. "We take turns on the bed. Tomorrow, I'll show you where you can buy a sleeping bag for cheap."

"Thanks."

"You're lucky you found JJ. He's got his shit together. If it weren't for him, we'd be in the park."

I shift among the lumps in the sleeping bag that serves as a mattress. It's probably better than sleeping on the threadbare carpet, but it smells like body odor.

"Hey, Lennon," Carl whispers, "Are you gay?"

"No." I stare at the ceiling.

"Oh. I am. So is JJ."

"Okay."

"Does that bug you?"

"No."

There's a silence, long enough that I think he was asleep. Then, "Are you sure you're not gay?"

"Yeah."

Carl sighs and rolls over. I exhale. Being gay in the Two Dragon Clan is unacceptable. You have to either be straight or act straight, no other choice. I would've freaked out just now if I hadn't grown up in San Francisco. In school, we get taught a lot about tolerance and acceptance, which I totally agree with. A lot of artists I admire are gay. It still feels pretty weird. Then I think about Head Elder. He'd freak out if he knew I was sleeping next to a gay dude. For the first time since my parents died, I smile.

The sound of the freeway rumbles through the room. Big rig trucks make the walls vibrate. In the street below, two men start a shouting match in a language I don't recognize. A siren wails and the men take off. In the room, other sounds begin:

snoring, coughing, weeping. Loneliness burrows a hole into my gut. I've barely thought about my parents today, but that's good, right? I can't let grief get the better of me. Concentrate on survival and stay clear of the clan. I feel bad about Auntie Cat, but to hell with the rest of them.

Even Tony?

Tears cloud my vision. I roll over and they dribble onto my forearm. Someday, I'll get revenge by killing his parents. And then he'll get his revenge by killing me.

Penny

Piece of shit waits for me on my locker door.

Kayla arrives and turns her combination in silence, like I'm not there. Then she glances over her shoulder before whispering to her locker, "It's Dani. I saw her."

Dani.

Okay, then.

"Don't tell her I told you."

This is why I don't fit in. I don't understand Bleaters at all. Telling Dani would break our pact, feeble though it may be. Don't Bleaters have any sense of honor?

"Okay," I whisper without looking at her. Then, even though I don't want to, I add, "Thanks."

Kayla sniffles. I glance over. Her shoulders are shaking. A tear dribbles down her acne-pitted cheek. She must be fresh from a round of Daisy Chain taunts, which makes me suspicious. "Was it really Dani?"

"Yeah." Her voice gets resentfully louder.

"When did you see her do it?"

Her voice shrinks to a whisper. "Last week."

Nope. No honor at all. Why should I fight her fight? I open my locker and stare at the wall of insults.

lezbo

ugly cunt

die already

Piece of shit sticks to my fingers. I can suck up so much for the sake of my family, but this is the limit. So. Done. I slam the door shut. Kayla squeaks and jumps as I stride away.

Dani is standing at her locker with two other Daisy Chains, all cackling about something. As I get closer, I spot a pink sticky note in Dani's hand.

I see red. I am a Strowler, the descendent of a dragon and a fairy. It's time they find out who they fucked around with.

My backpack, heavy with the books I didn't put away, slides off my shoulder. I'm about to slam it into them when I spot Ms. Gagliardi unlocking her classroom door at the other end of the hall. If I do this, she'll be the one to break up the fight. I'll lose my only ally. Are they worth it?

No.

I push my way through them and stick *piece of shit* on Dani's locker.

I don't speak or fold my arms because that would look weak and defensive. Gerry told me, in a fight, let the other person get lathered up. Dani's mouth flaps like a fish with her outraged sputters. Her friends gape, but I can see the gleam in their eyes, eager to enjoy a show. Dani glances at them. Her arms fold. For a brief moment, she looks uncertain. Then she speaks in that nasally, Daisy Chain way. "I'm so telling on you." She nods at her friends. "Avery and Emma are my witnesses." Satisfaction curls her lips. "You're going to be in so much trouble."

"Go on, then. Do it." I take a step so she has to back up. "I'll go with you. And after you tell Ms. Ikeda, I'll show her all the notes you stuck on my locker."

"She won't believe you."

"She will when she compares our handwriting."

Dani blinks.

I don't.

"You do that and you'll be sorry. I'll get you expelled."

I take another step. "If I'm expelled, the first person I come looking for is you."

Her back presses against the lockers. "I'm telling Kevin."

"I'm telling Kevin. I'm telling Ms. Ikeda." I mock her nasal tone. Then I sneer. "Snitch."

The other girls' eyes pop and their mouths go "O" at the taboo word.

Dani's face turns red and her oily eyes well up. If it were anyone else, I'd back off, but it makes my blood boil that she dishes it out, but can't take it. I point three fingers in the sign of the pitchfork and sweep my hand so they get it's meant for them all. "I curse the day you were born and the ground beneath your feet. May you never find peace as you walk upon this earth."

Their eyes go wide. Emma presses her hand to her heart. Avery gasps, "Are you a witch?"

I smile, turn and swagger away.

My heart is still pounding in my ears when I get to English class. I want to feel elated. I gamed them and won. Instead, I'm uneasy. Gran taught me there are two kinds of Strowler curses. The ones we sell to Bleaters, which are rubbish, and the ones we use against our enemies, which are real. True curses have power, but they darken the soul. The only remedy is to bless those I've cursed, but I don't want to. I want to scorch their earth the way they've scorched mine.

When I get home, first thing Bridie asks is, "How was school today?"

I haven't told her about the notes. What's the point? All she'll do is sigh, shed a tear or two, and ask me to bear up for the sake of the family. I can't tell her about the curse. She'll go into hysterics and say this is why she took us off the Crossroads, blah, blah, blah.

I shrug. "Same-same."

"Are you sure?"

"Yeah. Why?"

"Oh, nothing. Kai sometimes stays after school for activities or to hang out with his friends. You don't seem to do that."

I can't even begin to say how not in the mood for this I am right now. I answer in a dead monotone, "I don't have any friends. I don't like the activities."

Her lip wobbles. "Maybe you should give it a try."

Maybe if you hadn't dumped me into deep water and told me to swim to save your life. I bite back on those words to avoid her tears. Besides, I have other bones to pick with her. "Right. Look. Kai started middle school with the rest of his class. It's new for all of them. I started high school as a sophomore with people who already know each other."

"I can see how that might make things a little harder…"

"You don't. See. Shite."

Her eyes storm over. At least that brought out some fight in her instead of Miss Pity Poor Me. "Don't talk that way to me, madam. Another word and you'll be spending the evening here instead of the Auld Sod."

"Good. I don't want to dance for that chav."

"Don't call him that. It's insulting."

"You're right. I apologize to all the chavs everywhere."

I leave Bridie gawping and head upstairs. I'm so sick of it. We're not on the Crossroads, but we're still supposed to respect Kingfisher. Please. Done. I slam my door shut and take a deep breath. What's wrong with me? Why am I getting worked up over a load of bollocks? I can feel Gerry and Matthew's eyes on me from across the room.

Be kind to our Bridie, they whisper.

I glare at them. What about your Penny? Don't I count, too? You're stronger than her.

No. She's the mother. She's supposed to be the strong one, but she's not and I know it. Why all this anger? Is it the curse? I hurry over to the mirror and examine my face. I don't look any different than this morning. Maybe it takes a while before the darkening of my soul begins. Or maybe it's a load of bollocks and I'm a gom for believing a word of it.

I knuckle down to my homework, ignoring Bridie's call to dinner. A little later, she opens my door without knocking and sets a plate on my desk. "Eat."

I don't look at her or the food. "I'm not hungry."

"Then you'll be dancing on an empty stomach because you're coming with me and your brother, whether you like it or not." She gives a firm nod before leaving the room.

I glance at the plate. Cottage Pie. My favorite. I want to ignore this peace offering, but the aroma of those creamy mashed potatoes covering beef and vegetables sautéed with tasty gravy makes my mouth water. Maybe just a few bites. She's right. I don't want to dance on an empty stomach. Besides, I like it when she acts like an adult instead of a damsel in distress.

I dress without enthusiasm, wearing the same costume as last time. Bridie gives me the cold shoulder when I climb into the backseat of the car. Kai is too busy playing a game on his phone to notice. Nobody speaks until we arrive at the pub and Bridie fakes a cheerful smile as she greets the punters at the bar.

As usual, Kingfisher is seated front and center, only this time he isn't alone. There's a woman beside him with sour eyes and twisted lips, as if she can't stand the taste of her own mouth. Her red dress hangs loose on her thin shoulders and she looks gaunt despite the bright makeup penciled on her face. A teenage boy is with them. I guess he's Kingfisher's son with his shaved head, squinty eyes and teal Sharks' hockey jersey. Also, he looks an arsehole. The three of them watch us set our instruments and adjust the microphones like it's part of the show. Kai and I exchange wary glances while Bridie goes about her business as if all is right with the world.

Kingfisher whistles.

Her shoulders hunch. Then she pretends she didn't hear and continues tapping the mike. "One-two, one-two." Her voice echoes through the pub.

Kingfisher whistles louder. "Bridie. Over here. Bring the kids."

Mum and I look at each other, all the tension between us dissolving. We need a united front against the Upright Man.

"Do we gotta?" whispers Kai, his face scrunching.

"We gotta." Bridie forces a smile.

I don't bother looking pleasant. The role of surly, reluctant teenager suits me better. Kai puts on a middle school version of the same attitude.

"Mr. Kingfisher, how nice to see you," Bridie says as we stand before his table.

"Just Kingfisher." He points his chin at the woman. "Doreen."

Bridie bobs her head respectfully. "Walk in peace, Mother Bird."

"She ain't the Mother Bird."

There's a tense hush at this rude way of saying she's not his wife.

Doreen looks Bridie up and down. The tense lines in her face deepen. "So, you're the rum piece all the crew are prattling about."

Bridie's smile fades. I almost chew off my lip at this insult. Piece means a loose, available woman.

"Shut up, Doreen." Kingfisher nods at the boy. "My son, Mikey Boy."

"Walk in peace, fair lady." Mikey Boy makes the polite words sound rude.

"Walk in peace." Bridie nods her head graciously. "How delightful to meet your family."

Kingfisher takes a swig of beer and speaks through the foam on his lips. "Doreen ain't Mikey Boy's ma. She died a while back. Doreen's my convenience."

I stiffen. It's rare for a Strowler man to out-and-out call a woman his mistress, though the word is worse than that, a convenience being a woman a man uses or not, at his convenience.

Doreen's eyes burn. "We have two daughters."

Kingfisher turns to his son. "Them's her kinchin. The ewe is Penny and the whelp is Kai."

Mikey Boy looks me up and down like he's examining merchandise. "She's a rum dell."

A dell is a girl ready to lose her virginity. He and Kevin Anderson would make great mates. Manky bellends, the pair of them. I wish I could paste him like I did Kevin, but all I can do is look at him like he's got B.O. He doesn't return the compliment. He's too busy pouring himself a pint from his dad's pitcher.

"Enjoy the show." Bridie's cheery tone is as false as her parting smile. She places her arms around Kai and me, and leads us back to the stage. I glance back. Doreen is ordering something from the waitress. Kingfisher and his son are eyeing Bridie's arse. I want to go over and punch them.

Bridie's grip tightens. She whispers, "Never mind them."

"We should scuttle," I whisper back.

"We can't, not with them sitting right there. Concentrate on the show."

Easier said than done. The show starts and Bridie's timing is off. Kai and I can't harmonize with her and sound awful. Bridie sets down her guitar, picks up her fiddle and closes her eyes as she plays. I do the same with my penny whistle and we sound a little better, though Kai's drumming is still off. By the third song, and my first dance, we perform in harmony despite the presence of the Upright Man, his leering son and seething mort.

As I bow to the crowd's applause, Doreen slams down her glass after draining the contents. "It's disgusting the way you're looking up her skirt."

Kingfisher's head turns slowly. His glare makes her shrink back in her chair. "You accusing me of looking up that little girl's skirt?"

"Not the ewe." She jerks her head toward Bridie. "The doxy."

"Get lost, Doreen." He empties the pitcher into Mikey Boy's glass and thumps the table twice with his meaty palm. Moments later, a male Strowler hurries over with a full pitcher.

Bridie's knuckles whiten around the neck of her violin. The rest of the set proceeds at a miserable pace. Her fiddling is so off I stumble at the end of my third jig. My cheeks burn through the sympathy applause.

Bridie comes up to me, motioning Kai to join us. She whispers, "You've sprained your ankle. Choose a foot."

I lift my right foot, touch it to the floor as if testing it and wince.

Bridie goes back on stage and leans regretfully into the microphone. "Well, everyone, I'm afraid my daughter hurt her ankle and I've got to get her home. Sorry to cut things short. See you next time."

I limp off the dance floor to another round of sympathetic applause, though this time I feel happy rather than humiliated, since it signals the end of our ordeal.

Kingfisher stands. The tiny stage shakes as he comes up the stairs and walks over to where Bridie is packing away her fiddle. "Join me for a drink."

She shakes her head. "I can't. My children."

"The kids can join us. I'll buy them dinner."

"They've already supped. I need to get Penny home so I can look at that ankle."

"It won't hurt her to sit for a bit."

"I think it will. Besides, your mort," Bridie nods toward Doreen, who glowers at them while tipping back her glass. "Won't appreciate me keeping you company."

"I told you, Doreen's my convenience, and she's becoming inconvenient."

"That's between you and her. I have to get home to my husband." Bridie lifts her guitar case in one hand and her fiddle in the other. She turns to Kai. "Help your sister."

I put my hand on Kai's shoulder and do my best to limp without milking it.

Kingfisher calls after us, "It won't last. Bleaters don't understand our kind."

Inside the car, Bridie locks the doors. As we pull away from the curb, she lets out a breath. "Oh, that dreadful man! Sorry, children, but we'll have to stash our game at the Auld Sod. We'll wait a few weeks and find another pub."

I bite back on saying Kingfisher will eventually find us wherever we go. Unpleasant thoughts poke at my mind, until I finally have to speak. "Mum, have you thought about cursing Kingfisher?"

The light from the car's console casts shadows over Bridie's face, making her cheeks hollow and her eyes dead. "I've thought about cursing a lot of people, but I don't."

"Why not?"

"You know why not."

"The darkening of the soul. Is that for real?"

"Real enough."

My heart starts fluttering. "Why even have curses if they bite you in the arse like that?"

"A curse isn't to be cast lightly. It's a last - not a first - resort. You're darkening another's road and you pay by darkening your own."

"But what if the other person really deserves it?"

"You mean Kingfisher?"

Sure, why not. "Yeah."

"He'd have to have a well of darkness so deep within that the curse can't reflect back on you. I don't know if he's that foul. He's not worth chancing my soul."

I cross my arms as a chill runs up my spine. I hate Dani and the whole Daisy Chain. I want to curse each and every one of them, but not enough to harm myself. I chew my lip before saying, "Mum…"

I start with the notes and describe my life as the school's toadeater. Kai slides forward and offers to thrash anyone who's tarnished my name. His face is wound tight with outrage. It's touching he wants to defend my honor. Bridie, on the other hand, listens with her eyes on the road and her face blank.

That changes when I get to the curse. She immediately flicks the turn signal and pulls into the first available parking spot. "Who taught you to curse? Was it Gran?"

I squirm, wanting to say, but not wanting to grass.

Her voice rises. "It was for me to teach you the ways of Liansidhe, not her."

"Then why don't you?"

Bridie rubs her forehead while muttering, "Selfish gobby cow. She doesn't trust me to raise you. Another reason we had to leave." Then she looks at me with no-nonsense eyes. "Fairy magic isn't to be trifled with. Did she teach you that?"

"No. I mean, sort of. She said not to throw curses about willy-nilly, but I didn't. They deserved it."

"Do you deserve it, to have your soul darkened because of them?"

My voice becomes small. "No."

She takes a breath. "Right. Now, you're going to reverse the curse and bless those girls, right this moment."

I huff and look out the window.

"Penny…"

"No. Why should I? I bless them and they go back to making my life hell. That's what you want, right? For me to take it up the arse no matter what so you can have a comfortable life."

Kai gives a long whistle from the back seat. The tension between Bridie and me feels like a razor's edge. One slip and someone is going to get hurt.

Her voice is very quiet. "You should have told me about those notes. I don't expect you to take a load of shite from those toffee-nosed minxes, not for any reason, least of all to spare my feelings." She's not hysterical, so I suppose that's something, but I can't believe her words. She must know it, too, from her long sigh. "After the Beggars' Banquet, I'll work another Charm on Bill and get him to transfer you to another school."

"Really?" I swivel around to face her. This is not what I expected at all.

"My word," she replies solemnly. "Not until next semester, if you can hang in there that long."

"I can. I even know another school I'd like to go to."

She looks surprised. "Well, that's a change. I'll find a way, but first you have to bless those girls."

Gall builds up in my throat again. I swallow it hard. I'm not going to let anything get in the way of getting out. "Which blessing?"

"What are the girls' names?"

"Dani, Emma and Avery."

"Repeat after me. Dani: may kings respect you, the devil neglect you, the angels protect you, and heaven accept you."

I repeat the blessing three times, once for each girl. It makes my stomach churn, but when I'm finished, I feel better, lighter. The darkness on my soul must be gone. I breathe easier. "So, that's it?"

"That's it." Bridie pushes the ignition and speaks over the rumble of the engine. "Curses like that only stick to the darkest of souls. Then, even blessings won't work because their well is so deep, the blessing is swallowed by the darkness."

I don't know about the other two girls, but Dani... something tells me her well is that deep. Kingfisher, too. I'm done with Dani. Kingfisher, though, I'm certain he's not done with us.

Lennon

I'm hungry all the time.

For the past few days, I've had to choose between eating and having a place to stay. My drawings earn more than just asking for spange, but the chalk is almost gone, along with the money I stole from Auntie Sylvia. I've scrounged through all of my pockets at least twice and all I can come up with is $7.28. I can spend it on food or chalk, but since I need the chalk to make money, the choice is already made.

My food comes out of the trash. Nix showed me how to dumpster dive behind places that discard unused food at certain times of the day. It's not as gross as it sounds. Yesterday, we ate expired sandwiches and bruised bananas behind a convenience store. Problem is, lots of people know this trick, so you have to get there first.

A man stops to check out my latest drawing, a Tyrannosaurus holding a bobbing, pink balloon. I drew it in front of a toy store, hoping the kids passing through the door will get their parents to throw some spange my way.

"Nice." He drops a dollar into my cup.

Three more dollars and I can buy chalk and maybe afford a

burger at McDonald's. One thing I can't afford is to bunk with the crew tonight.

The sun beats down on the pavement. I press against the wall to catch the dwindling shade. My scalp itches. I want to yank off my beanie, but I can't take the chance. Instead, I shrug off my jacket, laying it in a heap at my feet so no one will grab it. Grime streaks my ripped jeans and the Metallica t-shirt looks as bad as it smells.

An Asian mom and her son leave the toy store, smiling and holding hands. She glances at me and quickly looks away. My throat aches. What would Mom think if she saw me? Would she look away, not recognizing me? Or would she be ashamed at the sight of her son living like a bum? And Dad… I swallow hard. I don't want to think about my father.

I tug at the blond tufts sticking out from my beanie. Carl bleached my hair in exchange for me touching up his roots. The extra camouflage can't hurt and I enjoy the bitter pleasure of knowing Head Elder would shit bricks if he saw me.

I shade my eyes as I stare at the bright blue sky. *Hey, Jade Dragon. Would it hurt to send some clouds my way?*

No answer. Is he ashamed of me? Who gives a shit? Not Jade Dragon.

Thanks for nothing. I flip the bird at the sky, hold my breath and wait.

Nothing.

Maybe Jade Dragon isn't real. Maybe the whole summoning ceremony is a big hoax that Dad was going to let me in on eventually. Between learning the Dragon Shout and hiding from Head Elder, my *chi* had gotten all messed up. Maybe what I'd heard and felt in the ancestral hall had been a weird fantasy. I'd rather believe that than believe Jade Dragon is real and doesn't care enough to help me get revenge. I squat by my drawing for another hour, using shards of chalk to clean up what's stepped on and smeared. A few more people toss in their spange. As I rub the last bit of green into the T-Rex's body, a pair of familiar boots comes to a stop beside me.

"How'd you do?" asks JJ.

The others circle me and look down. "So cute," says Nix wistfully. Amethyst looks sad. So does Carl. They know.

I shake my head.

Sway smirks. "You don't gotta spend the night outside, y'know."

I shrug.

The smirk tenses into a frown. "You think you're too good to hustle?"

I want to tell him, yeah, I am too good to hustle, but under the anger, there's so much pain in his eyes. "I've never had sex, okay? Not with anybody. I don't want to start by doing it like that."

Maybe they get it now. Or maybe they think I'm even more of a twerp than they thought. Doesn't matter. I stand and pocket my spange. "I'll come by later to get my sleeping bag." I bump fists with Carl and manage to smile at Nix and Amethyst's little waves before walking away.

"Hey, Lennon," JJ calls out. I stop and turn. "You can stay one more night."

"We ain't runnin' a charity," Sway protests.

"Okay, let's put it to the vote. All in favor?"

Nix, Amethyst and Carl raise their hands along with JJ. Sway shoves his hands in his pockets, but doesn't protest when I rejoin them.

"Just tonight," JJ says.

"I know." My stomach relaxes a little. I can eat, buy some chalk and maybe make enough for tomorrow night. If not, I'll have to find a doorway to squat in.

At McDonald's, I reluctantly hand over enough change for a cheeseburger. I should dumpster dive to save money, but I've got to stick with the crew. I'll allow myself the luxury of one more night indoors. After that, I've got to figure out a way to make enough money to leave San Francisco and head someplace Tony won't think to look for me. Not Los Angeles. The Two Dragon Clan has a large presence there. Same with Seattle. Maybe Portland. Lots of runaways there and the clan has no chapter in Oregon. Yeah, Portland will work, except I heard a bus ticket costs about a hundred bucks. I should've stolen Auntie Sylvia's credit cards, too.

We leave McDonald's, but instead of getting on the bus, we cross the street and head into the park.

"Where are we going?" I ask.

"Party on Hippie Hill," JJ replies.

Hippie Hill? "Will there be a hippie drum circle?"

Carl drapes his arm across my shoulders. "What do you think?"

It's weird. A few weeks ago, I would've squirmed if a gay dude put his arm around me. Now, it doesn't bug me at all. Carl isn't trying to hit on me. He's lonely. I get that. If I were to stop and think about how alone I am, I'd probably curl into a ball and cry.

The distant sound of tribal rhythms gets louder as we go deeper into the park, until we get to a bench where a bunch of adults are pounding on drums or playing other instruments. One has a didgeridoo and sits cross-legged while blowing through the long tube. Most look too young to be real hippies, even though they're dressed in tie-dye and fringe. We head up a grassy slope where people are lounging on blankets, passing around bottles, pipes and joints. Dancers dot the hill, eyes closed, swaying and flailing their arms as if in a trance.

What would Head Elder and the clan think if they knew I was here, surrounded by people who are drunk and high? Disgrace. My lip curls. Yeah, they kill my parents, but I'm the disgrace. The thought makes me want to grab a joint and inhale.

At the top of the hill, a hairy hippie has a Styrofoam cooler full of Pabst Blue Ribbon. JJ pays and hands out cans to the crew, including me.

I shake my head. "I can't afford it."

"My treat."

I've already admitted I'm a virgin; I don't want to say I've never had a drink. We clink cans before tipping them back. Bitter, sour bubbles sting my mouth and it takes all my willpower not to spit it out. My eyes water as I force myself to swallow.

JJ cocks his head. "What are you doing out here, bro? I mean, you look like you belong in prep school."

"I don't belong anywhere."

"What about your family?"

"Don't have one."

"Yeah, well, what about what about a shelter? You're clean. They'll take you in."

First place Tony would look. "I don't want to stay in a shelter."

"You might change your mind if it gets cold enough." JJ starts to take another swig when the can is grabbed out of his hand.

A man with a sunburned face, greasy hair and a scraggly beard shoves JJ aside before draining the can. I recognize him. One of those hardened bums who prey on the younger runaways, knocking them around and stealing their spange.

JJ shoves him back. "Fuck off, asshole. You owe me a beer."

The bum reaches into his grimy jean's pocket and pulls out a balisong. With a flick of his wrist, the knife slides from the handle. He holds it out so the blade gleams in the setting sunlight. His lips curl back, revealing a jagged grin. "C'mere, bitch."

I shove JJ out of the way. My front snap kick connects with the bum's wrist, jerking the knife from his grasp. I follow through with a sidekick to the groin. He doubles over, cupping his dick as he screams in agony. A left uppercut sends him rolling down the hill. When he reaches the bottom, he curls into a fetal position and rocks back and forth.

I grab the balisong and flick my wrist, watching the blade whisk in and out of its sheath. As I slide it into my pocket, I realize the drumming has stopped. Everyone on the hill is staring at me. My face heats as whistles and cheers fill the air. My crew stares as if seeing me for the first time. Then the girls clap their hands, while Carl and Sway make kicking and chopping motions while yelling, "Hi-yah!"

JJ rubs his chin. "I just thought of something."

I shove the knife in my pocket. "Yeah?"

"A way you can contribute."

The next night, I stand with JJ, Carl and Sway at the north corner of Buena Vista Park.

"You sure you know what to do?" JJ asks for the fifth time.

I nod.

"We'll follow. If it goes down wrong, give the signal."

I take a deep breath and tense as a car slows to a stop. The driver peers out the window. He's an older guy, at least thirty, with a long nose, beady eyes and pasty skin. He looks like he spends all day staring at a computer.

Carl groans, "Ah, shit. It's Moby."

"Moby?" I ask.

JJ answers, "We call him Moby because he's such a dick. He pays good, but he's rough. No one wants to go with him."

Carl tugs my shoulder. "Better pass on this one."

Sway smirks. He still believes I can't handle myself on the street. Time to buy him a clue. "I can do it."

"You sure?" asks JJ.

"Yeah." My stomach clenches as the passenger side window unrolls.

JJ struts over and leans in. "Wanna date?"

Moby juts his chin toward me. "He new?"

"Yep." JJ turns and whistles.

I climb in and my feet slip on something long and round. Empty bottles cover the floor mat and I have to hunch my knees to settle on the seat. I close the door and Moby rolls up the window. Immediately I gag on the smell of old wine and stale semen. I'll bet he lives with his mom and uses the car to jerk off to pornos on his phone. He doesn't look at me. He's a mouth breather and his chest rattles with something I hope isn't contagious. So this is the kind of guy who picks up homeless kids for blowjobs. I guess he doesn't care I haven't brushed my teeth in awhile.

Moby drives up Buena Vista Avenue to a turnout surrounded by trees, and parks in the City Vehicles Only zone. He fumbles with his pants, pulling down the zipper. Show time. I reach into my jacket. He grabs hold of the scruff of my neck. Using both hands, he forces my head toward his erect dick. I'm afraid he's going to poke me in the eye with it.

I jam my elbow into Moby's ribs. He cries out and loosens his grip. I yank free and thrust my elbow at Moby's chin, knocking him back against the headrest. I pull the knife from my jacket and spin out the blade.

"Don't! Don't!" Moby's beady eyes bulge. Fear sweat dampens his forehead. "What do you want?"

What a stupid question. "Your wallet."

Moby reaches into his pants and I poise the knife under his ear. A moment later, the wallet is in my hand. Without looking back, I fumble for the door handle. It won't open. It's got one of those childproof locks. This Moby guy really is a dick. I look at him. He looks at me. I touch the point of the knife to his neck. He does something with his left hand and the door unlocks.

I jump out of the car and inhale the fresh cold night air. The crew is standing on the sidewalk, laughing and flipping off

Moby. The headlights go on. He turns them too bright, blinding us. The engine revs, roars and jerks, like he punched the gas pedal, but forgot to take off the emergency brake. I have no doubt he's about to mow us down.

We dart into the park. A door slams and his shouted curses follow us as we scramble through the dense foliage. Night training in the forest surrounding the Two Dragon Clan compound prepared me for worse than this. I duck around the branches that catch and snag the other guys, and soon run past them to lead the way. When we reach a clearing on the other side of the park, we stop. I bend over, grasp my knees and pant like the other guys, even though I'm not winded. After some high fives, I toss the wallet to JJ.

He holds it up to the light from the nearby tennis courts and hoots gleefully over the contents of the billfold. "This'll last us a few days." He pockets the cash and rifles through the credit cards.

"What about the cops?" I peer through the trees. "Isn't he gonna call the cops?"

The other guys laugh. Sway makes a hand phone and presses it to his face while speaking in a deep, pompous tone. "Hello, 911? Yeah, I'd like to report that while engaging in, uh, sexual intercourse with a, uh, child prostitute, I got robbed."

I've got to admit, that's pretty damn funny.

JJ plucks out Moby's driver's license. "I know a guy who'll give us good money for this shit."

"What about the credit cards?" I ask. "Can we use them?"

"Nah, too risky. Store clerks can finger us to the cops." He tosses the wallet into a clump of bushes and we make our way out to a path.

After buying pizza and beer, we return to the hotel, where Amethyst and Nix greet us like heroes. Nix finds a hip-hop station on the clock radio she'd rescued from the trash. Everyone digs in, dancing to the beat as they chow down. I eat little, my stomach tied in knots. So, now I'm a thief. But that Moby guy got what he deserved, right? I can rob guys like him and still be a righteous *Xia*. Maybe not as Paul, the Dragon Son's heir, but as Lennon, I can walk whatever path I choose. I close my eyes, leaning my head against the wall, and reach out, though there's no one left to hear me.

Mom, Dad, I'm walking the Wayward Way now. Forgive me if this disappoints you, but this must be my path until I can avenge you.

Something touches my mind... fuzzy... distant... familiar...

Paul?

Tony.

I bolt upright as I clamp my mind shut.

"Damn, you're jumpy, bro," JJ says as he hands me a beer.

I take a long swig, grimacing as the bitter liquid fills my mouth and burns my chest. The after buzz slows the pounding of my heart. Tony must be using another person's *chi* to boost his power, seeking the opening I had just given him. Now Tony knows I'm still in the city. Shit.

After paying the rent, JJ divided the loot among the four guys. It'll take a few more robberies before I can make enough to head for Portland. Until then, I'll lay low and keep my thoughts to myself.

Penny

The bell rings as I'm about to head out the door for school. It's a postman, who hands me a priority mail envelope addressed to Bridie. It's from the United States Citizenship and Immigration Services. This could be it. Once she gets her green card, it's official. We're here to stay. I get a weird feeling in my stomach. I'm so tempted to hide it or throw it in the trash.

Bill comes up behind me. "What's that?"

"Something for Mum from the government." I show him the envelope.

"I'll take it." He avoids eye contact with me as he snatches it away and heads upstairs.

Looks like someone else wants to hide it, too. Of course, he doesn't want her to have a green card, not when it means she can get a job, earn her own money and have some independence from him. I'm not about to play his game. I go to the kitchen where Bridie is packing Kai's lunch.

"Shouldn't you be on your way?" she asks. "You're going to be late."

I tell her about the envelope. Her face goes blank. Then she shrugs. "Well, whatever it is, I'm sure Bill will take care of it."

"What if it's your green card?"

"If it is, he'll give it to me. If it isn't, well, it isn't. Bill's letting his lawyer take care of all the paperwork. I don't want to bung things up by sticking my nose in. Now, run along. I don't want to have to drive you both to school."

Willful ignorance. What a fine way to start the day. I'm sure it will only get better.

And it does.

I find *witch* stuck to my locker before second period. It's not in Dani's handwriting. I rip it off and crumple it in my fist before glancing around. No one in the locker bank is paying any attention, but then again, me getting a note is hardly news.

"Hi Penny," Kayla sings out as she spins her combination lock. Her smile makes her look like the cat that swallowed the canary. "Hey, a bunch of us are playing *Cards Against Humanity* at lunch if you want to join."

I do her dirty work and she invites me to the Goth table. Isn't that grand? I want to tell her to sod off, but it's not worth the effort. "Can't. Have to study."

"Okay. Maybe tomorrow."

I shrug and sort through my books. She sticks to my side all the way to class, prattling about her silly game. I tune her out and eye the people we pass. A guy gives me a thumbs-up. A couple of people swerve to avoid me. A girl crosses herself.

My stomach twists. Oh bugger. Really? "People think I'm a witch?"

Kayla's cheery façade becomes cautious. "Are you?"

"No."

"I heard you cast a spell on Dani and her friends."

"What?" Bloody stupid Bleaters can't tell the difference between spells and curses. "I didn't cast a spell."

"Okay." She doesn't look convinced.

I want to think it's funny, but I can't. Back in the day, Strowler women were burned at the stake as witches for telling fortunes, and selling curses and charms. People like to think things have changed, but those people have never been called pikeys and gyppos, or been chased out of town and off public land. Traveling people are still plenty persecuted. It's easier to call us witches and thieves than to accept us for being different.

After class, I dash out so Kayla can't glom onto me. When I get to sewing, Ms. G. greets me warmly. My classmates busy themselves with fabric and yarn. Some even talk to me. It's been a much better place since Dani and Sarah dropped out. Nobody makes the sign of the cross or the evil eye in my direction. Maybe only Kayla and a few hobs listened to whatever rumors Dani and her friends are trying to spread. Still, I'm cautious as I approach the cafeteria. Parkside Academy has a closed campus, so we're all stuck in the same room, from the popular jocks to lowly outcasts.

I hesitate at the entrance, clutching my lunch bag. No one pays me any mind, not when there's a show to watch.

The Daisy Chain has become a prayer circle. Dani, Emma and Avery are standing in the center while the other girls lay hands on them with their eyes closed. One girl speaks aloud of "binding Satan" away from them.

What a joke. How can they bind Satan when they're the ones doing the devil's work?

Kevin and his crew are lounging at the next table, staring at one guy's phone while passing around the tiny bottles. It's as if their girlfriends don't exist.

The black-clad kids at the Goth table are also holding hands and moaning prayers between giggles. Then one guy stands, raises his hands, and hollers, "Praise Jeebus!"

Laughter bursts out all over the cafeteria. Even Kevin joins in.

Much as I enjoy watching the Daisy Chain fail, I know it can't bode well for me. Lunch in the library sounds like a really good plan. I start backing out. Dani's eyes pop open. She stares at me across the room. I stare back, into a well of darkness so deep. I can taste her hatred in the back of my throat. It burns like hot coal.

Before, I was her victim. Now, I'm her enemy.

Lennon

A sharp whistle pierces the air, followed by a hollered, "Lennon!"

JJ can be a real pain in the ass. If I weren't trying to make a good impression, I'd turn around and flip him off. Instead, I stay squatted in front of the Café Gran Via chalkboard, putting the finishing touches on the bunch of grapes I'd drawn next to the wine of the day. When I finish, I take a step back, examining my work with a critical eye. The lettering looks good, all the small plate specials spelled right, including *'Gambas a la Plancha'*, whatever that is.

"Very nice," comments Edgar, the café owner, a middle-aged guy with a shaved head and small, gold hoops in his ears. His suit has a shiny texture that sparkles in the sunlight. "Tomorrow afternoon, same time. If you can keep up the good work for the week, you've got the job. I can even recommend you to the other restaurants in the area." He hands me ten bucks.

"Thanks." Money earned instead of spanged or stolen. It makes me feel good about myself for a moment.

"Lennon!"

Edgar looks across Haight Street at JJ and the crew. He grimaces. "You should stay away from troublemakers."

I push my glasses up the bridge of my nose. Easy to say if you have a roof over your head. "I'll be back tomorrow." I shove the cash in my pocket and run across the street. I glare at JJ. "Don't bug me while I'm working."

JJ grins. "What'd ol' Edgar give you? Chump change? Screw that. We're gonna make bank."

We head for the Panhandle, a long, narrow strip of parkland that runs parallel to Haight Street.

"Wait. Where we going?" I ask.

JJ answers, "Creepster Alley."

"Again? We were there yesterday."

He gives an impatient sigh. "Bro, we gotta go where the tricks can find us. There are only a few places we can pimp ourselves."

"What if that guy comes back?"

"What guy?"

"That guy we jumped yesterday. The one that said he's gonna get us."

He snorts. "Yeah, what's he gonna do?"

And I thought I was the newbie. "I don't know, like, get a gun."

"A gun?" Carl's eyes go wide and shiny.

"Pussies," Sway sneers, but his pace slows.

JJ rubs his chin. "Okay, look. We'll go check out the scene. If that guy shows, we'll bounce back to the crib and wait a few days before we hustle again."

That sounds reasonable. The money is too good to walk away from. A couple more robberies and I'll have enough for a fake ID and a bus ticket to Portland. Once up there, I want to go straight. Earn money drawing chalk signs and whatever else. Being a fake hooker for much longer is too risky. If I'm picked up by the cops, they'll turn me over to my family.

We cross over the Panhandle and down another couple of blocks until we get to an elementary school. Creepster Alley runs between the school and an apartment complex. It's narrow and dark, even at noon, and deserted nights and weekends. That's when the creepsters roll in, looking for homeless kids turning tricks.

When we reach the middle of the alley, Carl and I lean against the apartment wall. There aren't any windows on this side of the building, which is probably why no one complains. JJ lights a cigarette. Sway uses a red Sharpie to add to the graffiti to the wall. I can't tell if he's drawing a devil, a goat, or a devil-goat.

About ten minutes pass and still no action. A bird chirps in the bushes on the other side of the tall chain link fence separating the alley from the school parking lot. It sounds like a slow alarm. I start shifting from shoulder to shoulder. Carl paces. JJ lights another cigarette. Sway finishes his devil-goat and writes beneath it: "See me bleed".

JJ takes a last drag and flicks away the butt. "This is weird. Let's split…"

Men come barreling at us from both ends of the alley. I freeze, just like the others. Then JJ calls out, "Shit, it's Payroll. Run."

Payroll. I'd heard other kids whisper about him, a pimp who doesn't mind damaging the goods.

The four of us sprint to the chain link fence. I can easily leap over it, but that would mean leaving the others behind, like a coward, someone unworthy to be called a *Xia*. As soon as we jump onto the links, the men are upon us. They yank my friends down. The one who tries grabbing hold of me gets a kick in the face. Another gets a boot to the chest that sends him sprawling.

"Cut that shit out," orders a voice with a twangy accent. It belongs to the shortest guy in the alley. Unlike the other gangsters, who are all wearing hoodies and jeans, he's dressed in trousers with suspenders over a white wife beater. His brown hair is greased back in a slick mullet and he has one of those weird beards that only covers part of his chin. His eyes are stone cold as he presses the business end of a revolver to Carl's forehead.

"Get down, bitch, or he dies."

Carl turns sheet white. His blue eyes plead with me for his life. The rest of the crew are being held lock-armed.

My heart pounds wildly. One wrong move and he could kill all of us.

JJ's voice trembles through an attempt to sound persuasive. "Hey, Payroll, it's cool. We'll do what you want."

Payroll gives a rasping laugh. "Hell, yeah, you'll do what I want, bitch. You're all my bitches now."

Only one thing can save us: the Dragon Shout. It's hard, channeling my *chi* while clinging to the fence. I try taking a deep breath through the panic clutching my chest. Power roils through my abdomen before surging up like vomit. It sticks in my throat. My limbs trembles and I would have fallen off the fence if two of the goons hadn't hauled me down.

A gray haze covers my vision. I blink hard and shake my head. Payroll now stands before me. He presses the gun to my forehead, hard, indenting the skin into the bone. My breath starts coming fast. If he kills me, it's over. Head Elder wins. I'll never get my revenge.

"Heard some chink punk was rolling the tricks, scaring off the paying customers." Payroll steps back.

His men pat me down. My heart sinks further as one pulls the balisong from my jacket. They shove me to the ground so hard my glasses fly off my face. Pavement scrapes my chin and the septum ring yanks from my nose. Two more men catch hold of my legs and the others my arms, so they hold me spread-eagle.

A pair of biker boots appears beside my head. I flinch and twist, certain Payroll is about to kick me in the face. Instead, he grabs hold of my hair and yanks so hard my eyes water.

"Oh, no. We're not going to mess up that pretty face, even though you messed up my boys with the kung fu karate shit of yours." The handgun waves in my face. "That shit ain't shit against bullets, bitch." Payroll strokes the barrel down my cheek. "We're done fucking around with you."

The barrel traces down my neck and spine, making me tremble. The business end is shoved up my butt. I scream into some guy's grimy hand.

"My boys are gonna do you prison style until you beg me to let some trick come in your mouth."

Rough hands seize the waistband of my jeans and try yanking them down without undoing the buttons. I squirm and kick, but my legs feel like rubber. They're going to rape me in the ass and I can't stop them. No. I have to stop them. I reach out with my mind, groping desperately for Jade Dragon.

Ancestor, help me. I need your power. Now.

Nothing. My eyes squeeze shut and I take a shuddering breath, trying to re-channel my *chi*.

The click of weapons echoes through the alley. Scuffling noises sound, but no one speaks, not until a voice booms out, "Let them go and we'll let you live."

The gangsters release me and back away. A pair of laced-up leather boots and the tip of a staff appear beside my head. I roll over. A patchwork coat covers the man's ragged clothes. The wind whips through his wild hair and beard as he stares down at me with inquisitive gray eyes. My heart starts pounding again. Oh shit. I grope for my glasses and shove them on. My septum ring has disappeared.

The Beggar Chief holds out his hand. "It's all right, son. You're safe."

I wobble as I stand and quickly let go of the calloused hand. Then I tip over and stumble to regain my footing. A group of the raggedy men and women hold Payroll and his crew at gunpoint. I try sounding clueless as I ask, "Are you the police?"

JJ gives a nervous laugh. "You kidding, bro? It's the Beggar Clan. He's the Beggar Chief."

"The what?" I tug my beanie farther down my forehead.

"John Walks Long, at your service." The Beggar Chief bows.

JJ, Carl and Sway all bow back. JJ says, "Walk in peace, Beggar Chief."

"Walk in peace, children." He shakes his shaggy mane. "Though peace is far from this place." He turns to Payroll. "I know I promised you your lives, but I wish you'd fought back. I only need a single excuse to kill predators like you."

"Kill us, you're a dead man." The pimp's shaky voice doesn't match his words.

The Beggar Chief turns to a tall woman with a grim face. "Make sure they can't easily walk away when you're done with them."

The gangsters look alarmed as the Beggars herd them toward the wall while forming a semi-circle.

John Walks Long makes a sweeping gesture with his staff and start walking toward the end of the alley. I exchange wary glances with the crew before following the Beggar Chief as if he were the Pied Piper. My legs are still trembling, but I can walk without swaying.

When was the last time I'd seen John Walks Long? Maybe six months ago. That time my parents and I had gone out for pizza on the Italian side of Grant Avenue. We were leaving the restaurant when the Beggar Chief walked by. He and Dad had greeted each other politely. The Two Dragon Clan and the Beggar Clan aren't allies or enemies, though Dad had allowed the Beggars to look after their interests in Chinatown, as long as it didn't affect the community.

John Walks Long had greeted Mom with a polite bow before remarking how much I had grown. Shit. Still, he won't be expecting the son of the Dragon Son to be turning tricks in a dark alley.

A cry of pain echoes off the walls. I look over my shoulder, but can't see beyond the broad backs of the encircled Beggars.

"What are you gonna do to them?" asks JJ.

"Broken arm, broken leg, nothing to concern you." The Beggar Chief raises his bushy eyebrows. "The question is what to do with you?"

"What do you mean?"

"We didn't just happen to be here, my son. I've been getting reports about a gang of boys who attack and steal from the men who solicit them. Today, I was told Payroll and his thugs were planning retaliation against those boys. It seems we got here just in time."

"How can we repay you?"

"You can't." The Beggar Chief's voice goes cold. "I don't want payment from criminals. You robbed those men. Your motives don't matter. Now those gangsters know who you are. You can't return to Haight Street. Payroll will come after you when we're gone."

We get to the end of the alley and two Beggars step out of the shadows to stand on either side of their chief.

"You want us to clear out?" asks Sway.

"I want you to go home. Your real homes. My people will escort you to the Youth Crisis Center. You will stay and let them help you. If possible, reunite with your families. I don't want to see any of you on the streets again."

Sway clears his throat. "Um, there's a couple of girls. They're with us."

"They can go with you to the shelter. You can collect them

on the way." John Walks Long examines our reluctant faces. "I'm not asking, boys, I'm telling you. Leave now."

I shove my hands in my pockets and scowl with the rest of the crew at the thought of being forced into a youth shelter. I shuffle with them out of the alley toward the Beggars waiting to escort us.

The Beggar Chief holds out his staff, stopping me in my tracks. He speaks gently. "No, son, you're not going with them."

I go all "huh?" with open mouth and wide eyes. Look at how clueless I am, man.

I know he isn't buying it.

The crew surrounds me. "Why can't Lennon come with us?" asks Carl.

"Lennon?" John Walks Long turns to me with a grin that reveals uneven, yellow teeth. "Because he's coming with me."

JJ leans over and whispers to me. "Bro, he must have heard about your kung fu stuff. Maybe he wants you to join the Beggar Clan." Envy glints in his eyes.

"Can't my friends come with me?" I ask.

The Beggar Chief shakes his head. "Only you."

JJ and Sway give me farewell head nods. Carl and I hug.

"Thank you." His voice is hoarse in my ear.

"Bye." I step away without looking at him. Will I ever see any of them again? Probably not. I wish I could have said goodbye to Amethyst and Nix.

While they walk away, I try taking deep breaths without being obvious. The sluggish flow of my *chi* makes me dizzy. I need a little more time, just a few more minutes, so I can recover enough to attempt the Swift Step or some other means of escape.

A hand clamps down on my shoulder. The grip feels like an iron band. "Come along, Michael Lau's son."

My stomach drops. The Beggar Clan didn't arrive in the

nick of time to rescue some crappy homeless kids from Payroll. They came to get me.

I yank free and step back. "I'm not going with you. I don't know you."

The Beggar Chief's massive chest expands in a disappointed sigh. "What would your parents say if they knew how you'd fallen among thieves?" Though his voice is stern, his eyes are full of pity.

I don't want or trust his sympathy. "I don't know what you're talking about."

The slate gray gaze becomes unwavering. "After the Dragon Son and his wife died, the Two Dragon Clan let it be known that the heir, Paul, was now residing in the clan compound on Chisel Knife Mountain, and being raised by his grandfather."

I can't keep my hands from clenching into fists.

"However, I heard a different tale," John Walks Long's bushy eyebrows raise with his words, "of the Two Dragon Clan frantically searching for a fifteen-year-old boy. About a week ago, a remarkable young man came to see me. His name was Tony Lau."

I force myself not to blink.

"I'd met him before, always in the company of his uncle. A stern, cold boy, though he became agitated as he spoke of his missing cousin, Paul. He swore me to secrecy before giving me this photo." He reaches into his massive coat, pulls out a piece of paper and unfolds it.

It's a photo of my grinning face, taken when my family had spent the day at Clearwater Bay beach in July. Had I once been so happy? I can't remember what that feels like anymore.

"I can see why your family has had trouble finding you. You look almost nothing like the boy in this picture."

"I'm not the boy in that picture." I try giving a casual shrug. "So, were you offered some kind of reward for this kid?"

"Ten thousand dollars for his safe return."

I take another step back.

"However, this kid's father was a friend of mine, a real hero, one of the finest men to walk the Glory Road. I find it hard to believe his son would choose the Wayward Way without reason."

I bite my lip. For a moment, I want to blurt out everything that had happened and ask the Beggar Chief for help, but I can't betray my clan to another, not for any reason. "What would you do if you found this kid?"

"I would offer him refuge, a place to hide." John Walks Long grasps his staff with both hands and lifts it with outstretched arms. "This, I do swear on my honor as the Beggar Chief of San Francisco. I will not return Paul Lau to those who seek him, even if they are his family."

John Walks Long won't – can't betray that oath. Now that the crew has disbanded and Payroll is out for my blood, I need a safe place to stay. "On one condition."

The Beggar Chief cocks his head.

"Call me Lennon."

Penny

I feel Dani's oily glare as I enter fifth period maths. It spreads across the room and pools at my feet. I mutter the blessing, "May kings respect you, the devil neglect you, the angels protect you, and heaven accept you."

It's not for her. It's for me. The notes have stopped, but I'm not thick enough to believe she and Jesus are BFFs. Beneath that dark gaze I sense a bitter brew coming to a boil. When it hits the surface, she'll strike.

Avery and another girl – Madison, I think – sit beside her with huge Bibles on top of their textbooks. They chatter loud enough so everyone can hear about some church youth group they went to last night. I roll my eyes. Great. It's my fault the Daisy Chain got religion.

Avery gives me shady side-eye before declaring, "I asked Pastor Steve and he says witches definitely go to hell."

"Christ on the cross, you're so full of shite," bursts out of me. Bollocks. I want to hit myself. I let them get to me and I can't, especially not today. One complaint from the school is all the excuse Bill needs to cancel our plans for tonight.

The class goes silent. A few titters circle the room. Avery

and Madison's faces are filled with anything but Christian love. The Goths smirk, waiting for them to open their mean mouths and prove themselves hypocrites. Ms. Alvarez raps her knuckles on the desk, signaling the beginning of class. Luckily, she's the no-nonsense type. She doesn't care who started it, but if you try getting the last word, she'll hit your ass with detention. I keep my head down and nose in my books for the rest of the day. I don't breathe easy until I'm on the bus heading home.

Bridie is preparing a king's feast for Bill, consisting of roast beef, mashed potatoes and gravy, a crisp green salad with buttermilk dressing, and apple pie, all his favorites. I chop vegetables, peel potatoes and roll the dough. The savory smells make my mouth water and I'm sorely tempted to dig in. Kai whimpers like a puppy until Mum gives him a bowl of potatoes and gravy.

Bill comes home, goes to his office, shuts the door and doesn't come out.

"He's being a grump," Bridie whispers. "He'll get over it after he eats. Carry on getting ready."

I have to admit she knows him pretty well. By the time we're heading out the door, he's seated in front of the Giants' game on telly, his plate overloaded with food. He doesn't even grunt in response to our farewells. For a moment, I wonder if he's feeling jealous or suspicious because Bridie looks so young and gorgeous in the miniskirt I made to match my costume. Then potatoes spew from his mouth as he protests an umpire's call. Bridie gives a pained smile. I shudder. We both know she'll have to have sex with him when we get home. Right now, though, we're free and we flee before he has a chance to stop us.

I have a hard time sitting still during the drive. I practice dance moves with my feet. Bridie and Kai go over the set list even though it was decided weeks ago and we all know it by heart. The ride becomes bumpy after we get off the freeway. We haven't been to this part of the city before, the part along the southern shore of the bay. We pass weedy vacant lots, container yards, and rows and rows of warehouses. It's getting dark and the streetlights are sparse, making it hard to read the few street signs we pass.

I turn on my phone and use the light to read the directions that came with the invitation. "I'm pretty sure we're going the right way. It says to keep going, to the end of this street and then turn left at the cement factory."

After bouncing along another couple of blocks, we get to a structure with huge, concrete towers surrounded by a tall chain link fence wound with barbed wire. We can't see any signs, but guess it's the factory and make the turn. This leads to another street lined with warehouses. We keep going until it dead-ends. To the right, there's a gravel road with an open gate. Leaning against the gate is a weatherworn plywood board spray-painted with the road marker of a Beggars' Abode: an open-bottom rectangle covering three parallel circles, and the symbol of the Glory Road, a straight, vertical line topped with a crown.

This means the Beggars within walk the Glory Road, however, all Beggars are welcome. If there was a diagonal slash through the symbol, it would mean those on the Wayward Way are forbidden to enter.

This makes me wonder how much John Walks Long knows about us. Does he know we walk the Wayward Way or even care, since we're not Beggars? I hope he didn't ask Kingfisher to vouch for us. If he did, the Upright Man will definitely hold that over us the next time we see him.

The gravel road ends at a gate guarded by two women in ragged military fatigues. Beyond them is a huge metal warehouse, at least two stories high, its front entrance lit up with bright lights. The guards use high-powered flashlights to wave us forward.

Mum unrolls the window. "Hello. Bridie Sparrow and children."

The guard speaks into a shoulder-mounted walkie-talkie, listens, and leans down. "Go around to the back entrance and park next to the caterers. Jeremiah will escort you in."

Bridie's eyebrows lift. "Caterers. This is posh."

After unloading our instruments, we walk around a large truck set up as a mobile kitchen. Chefs are preparing and plating skewers of shrimp that look super yummy. Kai smacks his lips. "Mum…"

"Later," she replies firmly to his pout.

Two more Beggars in military fatigues guard the back entrance. Between them stands a tall man wearing camouflage trousers, combat boots, and a black tank top. From the neck down, his left side is covered with the mottled, puckered flesh of old burn scars while swirling, dagger-like tribal tattoos decorate the intact skin of his right side. He's talking into one of those shoulder walkie-talkies, but looks up as we approach.

"Bridie Sparrow? I'm Jeremiah Walks Long."

"The Beggar Chief's son?" Bridie asks. He nods. "Walk in peace, Jeremiah." She sets down her guitar to shake his hand. "These are my children. Penny."

"Walk in peace." As we shake, I feel his callouses press into my palm. He's kind of sexy with those gray eyes and that square jaw, and he looks as fit as if he were still in the military, despite the scars.

"And Kai."

Kai stares with big eyes. "Were you in the war?"

Jeremiah nods. "Two tours of duty in Afghanistan."

"Is that where that happened?"

Bridie's face reddens as she tugs Kai's arm. "Shush."

"It's all right, ma'am. I prefer people notice than pretend

they don't." He turns so more of his scarred flesh is visible. "It happened in Kabul. A car bomb took out a whole building and burned half my body."

Kai chews his lip like he wants more details the way he wanted a skewer of shrimp. I step on his foot. "Ow!" He glares at me before glancing more meekly at Jeremiah. "Um, walk in peace."

"Walk in peace. You are most welcome to our Abode." Jeremiah picks up Bridie's guitar. "Follow me."

As we enter, we pass two storage areas on either side of the door. The area to the left contains shopping carts piled with threadbare blankets and dirty plastic bags filled with crushed aluminum cans and plastic bottles. Ripped and torn overcoats hang on pegs, along with equally worn scarves and hats. Cardboard signs are stacked against the wall, the top one scrawled in blocky words:

Homeless

Anything helps

God bless

The other area holds sparring equipment like boxing gloves, helmets, padded mats, punching bags and a table of hand-held weapons, including broken bottles and knives. Beggars might appear helpless, but believe me; you don't want to mess with them.

The warehouse is huge with two levels of corridors and rooms. Bright, fluorescent lights flood the interior, giving everything an artificial glow, until I blink a few times to adjust my vision. Jeremiah leads us past an octagonal fight cage and a workout area with exercise equipment, toward a boxing ring in the center of the building. The ring is surrounded on all sides by long tables, several rows deep, each covered with gold tablecloths and set with silverware, cloth napkins, wine glasses, and gold-rimmed plates. Square metal lanterns with lit candles adorn the center of each table. Men, women and children are mingling around, chatting with each other, all of them dressed in thrift store finery rather than rags.

"This place used to be a steel shop." Jeremiah raises his voice to be heard above the echoing hubbub. "It was shut down about thirty years ago, after a construction crew ruptured a nearby pipe that caused toxic waste to spill into wetlands out there. It cost too much to clean up, so the city left the area to rot. My father bought this place for a song, and we've been here ever since."

"I'm surprised you're allowing caterers in here," Bridie remarks. "Don't you have a kitchen?"

"We have two kitchens, a laundry, an infirmary, even a school. Father wants as few of our people as possible to work during the banquet. The caterers are cooking, but not serving. The servers are chosen by lottery from among our people. We have a system so no one winds up serving for two years in a row."

I sigh. Why can't the local Strowlers have a bang-up chief like John Walks Long instead of a bounce like Kingfisher?

As if he heard my thoughts, the Beggar Chief steps out from among his people. He's wearing a deep blue velvet blazer with leather-patched elbows, a brocade vest, a white dress shirt and seamed black trousers. Polished black boots have replaced his fringed leather ones. His wild mane has been neatly brushed and even his beard and mustache look trimmed. He looks so majestic, if I was older – a lot older – I might think he was handsome.

"Dear lady." He bows over Bridie's hands. "You and your family honor us with your presence."

Bridie inclines her head. "You honor us with your invitation."

He holds out his arm to her. "I'm afraid we have but a makeshift stage," he says, as he leads us to the boxing ring. "We took down the ropes just for you."

"We're used to performing on the street and in pubs. A boxing ring will make a lovely change." She glances over her shoulder. "Isn't that right, children?"

"I think it's brilliant," says Kai.

I don't answer. Jeremiah has walked ahead and is handing Bridie's guitar to an Asian boy standing beside the ring. He's about the same height as me, and skinny, but with broad shoulders. His full lips and high cheekbones are to die for, and he's got cool, spiky blond hair with black roots. I wish I could see his eyes, but he's wearing round, tinted glasses.

John Walks Long calls out, "Lennon."

Really? Did he get the name because of the glasses or the glasses because of the name?

Lennon hurries over. He's wearing army fatigues, though he looks too young to have been in the military.

"These are the Sparrows. You can take them to the dressing room now." John Walks Long turns again to Bridie. "Would you like to eat before or after your performance?"

"After," Bridie replies, ignoring Kai's groan. "Never perform on a full stomach. It slows you down."

"I understand. You must join me at my table when you're done."

"Thank you."

"If you need anything, ask Lennon." He gives a benevolent nod before strolling away.

Bridie smiles at the boy. "Do you like the Beatles?"

The boy looks surprised, as if he hasn't been asked this a million times before. "They're okay."

"I guess you didn't give yourself the name."

He shakes his head.

"I'm Bridie Sparrow, and these are my children, Penny and Kai."

"Hello." I smile.

The boy gives a quick nod and looks away as he gestures us

to follow him. So, he's not a talker. No big deal. We're not here to talk.

The dressing room is more suitable for boxers than musicians with its gym lockers, massage table and metal folding chairs. The hooks in the wall hold robes and there's a stack of towels and a medical kit on top of a stainless steel table.

Kai swings himself onto the padded table. "Hey, can I get a massage?"

"Only if you're going to fight." A whisper of a smile lifts Lennon's lips for a brief moment.

"Performing is exactly like fighting, only tougher. That's what Gerry used to say."

"Gerry?" Lennon's puzzled expression becomes hesitant as he says the name, like he doesn't want to be nosy. He glances at the metal table. "They forgot your water. I'll be right back."

While Bridie and Kai tune their guitars, I check my new dress in a mirror that's leaned against the wall as if by second thought. I like the emerald green, stretch velvet fabric and the simplicity of the design, with its tight bodice, flared skirt, and spaghetti straps. Long sleeves are attached below the armpit, leaving my shoulders bare and sort of sexy. I perch on a chair and lace up my gillies. My skirt rides up my thighs and I tug it down in case Lennon walks in. Does he like my dress?

Whoa.

Where did that come from? Why should I care if he likes my dress? But I do. I want him to think I look cute.

Cute? Really?

There's a tap on the door and Lennon enters, carrying a pitcher of ice water and three stacked glasses, which he clutches to his chest as he closes the door. I duck my head so he won't see my cheeks burn. What is wrong with me? It's not like I haven't been around dimber lads before. Most were Strowlers and I had avoided them like the plague, not wanting anybody to get ideas about setting me up with anyone. Lennon

– he's different. He's a Beggar kid. No one's going to try marrying me off to him, so I'm free to think he's completely adorable.

Oh god. Seriously, what is wrong with me?

Lennon sets the pitcher and glasses on the metal table. Then he moves to the center of the room and shifts awkwardly before sticking his hands in his pockets. "Um, I'm supposed to stay here in case you need anything."

"We should be fine, but stay if you must." Bridie opens the door a crack and peers out. "Any other Sharpers here besides the Beggar Clan?"

"Sharpers?" The boy looks puzzled.

"Sorry." She turns and smiles. "That's our word for the people of the Crossroads. You see, we're Strowlers and I just wondered if any other Strowlers were invited. Say, a man named Kingfisher?"

Lennon shakes his head. "Not that I heard."

Bridie's smile brightens. "I see. Well, just wondering. Do you know when we go on?"

"The Chief said to send you out after the appetizers are served. I'll let you know." He takes Bridie's place, opening the door slightly more so he can lean against the frame.

While my mother and brother finish tuning their instruments, I do some warm up exercises. After a series of plies, I rest my ankle on the edge of the metal table and bend over, wrapping my hands around the sole of my foot. My skirt rides up my thighs again, revealing my dancing shorts. I glance at Lennon to see if he notices. He remains in the doorway, facing outward with a solemn, vigilant profile. What an odd boy. Why doesn't he take off those silly glasses?

Kai sets down his guitar and peers out the door. "Wow!"

"Yeah, they do it up big," says Lennon.

I join them. Lennon opens the door a little wider so I can see out as well. The warehouse lights have been lowered and candlelight glows off the faces of the seated Beggars. The servers seem cheerful as they greet their comrades while setting down white porcelain platters piled with beef and shrimp skewers.

Kai smacks his lips.

Lennon grins. "Don't worry. The chief is setting aside plenty of food for you."

He looks different when he smiles: warmer, kinder, as if he hasn't always been so quiet and solemn. My heart beats a little faster. I try to think of something to say that isn't stupid. "Um, so is there always live entertainment like us?"

"Someone told me they usually invite street musicians to perform."

"They?" My brow wrinkles. "Aren't you with the Beggar Clan?"

He shakes his head and looks away. More questions compete in my mind, but I bite back on them. He has no reason to confide in me. Jeremiah, who sits beside his father at the main table, stands and turns toward us. As he makes a beckoning gesture, a spotlight shines down on the boxing ring.

"Time for you to go on," says Lennon.

Something mischievous wiggles up in me. I look him in the eye, or as best I can with those glasses. "Are you going to watch our show or stay in here?"

His faced reddens. "I'll watch the show."

"You better. We're pretty good."

He ducks his head. "Okay."

Feeling oddly pleased with myself, I turn to Bridie. "Mum, it's time to go on."

Bridie stares with narrow eyes at her vibrating phone. "Oh, bother, it's Bill. What does he want?" She gnaws her lip. "Just for once, I'd like an evening without him checking up on me." She hesitates a moment longer. Then she powers it off and drops it in her purse. "Whatever he wants can wait until later. I'll say I forgot to turn my phone on."

I knew coming here would do her good. About time she stood up for herself and not come to heel every time he snaps his fingers.

Bridie and Kai pick up their cases, while I gather my penny whistles and the bodhrán. Then we follow Lennon out the door. As we reach the stairs, the Beggars start clapping. Bridie goes up first, followed by Kai.

Lennon speaks above the noise. "Good luck."

I tilt my head. "You're supposed to tell me to break a leg."

Lennon's almost smile returns with a vengeance. Does he have dimples? My heart starts hammering. I turn away and hurry up the stairs.

I'm a moron. The prettiest girl I've ever seen and she's actually talking to me, and I can't think of one intelligent thing to say.

What can I say? I can't even tell her my real name. I've already said too much by admitting I'm not a Beggar. She has to be wondering what I'm doing here. I know I should avoid her for the rest of the banquet, but I don't want to. I like listening to her. That Irish accent is kind of hot and she gets this sparkle in her green eyes when she says something funny. Man, green eyes. How hot is that?

I hurry around the ring to the tables set aside for the Beggar Clan kids. Everyone assumes I'm some runaway the Chief is grooming for membership. I wonder if they're right. Most single people live in dorms, but I've been given my own room on the excuse I'm too young to be with the adults. I've also been assigned daily duties, workout regimens and been attending the three hours of schooling for kids my age. John Walks Long has told me I can stay here as long as I want. He wants me to think he's kind, that he's following the Beggar creed of caring for widows and orphans. I cry bullshit. Gaining my trust is part of his power play. If he can convince me to join the Beggar Clan, it would be a killing blow to the Two Dragon Clan.

To be honest, it's tempting to go that route. I'd have the full muscle of the Beggar Clan backing me up when I accuse Head Elder of murder. Shit would get done and the damage would be permanent. I could never go back to the *kongsi*, or live with Auntie Cat, or call Tony my brother. I'm okay with that. Really. I don't have ice in my veins and I'm not numb to what it means to lose what's left of my family. If I let myself think about it, it feels like I'm being stabbed in the gut, but I'd do it. I'll do almost anything for revenge, except one thing. I'm done being a puppet. Head Elder can't pull my strings and neither can John Walks Long.

There are three empty spaces at the end of a table. I sit next to Tyler and his twin brother, Cody, who are a year older than me. Their parents have been members of the Beggar Clan since before they were born. At the age of eighteen, kids are given the choice to become members of the clan or live in the mundane world. Even John Walks Long had to respect Jeremiah's decision when he decided to leave the clan to join the military. The other two seats must be for the Sparrow kids. Maybe Penny will sit next to me. My heart beats a little faster. I grab a skewer from a serving tray and cram some shrimp in my mouth. I barely taste it because Penny has stepped into the spotlight. Her green dress sparkles and she looks like a shimmering fairy.

Bridie Sparrow adjusts the strap on her guitar as she steps up to the center microphone. I can see where Penny got her green eyes, but that red hair – wow. It's like a flame under the bright light. She seems so young for a mom. She even dresses young, in a miniskirt and fringe leather boots. I can't remember Mom ever wearing a miniskirt. A lump forms in my throat. I grab a glass of water and take a deep gulp to wash away the pain.

As the applause dies down, Bridie speaks. "Thank you for inviting my family to share this special occasion with you. It's a great honor. Strowlers and Beggars aren't so different and we share with you some songs." She strums a few chords on her guitar before leaning into the microphone to sing.

> *"Of all the trades in England, a-beggin' is the best*
> *For when a beggar's tired, you can lay him down to*
>   *rest.*
> *I got patches on me cloak, and black patch on me knee.*
> *When you come to take me home, I'll drink as well as*
>   *thee."*

The Beggars clap their hands to the beat of Kai's drum as they join in with the chorus, "And a-begging I will go, a-begging I will go."

At the feast after the Summoning Ceremony, Brother Ash, red-faced from too much beer, stood and sang a song not so different than this one. Mom and Dad had laughed along with me at the sly lyrics about a beggar wooing and winning a landowner's daughter. The lump returns to my throat. Being Lennon, a homeless street kid, has kept me on edge, but also dulled some of the pain. The more I'm Lennon, the less I'm Paul and the harder it is for the Two Dragon Family to find me. I have to ignore the part of me that's still Paul, grieving for his parents and crying for justice.

The Sparrows sing two more songs before Bridie announces that Penny will dance a slip jig. The servers start setting down the plates for the main course, but I keep my eyes fixed on the girl in the green dress as she steps forward and bows.

Penny dances like a fairy, moving in light-footed, intricate patterns to the music made by the fiddle and drum, kicking up her legs and leaping, light and strong, one leg thrust outward and the other tucked beneath her.

"She's hot," Tyler says in a loud whisper.

"Hell, yeah, she is," replies his brother.

Heat spreads across my neck. I want to tell them to shut the hell up, but why? I barely know Penny and it's not like they were insulting her.

"You can look, but don't touch," says Tyler. "Remember, she's a Strowler."

The music ends and Penny bows to the applause. As she lifts her head, she peers out at the crowd as if searching for someone. Me? Yeah, right.

I turn to Tyler. "What's a Strowler?"

Cody leans forward to stare at me. "You don't know what a Strowler is, dude?"

Tyler nudges him back. He picks at a zit on his chin as he answers. "Strowlers are, like, the Gypsies of the Crossroads. They're all over the place, even here in San Francisco. Thing is, Strowlers stick with their own kind. Don't even think about hitting on their women."

Penny plays her pipe while her mother and brother strum their guitars and sing a lively song about whiskey in a jar. I'm a Hakka, a Gypsy, sort of. For more than a thousand years, the Hakka migrated across China before settling in the southern region. The name, Hakka, means 'guest people.' I was thinking Kai looks kind of Asian, so maybe "their own kind" means other Gypsies, too… I shake my head. What am I doing? I can't be thinking about a girl, any girl, whether she's a Hakka, a Gypsy or whatever.

After about another half hour of song and dance, the Sparrows leave the stage to roaring applause.

I turn to Tyler. "What now?"

He rolls his eyes. "Cloudy."

"Cloudy?"

"Yeah, he's, like, the oldest member of the clan. He'll sing the Beggar's Anthem, and then there'll be a speech by the Chief. Then there'll be the Beggar Oath…"

"And then we can have dessert," Cody finishes cheerfully.

The Beggars start pounding on their tables. An old man stands. I've noticed him around the Abode. His long white hair and beard, along with his potbelly and ragged clothes, makes me think of Santa on the skids. Tonight, Cloudy wears a light blue suit with wide lapels and matching vest that makes him look like a refugee from the seventies. He clears his throat loudly before singing in a surprisingly strong voice.

> *"A Beggar I was, and a Beggar I am,*
> *A Beggar I'll be, from a Beggar I came;*
> *If, as it begins, our trading do fall,*
> *We, in the conclusion, shall Beggars be all."*

The rest of the Beggars join in, including some of the kids at our table, though Tyler and Cody and most of the other teens bend over their phones and start texting or playing games. I continue eating slowly.

"Hello," Penny whispers as she slips into the seat beside me.

I freeze. I even stop chewing. I need to say something, but not with a wad of food in my mouth. As I swallow, Kai sits beside Penny and they turn eagerly to the servers who are bringing their food.

"I thought I was gonna die up there," complains Kai as he digs in. "Next time, we eat before we go on."

"You eat. I can't dance after eating a bunch of heavy food."

"Delicious food." Kai isn't shy about talking with his mouth full.

Cloudy finishes his song and bows to applause that grows louder rather than dying down. Across the room, Jeremiah escorts Bridie through the crowd to the center table. The

Beggar Chief stands and bows as he offers her the seat beside him.

I take a gulp of water and hope there isn't any food in my teeth as I turn to Penny. "Your mom is really being honored."

"I know. It's wonderful." Her head tilts and her green eyes sparkle as she asks, "So, how did you like our show?"

"Wonderful." Wait. She just said that. My cheeks heat and I give a fake cough to buy time. "It was really great. Your mom's voice is amazing. And your dancing was pretty amazing, too."

She shrugs. "Thank you, but really, I'm just okay. I'm an amateur. I've never competed."

There's a competition for that? I'm about to ask, when Jeremiah speaks. "The Beggar Clan offers poor thanks to Bridie Sparrow and her children for the rich entertainment they provided."

Bridie smiles brightly as she acknowledges the applause. Penny ducks her head while Kai keeps eating. Then their mother sits and Jeremiah continues talking. "We're plain people. We don't need fancy introductions. You know who to thank for all that we have. He's my father, but he's the father of us all, our chief, John Walks Long."

Applause thunders through the warehouse, accompanied by stamping feet and roars of approval. Jeremiah sits as his father stands.

John Walks Long waits for the ovation to die down. When he speaks, his majestic tone echoes off the metal walls. "We may be beggars, but poverty is our strength and our shield, and with it we shall always prevail."

He keeps talking like that; using grand phrases that bring on bursts of applause. He sounds like a politician, but maybe he has to. Beggar Chiefs are elected, not born into their position. The Two Dragon Clan can't replace me, no matter how long I'm gone.

After the Chief finishes his speech, Jeremiah stands. "Brethren, all rise and give voice to our oath."

All the adults in the clan stand. Everyone at the kids' table stays seated, though the twins and the rest of the teens put down their phones. The tables thud as huge black books with gold-edged pages are placed on their surfaces. The Beggars scoot around so each can lay their hand on a portion of the book.

"What are they doing?" I ask Tyler.

"Swearing on the Bible, dude, what do you think?"

I think the Beggar Clan in China does something different, but I don't bother saying.

Jeremiah speaks loud and strong, pausing frequently so the Beggars can repeat his words. "I do swear to be a true Beggar and that I will in all things obey the commands of my great tawny prince, John Walks Long, and keep his counsel and not divulge the secrets of my brethren. I will never leave nor forsake our company, but will observe and keep all the times of appointment, either by day or by night, in every place whatever. I will take my prince's part against all that shall oppose him or any of us, according to the utmost of my ability. Nor will I suffer him or anyone belonging to us to be abused by our enemies, but will defend him, or them, as much as I can, against all other outliers. A bloody end to me should I break this oath, God strike me blind."

May Heaven, the all-ruling, and Earth, the all-producing, read our hearts. If we turn aside from righteousness or forget kindliness, may Heaven and Earth destroy us.

My shoulders stiffen. I didn't break my oath to Tony. I would have turned aside from righteousness if I had played along with Head Elder and pretended my parents hadn't been murdered.

"Dessert," Cody announces. He and Tyler join the growing line at a buffet table set up during the feast.

A couple of middle school kids come up to Kai. One asks, "Can we see your guitar and your drum?"

"I guess." Kai stares longingly at the buffet. "Can I get dessert first?"

Penny waits until her brother and the kids take off, then says, "That was pretty cool, us being allowed to witness the Beggar Oath."

"Um, yeah." I stare at my plate, trying to think of something to say. "Um, do Strowlers have an oath?"

"No. You're born a Strowler. You can't become one, so there's no reason for an oath of allegiance, especially one you repeat every year, you know what I mean?"

I know exactly what she means. It'd be nice to talk to someone who understands, but that isn't an option, so I shrug.

"We do have other kinds of oaths, though: brotherhood, sisterhood, repayment of debts, vengeance, that sort of thing."

We will rescue each other in difficulty; we will aid each other in danger.

My fingers dig into my knees.

Penny leans closer to me. "Are you all right? You don't look so good."

I have to be Lennon, not Paul. Lennon doesn't care about some stupid, bullshit oath. "I'm good. I think I ate too much."

"Oh. I was going to ask if you wanted to get dessert, but…"

"No - I mean, yeah. Always room for dessert. Let's go." Yeesh. Even Lennon isn't good with girls.

While we wait in the buffet line, four Beggars carrying violins and a cello climb into the ring. Tables are hauled aside to form an open space. As the musicians begin playing a waltz, John Walks Long leads Bridie onto the makeshift dance floor. I expect the Beggar Chief to lumber like a trained bear, but he dances almost as gracefully as his partner. More couples join them, until the space is almost full.

"Can you waltz?" asks Penny.

"What?"

Her eyes roll. "I'm not asking if you want to. I'm asking if you can, if you know how."

"Oh." Heat spreads across my neck again. I have to stop acting like such a moron. "Um, not really. I guess you can, though, huh?"

"Uh-huh." She sounds bored.

We reach the front of the line. Penny's small white hand plucks a chocolate cupcake off a tower of silver platters. Her pink tongue darts out to lick the frosting before she sets it on her plate.

I don't how to describe what's going through me. I mean, I've been turned on before, but damn. I feel like I'd been hit by lightning, but it's not just lust, it's something else that makes me feel… damn. I barely notice what I grab as we move along the buffet line. Penny will probably ditch me and go find someone who can talk. And dance. Maybe Tyler or Cody.

At the end of the buffet, she balances her plate in one hand as she pours herself a cup of tea with the other. "Would you like some?"

My heartbeat quickens. "Yeah, thanks."

"Milk and sugar?"

"I like it plain."

"Plain?" Her nose wrinkles. Then she shakes her head. "Americans."

"Chinese American."

Her whole face crinkles in the cutest grin ever. I try thinking of something else clever to say, but my tongue ties into a tight knot. All I can do is nod as she hands me a cup of plain tea.

She glances around. "It's so noisy here. Is there someplace more quiet?"

Would it be weird if I asked her to my room so I can draw

her? Yeah, really weird. She'll probably think I want something else. I turn away so she won't see me blush. "Yeah, over here."

I lead her to a set of stairs behind the boxing ring. We sit halfway up, still in the light, but out of view of the party.

Penny picks off the cupcake wrapper. "Can I ask you a question?

I stick a forkful of chocolate cake in my mouth before nodding.

"Are you called Lennon because of those glasses?"

I nod, barely tasting the cake.

"Can you tell me your real name?"

I shake my head.

Penny takes a bite of the cupcake. I shovel in another forkful. We chew in silence. Then she licks a dab of frosting off her thumb and another tremor powers through me. She is so... hot, cool, pretty, sweet, smart – none of the words seem right. Maybe all of them are right. I've never met a girl like her before. I could sit here and listen to her talk all night. If only I didn't have to talk back.

Penny sighs. "I guess I'm being nosy. I know how it is on the Crossroads." Her frown becomes pensive. "You don't have a problem with me being a Strowler, do you?"

"What? No." I hesitate. It can't hurt to tell her and might earn me some points. "I'm kind of a Gypsy, too."

"What do you mean?"

"I'm Hakka. That's Chinese for..."

Her mouth gapes open before she interrupts. "You're Hakka?"

"You know what that is?"

"Of course. Kai's father was Hakka." She squints. "You're not a member of the Two Dragon Clan, are you?"

How did she guess that? Because you have to be Hakka to be a member of the Two Dragon Clan, dumb ass. I want to smack myself. I take a shallow breath and try sounding cocky. "Hell, no. I got nothing to do with those losers. Why?"

She stares at me for a moment, as if trying to figure out my reaction. Then she shrugs. "Kai's father was, until he decided to walk the Wayward Way."

Talk about a loaded sentence. I take a sip of tea to cover my surprise. She gnaws her lip as if wondering if she'd said too much. I rest my head against the rail attached to the banister and try looking casual. "Why did he do that?"

Penny leans against the wall, shifting so her skirt covers her thighs. "He was a musician. I guess that's not acceptable to the Two Dragon Clan. I mean, not as a profession. They're not real supporters of the arts, so to speak."

Tell me about it.

"Anyway, he dropped out and busked around London until he met my parents."

"Busked?

"Played music on the street."

"Um, what about your dad? I mean, um... I guess I shouldn't ask that."

Penny cocks her head. "You mean since you won't tell me anything?"

I shrug.

So does she. After a sip of tea, she sets down her cup and looks me in the eye. "My father was gay. Does that bother you?"

"Why should it? I don't care if someone's gay or not."

The hunch slips off her shoulders. "I knew I liked you for a reason." She pops the last bit of cupcake into her mouth.

She likes me. My head spins. How can she like me when I'm so gloomy and silent? But she does. She just said so. I want to say I like her, too, but my tongue is stuck to the roof of my mouth. I slurp up some tea and a drop dribbles down my chin. Smooth move.

Penny doesn't seem to notice. She keeps on talking in that brilliant accent. "I wish more people on the Crossroads felt the same way. Bloody macho culture. It's probably more acceptable here in San Francisco. As for London, well, nobody really cared. It was a great place to walk the Wayward Way."

Can she be more perfect? "So, you're on the Wayward Way, too?"

She spears her fork into the lemon bar on her plate. "I was born on it."

"I'm supposed to be on the Glory Road, but it's bullshit. I'm on the Wayward Way now."

"Did you run away?"

I give the slightest of nods.

"From far away?"

I rest my chin on my knee. I want so much to tell someone, to trust someone. "I'm from here."

"San Francisco?"

I nod.

"You can't go home?"

I shake my head.

She sighs. "I know how that feels. I want to go home, but I can't."

"Home? You mean back to Ireland?"

"Not really. I'm Irish, but Strowlers don't really have nationalities. We move around a lot. But if there was a place I'd call home, it would be London."

"How come your dad – dads? – aren't with you tonight?"

I said the wrong thing. The sparkle in her eyes fades and she stares at the plate resting on her knee. I'm about to say never mind when she speaks in a soft voice. "They're gone. My mother married a Bleater. That's why we're here instead of London."

Gone as in dead? I don't want to ask because I don't want

to talk about it, because if I do, I might spill my guts. Instead, I ask, "What's a Bleater?"

"It's what we call outsiders, people not on the Crossroads."

"Oh, yeah. The Beggar Clan calls them Mundanes."

"I know."

I wait for her to continue, but she takes a glum bite of lemon bar. Then she sets down her plate and leans her cheek on her knee so we're face to face. "I like talking to you. It's easy."

"I like talking to you, too."

She smiles and my heart dances. "You haven't said much."

"I feel like I have."

"Quiet boy. How old are you?"

"Fifteen."

"Oh. I'm sixteen."

"I'll be sixteen in October."

"Really?" Her smile widens. "That makes us both monkeys."

For a moment, I'm impressed she knows she was born in the Year of the Monkey. Then I remember her Chinese stepfather. "Yeah, it does."

"I like monkeys."

"Me, too."

Her green eyes sparkle before me. Her mouth looks like a rose bud. I want to kiss her. Want it so bad, I can't stop myself. I arch my neck, leaning into her. She looks startled. Then she gives a little gasp and closes her eyes. I close my eyes, too. Somehow, our mouths meet. The soft press of her lips and the faint taste of lemon and chocolate make my mind spin.

She ducks her head. "I've never kissed a boy before."

"Me, neither."

Penny grins. It takes me a moment to realize what I'd said. Oh, man. My cheeks burn.

She gives me a little nudge with her shoulder. "It was nice."

"Yeah," I whisper. "I like you."

"I like you," she whispers back.

We share a smile. I want another kiss, but don't want her to think I'm a pushy creep. Maybe if I wait, she might… I take a breath as she leans a little closer, shy mischief on her face. My eyes close and I hold my breath. Our lips touch and then part. I taste the tip of her tongue and my body sets on fire.

Bridie's voice echoes through the warehouse. "Penny. Penny. Oh, bother, where is the girl?"

Penny draws back and sighs. She peers out between the iron railings. I follow her gaze. Her mother and brother are standing outside the dressing room, instruments in their hands. "Looks like we're leaving."

My head drops. I stare at my knees to hide my disappointment. If only we could have had a few more minutes.

"I'd…" Penny pauses and takes a hesitant breath. "I'd like to see you again. I mean, if you feel like it."

I look up, eyes wide. "Yeah, I do."

She gnaws her lip and casts a guilty glance toward her mother. "Do you know where Parkside Academy is?"

I do, but I shake my head.

"It's in the Sunset, on Fifth Avenue, close to Golden Gate Park."

Close to Auntie Cat's place, in walking distance, but not too close.

She speaks quickly. "When you cross Lincoln, there's this walkway that leads into the park. About halfway down, to the right, there's a dirt path. You want to meet me there? My lunch is at eleven-thirty. I'll cut out and meet you at the top of the hill. Do you think you can find it?"

"Yeah." I know exactly where she means. "I'll be there."

"See you tomorrow." Penny glances over at her mother. Then she plants a quick kiss on my cheek. I barely feel it before she's on her feet and flitting down the stairs. Then she turns, skirt swirling with her movement, and waves.

I wave back. Then I blink and she's gone. Through the railing I see her join her mother and brother. John Walks Long gives a gallant bow over Bridie's hand. Then Jeremiah escorts the Sparrows toward the back of the warehouse.

She kissed me. And she likes me. I run my fingertips over where she'd sat. The cement is still warm. I let out a shaky sigh. Bad timing – the worst. Why did I have to meet her now?

I amble down the stairs, carrying our dishes like I'm helping with clean up. After dumping them onto a cart, I start clearing one of the tables. No one gives me a second look until Jeremiah comes striding over. He gestures me closer and speaks in a low voice. "There's been a breach in our security."

Oh, shit. "What do you mean?"

"One of my men caught a caterer sneaking in to take pictures with his phone. Claims he'd been paid by a reporter who wants a scoop on the Crossroads. Don't worry. We checked. There weren't any photos of you."

I exhale. As long as it isn't about me, it should be okay. As I head upstairs, I stop at the step where I'd sat with Penny. The Beggar Chief won't want me to go meet with her. He'd forbid me if he knew. And if my family finds out…

I give a dry laugh. My family. After all they'd done, their opinion of who I kiss doesn't matter. And neither does John Walks Long's. One way or another, I'm going to make it to the park tomorrow and nothing can stop me.

I stare out the window at the headlights on the freeway. My first kiss. It had made me feel so… I don't know what. Funny? No, not that. Warm? Happy? Both and more. I blow hot breath on the window and draw a pair of round glasses. Maybe next time he kisses me, he'll take them off.

"Penny's got a boyfriend," Kai sings out.

"Shut up." I smear the glasses with my sleeve. He kicks my seat. I turn around and try smacking him, but he ducks away too fast and I only manage to swat his knee.

"Ow. Mum," he whines.

"That's enough you two." Bridie steers onto the off ramp before giving me a quick sideways glance. "A boyfriend?"

"Kai's making fun because I was talking to that boy, Lennon."

"What did you two talk about?"

"Yeah, what?" asks the little pest in the back seat.

Like I'm going to talk about my first kiss with him sitting there. I shrug. "I don't know. Stuff. He liked our show."

"How sweet," Bridie says absently. The mention of a

boyfriend should have her jumping down my throat with questions, but she's barely spoken since we got in the car.

"You have a good time tonight, Mum?"

A little sigh escapes her lips. "Best I've had since…" She pauses. Her voice becomes faint. "Well, since your fathers died."

I glance back at Kai. He's stopped gloating and stares at our mother with a solemn face.

"John Walks Long is such a gentleman," she continues, "and it felt good not having to sham anyone."

It's about time Bridie figured that out. How can she, how can any of us, have real friends or a real life as long as we're being fake? I touch the smeared glasses. Maybe that's why being with Lennon felt so special.

We drive the rest of the way in silence. Kai stretches out on the backseat and plays a game on his phone. I yawn and glance at the clock. It's past eleven, but for once, I'm looking forward to getting up for school. I still have to figure out what I'm going to wear. Maybe that pinafore I'd made in Ms. G.'s class. It looks really cute with my gray leggings and ankle boots.

As the car approaches the house, Bridie sighs again. "Back to being who we aren't." She presses the garage door opener, heading up the driveway as the door rolls open. Then she hits the brakes.

Piles of clothes cover the garage floor, some of them draping Bill's car, as if there had been an explosion that only affected our wardrobes. Kai and I jump out of the car. Blank-faced, Bridie climbs out more slowly. Then she leans against the bonnet as if she's about to fall over.

My brother and I exchange uneasy glances before entering the garage. I reach down and pick up a dress I'd made for Bridie. It's still on the hanger. About half the clothes are on hangers. Some look as if they'd been dumped out of drawers. I recognize a heap of clothes that had been in the laundry basket. Shoes lay haphazardly as if thrown.

What happened? Had someone broken in while we were gone? But if that happened, then where's Bill? I look back at Bridie, still frozen in place. "Mum?"

The back door swings open, hitting the wall with a bang. Kai and I jump. Bill stomps down the stairs, his face cold despite his angry movements. He knows. I can tell from that no-bullshit look in his eyes. He knew even before we'd left the house. Why hadn't he said anything then? Dinner. Must be. He wanted a final meal from his domestic servant before he showed her the door.

Bill stops at the foot of the stairs and glares at Bridie. "I want you and your brats out of here. Now."

Bridie's breath shakes as she inhales. She stammers as she walks into the garage. "Darling, what... what's wrong? Why..."

"Don't you 'darling' me. I'm onto you."

"Onto me? What do you mean?"

"I know, Bridie. You're scamming me."

This is it. Finally. The truth.

Bridie takes another tentative step forward. "Please, Bill. I don't know who told you what, but..."

"Where were you tonight?"

Bridie opens her mouth and closes it. Her gaze drops. "I'm sorry. We weren't at a PTA show. We performed at another place, a private party. I didn't think you would approve, so I..."

"Is this who you were with?" Bill yanks his phone from his pocket and thrusts it out at her.

I squint. It looks like a picture of Bridie dancing with John Walks Long.

Bridie cautiously approaches Bill, staring at the screen. "Yes, that's the host of the party."

"Host? That's what you call the man you're sleeping with?"

My mouth drops open. He thinks Bridie is cheating on him with John Walks Long? Maybe the cat isn't out of the bag. Bridie can wiggle out of an accusation of adultery. The picture isn't even incriminating... except where did Bill get that photo?

Anger flashes across Bridie's face and gives her voice more power. "I didn't sleep with him. What are you talking about? I would never cheat on you."

Bill swipes the screen, showing more photos of Bridie with the Beggar Chief. "Yeah, you wouldn't cheat. You'd lie to your husband and expect him to foot all the bills for you and your brats while you sneak off to party with some lowlifes, but you wouldn't cheat."

"No, you don't understand."

"Game's over, Bridie. I know who you are. I know what you are." His contempt deepens when he says the word, 'what.' "You're some kind of Gypsies. Strowlers. You scam people, collect what you can, and move on."

The game is over. We've been snapped. This is what I wanted, right? So why can't I breathe?

Bridie closes her eyes for a moment. An odd sort of calm seems to settle on her. She speaks in a quiet voice without emotion. "Yes, we're Strowlers. I'm sorry I didn't tell you. That was wrong of me."

"That's just the tip of the iceberg. What about living with two men at the same time? And being married to both?"

My breath comes back in a gasp. How does he know about that?

Bridie looks stunned. It takes a moment for her to stammer out a reply. "I... I was afraid you wouldn't understand."

"Understand?" Bill scoffs. "Understand that you didn't live on an Irish farm, that you lived in London? That you and those con artists traveled around, scamming people, while pretending to be a rock band? Understand that you scammed me, too?" He seems to relish spitting information at us.

"I'm not scamming you, Bill. I didn't cheat on you."

"You expect me to believe that? Sleeping with two men is like second nature to you."

Rage burns my skin. How dare he scumber my mother? "Shut your filthy gob, you chub."

Bill snorts like a bull. I'm sure he has some choice things to say to me.

Bring it. I'm so ready.

"Penny," Bridie grips my arm with a frantic strength and yanks me behind her. "Sorry, sorry. She's upset. She… Kai, it's my fault, not theirs. Let's not involve them."

"You brought your kids into this. Raising them to be little con artists. Making me pay for their food and clothing, and schools. Well, I'm not your patsy anymore. I want you out of here. Now." Bill jabs her in the chest.

Oh no he didn't.

I storm forward with my brother to defend our mother. She spins around and catches hold of us, drawing us into a desperate embrace. "No. Stop it," she whispers as we strain against her. "He'll call the *gardaí*."

No Strowler wants the police called for any reason. Much as I want to thrash him, I stand my ground and pant out my anger. Kai kicks the ground as he turns away.

Bridie wrings her tense white hands. "Bill, please. I'm sorry I lied to you. I don't know what you were told, but we're not conning you. Can we talk about this in private?"

His face doesn't change. "Out. Now."

She blinks. Tears spill down her cheeks. She stares at Bill a moment longer before giving a little nod. "All right, then." She takes a deep breath and manages to sound calm, though her fingers tremble as she wipes her eyes. "Children, fetch our suitcases out of that corner."

We do as Bridie asks, hauling over the baggage we'd brought with us from Ireland. We don't try sorting through the piles, shoving our things into the suitcases as quickly as possible under Bill's watchful glower. What doesn't fit, we dump into plastic garbage bags.

After zipping up the last bag, I stride up to the chub. "My sewing machine came with me. You didn't buy it. I want it back."

He gives a tight shrug. "I'm going with you. Make sure you don't steal anything."

Angry words flood my mouth. I swallow them, afraid he'll change his mind about letting me in. They burn going back down.

Bill marches me upstairs and looms in the doorway as I pack my sewing machine and fabric. I take a turn around the room. Have I missed anything? I get this feeling I should look in the bin. Gerry's smile catches my eye. The photo! My breath catches in my throat as I snatch it out. Bent, but not torn. Relief makes me dizzy. With ginger fingers, I slide it into the sewing machine's storage case.

"Who the hell are they?" demands Bill. "More of your mother's boyfriends?"

I look him up and down before answering. "Better men than you."

Bill's hands become fists. Is he going to hit me? He can try, but even the threat of the *gardaí* won't stop me from defending myself. I lift my chin and don't blink, daring him.

He points at me instead, though he doesn't dare jab me. "This is your fault. If you weren't here, your mother and I would have worked out."

Seriously? He's blaming all this on me? Like it was my idea for Bridie to fake? If he believes that, then he doesn't deserve the truth.

"Then I'm glad I was here." I brush past him out the door.

Back in the garage, Bridie and Kai have stuffed our bags into the car. I place my sewing machine on the floor behind the driver seat. Across the street, the neighbors have gathered to gawp at us. One guy holds up his phone like he's taking pictures. Damn nosy Bleaters. I can't wait to be shut of them.

Bridie looks at Bill with red-rimmed eyes. "I guess this is goodbye."

"This is get-your-lying-cheating-ass-out-of-here. I'm getting an annulment. When that's done, I'm going to make sure the three of you are deported back to Ireland."

With both hands, he shoves her against the car. By the time he draws back to shove her again, Kai and I are around the bonnet. Bridie ducks past Bill and grabs hold of us, dragging us back.

She whispers frantically, "The police, the police."

One part of my enraged brain wonders if the neighbors can overhear and think she wants them to call the cops. Not good. I calm down enough to help Bridie drag Kai around the car. It takes both of us to load him into the back seat. He kicks the door after we close it. Through the window, I see the reflection of my helpless fury in his eyes.

"Get in the car. Now." Bridie gives me a look that won't tolerate disobedience. I stride around the boot to avoid the chub and climb into the passenger seat, slamming the door closed.

Bridie talks to her ex-husband across the roof. "I tried, Bill. I really tried to be a wife to you. I wasn't perfect and you're right, I lied to you, but I never cheated on you and this wasn't a con. I wanted our marriage to work. I don't know what to say except I'm sorry. Goodbye."

Bill doesn't reply. He seems frozen in place, except for his eyes as he watches her climb in the car. She locks the doors and starts the engine. As she backs out of the driveway, he comes back to life, shouting, "I bought you that car. I want it back."

She manages to avoid him as she pulls onto the street. Bill runs alongside the car, banging on the boot. "Get out, you bitch. Cheating, lying bitch."

I don't know if he means get out of the car or out of his life. I expect him to continue chasing us like a dog down the road, but he stops abruptly. The streetlight shines down on his face. He looks stunned, like his rage is spent and he's left with nothing.

I sit back, my shoulders and neck stiff to the point of pain. My stomach feels like I've eaten something horrible and then been punched. It finally happened. I thought I'd be happy. How stupid is that?

Bridie holds the steering wheel in a white-knuckle grip. Her eyes look blank.

"Are you all right, Mum?"

"I'm trying to think where we can go."

"Maybe you better pull over for a moment."

Bridie pulls the car into the driveway of a dark house. She turns off the ignition and stares straight ahead. Then she reaches into her purse and pulls out her phone. She powers it up and frowns at the screen. "I have a text message from Jeremiah Walks Long. One of the caterers took photos of me at the banquet." She exhales a shaky breath. "Well. Bill must have hired a private detective. The Charm slipped between my fingers. I should have seen it coming." She presses her palm to her mouth, but the sob still escapes.

I glance back at Kai. He's sitting with his knees to his chest, staring at our mother with wide eyes. Plastic bags are heaped beside him.

I chew my lip. "Um, Mum, I know things aren't great between you and Gran and Grandda, but can't we," I pause as Bridie's hand drops. Her mouth pulls in a tight line. "Can't we call them?"

"No." Her voice gains some heat. "No, we cannot call your

grandparents. They told me if I marry Bill, I'm on my own." She pauses and whispers, "And here I am." After another pause, she gives her head a brisk shake. Then she pushes the ignition on the car. "We'll figure out something. Don't worry."

Don't worry. Why do adults always say stupid things like that? I glance again at Kai. He's picking at a hole in the knee of his jeans. "Are we homeless?" he asks.

Bridie attempts a weak smile. "We're Strowlers. We don't have homes."

I stare out the window. I got what I wanted. We're Strowlers again. Only this time, we have nowhere to go.

Penny

Bridie's aimless driving eventually leads us to a motel on the outer end of the Mission district. There's a liquor store across the street, and the men hanging around outside whistle and holler as she gets out of the car to go to the lobby. I gnaw my thumbnail while we wait. A few minutes later, she gets back in the car and starts the engine.

"There's a room available. Two beds. Not a bad price."

"How did you pay?"

"With my credit card."

"But Bill… won't he cut it off or something?"

"Maybe. He hasn't yet." She gives her head a brisk shake. "I can't think about that right now."

I bite off a piece of nail. What is it with her and denial? Does she really think it comforts us or makes things better? When is she going to face reality? "What about the car? Can he take it from us?"

Bridie steers into an empty parking space. "Don't worry about that, darling. The car is registered in my name. He gave it to me, so he can't take it back or claim we stole it."

Only a handful of cars are parked in the dimly lit lot.

Quickly, we unload all our belongings, not wanting to chance leaving anything in the car.

The stench of cigarettes lingers in the air, and curtains and bedspreads have a pattern that resembles fungus. Still, it's better than driving around. We talk little before settling down, Kai in one of the double beds, and Bridie and me in the other. She curls into a tight ball. I listen for tears, but she's silent and still. Kai burrows into his usual heaping nest of sheets and blankets. The men at the liquor store get louder and a fight breaks out. Buses rumble and squeal down the street. It figures the hotel would be along an all-night bus line. I stare at the ceiling. How could such a good evening go so bad?

I rub my forehead. Sleep is impossible. The mattress feels like a block of cement and the lumpy pillow smells of bleach and mold. I need to think about something else… that kiss. I close my eyes. My first kiss and it was so nice. Not weird or grope-y. Lennon is so sweet. Will I ever see him again?

My eyes pop open. I'm supposed to meet him at lunch. That won't happen now. How long will he wait for me, standing on the pathway amidst the trees and shrubs, looking like an owl with those round glasses as he glances around, searching for me? My chest aches. I have to think of something else… the ferry ride between England and Ireland. The rocking motion of the boat had always made me sleepy. I'd lay my head in Gerry's lap and feel so safe.

"Darling, wake up." Bridie strokes my hair.

My eyes blink open. I frown at the curtains, even more fungus-like in the light of day. "What time is it?"

"Almost seven." Bridie goes to the other bed and gives Kai a gentle shake. "Son, it's time to wake up."

"Why are we up so early?" I murmur.

"You have to get ready for school," Bridie states briskly.

"School?" I sit up. "How can we go to school?"

"Don't wanna go to school," Kai grumbles.

"That's too bad because you have to go." Bridie's hands go to her hips. "I'm sorry, darlings, but this is a real rough patch and I need to think my way through it. I'll be too distracted with the two of you here. I need you to spend the day someplace safe where I won't have to worry about you, so school it is. Now, get up and get ready to go. There's a McDonald's down the street. I'll get us some breakfast. I want you ready to go by eight. No excuses."

Bridie grabs her purse and walks out the door before I can say anything else.

Kai flops back on the mattress. "This sucks."

"Yeah, really." I pause. If I go to school, then I can see Lennon again. At least I can tell him goodbye.

School is full of suck. There's a lot of gawp and cackle as I walk down the hall. A couple of kids live on my block. It'd be just my luck if they were across the street last night. Whatever. I'm so done with this heap of shite.

During class, I doodle in my notebook and give the teachers blank stares when they question me. I intentionally flunk a test in American History, since I couldn't care less about the Founding Fathers of this or any other country. My only moment of regret comes during Ms. G.'s class when she compliments my pinafore and offers suggestions for the dress I'm designing. I work on the pattern with little enthusiasm, knowing I'll be leaving it behind.

At the end of class, I'm the last one out. I hesitate at the door before saying, "Bye, Ms. G."

She looks up from her knitting with a kindly blink. "Bye, Penny. See you tomorrow."

God, I almost want to tell her or at least thank her for being the only person to stand up for me. All I can do is bob my head. My throat burns as I force back an urge to cry. I hurry out the door.

There's one more class before lunch, but I don't give a toss.

I go to my locker and shove all my schoolbooks inside. Then I slam the door and lock it. Why make things easy for people who have made life so hard for me? I stride down the hall toward the stairway that leads to the parking lot.

Dani steps out of the loo in a cloud of cigarette smoke, her thumbs tapping away on her phone. Her oily eyes glisten as they track me. "Cutting class?"

I flip her off. "Up your arse, you manky bint."

Maybe I should have blessed her instead, but I'm in no mood. Her eyes don't change, but her mouth spreads in a smile. I expect her to go fake Christian on me, but instead she says, "Have fu-un."

She's probably going to peach on me to Ms. Ikeda. Like I care. I cross the parking lot, turning my back on Hellhole High forever.

A cold ocean breeze gusts down Lincoln Avenue. Makes me glad I wore leggings instead of tights. I button my jean jacket up to my neck. So much for looking cute in my pinafore.

I cross the street and veer off the sidewalk to an uphill dirt trail. Although it's autumn, leaves don't seem to fall off the trees in California and the underbrush remains thick, hiding me from view. I head for a huge, old elm, still standing amidst the stumps and fallen branches of lesser trees. It was one of my favorite hideaways back when I cut class. I perch on a branch at the foot of the elm and rest my feet on a stump. Then I reach into my pocket and pull out my phone. It's almost eleven a.m., seven p.m. in Ireland. The perfect time to call my grandparents, but should I? Bridie will be furious. Plus, I don't want them thinking they can marry me off because I'm skint. I take a hesitant breath. This isn't about Bridie or me. Kai is twelve years old. There's no reason for him, or any of us, to be homeless if we can get help. I press my hand over one ear to block the traffic noise on Lincoln and hold the phone to the other ear. Nothing. I check the screen. Call Failed. I'm in a dead zone.

Maybe I'll have better reception on the walkway. I slide off the branch and head for the trail.

Kevin Anderson steps out from behind a tree. His leering grin shows sharp white teeth against his red face. "Hey, cunt."

I manage not to gasp, but my steps falter. What is he doing here? I glance at my phone. Still no reception. I shove it in my pocket to free my hands. I have two choices: fight or flight. If I run, there's a good chance he can tackle me from behind and drag me into the dense bushes. Fight it is. I stride forward. If he touches me, if he even says one word, I'll kick him in the balls.

Two of Kevin's crew appear from behind the trees to join him. Mischief glints in their eyes and something worse, something that makes my heart pound. Behind me, footsteps crunch on leaves and twigs. Two more boys bear down on me until I'm surrounded.

"Dani says hi," says Kevin.

Have fu-un.

"You made me look like a pussy, bitch, and now you pay."

I slide my backpack off my shoulders. If only I hadn't dumped my books, it would make a better weapon.

"You're giving us the blow jobs you owe us. If you do it real nice, we might let you go."

"Go to hell." My voice shakes. I take a deep breath. If I scream, will anyone hear? I swing my backpack at the first boy groping for me. He catches hold of it and tosses it away, leaving him open in front. My knee makes contact with his groin. He doubles over, groaning in agony. His friends laugh.

Kevin smirks. "Okay, not nice. Fine with me."

Two boys grab me from behind. I lift my leg and kick down on the side of one boy's knee. He cries out as he crumples to the ground, dragging me down with him. The other boy stumbles down as well, but doesn't loosen his grip. He kneels on my upper arm and shoulder.

Pain and panic close my throat. The other boy rolls over and kneels on my other arm. Kevin and the two other boys loom over me. Red-hot rage fills the eyes of the one cupping his groin. My throat opens and I scream.

Kevin raises his fist.

A blur darts out of the brush, grabs hold of Kevin and disappears into another clump of bushes. Everyone freezes, even me. The bushes shiver with the sound of a one-sided struggle. After a final violent shake, they go still.

The two standing boys back away. The kneeling boys jump up. "What the hell was that?" whispers one of them.

I scramble to my feet, ready to run. Then the blur darts out again and takes shape. A soldier wearing a camouflage hoodie, olive green beanie and khaki trousers peers at me through round glasses. Not a soldier. Lennon.

The four boys stare at him cautiously. One comes forward, raising his fists. Lennon's roundhouse kick sends him sprawling. The others have no time to react. Lennon makes quick work of them with a series of punches and kicks, until they've fallen into groaning heaps around him.

My lids flutter with rapid blinks. My mouth is gaping open. Lennon comes up to me, his round glasses darkened by the shadows. My knees shake and I grip his shoulder to steady myself.

"Are you all right?" he asks softly.

I gasp in air so I can speak. "I'm great."

He gives a grim nod. "Which one?"

It takes me a moment to realize he means which one is the ringleader. I point at the bushes. Lennon goes back in and hauls Kevin out by the collar, forcing him to scramble on his hands and knees. Scratches cover his arms and face and his clothes are ripped. Lennon wraps his arm in a chokehold around Kevin's neck so he has to look up at me.

My mouth feels dry as a bone. I cough several times to

work up enough phlegm and spit in his eye. He recoils, anger clear on his face, though he doesn't dare speak.

His crew stumbles to their feet and scarper down the trail without a backward glance.

"Shit holes," I shout after them. Then I look down at Kevin. "Listen, you gobshite, we hear you do this to another girl, you won't just get an arse-kicking. You'll disappear. Got it?"

He stares at me, bug-eyed. So I smack him across his manky mouth. The impact of my hand, his recoil and squeal of pain… these send a wild fury zinging through me. I know if I hit him again, I won't stop, and we don't have time for that.

I wipe his slobber on his sleeve and repeat, "Got it?"

Lennon grabs a fistful of Kevin's hair and bobs his head up and down. Then he hauls him to his feet and shoves him down the trail. I put my boot to his arse to give him further momentum. After lurching forward, Kevin stumbles into a frantic run.

Lennon picks up my backpack and hands it to me. "We better get out of here."

With his eyes hidden, he looks so cold and righteous. Not at all like the sweet boy who gave me a shy first kiss. Who is he really? If he hadn't shown up when he did, those boys, they would have… I dig my knuckles into my forehead. How could I have been such a gom? I cast a curse. I knew there were repercussions. Dani must have been biding her time, waiting for me to cut class so she could tell Kevin. And now it's done. Her well of darkness is too deep and the curse will rebound onto her. I'm truly free of that awful place. I rub my forehead hard so I don't cry.

"Penny?" He sounds worried.

I clear my throat. "Where to?"

"How about the de Young Museum? We can hang out in the café or something."

"That'll work."

We head downhill, winding through the trees and brush,

and cross a street that leads to the baseball field. Even with no one else there, it feels too exposed to cut across, so we stick to a trail that winds around the field.

We walk in silence for a few minutes. Our hands brush, then clasp. His skin is warm and a little dry. My hand must feel like a block of ice. He doesn't seem to mind. The touch of our palms, the secure grip of his fingers makes my heart beat a little faster, in a good way.

"Thank you."

"You're okay?"

I nod.

"Who were those assholes?"

"They go to my school. They've been harassing me. Slagging me off. Especially Kevin, ever since I beat him up."

"You beat him up?" Lennon doesn't sound surprised. "Good. I'm just glad I got there when I did."

"Why were you early?"

"You can thank MUNI. You know how it goes. You leave early, you arrive early. You leave on time, you arrive late. So I chose early."

"Glad you did." I take a hesitant breath. "Um, did you learn to fight like that in the Beggar Clan?"

He shakes his head. There's a long enough pause, I think that's the end of it. Then he speaks and there's an edge to his voice, like he's choosing each word. "Something happened to me. I got jumped, kind of like what happened to you. John Walks Long saved me. Since then, I've been thinking about what I should have done different. I blamed myself instead of blaming the assholes that jumped me."

Totally changing the subject, but that's okay. He's right. In the back of my mind, I'm blaming myself instead of Kevin and Dani. I kick a rock in our path. "Victims always blame themselves, or get blamed. It sucks."

"I'm not gonna be a victim, not ever again."

"Me, neither." Our hands squeeze tight. "My dads taught me to fight. Well, Gerry taught me boxing. I sparred with Matthew, but even though he was on the Wayward Way, he couldn't teach me any Two Dragon Clan skills. He couldn't even teach them to Kai."

"Why not?"

"Strowlers are matrilineal. It's funny since they're so bloody macho, but that's how it's always been. If your mother's a Strowler, you're a Strowler. Kai can't be a member of the Two Dragon Clan. Matthew didn't want us to get in trouble for learning the–" I use my fingers to make quotation marks and whisper dramatically, "secret skills."

Lennon snorts. "Rules and secrets are stupid. They don't help anyone."

I sigh. "Yeah, but they can make your life pretty miserable if you don't obey."

He snorts again.

After leaving the trail, we walk around the California Academy of Sciences building, across a tree-lined music concourse and up the stairs to the de Young Museum. The building looks like a copper-colored shoebox with an inverted chimney. Not at all like the grand museums in London. Not even the Tate Modern, which is located in an old power station. "It's so ugly."

Lennon shrugs. "What matters most is what's inside."

I suck back a sigh. He has to stop saying things like that before I develop a major crush on him.

We head through the lobby, passing the gift store and exhibits until we reach the café. I pull out my wallet. I don't have much, but this is no time to be cheap. "My treat. I insist, so don't say no."

Lennon ducks his head, making him seem more like the boy from last night. "I guess I'd like a mocha."

"Me, too. You like whipped cream and cinnamon?"

"Cinnamon?" His nose wrinkles in the most adorable way. "I'll give it a try."

"You won't be disappointed." As I head for the espresso bar, I glance around at the tables. All the punters look at least fifty. The longer we linger, the more we'll stand out, so I order our drinks to go.

"Maybe we shouldn't stick around here," Lennon says as I hand him his drink.

"I was thinking the same thing."

"Let's go outside. I know a place we can sit."

We head for the sculpture garden outside the café. Lennon leads the way as we stroll under a gigantic safety pin suspended on its head and past a lawn covered with huge, ceramic fruit. A boy who likes museums. Interesting. Matthew liked museums. He took Kai and me to all the free ones in London.

We go around a grassy knoll and down a slope, into an embedded cement structure. After passing through the arched entryway, we come to a round corridor. I listen, but hear no voices coming from within. We're alone. My heart starts hammering. Am I crazy to trust him? Even if he did save me from being raped, what if he's setting me up for another assault? No. That can't be. John Walks Long would literally murder him. I rub my eyes.

Lennon looks at me with owlish concern. "You okay?"

Fear, anger, lack of sleep, it's all making me paranoid. What I need right now is a friend and he's the only one I've got. I nod and keep walking, clutching the hot paper coffee cup close to my chest against the cold air trapped between the walls. Despite being under a hill, there's plenty of light shining off the smooth, adobe-colored walls.

When we reach the middle, there's an archway that leads to a cement chamber. The walls curved upward into a dome with a hole in the center. We stand beneath it and gaze up at the sky.

Then Lennon points to a circle of light on one of the walls. "See, sunlight shines through the hole to form a circle that moves with the Earth as it rotates around the sun." He looks up again and I follow his gaze. Blue sky peeks through gusting gray and white clouds. "Doesn't it look sort of like the moon?'

"Yeah, it kind of does." So beautiful. For a moment, I feel at peace. Then I lower my head. There is no peace. My life is nothing but turmoil.

Lennon lowers his head, too. Our eyes meet. If all that horrible crap hadn't happened in the woods, I might have wanted a kiss. Now, I wrap my arm around myself.

"Want to sit?" Lennon nods toward the circle of cement benches built into the wall.

I perch on the center bench and take a sip of mocha. The sweet, familiar flavor makes me feel a little calmer.

"You're right. The cinnamon is good." Lennon leans back, drawing his knees to his chest. He stares at the hole again.

I sigh. "On a scale of zero to suck, this might be the suckiest day of my life. At least I don't have to go back to that shithole."

"Won't your mom make you?"

I twist so I sit with one leg tucked beneath me. Lennon is close enough that I can feel his body warmth. My reflection stares back at me in his lens. "Can't you take those things off? Please?"

He hesitates a moment before pulling his glasses off and sticking them in the pocket of his hoodie. What gorgeous, warm brown eyes. If that's what he's trying to hide, the glasses work.

I hold my cup under my nose, breathing in the soothing, cinnamon-chocolate smell. "No, my mother won't make me. Last night, after the banquet, everything went to shit."

"What happened?" Those brown eyes immediately go from concerned to wary. "Sorry, I shouldn't ask."

"No, it's all right. If you don't mind listening."

"I don't mind."

It all comes pouring out, starting with arriving home from the Beggars' Banquet and finding the mess in the garage, and ending with spending the night in the motel. Lennon doesn't show much emotion until I tell him about Bill jabbing and shoving Bridie.

"What a tool. I hate that the most, people with power picking on people without any. I was thinking it was too bad your mom didn't get Jeremiah's message so she could do damage control, but now I think you're better off without him."

"We're homeless without him, but that's still better. He never hit Bridie before. I think." Could he have hit her when Kai and I weren't around? She wouldn't have told us and, let's face it, she didn't look surprised when he shoved her. My breath starts coming in spurts. If Lennon weren't there, I'd punch the wall.

"You okay?"

I nod.

"You know what I don't get? All those pictures showed were your mom and the Chief dancing. Why would the detective tell Bill they were sleeping together?"

"I don't know. Maybe he didn't. Maybe Bill just decided Bridie was cheating on him." Maybe, with the Charm fading, Bill decided he didn't want a family and this was the best way to get rid of us. A gust of wind blows through the hole in the dome. I rub my arms.

"Are you cold?"

I nod.

Lennon scoots a little closer and puts his arm around my shoulder. I lick my suddenly dry lips and scoot closer, too. Our heads touch as we lean back against the wall. It's funny how it doesn't feel awkward or sexual. It feels nice. I don't want to leave. I wish we could make this our place. Nick some blankets from gift shop and food from the café, and stay here all night.

He speaks and his breath stirs the hair covering my ear. "Hey, isn't there a movie where a couple of kids sneak into a museum and stay there all night?"

I grin. See? We even think alike. "Yeah. Probably."

"We could go all over the museum. I could show you the best paintings. And we could spend the night in the observation tower, looking at the stars."

Such a dreamy boy, wanting to show me paintings instead of seducing me. No wonder I feel safe with him.

His arm tightens around me. "I – I wish I could keep seeing you."

My heart starts pounding. A tingling sensation spreads through me. A night alone in the museum would be a really bad idea. Or a really good one with bad consequences.

"Can your mom ask John Walks Long for help? Maybe you can stay at the Abode for a while."

"No. There's a Strowler Nest here. We have to go them for help before we can go to anyone else." Not that we will, but Lennon doesn't need to know that.

"Nest?"

"That's what we call our campsites, because, you know, we all have bird names. There's a main caravan, the home of the Mother Bird, and the smaller caravans come and go."

He gives an owl blink. "I didn't know that."

"Anyway, you know how it goes on the Crossroads. If you ask someone from another clan for help, you're beholden to them, more than someone from your own clan."

"I hope you don't think you're beholden to me."

Heat rushes to my cheeks. I do, but I'm not sure how to say it or what to do about it.

He lifts his cup. "Even if you do, this is payment enough."

Not hardly, but I can't help laugh. "Can I at least get you a refill?"

"Next time?"

Two words with so much promise that will never happen. This really is the suckiest day ever. As if to rub salt in my wounds, my phone rings. It's Bridie.

I gnaw my lip, so tempted not to answer, but she never calls in the middle of the school day. It has to be important. Maybe Kevin and his crew have peached on us.

"Hi, Mum."

"Where are you? I'm at your school and no one has seen you since third period."

"What are you doing at my school?"

"I came to pick you up. I've already collected your brother."

"Pick me up? Why?"

"Never mind that. Where are you?"

"Um, I cut class."

My mother huffs out an impatient sigh. "Obviously."

"Did they say anything about it?"

"They? You mean, the school? Well, aside from giving me grief about you cutting, no. Why?"

"Nothing."

She snorts. "I wasn't born yesterday, Penny."

"I can't talk about it on the phone. I'm in Golden Gate Park, at the de Young Museum."

"How nice you're getting culture while running truant. I'll be out front in five minutes. Be there."

As I hang up, Lennon's arm slides away. I already feel colder without it. "I've got to go. My mother's coming to get me." I hold out my phone. "Give me your number and…" My voice trails off as he ducks his head.

"I can't. I don't have a phone and I can't use my email." He leans back and stares up at the hole in the dome. The gray clouds have grown thicker, blocking out the patches of blue sky. "There are people looking for me. I can't let them find me. If they hack my email account, it could lead them to you, and I don't want you hurt by my crap."

So many questions and no time to ask. Lennon won't answer anyway. I take a sip of mocha to ease the ache in my throat. He tugs up his hood and his warm brown eyes disappear behind his round lenses.

I slip off the bench. "Walk me to the front?"

Lennon stands and holds out his hand. My fingers wind in his. I don't want to think about letting go. Instead, I imagine we're going to sneak into the museum and find a place to hide until everyone is gone. I manage to hold onto that thought all the way through the sculpture garden, until we come to a stop under the safety pin. He squeezes my hand. I squeeze back.

"I should have kissed you back in there." I try to sound like I'm joking.

"Yeah," he breathes out, not smiling either.

I can't let it end like this. I unzip my book bag and take out a pen. Then I reach for his mocha cup and write my phone number on the cardboard sleeve. "Message me when you can, yeah? Let me know how you are."

He takes back his cup and holds it to his chest as he nods.

Bridie is already parked outside the museum. She jumps out of the driver's seat as we approach.

Kai unrolls the back window and smirks. "See? I told you she had a boyfriend."

Bridie's hands go to her hips as her eyes shift from me to Lennon. "What is going on here?"

"I'll tell you in the car. Don't get mad at Lennon. It's not what you think. Kevin Anderson and his crew jumped me. Lennon saved me."

Bridie's face drains of expression. "What-what are you talking about? Who jumped you?"

"I'll tell you in the car," I repeat firmly. "Um, can we give Lennon a ride back to the Beggars' Abode?"

She blinks. "Well, yes, of course. I want to hear what you both have to say."

Lennon shakes his head. "I can't come with you. There's stuff I gotta do before heading back."

Disappointment squeezes my chest. I don't blame him for not wanting to be in the middle of a family brawl, but doesn't he want to spend a few more minutes with me? "Are you sure?"

"I can't. Thanks anyway." The way he says it, there has to be something else going on.

"I can't stay parked here," Bridie says as she gets back into the car. "Let's go."

"I hope I see you again," he whispers.

I nod, my throat too tight for goodbyes. I climb into the front seat and keep my eyes straight ahead as Mum drives away. Then, unable to help myself, I look back. Lennon is already gone.

"All right, we're in the car," she says. "Tell me what happened."

I was so wound up about Lennon, I didn't notice the plastic bags piled up in the back seat until now.

"Penny?"

"We're not going back to the hotel?"

She keeps her eyes on the road. "No. We have someplace else to stay."

"Where?"

"The local Nest."

"What?" I gasp out the word. "But isn't that run by–"

"Yes. And I don't want to hear anything about it. We don't have a choice. We're going to go stay with Kingfisher."

Lennon

One of the biggest regrets of my life will be that I didn't spend the night in the museum with Penny Sparrow. I mean that in a non-sexual way. Sort of. I'm way into her, but hanging out would be enough. She's so cool. If things were normal…

Normal. Now, that's a laugh. Maybe what I mean to say is if she and I were normal, but we're not. If my life hadn't been so rudely interrupted by murder, I never would've met her. My parents would be alive and I'd be chugging along on the Glory Road. As much as I like Penny, I'd give up ever meeting her to have my parents back. Will I ever see her again? Pain spreads across my chest. Maybe it would've been better if I never met her. I'm tired of losing people I care about.

I start to toss my mocha cup into a trash bin, but I can't let go. Not until I remove the sleeve. Even if I never call her, at least I'll have this to remember her by.

I cram my hands in my pockets and head down Irving Street. There are lots of restaurants in this neighborhood. My favorite is Dolsot House, conveniently located right across the street from Auntie Cat's place. There's always a line out the door at lunchtime, so it's easy enough to tag onto the end.

Between my beanie, the hoodie and my glasses, I'm pretty sure I look nothing like Paul Lau. Some older kids, maybe college age, queue up behind me. I shift toward them and even nod a few times while one talks, hoping they don't notice. The aroma of barbecue beef and crunchy burnt rice makes my mouth water. Man, I love their kimchi pancakes. Sometimes, Auntie Cat and I would come over after her noon class and split one because they're so huge.

I try looking casual as I peer across the street. The front window of her Tai Chi studio looks dark, but that's not unusual. Sometimes she turns off the lights to make things more tranquil. I wish I could see some kind of movement. Shit. I didn't risk coming here to walk away with nothing. I take a sideways step so I'm behind the college kids. Then I take off my glasses. That's when I spot the closed sign on the door.

Noon classes are her bread and butter. Something is definitely wrong. Did the clan punish her because I ran away under her watch? That can't be it. I ran away from the funeral home, not her house. What if she's sick or injured? My heart starts slamming in my chest. If she is, it's my fault. She'd sheltered and comforted me and I'd paid her back by running away without a word. I've tried thinking of a way to contact her and let her know I'm all right, but anything – a phone call, email, a postcard – can be traced by the clan.

A familiar presence brushes my mind. I suck in my breath. It's Auntie Cat. She knows I'm here. After a moment's hesitation, I let her in.

Paul. I feel the urgency behind my name.

Auntie Cat, I'm sorry. I…

He's here. He's coming for you. Run.

The studio door swings open. Tony steps out.

Our eyes meet. I freeze.

Tony doesn't move, either. He looks exactly the same, wearing the usual jeans and black T-shirt. He doesn't like patterns or designs, or anything with logos. Last Christmas, as a joke, I got him one of those cheap, cheesy Bruce Lee T-shirts sold in Chinatown. Tony had actually laughed.

His mind brushes mine. *Little Brother.*

Tony is my brother. I had promised Dad to obey my brother.

Brotherly ties hadn't kept Uncle George from murdering Dad.

He keeps his eyes locked on mine as he steps off the curb. An oncoming car blasts its horn and he halts.

I push past the line and bolt into Dolsot House, jostling through the tightly packed tables, knocking into people who are trying to eat, and duck past a waiter gingerly balancing a hot stone bowl. People holler after me, but that's okay. The more confusion, the better. Tony will have to wade through all that.

Tactical advantage: I've been here many times. I know exactly where the bathrooms are, through the kitchen and around a corner. I take a chance and try the women's room door. Open. I enter and lock it. As I hoped, the set-up is the same as the men's room. It has a large enough window I can squeeze through. I drop down into a dark, narrow alley, where I can run in either direction or go up. I can hear the hubbub inside the restaurant. Someone – Tony – is pounding on the door of the men's room.

I'm seconds ahead of him and those seconds are everything. He taught me that. He'll lose more seconds once he makes it out here if I'm gone. Using the Climbing Skill, I scramble up the wall to the roof. With Silent Steps, I run across its surface and when I reach the edge, I push myself off using the Flying Skill and propel myself half a block to the tree-thickened foliage of someone's backyard.

Tony will see if the branches shake, so I land beside the fence. My feet don't hit the ground. Instead, I splash into a filthy bathtub. It tilts to and fro. I almost pitch over and lose seconds balancing myself. I hop out of the tub, soaked to my calves and step carefully around numerous stacks of rancid plastic bins overflowing with all kinds of crap. Every inch of ground is covered with trash that crackles beneath my feet despite my Silent Steps.

Okay, time to practice the Shadow Skill and I can't think of a better place than this hoarder's paradise. I hunker down behind a haphazard pile of bins and blend into the deep shade of a mossy tree. The ground is oily slick and smells like some kind of shit. I peer through the branches until I spot Tony standing on a nearby rooftop. He's looking this way.

Tactical mistake. With its thick foliage, this backyard is the most obvious place to land. Get out now. I slither against the house and wind around to the left. Another advantage, I know the houses in the area are pretty similar. I open a gate that leads to a narrow side alley. I'm expecting to have to crawl through more hoard, but the corridor is clear except for the garbage and recycling containers. I silently scoot through, open another gate, close it, and listen.

A crashing sound tells me that Tony has landed in the bathtub. Now he's got to search the maze of bins. My seconds are adding up and I can't lose a single one. With Swift Steps, I blur up 10th Avenue until I reach Judah Street. The light rail is clanking toward the stop in the median. I rush across the street and climb aboard. Ignoring the open seats, I head for the windowless space between two of the cars.

Breath wheezes through my chest. I clutch the handrail, my legs trembling as the train shudders into motion, and glance up and down the length of the train. Old people, a handful of tourists and some homeless kids. I can try blending in with the kids, but my military gear is like an arrow pointing right at me. I pull off the hoodie and beanie, roll them in a tight ball and casually shove them under my seat. Then I put on my glasses and tug my hair into spikey blond peaks, using my sweat as a sort of gel. Hopefully my wet feet and mud-stained pants make me look like just another street kid.

The N-Judah is slow as all fuck and stops at every block so more old people can turtle their way on board. After the fourth stop, I want to jump out of my skin. When we reach the UCSF Medical Center, I jump off.

Tactical advantage: since Tony rarely visits Auntie Cat and never takes the bus, he won't know that I can cross through the medical center lobby and catch the 6 on Parnassus Avenue. I linger next to the door, trying to look casual and not frantic, until the bus comes. Again, I stand in the center rather than take an open seat near a window. This bus goes faster and skips a few empty stops. I hop off at Van Ness and head underground for the light rail. The station is crowded and I thread my way to a spot against the wall. I look all around, scanning every face on the platform. No Tony. I can't shake the feeling I'm being followed, even though it doesn't make sense. Tony wouldn't bother tailing me. He'd grab me by the collar and haul me away.

I take the K train, which stays underground until we get to Third Street. Some of the tension eases out of me, which makes my legs ache. I want to sit, but I don't dare drop my guard for a single second. I get off at the stop closest to the Beggar Abode and duck into a gas station convenience store. I stay for about five minutes, staring out the window. No sign of Tony or anyone who might be with the Two Dragon Clan. I feel a little dizzy. Kind of euphoric. I beat Tony. That never happens. I guess I was never desperate enough.

I spot a group of Beggars heading back to the Abode and join them. A strong wind is gusting off the bay and one of the Beggars offers me a plastic rain poncho from her shopping cart. I gratefully tug it on, pulling the hood past my forehead to shade my face.

As we entered the warehouse, I yank off the hood and wipe my forehead, safe, at least for the moment.

Then a guard at the entrance says, "Hey, Lennon. Chief wants to see you."

And the moment is over.

I head for the octagon where Jeremiah is sparring with another Beggar. He's wearing only boxing shorts and his scars stand out like bright red welts even from a distance. John Walks Long is standing nearby, talking to some enormous bald guy wearing a satin Raiders jacket. Dude's not exactly fat or even tall, more like a bull, all square and bulky on top with skinny legs. Something about him, even from a distance, I don't like. I wonder what he's doing here. Hope it's nothing to do with me.

The Beggar Chief turns, his coat sweeping around with him. His eyebrows knit into one shaggy line of disapproval. He says something to Raiders Guy before striding toward me. He places a heavy hand on my shoulder and drags me to a private corner

"You left without my permission."

I duck my head. "I'm sorry. There was something I had to do."

"What was so important that you would risk our safety and yours?"

I'm not about to tell the chief about Penny. I owe him a lot, but not the whole truth when half will do the trick. "I went to see my Auntie Cat. I haven't talked her since I ran away. I'm worried about her, like, maybe I made her sick or got her in trouble by taking off."

The chief's scowl softens. "Auntie Cat. Do you mean your father's sister, Catherine?"

"You know her?"

"I've met her. Tony Lau said you were in her custody when you ran away."

"Yeah." I hesitate. I have to tell John Walks Long. Whatever the chief's motives, he doesn't deserve Tony breathing down his neck. "I went to where she lives and stood across the street. I thought maybe I could see her through a window or something. While I was standing there, Tony came out."

John Walks Long's breath whistles through his teeth. "Did he see you?"

"Yeah. He chased after me, but I managed to shake him off."

"You're sure he didn't follow you here?"

"I transferred buses three times. I didn't see him once."

He scratches his beard. "Not good. Not good at all. He could still track you here."

My heart sinks. I got used to living indoors and eating regular meals. "I'm sorry. I don't want to bring any trouble to you. I better go."

"Where?"

"I don't know." Actually, I do, but I'm not about to tell him.

He guesses anyway. "The Two Dragon Clan has a twenty-four-hour watch on the Greyhound bus station."

Well, shit. "There are other ways out of the city. I can take BART somewhere."

"Your cousin, having lost you again, will cast a wide net across the Bay Area. It might already be too late."

"I'll figure something out."

"I can find another refuge for you." John Walks Long returns to the Octagon, motioning Raiders Guy to join him. He shakes the cage. Jeremiah drops the opponent he's got a choke-hold on and hunkers down next to the chain links to confer with them. All three look at me and shake their heads. That's okay. They can go ahead and think I'm some snot-nosed punk who messed up.

The Beggar Chief and Raiders Guy shake hands. Oh hell no. I'm not going anywhere with that dude. I'm about to tell

John Walks Long when he comes striding back over to me, but he speaks first. "That man over there is Kingfisher. He runs the local Strowlers' Nest and he's agreed to take you in."

And that changes everything. "Does he know who I am?"

"No, and you'd be wise to keep it that way."

"What does he want in return?"

"Kingfisher owes me plenty. Don't worry about it."

I think I'll worry anyway. "What's he doing here?"

"The Sparrows came into some trouble last night. Remember the caterer who was caught taking pictures? His target was Bridie Sparrow. Since the Sparrows are Strowlers, Kingfisher wanted to find out what happened."

This must be the guy Penny said her family has to go to for help. Too bad he seems like such a dick. Still, if it means seeing her again… "If you think I should, then, okay, I'll go."

"Once you're there, lay low. Don't leave the camp. I'll let you know when it's safe to return."

"Return where?"

"To the Abode, to join us, if you want." Funny, how he manages to sound casual about something so huge.

I decide to play dumb kid since that's what he takes me for. "What do you mean, join the Beggar Clan? How can I do that?"

"Your parents are dead and you've run away. Obviously something is very wrong. If it weren't, you'd be the Dragon Son and we wouldn't be having this conversation. When you return, tell me everything, and I will help you sort it out. If it's revenge you want, I can guarantee it."

Using that grand voice, he makes it sound a generous offer. Except, "The only cost is to defect and join the Beggar Clan."

The Beggar Chief shakes his mane regretfully. "We can only avenge those who belong to our clan."

No. Shit. I suck down my anger even though I kind of want to punch him. It's no surprise he was hoping to use me.

Despite this, he's dealt with me kindly. He could have turned me over to Tony for a considerable sum. He could have left me in Payroll's hands. If he wanted to really fuck things up for the Two Dragon Clan, he could have killed me.

The Beggar Chief waits before taking my silence as an answer. He turns away.

I speak to his back. "How can I repay you?"

He looks over his shoulder. "Children, especially orphans, are under no debt of obligation on the Crossroads, regardless of who aids them. You should know that."

I do know that. I also know it's bogus. Fine words that sound kind, but mean nothing. I owe John Walks Long big time, and someday, I'll have to repay him.

Penny

"Those manky little cunts." Bridie snorts her rage. "I wish I'd been there. I'd have cut off their cocks and strung them up by their balls." I glance back at Kai, whose mouth has also dropped open. Bridie's been playing Bill's doormat for so long, I almost forgot she can swear a blue streak when provoked. "When I think about what they might have done." Her hands grip the steering wheel as if it were Kevin Anderson's throat. "Well, it's a good thing Lennon showed up when he did. I wish I'd known so I could thank him." She pauses. "Don't take that as approval for cutting class to meet a boy in the park."

I roll my eyes. Really? She's going to go there? "I haven't had any friends since we left London. Lennon was someone I could talk to, yeah? Don't make a big deal out of it."

"I'm not making a big deal out of it. Anyway, I'm sure you'll make new friends at the Nest."

Now she's trying to make this seem like a good thing, when we all know better. I want to punch the dashboard. Instead, I stare out the window as we drive past desolate container yards and weedy vacant lots.

"I thought you wanted to be back on the Crossroads."

That's not what this is about and she knows it.

"I can handle Kingfisher. Give me some credit. We don't have any choice."

"We do, too. We can call Gran and Grandda."

Bridie swerves the car with such force I'm jammed against the door. This is less hazardous than it sounds since there's no traffic and plenty of parking. Okay, she wants dramatics. She doesn't mind that her son is sliding around in the back seat with all our things. She cuts the engine and stares out the window, her hands still gripping the wheel.

Kai scoots forward. "What's going on?"

"This is between me and your sister." Bridie's eyes shoot fire at me. "I've told you what'll happen if you go back to Ireland. Are you that eager to get married?"

Heat rushes to my face. "I don't want to go back and live with them. Just… maybe they can help us."

"I'll tell you what your grandparents will do to help. They'll buy two plane tickets, one for you and one for your brother. They won't give you any choice about where you can go or what you can do. You'll be married by Christmas."

The ball in my stomach tightens painfully.

"Won't they send a ticket for you?" asks Kai.

The fire in my mother's eyes dies, leaving her grim and sad. "No. I made my bed and I lie in it."

"What…" He clears his throat and his voice goes smaller. "What about my grandparents? They'll help us."

Bridie heaves a pained sigh. "Your grandparents didn't offer any help when your father died. What makes you think they'll help us now?" She sighs again. "Well, they'll send a plane ticket for you and offer to take you in. They've no reason to help me or your sister. Still, if that's what you want, I won't stop you."

His hands grip her seat. "I'm not going anywhere without you, Mum."

I'm not ready to give up that easily. "What about Auntie Helena?"

Bridie freezes at the mention of her best mate, also known as Mad Maud, the Chief of the London Beggar Clan. Then she shakes her head slowly. "No."

"But she'll help us. You know she will. No one has to know."

"We can't risk it. Not after what happened. Do you want Gareth to die?"

My heart sinks. She's right. After Gerry and Matthew died, Helena and her brother, Gareth, gave us shelter. They were repaid for their kindness by a murder attempt on Gareth. That's when we fled to the cruel mercy of my grandparents' Nest.

There has to be another option. As I wrack my brain, Bridie pushes the ignition. "It's only temporary. We need a roof over our heads until I figure out what to do next."

Like the Beggar Clan, the traveling community lives on the industrial edge of the city. The wind whips the car as we drive closer to the shore. At the end of the street we come to a gravel road. Leaning against a pile of rocks is a wood pallet spray painted with two road markers. The first is the Strowler symbol, an open rectangle with two circles at the bottom, sort of like a wagon. The second is the symbol of the Glory Road, almost identical to the one at the Beggars' Abode except for one difference. This one has a slash through it, meaning those on the Wayward Way aren't welcome.

"Uh-oh," says Kai.

I open my mouth, but she beats me to the punch. "Don't. Start. We're going in and that's final."

How can she not have a bad – no, the worst feeling about this? My teeth jar as the car rattles through the potholes. At the end of the road, we come to a chain link fence topped with a tangle of barbed wire. Bridie pulls up beside a small boxy caravan parked outside the gate. 'NO VACENCY' is written in faded red marker on a torn piece of cardboard taped to its rusty side.

The door springs open and a grizzled man in a stained white t-shirt pops out like the world's meanest Jack-in-the-box. He even bobs a bit as he thumps the sign and yells, "Get lost."

Bridie unrolls her window. "We're the Sparrows. Kingfisher is expecting us."

He spares us a suspicious squint before reluctantly exiting his box to jerk open the gate. "Keep going straight until you get to a fork in the road. Veer left. When you reach the end, you'll see some empty trailers. You're in the first one."

"Thank you. What's your name?" Bridie smiles pretty.

Is he blushing? It's hard to tell through the stubble he's scratching. "Everyone calls me Mac."

"Walk in peace, Mac."

He grunts, shrugs and heads back into his box.

Bridie rolls up her window. She gives me a sideways glance. "It never hurts to be friendly."

I roll my eyes. Bridie is always friendly, for all the good it does her or us.

She follows Mac-in-the-Box's directions, passing caravans parked in slots along the road. In the center, we come to a large common area with a fire pit, picnic tables and barbecue grills. Kids are romping around the playground. The women watching them turn and wave as we drive past. We wave back.

Back on the Crossroads, living among our people. Just what I wanted, but not like this.

She parks in front of a medium size caravan with a 'For Sale' sign tucked in its windshield. It's at least twenty years old, judging from its square shape, beige paint and orange and brown pinstripes. "Kingfisher refurbishes caravans and sells them. He said we can rent to own this one if we like."

"How are we going to pay the rent?" Kai asks as we climb out of the car.

"I'll find a way." Bridie reaches under the first wheel well, pulls out a key and unlocks the door. "This is nice."

The interior has definitely been updated with a stainless steel kitchen, refinished cabinets and new upholstery. It would be better if it looked worn-out and junky. How can we pay for this?

Bridie opens a door and gives a pleased little gasp. "The bathroom is in lovely condition. Plenty of towels." She returns to the kitchen and opens the cabinets, revealing an assortment of dinnerware. Her expression becomes less pleased. She clears her throat. "Well, it seems Kingfisher thought of everything. How nice."

Except that "everything" adds to the overall cost of the caravan and Kingfisher will want payment in full. We have to get out of here. Now. I chew my lip. I know she'll shoot me down, but I have to try. "Mum, what about a shelter, you know, like, for battered women."

"I'm not a battered woman." She slams her hands on the counter. I guess I hit a nerve. "Besides, those shelters are full to bursting and we're not U.S. citizens. You think they'll throw open the doors for us? I've had all I can take from you, Penny. Shut it."

I'm so tempted to walk out that door, but I can't leave Kai behind. I cross my arms tight to hold back my anger.

She turns to Kai. "Son, you can have the cabover. Penny and I will share the bedroom. Now, let's get unpacked."

It takes about an hour to sort through and put away our clothes. It's a typical caravan, meaning every available nook and cranny had some sort of drawer or cabinet. I bring in my sewing machine last, cradling it in my arms. When will I be able to sew again? I can't afford to buy fabric or even thrift store rags. Maybe I can get a job and use what's left after expenses.

Kai climbs the ladder to the space above the cab, rolls in, and yanks the curtains shut. A moment later, he pops out. "Someone's coming."

I go to the front of the cab and peer out the windshield. A huge black SUV with tinted windows bumps along the gravel road toward us.

"That must be Kingfisher." Bridie says this as if she's expecting him.

The last thing I want to do is go out and thank him. Bridie offers no choice. She opens the door and points out. My brother and I exchange wary glances before following our mother.

Kingfisher stands with his legs spread wide. He nods at each of us, like a screw counting inmates. "How are we doing here? All settled in?"

"We just arrived. I can't thank you enough for all your help." Bridie sounds breathless. Helpless. I want to scream.

"Think nothing of it. Having your lovely presence here is thanks enough. Perhaps you can join me for a drink tonight." The passenger door of the SUV opens. Kingfisher's smile disappears and he hollers, "Not yet, boy."

I gasp as Lennon climbs out, wearing a military pea coat instead of the camouflage hoodie. How can it be him? But it has to be with those silly glasses. "What are you doing here?"

He takes a step back and gapes at me.

"My goodness. Is that Lennon?" asks Bridie.

Kingfisher's frown deepens. "You know this boy?"

"I should say so. He's our hero."

He glances at Lennon with skeptical eyes. "Hero?"

"Some horrible boys at Penny's high school…" Bridie pauses and coughs. "Excuse me. Some horrible boys were bullying Penny. Lennon caught them at it and gave them a thrashing."

Kingfisher's stance widens. His voice lowers. "What do you mean, bullying?"

"You know, teasing her because of her accent, calling her names because she's foreign, that sort of thing."

"Told you not to put your kids in them Bleater schools. Waste of time."

Bridie turns to Lennon. "What are you doing here, darling?"

Kingfisher answers. "Seems the boy got himself into some trouble and John Walks Long asked me to plant him."

We all stare at Lennon, who remains silent and wary.

Bridie gives a dramatic gasp. "Is it those boys? Did they go to the police?" She's got a plan. I look at Lennon, willing him to understand.

He blinks. "Um, I'm not supposed to say."

"You don't have to. I'm beyond grateful that you came to our Penny's aid. We are beholden to you. The only way we can pay you back is to offer you shelter, here, with us."

I can almost forgive Bridie everything for that. Despite wanting to yelp for joy, I cast demure eyes at the ground.

"I don't know about that," says Kingfisher slowly. "Ain't proper, the girl's boyfriend staying with you."

Bridie waves a hand. "Oh dear, no. He isn't Penny's boyfriend. We know him through John Walks Long. We are obliged to him for defending her, especially since he now has to hide. It's a matter of honor. I'm sure you understand."

I bite my lip to keep from smiling. She can't use Charm on a fellow Strowler, but the strict code of the Glory Road is almost as good a weapon. Kingfisher knows it, too. I can see it in his shark eyes as he concedes defeat. "Just for a few days, until the coast is clear."

"He can stay with us as long as he needs." Bridie slides her arm across Lennon's shoulders. "Come along, darling."

"Hey, what about that drink?" Kingfisher calls out.

Bridie glances back without stopping. "Not tonight. I've got children to take care of. Tell Doreen I'll be glad to have a drink with the two of you another time."

His eyes narrow into slits.

We follow our mother and Lennon into the caravan. Bridie gives Kingfisher a cheery little wave before closing and locking the door. Kai clambers up the ladder to the cabover.

I want to hug Lennon and dance for joy. This horrible day has finally gotten a little better. "You don't know how happy I am to see you." That shy smile comes to his face and he ducks his head. "What happened? Why are you in trouble? Is it the *gardaí*?"

His brow crinkles. "The what?"

"*Gardaí*. The police."

"Oh. No. Something else."

"He's gone," Kai calls out.

Bridie exhales. "Good." She turns to Lennon. "I hope you don't mind the couch."

"It's great." He pauses. "It's way better than sleeping outside."

Her face scrunches with sympathy. "Why don't you settle in, though you don't have much, do you?"

Lennon holds up his backpack. "Just some clothes and my notebook and, um, some chalk."

"Chalk?" I ask. What does he need chalk for?

He shrugs.

"I'm sorry I had to downplay your heroism in front of Kingfisher," says Bridie. "If he knew what really happened, he'd send someone to do serious damage to those boys. Personally, I'd like to string them up by their manky bollucks."

Lennon's eyes widen. I don't think he needs a translation.

"But they're Bleaters and they'll call the *gardaí*, who'll come after the two of you." Her arms open wide. Lennon's face reddens with her embrace. "I can't thank you enough."

He clears his throat and stammers that it was nothing.

"Nothing? It was everything…" Her voice trails off as she reaches for her phone. It vibrates in her hand as she stares at the screen. She gnaws her lip and shoves it back in her pocket. Her voice comes out faint and distracted. "We've nothing to eat. I'm going to the grocery store. Settle in while I'm gone." She grabs her purse and hurries out the door.

"Mum?" I run after her.

Bridie won't look at me. She gets in the car and drives off without another word. The boys join me outside. Kai stares at the lingering dust.

"It's okay," I say softly.

"No, it's not," he snaps. He stomps back into the caravan and slams the door shut.

"What happened?" Lennon asks cautiously.

My sigh hurts my chest. "I guess Bridie got some sort of message, probably from either Bill or Kingfisher."

"You okay?"

"No. Want to take a walk?"

"Sure."

We stroll past the empty caravans and head into a small forest of leafy trees that surround the Nest. Birds hop and twitter among the branches. Dry twigs snap beneath our feet. It feels like another world. Lennon looks half-owl, half-boy with his solemn face, round glasses and shaggy, black-blond hair.

"What's with the chalk?" I ask.

"I draw pictures, you know, chalk art, to get spange – spare change."

"That's something we have in common, working for spare change."

One of his almost-smiles lifts his lips. "Yeah."

"I draw, too. Mostly ideas for clothes I want to sew."

"Like, a fashion designer?"

"Yeah." I swallow the ache in my throat.

After passing through the trees, we reach a rocky beach that overlooks the bay. An oily smell from the container yards wafts across the cove. We stop at the farthest point, just short of the waves lapping against the shore.

"What's with your mom and Kingfisher?"

The sun glares off his glasses, hiding his eyes, making it easier to say what I'm feeling. "It's weird. Bridie's the kind of person who hates asking for help, but always manages to put herself in the position of being dependent. Kingfisher wants her. She thinks she can handle the situation; hold him off. She can't. He's going to force her…" I look away. The words choke out. "Force her to become his convenience."

Lennon doesn't ask what that means, either. A few moments pass and I wonder if he's having second thoughts about staying with us. Then he reaches out and gives my hand a quick squeeze. "That won't happen, not while I'm around." He pauses. "Thing is, I'm being chased. I don't know how long I can stay. If they catch up with me, I'm going to have to run."

"Who are they?" I ask without thinking.

He surprises me by answering without hesitation. "My parents were murdered. The people who killed them are after me."

I'm not surprised. There are lots of orphans on the Crossroads. Still, my heart aches for him. No wonder he's always on edge. "Do they want to kill you, too?"

"No. My parents were…" His brow wrinkles, like he's searching for the right word. "Wealthy. The killers are my relatives. They want to get custody of me so they can control my parents' money."

That's different. Most people on the Crossroads die in some kind of fight or working a dangerous sham. He can't be with the Two Dragon Clan. He would have turned to them for help, not the Beggar Clan. There are plenty of Crossroads tribes out there. He must belong to one of the smaller, less powerful ones. I wish he'd say more. Maybe he'll open up if I share, too.

"I know how you feel." I breathe through a tight chest. "My father and Kai's father, they were murdered, too. That's how we wound up here." I pick up a rock and skim it across the water. It skips three times before sinking.

Lennon picks up a rock. "I'm sorry about your dads."

"I'm sorry about your parents."

"I can't talk about them." He flings the rock across the water.

"I know." I sit cross-legged on the warm sand and toss another stone. This one sinks without skipping. He hunkers down beside me. "Can you take off those glasses so I can talk to you?"

His shoulders hunch. Then he slides the glasses into his pocket. "You don't have to talk if you don't want to."

"No. I mean, I want to. It's hard to know where to begin." I stare at a rock formation out in the bay, craggy and eroded, too small for an island. How long before the wind and water wear it away? "My parents, Gerry and Bridie, they didn't like the conventional Strowler life. They left Ireland and moved to London to walk the Wayward Way. During the day, Gerry worked shams and Bridie told fortunes. At night, they'd either busk on the streets or perform in pubs. By the time they ran into Matthew, they'd already had me. And Gerry had confessed to Bridie that he was gay. Bridie and Matthew fell in love, but Gerry continued living with them, all of us in the same caravan. It caused a big scandal for the Glory Road people, but no one on the Wayward Way cared."

I hug my knees. "Gerry and Matthew didn't just sham Bleaters. They also did side jobs for Sharpers, Crossroads people, usually those on the Glory Road who don't want to get their hands dirty. One day, they were offered a lot of money to retrieve stolen property. I don't know what and Bridie claims she doesn't know, either. Something went wrong, and they were shot and killed. Since it was on the Crossroads, it was kept quiet, no police involved, and since Gerry and Matthew were outcasts, their clans didn't seek revenge."

I pick up another rock, slick and fuzzy with oil and moss. I drop it and rub my fingers on the sand. "That day, when they died, I felt like I'd lost everything. Then, when we left Ireland, I lost my identity. I didn't think I had anything more to lose, but I was wrong. Now, we're homeless."

Lennon listens with his head cocked and his brown eyes warm with concern. "Can your mom get a job?"

"She doesn't have a green card." I grab a fistful of sand. "Which is weird. She should have one by now. I'm pretty sure Bill's hiding it from her."

"What a tool."

"Yeah." I release the sand slowly so it makes a little pile.

Lennon picks up the mossy rock. This time his throw is half-hearted, barely making it into the water. "I know how you feel. I've lost everything. Everything. There's nothing left."

I reach over and squeeze his hand. He squeezes back. Neither of us let go.

Footsteps crunch behind us. Our hands drop away. I swivel around and see Kai ambling toward us. Lennon slides his glasses on as if by habit.

"Is Bridie back?" I ask.

"Nope." Kai plops down on the sand beside me and takes out his phone. "I'm gonna call my grandparents anyway. It doesn't hurt to ask."

That's where he's wrong. It can hurt a lot to ask for help from people you love, who you think love you back, only to be told to bugger off. I hope he's not about to learn this the hard way.

After a few moments, he takes the phone from his ear and scowls at it.

"What's wrong? They didn't answer? It's kind of late there, you know."

"No. The call's not going through."

"We're probably in a dead zone," says Lennon. "Let's go back to the camp."

When we reach the row of empty caravans, Kai tries again. "It's totally dead."

"Can you get online?" I ask.

"Nope." He taps the screen a few times. "I can still play Tetris."

"Good to know." Did Kingfisher put us in a part of the Nest that has no Internet or phone access? I shiver. In the distance, Bridie's car comes rolling down the gravel road. "Let's help Mum with the groceries. Then we'll try another part of the Nest."

Bridie climbs out of the car and leans against the door as we gather around her. "I've got some bad news and some good news." She takes a deep breath, not looking any of us in the eye. "Good news first. While I was at the grocery, I met a lady named Lily Lark, whose family has been nested here for a while. She works as a maid, cleaning apartments around the city and she needs a new partner. We're paid in cash and there's no paperwork involved. It's not exactly legal, so the wages are low, but it's money coming in." She manages a smile that quickly fades.

I lick my dry lips. "The bad news?"

"Just before I left, I got a very nasty text message from Bill. He said he's cutting off my credit card and our phones. He works fast. When I tried to pay for the groceries, my card wasn't accepted. Luckily, I had enough money in my bank account to cover everything. As for the phone..." Bridie reaches into her purse. I exchange looks with Kai and Lennon as she stares at her screen. "All right, then, no phones. Let's concentrate on keeping a roof over our heads and food on the table." Still not looking at any of us, she walks around the car and pops the boot. "Let's get these groceries unloaded."

I force my feet to move. My arms tremble as I grab a bag, though I barely notice its weight. No way to ask anyone to help us. We're exactly where Kingfisher wants us: trapped.

Two weeks have passed and still no sign of Tony. I know he hasn't given up, that he must be searching every square inch of the city and beyond. Does he even know about this place, or about Strowlers?

I've learned a lot about them. They're migratory. Only the Mother Bird and her husband, the Upright Man, stay in one place, running the Nest. They don't take part in local politics and pay minimal tribute to the Two Dragon Clan or whatever tribe rules their district.

Which leads me back to Tony. Eventually, he's going to find out about this place. I don't know what the deal is between John Walks Long and Kingfisher, but I know Kingfisher would sell me out in a hot second if given half a chance. I wish I had enough money so the Sparrows could buy this trailer. Then they could hit the road and me along with them.

"Lennon." Penny's whisper comes from outside the curtains. "Are you awake?"

"Yeah." I sit up on my forearms. I only spent a couple of nights on the kitchen bench. Then Kai offered to let me share the cabover with him, which is way more comfortable. The curtains part and my heart does a one-two punch at the sight of Penny's crinkle-nosed smile. I don't want to be Paul Lau. I want to be Lennon, a lost boy who ran away with the Gypsies.

"Bridie's home from work. You want to come down?"

"Sure." I roll across the mattress and settle on the edge of the cab, my legs dangling over the side. Kai sits at the table, playing a game on his phone.

The front door opens and Bridie enters wearing jeans and a Maid Brigade T-shirt. "Hello, darlings." She rustles a bag. "I got some lovely biscuits for tea."

Penny groans. "Mum, you've got to stop spending money on things like biscuits. We're skint."

"Stop being such a killjoy." Bridie collapses onto the bench that used to be my bed. "Be a dear and make us a cuppa. I'm knackered."

Penny goes to the sink and fills the kettle with water. She looks up at me. "How was your nap?"

I shrug, since staring at the ceiling while my mind churns doesn't constitute a nap.

She drops a PG Tips bag into a teapot before turning to her mother. "Lennon and I cleaned the Tern caravan today."

A tired smile lifts Bridie's lips. "Thank you, darlings."

"I collected a whole bunch of bottles and cans around the Nest," adds Kai, not looking up from the screen.

"Good. I'll take them to the recycler." She sighs. "You've all been so wonderful."

The kettle whistles. While Penny pours the boiling water into the teapot, I get the cups and place them on the table. Bridie tears open a package of McVities Digestive Biscuits and puts four on a plate. I don't know why they're called digestive biscuits, since they look like chocolate cookies. They were made in England and apparently cost more than regular cook-ies. What I do know is that the Sparrows always have tea before dinner, and from what Penny told me, it usually involves a lot more food.

Bridie's work-reddened hands wrap around her cup and she sighs before taking a sip. Penny reaches into her pocket and pulls out the three twenty dollar bills we'd earned. Bridie takes the money and puts it in her purse without a word. Then she closes her eyes and breathes in her tea.

Penny leans forward. "How are we doing?"

Her mother's eyes remain closed. "Let me worry about that."

"Will we have enough to pay the deposit and the rent?"

"Too early to tell."

Kai gobbles his biscuit and stares longingly at the other three.

"I'm not that hungry." Penny picks up hers and hands it to him.

"Me, neither." I reach for my biscuit, break it in two and give the other half to Penny. Her smile makes my half taste all the sweeter.

Bridie sniffles. A tear runs down her cheek. She wipes it away with the back of her hand. Kai rubs his nose. Penny sucks in her breath. I stare into the depths of my tea. If only I had access to my parents' bank account. I could make the Sparrows' troubles go away. Maybe if I ask Auntie Cat. She'd do it, I know she would, but if Head Elder found out, he'd ream her. And he'd find out about the Sparrows. I don't want him knowing about them. He'll give them shit for helping me and might even retaliate against Matthew's family. Might. Ha. Will. It's not fair. It's my money now. Mom and Dad would want me to help the Sparrows.

Guilt squeezes my chest. I still have cash from robbing tricks. When Tony catches up with me, I have to be ready to run, and I need money for that. To be fair, I've been working odd jobs around the Nest and giving everything I earn to

Bridie, but is that enough to pay my obligation to the Sparrows? Not even close. There has to be something else I can do.

Outside, a horn blares three times. We exchange wary glances. Bridie wipes her cheeks and brushes back her hair before she stands. "Let's go outside. I don't want him in here." She picks up her purse as she heads for the door.

Kingfisher leans against the hood of his black SUV. Some teenage kid stands beside him, tall and skinny, wearing a teal tracksuit and looking like an utter tool.

"Evening," Kingfisher calls out. For a second, I want to be the Dragon Son, so I can wipe the smug look off his face.

"Good evening." Bridie smiles brightly. "You brought your son. How nice."

"Mikey Boy's come from his boxing lesson. He'll be competing for the Silver Gloves this year. Coach says he's one of the toughest contenders he's ever seen."

Mikey Boy doesn't seem to be listening to his father's praises. He stares at Penny in this weird way, like he's checking her out, but not sure he likes what he sees. That's fine. I don't want him to like her. He probably prefers girls who giggle around him like he's hot shit, something Penny will never do.

"You ever do any boxing, boy?" Kingfisher asks me. I shake my head. "Too bad. You and Mikey could go a few rounds. See who's the better man." I shrug like I have no fucks to give. Kingfisher turns to Kai. "You had boxing lessons, right, boy?"

Kai lifts his chin. "Yeah. My Uncle Oisin is one of the top bare knuckle fighters in Ireland."

"Good lad. Maybe Mikey Boy can teach you some moves." He turns to Bridie. "Boy needs a father."

Bridie's smile becomes strained.

After a moment of silence, Kingfisher clears his throat. "You know why I'm here. You said you'd have the deposit today."

"Of course." Bridie opens her purse. As she counts out the

money, I realize it's all she has, except for a couple of dollars and some change.

Kingfisher shoves the cash into his pocket without counting. "Rent's due at the end of the week. I'll prorate it for how many days you've been here. Should come to $600, not including water and electricity. I'll connect you to the Wi-Fi for an extra $30 a month."

Bridie nods. Kai looks down. Penny's face drains of expression. My chest tightens.

"There's a party tomorrow night. Adults at the fire pit. Lots of food and drinks. The kids will have their own party at the Wren trailer. Pizza and pop, of course. Attendance ain't optional."

Bridie takes a deep breath. "Do you want us to perform?"

Kingfisher grins. "You and I can discuss your performance later." He motions with his thumb. "Get in the car, boy."

Mikey Boy spares a final glare at Penny before climbing into the SUV.

As soon as the car backs away, Penny swivels around to face her mother. "We've got to get out of here right now."

Bridie replies in a dull voice. "We can't. There's no money, the car's almost out of gas and I don't have any more cleaning jobs lined up until the weekend." She gives her head a little shake and her tone becomes firmer. "Besides, I don't know what you – or he – thinks is going to happen tomorrow. We'll go to the party, get some free food, and get on with our lives. I'll find a way to get enough money to pay the rent. I... I just need some time to think." She takes a shaky breath. "I'm going to start dinner." She goes into the trailer and closes the door behind her.

Penny leans against the metal siding, her arms folded tight. "There's no way we can earn that much money by Friday."

I lean beside her, my hands crammed into my pockets. If I can find a way to sneak back to the city, maybe into the Tenderloin or another bad area, I can try turning tricks again. All I have to do is avoid Payroll, and the Beggar Clan, and Tony, and the Two Dragon Clan. I bite my lip to keep from saying, "Shit."

"This is bullshit," Kai announces. "I'm gonna find a way to contact my grandparents. I'll tell them I won't take their help if they don't also help you and Mum." He stalks off down the gravel road.

Penny's arms rise and fall with her chest. "His grandparents hate our mother. They might agree to help me, but they won't help Bridie." Her family's starting to sound almost as bad as mine. Except the grandparents probably don't want to kill Bridie, but what do I know? Her eyes shine, but tears don't fall. "She's going to sell herself to him."

"What? No. She just said…"

"I know her. She'll talk herself into it, the same way she talked herself into marrying Bill, only this is so much worse. I can't let her do it. I have to stop her. Somehow." She shakes her head. "I don't know how."

"I'll help."

"You've already done so much." She gives a humorless laugh. "You're probably sorry you took up with us."

I tip my head back, resting it against the cold metal siding. Red clouds fill the darkening sky. "Living on the street, you lose your way. One day feels like the next and every day feels like a waste. Being with you, with your family, I feel like there's some point to my life again."

Penny leans her shoulder against mine. "Too bad we're facing east. It'd be nice to see the sunset."

We haven't kissed since the Beggars' Banquet. It's weird. We started out by crushing on each other. Now, we're more like friends or allies, but with this thing between us. Like right now, I want to kiss her, but I don't want to ruin the friendship.

The front door opens and Bridie holds out a tray. Without a

word, Penny takes it and places it in the small circle of stones beside the stairs, like she does every evening. It holds a saucer of milk and a piece of bread. When I asked, she shrugged and told me it's an offering for the fairies.

It's empty every morning, but I'm pretty sure that's because it's more like an offering for the raccoons.

"Do you really believe in fairies?" I ask as she leans beside me again.

"Sure, why not?"

"Does it help?"

"Not so far."

I almost tell her I used to believe in an imaginary dragon, but I can't without cluing her in to the Two Dragon Clan.

We wander to the shore without saying much. Penny throws rocks into the water with a soundless fury. I feel like a real shit, holding onto my cash. If we can't figure out something else by tomorrow morning, I'm giving it all to Bridie.

Eventually, Kai joins us, his hands shoved in his pockets. He stares at the water lapping the shore as he speaks. "I went to the playground and asked one of the kids if I could use his phone to email my grandparents. He was about to give it to me when his mom told him no. Then I asked another kid and her mom said no, too. They looked at me all funny. I think Kingfisher told people not to help us."

Penny snorts. "What a surprise."

He turns to face her. "Should I tell Mum?"

"Don't bother. She'll say it's your imagination. She doesn't want to face reality."

"There's gotta be a way to get online. Next time Mum drives somewhere, I'll go with her. See if I can get on someone's Wi-Fi."

"Good idea." She smiles and pats his arm, but when he faces the water again, her smile evaporates.

At least giving them the money won't make me feel so

goddam useless. If Tony shows and I've got to run, so be it. I can start again with nothing. Go back to being a thief and try not to think about how much that shames my parents.

We head back to the trailer. Penny helps her mother make dinner while Kai and I wash the dishes and set the table. It's a routine we've settled into. Sometimes I help peel and chop vegetables as well, though the food they eat is a mystery to me. Tonight it's something called 'bubble and squeak', which involves sausage, onions and leftover mashed potatoes. Actually, most of what they eat involves potatoes. Mom's attempts at cooking potatoes had never turned out so good. Bridie's potatoes, though, are tasty. Would Mom have liked Bridie? I have a feeling Mom wants to thank her for taking care of me. It makes my throat hurt. When we sit down to eat, I make sure to tell her how good everything is. Bridie smiles, but tension soon clouds her eyes once again. She barely eats and carefully scrapes everything on her plate into a container. Then she heads into the bedroom and closes the door. Kai retreats with his phone into the cabover, leaving Penny and me to flip through the few TV stations available with the trailer's antenna. A strong wind picks up, making reception bad except on one channel with nothing worth watching, so Penny goes to bed.

I turn off the lights and stare out the window, even though there's nothing much to see. There's no point in tossing and turning in the cabover. I haven't slept in two days. Insomnia is turning me into a zombie. I can't think straight. Thoughts and images scramble through my mind. Was running away really my best and only option? Sure, it kept me out of the clutches of Head Elder, but I'm no closer to gathering the evidence I need to accuse him, and my aunt and uncle, of murder. Do I really have to wait until I'm eighteen? What else can I do? No one will listen to me while I'm a powerless kid.

Outside, the wind howls and shakes the trailer as if trying

to keep me awake. I stand and stretch, rubbing my neck, sore from tension. The trailer's walls are closing in around me and I feel like I want to jump out of my skin. I grab my coat, open the door a crack and hold it tight against the wind as I slip outside.

Cold gusts slap my face, clearing some of the fuzz from my brain. Dark storm clouds gather overhead. Good. I'm tired of beating myself up. Let the weather do it instead.

Within the circle of stone, the milk and bread are gone. At least there's a happy trash panda out there somewhere.

I walk against the wind, past the trailers and through the wooded area to the little beach on the point. I perch on a thick log of bleached driftwood and stare at the dark sky above the choppy waters of the Bay. In the distance, I can see the blinking lights of planes taking off from San Francisco International Airport. Bet they're in for some turbulence.

A thick drop of rain splatters on top of my head. I pull up my hood. More thick drops fall, not enough to wet the ground before they stopped. Thunder rumbles in the distance. The possibility of lightning stirs my heart. If only Penny was here to watch it with me. If only we can talk. Maybe she could help me figure out what to do. Or maybe I could just lay my head in her lap and feel her fingers stroking my hair. Then I could sleep. I close my eyes. Sharp, sweet feelings move through my body, feelings forbidden toward someone from another clan. Such stupid shit. Why should I care? I like Penny. Maybe I even…

I suck in my breath. No, I can't love her. It's the wrong place, the wrong time – everything wrong. And yet, when I'm not thinking about my parents, I'm thinking about how to protect her and her family.

"What should I do?" My whisper comes out as a sigh.

Do as you should.

I almost fall off the log.

Jade Dragon?

No, it can't be. He doesn't exist. Yet the whisper echoes through my mind. I give a tight shrug. "What's that supposed to mean?"

You run, hide, cry. You don't act.

"Bullshit!" I snort. Okay, not Jade Dragon. It's my conscious bothering me. "What else am I supposed to do? I don't have any power. If they get me, they'll use me. Besides, not having me pisses them off, and I like pissing them off."

You have power. You don't use it.

I sigh. Maybe I should pretend it is Jade Dragon, just to get things off my chest. *You have power. You could have warned me. You could have warned Dad. Instead you let him and Mom die. Why should I listen to you?*

I warned you and your father. Kill the traitor. You did not listen.

Pain spreads across my chest. I jump to my feet and shake my fist. *You ordered me to kill my grandfather. You think that's easy?*

Thunder rumbles, much closer than before. *It was not meant to be easy.*

I grit my teeth. I need answers, not pointless bullshit. *Who killed my parents?*

Jade Dragon exhales. Steam blows from his snout. *I am not omnipotent. I cannot read minds. I know what I know and see what I see. I saw your grandfather plot to overthrow your father. I did not see who killed your parents.*

I saw my aunt kill my mother.

Will you kill her?

No. I can't. It's different than it was 500 years ago. Don't you get that? I need to prove they did it - that my grandfather ordered them to do it.

Did he?

Of course he did.

Will you kill him?

No. I just told you. I need proof and I can't get it. I don't have any power. I can't get justice.

Jade Dragon whips his tail. Shards of lightning illuminate the clouds. *Justice requires power. Power without wisdom is useless and you are not wise.*

My heart pounds with the ensuing thunder. *What should I do?*

Pay your obligation to the girl and return to your family.

No. I'm not going back to them. Weren't you listening? I don't have any power.

You have power. You fear it and will not use it.

Not anymore. I don't fear it. I want to use it.

Then do so.

A jagged bolt of lightning shoots down from the sky and strikes the beach. Electric heat thrums through my body. Power. I have power. I can do it. Thrusting my left hand toward a pile of driftwood across the beach, I breathe out the word, "Kaah."

Splinters fly as the wood breaks into pieces, scattering across the beach and into the water.

I suck in a gasp. The thrum of power dissolves, but doesn't leave me. I feel a weird mixture of weariness and exaltation. Gratitude fills me. Jade Dragon is real. He's going to help me after all.

A steady rain begins to fall. I lift my face so it cools my skin. I reach out to my ancestor. Jade Dragon is already distant. No longer over the bay, he soars toward the Pacific Ocean.

Wait. Don't go. I need you. You have to help me destroy them.

A sense of vague regret accompanies Jade Dragon's words. *The time of dragons is passed. We are few, always few, and now even less. The weapons of man can destroy us. Sky and water is where we belong. The choice was made. You are the Dragon Son. Use your power with wisdom, my hatchling.*

What do you mean choice? What choice?

Silence. Jade Dragon was gone.

The rain mingles with tears falling down my cheeks. I wipe both away. No more tears. No more sorrow. I have power and I'm going to use it.

A piece of paper blows against my ankle. I start to shake it off when I realize it's an envelope. It's damp and dirty, but that doesn't matter. I got the message. It's time to pay.

Bridie pads around the bedroom muttering, like she does when she's stressed out. She comes around to my side of the bed. Cold, gentle fingers sweep a lock of hair off my forehead and caress my cheek. My throat tightens, but I don't stir.

She closes the bedroom door with a soft click. After a few moments, the shower starts running. I sit up and rub my burning eyes. The storm woke me up in the middle of the night and I couldn't get back to sleep. "Oh, Bridie," I breathe out. How do you save someone from herself?

I open the drawer of my nightstand and take out the photo of Gerry and Matthew. Their eyes, which had once looked mischievous, now seem sharp and serious. Their voices whisper, *"You're strong, Penny. You can do it."*

"What can I do? I'm only sixteen."

Silence.

I shake my head. There are no voices. They left me alone to take care of the woman they loved. It's up to me to save the day, for their sakes.

Right?

I pinch the photo tight enough to bend the corner. They

made the choice to do something with fatal consequences, despite having had a wife and children who relied on them. They knew what Bridie was like and they went ahead and did it anyway. Did they really expect me to pick up the pieces?

Well, fuck them.

I drop the photo because if I don't, I'll wad it up and throw it across the room.

Wow.

Where did that come from? All this rage. I've kept it bottled up. I mean, I know it's been there, but I didn't realize how much is directed at Gerry and Matthew. I want to scream at the photo, "How could you do this to me?" even though I know. They were cocky rogues who thought they'd live forever. And I love them. I always will. But I can't do anything for them, not anymore. Whatever I do is for myself, and Bridie and Kai.

As soon as the shower stops, I hurry out so I can be first in line for the bathroom. The cabover curtain is closed, so the boys must still be asleep or playing possum so they don't have to get up and help with breakfast. Bridie opens the door, smiles and pats my cheek as we slide past each other.

Fifteen minutes later, when I step out of the bathroom, she's glaring daggers at me. "What is this?" She thrusts out a dirty envelope.

"Mum." I press my finger to my lips and nod toward the cabover.

Bridie lowers her voice to a harsh whisper. "What is this?"

"I don't know." I sit at the kitchen table and draw my knees to my chest. "Mail?"

"Don't be smart with me, madam."

"I'm not being smart. I don't know what you're talking about."

Kai pushes open the cabover curtains and yawns as he sticks his legs over the edge. He gives Bridie a bleary stare.

"What is this?" She waves the envelope at him.

Kai tries to grab the envelope and Bridie clutches it to her chest. He exchanges puzzled glances with me. "I dunno. What is it?"

"Money," Bridie spits out the word.

"Oh-kay." He slides down the ladder and sits across the table from me.

Her hands go to her hips. "Did you children go around the Nest, telling everyone we're skint?"

I roll my eyes. "Of course not. You think we don't know better than that?"

"Then where did this come from?"

"I don't know. Where'd you find it?"

"Someone shoved it through the mail slot during the night. No names, no note. Just money."

"Is there a lot of money?"

"It doesn't matter if there is. We're not going to spend it."

Lennon rolls into view, still tangled in his blanket. He rubs his eyes and asks, "What's wrong?"

Bridie holds out the envelope. "What do you know about this?"

He blinks and shakes his head.

She huffs. "As soon as I find out who put it there, I'm giving it back. Don't try to talk me out of it. And if I find out that any of you have been begging…" Her voice trails off as her expression became less certain. "Well, I'll be cross, but I'll forgive you." She takes a deep, shaky breath. "Enough of that. Let's make breakfast."

Lennon avoids eye contact with me as he heads to the bathroom. Interesting. Suspicious, even.

There's almost no talk as we go about our morning routine. Bridie stands at the stove in grim silence as she makes porridge. How's that going to taste when we can't afford milk and sugar anymore? And what about when we can't even afford oatmeal? I feel that rage rise up inside me. Bridie won't accept a bit of anonymous charity, but she will throw herself at the mercy of Kingfisher. If that's how she wants to live her life, whatever, but doesn't she realize that Kai and I are being dragged along?

We sit down to eat. The porridge goes down thick and forms a lump in my stomach. I push aside my bowl. "About the party tonight, I don't want to go. I'm going to stay here."

Kai pipes up, "Yeah, me neither. Me, too."

Lennon has gone owlish, peering solemnly at each of us from behind his glasses. He shifts in his seat before adding, "I guess I'll stay, too."

Bridie's grim expression doesn't change. "We are all going and that's final. We can't refuse Kingfisher's invitation, especially when we're living in his caravan." She stands and grabs my bowl along with her half-eaten porridge. "Outside. All of you. I need to straighten things up around here."

She turns her back to us while we file out. Her tense shoulders start to shake and her hand goes to her mouth. She starts sobbing as I shut the door. The sound breaks my heart, but barely takes the edge off my anger.

The boys trail after me as I head down the road toward the main part of the Nest. The ground is still wet. Not that we have much access to weather reports, but that storm came out of nowhere and seemed to leave just as suddenly. Too bad it hadn't stuck around and ruined Kingfisher's party plans.

Kai runs ahead and stomps on a puddle, sending a spray of mud everywhere. "Where do you think that money came from?"

"Gee, I wonder." I stop and turn so I block Lennon's path. Sunlight darkens his lens and I can't see his eyes. My hands go to my hips. "Any ideas?"

He shakes his head while looking down. I roll my eyes. He's a terrible liar. Then he speaks in a hesitant tone. "Um, why was your mom so mad?"

"Remember what I told you? She hates accepting help, but keeps putting herself in a position of being helpless. Getting money like that only made things worse. Now she's got to find a way to empower herself and she's going to convince herself the only way to do that is to become Kingfisher's convenience."

Kai stomps the puddle again, harder, splashing everything around us, including our clothes.

I spare him a glare. "Cut it out."

He stomps yet again, softer, so I let it pass.

Lennon looks up, solemn as an owl. "If I told her that envelope came from me, would that stop her?"

I shake my head. "Nope. She'll give it back to you."

"But I gave her the money I earned around here."

"That's different. Giving her twenty bucks here and there means you're helping out. Giving her a big lump sum means you don't think she can provide for us."

"She can't."

"That doesn't matter. She can't accept your money like that, especially if it's all you have. Is it?"

He nods.

Now we were getting somewhere. "How much was in the envelope?"

"Three hundred seventy-nine dollars."

Kai's mouth pops open. "Dude, where'd you get that much money?"

Lennon shrugs. For a moment I don't think he's going to answer. He toes at the mud. "I was sort of a hooker."

Kai's mouth becomes a gaping hole.

No. I can't have heard that right. "A… a what?"

"A hooker. You know, a prostitute, except I didn't do any of the prostitute stuff. I posed as one and when I'd get some place private with the guy, I'd rob him before anything happened."

My lips flap without sound. Kai seems frozen in place, his

feet stuck in the puddle. Quiet, heroic Lennon is a tag-rag, a thief. He crams his hands into his pockets and stalks down the road. Kai and I exchange glances before taking off after him. We catch up and stride along on either side of him. Grim-faced, he ignores us.

I grab hold of his arm. He's surprisingly muscular for someone so skinny. "Hey. You forgot something."

"Yeah, what?" At least he doesn't shake me off.

"Our dads were wide boys who shammed Bleaters. Not much different than what you did."

"I guess." His pace slows. "I was only trying to survive."

"We all do what we have to." I want to loop my arm through his so we can walk close together, but not with Kai there. My hand slides away. Did his fingers almost reach out for mine?

"Wide boys are the best," says Kai. "They're Sharpers who know what's what and how to survive on the street."

Lennon gives one of his fatal almost-smiles. "So, I'm a wide boy?"

I ignore my heart flip. "I'd say so."

He nods and some of the gloom falls off him.

"Okay, then, back to business. We need to cock up Kingfisher's plans. I figure they'll go to our caravan or his. Wherever they go, we'll walk in and stop them before, you know, it happens."

"Gross," Kai mutters.

"Kingfisher's gonna go ballistic," says Lennon

"Good. I want him vexed enough to kick us out. Then Bridie will be forced to use your money so we can go somewhere else."

Lennon rubs his chin like a proper wide boy, considering the next move in the game. "That could work. We better case his place and see how to get in."

Kai picks up his pace. "I know where Kingfisher lives."

Everyone knows where Kingfisher lives, but I don't bother saying so. We follow him up a row of caravans and around the fire pit until we reach a tree-shaded lot that contains a manufactured house with faded, pitted metal walls showing the wear and tear of bayside living. On the right side of the door is a small garden of carefully tended potted plants. To the left stretches a chest-high, chain link fence, divided into four separate kennels, each containing a dilapidated doghouse. Only one of the kennels contains a dog, a weary-looking Pit Bull with a stitched ear. It's common cackle that Kingfisher is part of a dogfighting ring. My stomach twists. How can Bridie even think of shagging someone like him?

As we get closer, the dog looks up, but doesn't have the energy or the desire for guard duty. Poor thing. Used and abused by that evil bastard. I'm half-way to opening the gate and letting it out, until I see the padlock. See our future if we don't stop Bridie. I might not be able to save the dog, but I will save us.

We duck behind the black SUV. A shrill woman's voice can be heard through the open kitchen window. "This is my home. You think I'm going to let that trull and her pack of brats move in here?"

Kingfisher's voice rises over hers. "This ain't your home. You ain't my wife."

"I'm the mother of your children."

"Don't matter. We ain't married. This is my Nest. You want to stay? You play by my rules. You cook, clean, mind the kids. I'm moving her trailer next door and I'll go there as I please."

"You can't walk all over me like that. I'm leaving."

"Fine by me."

"I'm taking the girls."

"No, you ain't. You want to leave, go. The girls stay. That's final."

"You go through with this, you'll be sorry. I'll make you sorry."

"How you going to do that?"

Doreen's answer is a choked sob. Then her voice regains strength. "I'm not going to that party and pretend I'm having a good time while you replace me. I'm staying here."

"Suit yourself."

We creep away. My chest aches. Poor Doreen. No wonder she's so bitter and this place is so messed up. Kingfisher wants to rule the roost. He doesn't want to share his power with a Mother Bird. I wish Bridie had been there. Does she think Kingfisher will treat her any differently? "Okay, we know they won't be going back to Kingfisher's house. That makes things a little easier. Let's check out the Wren place."

We make our way to a huge caravan parked at the edge of the woods. Two smaller caravans across the road block the view of the common area and the fire pit. We won't be able to keep an eye on Bridie from here. I motion the boys to follow me between the two caravans and across the grass to the playground, where we climb on the swings. Nearby, a group of women sit on the benches and watch their children romp around a huge, colorful plastic structure with tubes, climbing walls and slides.

"One of us could hide over there and have a good view of the fire pit," suggests Lennon.

He's right. As long as it's dark, it'll be easy to hide while still having a view of the party. "Except it might be noticed if one of us is missing from the party."

"We can take turns."

"Yeah, that could work. As long as no one is gone for too long." It's great having someone to bounce ideas off of, instead of just Kai, who's swinging back and forth, going higher with each swing. "Cut it out. We need to talk."

Kai's legs gallop beneath him as he hit the ground, slowing his momentum to a hover. "Yeah?"

"Here's what we're going to do. Lennon and I will take turns hiding in the playground and spying on Bridie and King-fisher. We'll trade places in short intervals, like twenty minutes, so no one is gone for too long. You keep track of time on your phone and cover for us when we're out trading places."

Kai pouts. "Why can't I spy on Bridie?"

"I just told you. We need you to keep track of time and cover for us. Besides, the only way we have to tell time is your phone. You want one of us holding onto it?"

"No way."

"All right then." I breathe out a little sigh, hoping he doesn't point out later that I can charge and use my own phone. The truth is I don't want him skulking around the play-ground, where anyone can wander by. He's not quite the wide boy he wants to be yet. I turn to Lennon. "Sound like a plan?"

He nods and a smile whisks across his face. "I like the way you think."

I duck my head so he won't see me blush. "Let's get back to our place. Bridie must be wondering where we are."

Back at the caravan, Bridie's car is gone. Kai runs to her parking space and kicks the gravel. "What the hell? I told her I want to go with her if she goes to the store."

Inside, there's no note. She never leaves without a note. What game is she playing? By the time I've worked up to a proper fret, her car comes rolling down the road. I try calming enough to seem uninterested, but as soon as she steps inside, I can't stop myself from saying, "Where were you?"

She holds up a bag and says in a breathless voice, "Lily told me there's a half-price sale on cold meats at Safeway and I wanted to get there before they run out."

Like that's going to happen.

Bridie places a couple of plastic packages in the fridge and heads for the bedroom, clutching her purse. Kai whines after her, complaining she was supposed to take him with. She shoos him away and closes the door. I stare after her, my arms folded.

"What's wrong," whispers Lennon.

I shake my head because I don't know. Maybe nothing.

Moments later, Bridie emerges. "What?"

"Oh," I do my best to look innocent. "I was just going to say, Lennon and I will make lunch."

Her tense frown becomes a weary smile as she sinks into a chair. "That would be very nice."

We dole out a single slice of meat and cheese per sandwich. Both taste like wax and I struggle to finish, even though I know there's nothing more to eat until dinner. While Kai does the dishes, I announce I have a headache and need to lie down.

Bridie's eyes go shifty as she takes a quick glance at the bedroom, but she doesn't say anything when I head down the hall. Inside, I close the door and creep around the room. Bridie usually keeps her purse on the shelf above the kitchen table. Maybe she wants to keep Lennon's money away from us. I hope that's what it is. I find it under her nightstand. Guilt flutters my chest as I poke inside. The envelope is there along with her wallet, phone, hairbrush, the usual. So everything's plummy, right? I want to believe that, so bad, but I can't shake the sick feeling in the pit of my stomach. Licking my dry lips, I slide open the nightstand drawer.

The box of condoms inside turns the pit into a chasm.

I slide the door closed before dissolving onto the bed in a puddle of tears and snot. My hand covers my sobs and I gasp for air between my fingers. I didn't cry when I first heard Gerry and Matthew had been killed, because I didn't believe it. My tears fell in an airplane loo somewhere above the Atlantic Ocean, when I had to accept they weren't coming back because they wouldn't have abandoned us to this fate.

After a while, I sit up and wipe away the gunk from my eyes and nose. Then I open the bedroom door. Bridie and Kai sit at the table, watching an episode of Friends. Or rather, Kai watches. Bridie stares out the window with a distracted expression.

I drink some water to clear my throat before asking, "Where's Lennon?"

Bridie blinks several times as she turns her head. "How's your headache, darling?"

The words grate on my nerves. I grit my teeth before managing to answer nicely. "Better. So where's Lennon?"

"He went out for some fresh air."

For a moment, I imagine going back into the bedroom, grabbing the condoms and throwing them in her face. Instead, I head out the door. Where has Lennon gone? Where else but the beach? I stride down the gravel road and weave through the woods. A loud noise stops me in my tracks. It sounds like wood cracking and breaking, but how can that be? I hurry through the woods and out to the beach.

Lennon stands close to the shore, holding out his hand and facing a pile of shattered driftwood.

"What are you doing?"

His arm drops as he spins around. His mouth gapes open before he says, "What?"

"What are you doing?"

"Um. Looking at the storm damage."

"Oh." The driftwood looks like it had been struck by lightning, but what was that noise? And why had he been holding out his hand? "Were you doing something?"

His face reddens. "Stomping on stuff."

I almost smile. Lennon seems so mature most of the time. It's easy to forget he's still a boy. Maybe he was venting some frustration. I wish he'd asked me to join him. I'd love to stomp on something right now.

"Are you okay?" he asks.

"No." I wait until he stands next to me, but then I can't look at him. Instead, I stare at the water. "Part of me wanted to believe Bridie, that she really wasn't going to lie down and become Kingfisher's convenience, but I found proof."

"What kind of proof?" Lennon's tone is cautious.

I shake my head.

"Sorry."

I shrug. "It doesn't change anything. Maybe she doesn't want to save herself, but she's not going to drag us down with her."

Lennon digs the tip of his shoe into the sand. "It's not that easy to make the right decision. I've made some pretty lousy ones."

"What do you mean?" I can face him now, but he looks away over the water. "You mean, like, when you were pretending to be a hooker and robbing people?"

"Yeah, that, and other stuff." He shakes his head. "I'm not wise."

"You're fifteen. Are you supposed to be wise?"

He takes off his glasses and wipes his face before turning to me. Those gorgeous brown eyes, so seldom seen, quicken my heart. "I'm gonna be sixteen next week."

I want to say we should celebrate, but the ache in the eyes stops me.

"I've made some big mistakes. I shouldn't have run away. I've got to go back."

My throat tightens, making my voice squeak. "Go back? When? I mean… now?"

"No." He shakes his head. "I'm not leaving until we get your family out of here."

I realize I'm shaking. I can't stand the thought of being

alone, even after we escape from this hellhole. "You know you can come with us."

"I know, but I can't. I have to find out who killed my parents. I need justice."

Justice. The word makes my mouth dry and bitter, maybe because I thirst for it so deeply and don't know if I'll ever taste it. One thing I do know is that I can't deny it to Lennon. All I could think to say is, "Be careful."

I start to turn away. He catches hold of my hand. A little tug is all that's needed to move closer, press against him, and wrap my arms around his neck. His arms slide around my waist. Our lips meet. The hesitant touch of his tongue makes me draw away, just a little. What if I never have a chance to kiss him again? My lips part. His tongue twines with mine. Fire sings through my veins. I don't want to stop.

He's leaving. He's leaving. The words echo in my mind, faint at first before becoming louder. My hands move to his shoulders and I step away, holding him at arm's length before letting go. He's breathless and his eyes are unfocused. Part of me is pleased, knowing that he wants me. If I let him have me, he'll stay…

I mentally slap myself. Just the sort of thing Bridie would think. I am not going to be her. I take another step back. "We shouldn't kiss like that, not if you're going to leave."

Lennon fumbles with his glasses before sliding them back up his nose. "I know. I'm sorry."

Me, too.

We head back through the woods, side by side, not touching, and me wondering if I'm one of his big mistakes.

Penny

"I can't decide. You choose." Bridie holds up two mini dresses.

Back in London, I would have loved making that choice. Bridie would have been stepping out with her lads, all of them dressed in rum riggings. Now, the sparkly, stretch satin fabric, meant to hug every curve, makes me feel ill.

"Neither."

Bridie huffs with frustration and tosses the dresses onto the bed beside me. Then she turns to the mirror and begins applying her blush with angry strokes of the brush. "I don't need this attitude. Things are hard enough."

No kidding. I grit my teeth to keep from saying the words aloud. Nothing motivates Bridie so much as opposition. If I want her to reject Kingfisher, I have to appeal to her motherly instincts. "I don't want to go to that stupid party. Mikey Boy's going to be there. He gives me the creeps."

For a moment, Bridie looks uncertain. Then she shakes it off. "Don't worry about him. You'll be with your brother and Lennon. He won't bother you with them around. If he does, come get me."

I grab fistfuls of bedspread to contain my anger. It's like

Kevin Anderson all over again. "You don't get it. I don't like him and I don't want to be anywhere near him."

"Well, it can't be helped." Bridie reaches for the shortest and tightest of the dresses. It's ice blue and trimmed with silver and pink flowers, and barely covers her bum after she tugs it on. "Give us a zip."

I zip up the back and tug on the hem. For an instant, it sits at mid-thigh before riding back up to near indecency.

Bridie pretends not to notice. She turns to the mirror to apply a thick layer of red lipstick. Then she puckers her lips as if blowing a kiss before addressing my reflection. "We've been over this. You have to go. We all do. We don't have a choice. Besides, you and the boys need to get out of this stuffy trailer for a while. Have some pizza and watch a couple of movies, and I'll…" She looks down as if unable to meet my gaze. "I'll come get you when the adult party is over."

My stomach twists. There's no avoiding it. All I can do now is deflect my mother's suspicions. I manage a reluctant smile. "I guess I wouldn't mind having some pizza."

"That's my girl." Bridie ties a silver and white shawl around her shoulders. Doubt flickers across her reflection and she teeters for a moment on her strappy, three-inch silver heels. Then she gives herself a hard stare and her face seems to age ten years. She turns away and speaks over her shoulder. "Now get dressed."

After the bedroom door closes, I pull out a plain black jersey dress with cap sleeves and a hem that falls to just above the knees. I reach for my white trainers before realizing they'll glow in the dark. Instead, I tug on my flat-heeled, black leather boots. Then I grab my black hoodie and head for the kitchen.

Bridie rolls her eyes at the sight of me. Then she looks at Kai and Lennon, who are both wearing dark T-shirts and jeans, and black beanies. Her hands go to her hips. "You lot look like a canting crew going on the dub."

Lennon's face goes blank. "What?"

"She said we look like gangsters." I cross my arms and tilt my chin. "I'm not putting on rum riggings to hang out with a bunch of people I don't know."

Bridie waves an impatient hand. "Fine. Suit yourself. Let's go." She turns away and opens the door.

Outside, the setting sun has turned the scudding clouds bright pink and blood red. Bridie allows Kai to lead the way down the path to the Wren caravan. Canned music and live singing pour out the open windows. I wince. I don't usually mind karaoke, but not tonight.

"Sounds like they're having fun in there," Bridie remarks brightly. No one replies. A shadow of hesitation crosses her face, quickly replaced by determination as she struts away.

Mrs. Wren, a plump, middle-aged woman with a warm smile, greets us at the door. She ushers us into one of the largest caravans I've ever seen. Her husband, bald, jolly Mr. Grosbeak, stands in the kitchen, handing out slices of pizza and cans of soda while calling out encouragement to the kids in the living area playing Rock On on the game console. After getting our food, we slip past the players, who stare at the TV screen intently as they work their fake musical instruments. Other kids are hanging around the kitchen table or lounging on the couch while they wait for their turn to play.

All the girls, even the youngest ones, are wearing sparkly party dresses while the boys are dressed in trousers and designer T-shirts. Aside from a few appraising glances, no one pays much attention to us as we make our way to the darkened back bedroom and squeeze into a corner next to a window. Kids sit on the bed or the floor, their eyes glued to the first *Pirates of the Caribbean* movie on the widescreen TV. At least Mikey Boy is nowhere in sight. Maybe he's nicked some beer from the adult party and gone into the woods to party with his friends.

Lennon glances at Johnny Depp before asking, "Any relation?"

It takes me a moment. Then I grin and shove his arm. "Lol. No. Back then, Strowlers didn't have surnames, not until the 20th century. We traveled in caravans, mostly with extended family, and called the caravans by bird names. When the officials forced us to use surnames, we used our caravan names." A sad feeling washes over me. I've been to plenty of parties like this before. Under any other circumstances, I'd be happy to sit on the bed and eat pizza, and watch the adventures of my non-relative, Captain Jack Sparrow. Instead, I'm hoping to flee this place and our people before the end of the night. It sucks and I let myself have a momentary pity party before getting back to business. I turn to Kai. "Got your phone?"

He rolls his eyes. "No, I forgot it." He pulls it from his pocket and shows it to me. "I got the alarm set for twenty minutes."

"Good. I'll go first. If..." I pause. I can't say 'when.' "If anything happens with Bridie and Kingfisher, I'll come back here and knock on this window. Then you two come out and meet me, and we'll go stop them. Okay?"

They nod. As I brush past them, Lennon catches hold of my arm. I stop. His fingers quickly slide away. He speaks in a hushed tone, his eyes hidden by dark lenses. "Be careful."

I shrug and continue on my way, though my heart is pounding. I can't think about it, that he cares about me, that I care about him, so much, and soon it won't matter because he'll be gone.

In the living area, Mr. Grosbeak has taken over on the guitar while his wife sorts through the pizza boxes. I saunter by with an excuse ready on my lips, but neither seems to notice as I slip out the door.

The sky has grown darker during the short time in the trailer.

The chill in the air has sharpened. I zip up my jacket and tug on the hood as I creep between the trailers. Then I head across the playground, sticking close to the shelter of the play set. I perch on the bottom of a slide and draw my knees to my chest.

The adult party doesn't look much different than the kids' party. The women all wear colorful, sparkly dresses and the men, trousers and dress shirts. Bridie stands close to the glow of the fire pit, talking to her fellow maid, Lily, and another woman. A man approaches them, carrying four bottles of beer. He hands them out before wrapping his arm across Lily's shoulder. The four of them clink bottles and drink before they continue chatting. Bridie seems happy and relaxed, though she's taking long pulls off her beer.

I slide up the slick plastic surface. After craning my neck, I spot Kingfisher at one of the grills on the other side of the fire pit. He's using tongs to turn some kind of meat. A group of men surround him, all talking and drinking beer.

Everything looks so ordinary, boring, even. I slide back down to a perch and rub my cold nose. Maybe I was wrong. Maybe those condoms had been in the drawer before we'd moved in and Bridie hadn't bothered to throw them out. Hope beats hard and painful in my chest. If only that was true, I could head back to the kids' party, but I can't let myself believe it. I stay put.

After what seems more like an hour, Lennon shows up. He's taken off his glasses, probably so he can see better in the dark. As he takes my place on the slide, he whispers, "Anything going on?"

"Not really," I whisper back. "How about there?"

"First movie ended. They're showing *Dead Man's Chest* now."

"Seen it."

We share a quick, faint smile. Then I head back to the caravan. I tug off the hood and unzip the jacket before going inside.

Though my stomach is in knots, the smell of pizza makes my mouth water. I eat the piece I'd left behind in the bedroom and get myself another. By the time I finish that, the twenty minutes are up. Mrs. Wren now sits on the bed, a girlish glow on her face whenever Johnny Depp shows up. Mr. Grosbeak mans the Rock On drum kit and has his eyes fixed on the screen as I slip out the door.

When I get to the slide, Lennon points out Bridie and her friends sitting at a picnic table, eating and drinking. Kingfisher remains at the barbecue grill. That didn't change from the time Lennon left and came back. As we exchange places again, the adults finish eating, but keep drinking. Their voices are getting louder.

When I return to the caravan, I find Kai playing a game on his phone. "What are you doing? You're supposed to be keeping time."

Kai rolls his eyes, his thumbs still tapping the screen. "I set the alarm. It'll vibrate. I can't miss it."

I cross my arms. "I need you to take this seriously."

He looks up, his thumbs sliding away. "I am taking it seriously. I'm bored." He nods toward the TV. "I've seen this movie, like, a million times."

"Whatever. I'm going to use the loo." I go out to the hall and find the toilet door locked. With a gusting sigh, I lean against the wall to wait. Tension and lack of sleep are exhausting me. Maybe I should drink another soda, but then I'll have to pee again.

The front door swings open. Mikey Boy saunters in, followed by his crew. I edge against the wall into a shadow, but he doesn't seem to notice me or anyone. He and his friends double over against the kitchen counters, clutching their sides as if attacked by a case of the giggles. Are they drunk? One of them lifts the lid on a pizza box and they grab at the slices as if starved. Okay, stoned. With any luck, Mikey Boy will be too buzzed to notice me.

After I use the loo, I rejoin my brother in the bedroom. "Mikey Boy's here."

Kai doesn't look up from his game. He snorts. "Is he wearing his silver gloves?"

"No. I think he's stoned."

"Yeah?" He snorts again. "Tool." His phone vibrates. He holds up his screen, which blinks with red zeroes. "See? I told you I set the alarm."

I hesitate. I'll have to walk past Mikey Boy and his crew, but what choice do I have?

They're still in the kitchen, devouring the pizza and swilling down sodas. As I squeeze by, the strong, skunky stench of weed makes my nose twitch. Mikey Boy stares at me with bleary eyes as he gingerly touches a purple and black bruise on his chin. Then he points at me with a bobbing finger. "That's Penny. She can dance."

The other kids stare at me for a blank moment before another fit of giggles has them choking on their food. I roll my eyes. Whatever. I step outside and close the door. After walking across the path between the trailers, I look back. The door remains shut. Looks like Mikey Boy prefers pizza and weed to pestering me and that's a good thing.

The faint sound of live guitars playing flamenco music grows louder as I approach the playground. When I reach the slide, I see a group of musicians standing by the fire pit, strumming away as couples dance in the clearing between the barbecue grills and the picnic tables. Bridie remains at the same table, by herself now, while her friends dance.

"Anything?" I whisper to Lennon.

He shrugs. "They all seem more drunk. That's about it."

My stomach tenses. "This could be it. Stay by that window."

Lennon gives a single nod. As he turns away, I grab his arm. I feel him tense under my hand and I let go. "Mikey Boy and a bunch of his friends showed up. They're stoned."

"Want me to stay here with you?" The concern in his voice sends a wave of warmth through me. I wish I could touch his arm again.

"No. If we're both gone too long, people might notice, and I don't want Kai there by himself."

"Don't stick around if he shows up."

"I won't. He's the last person I want to see." I pause. "Well, second-to-last."

The dim light shines off Lennon's brief, white-toothed grin. Then he takes off across the playground.

I tug up my hood as I settle on the slide. The musicians end their tune with a flourish of energetic strums. Then they reach for their drinks from a nearby table and stand in a semi-circle, talking as one of them replaces a guitar string. Kingfisher walks around the fire pit, carrying two beers. He goes straight to Bridie and hands her one.

I jump to my feet. Is this it? Should I go get the boys now? Then Bridie's friends return, laughing and swaying. Kingfisher strolls away. I exhale. My arms fold tight as a cold wind gusts across the playground. This could go on for hours. Maybe next time, I'll sneak out a cup of hot tea.

"You spying or something?"

I spin around. Mikey Boy is ambling toward me, his hands shoved in the pockets of his red and white leather baseball jacket. I back away from the slide and into the clearing so I have room to run. "None of your damn business."

He stops about five feet away. "You watching my dad and your ma?"

I don't bother answering.

Mikey Boy glances toward the fire pit for a moment. Even in the darkness, I can see the bitterness on his face as he looks again at me. "He wants to replace Doreen with your mom. I can't stand Doreen, she keeps trying to be my mom and she's not."

I want to leave, but he might say something I need to hear. The wind picks up again. He weaves in its wake. After a moment of silence, his voice gains heat. "My ma died a while back. Drunk driving. Him, not her, but he covered it up. Made it look like her. I. Fucking. Hate. Him." He kicks up a foot full of sand.

I step sideways to avoid the gritty spray while fighting an impulse to run.

"He's the reason I can't read. He never let me go to school. How am I supposed to be a prize fighter if I can't read a contract?" Another kick. "Fucking hate him. It's his fault you all wound up here."

"What?" I take a step forward. "What do you mean? His fault how?"

He opens his mouth as if he's about to answer and then starts vigorously scratching his head. What the hell? Does he have lice? I really want to leave, but I want to know what he's talking about.

The energetic strum of guitars makes me swivel toward the common area. Firelight flickered off the grinning faces of the musicians. Having everyone's attention, they now slow the tempo to a romantic ballad. I suck in my breath as Kingfisher approaches Bridie. He holds out his hand. Bridie sets down her beer. Her hands twist in her lap before she reaches out to him. His arm wraps around her waist, holding her close as they begin to sway in time to the music.

"He wants us to handfast," says Mikey Boy.

"What?" I reluctantly turn to him again.

"He wants us to handfast. Then he'll give me my own

trailer. We'll get married when we're old enough, provided that Chinese kid hasn't gotten in your pants. If you ain't a virgin, you'll be my convenience."

My mouth drops open. I blink hard. Kingfisher isn't only after Bridie; he's after me, trying to trap me in his Nest by making me sleep with his loser son. I give an incredulous laugh before anger heats my words. "Sod off."

He shrugs. "Hey, it's not my idea. I don't want to handfast with anyone. Soon as I get a manager, I'm gonna get the hell outta here, and I don't want no wife along."

"Why are you telling all this?"

He fingers his bruised chin. "Anytime I don't agree with him, or he just feels mean, he lets me have it."

I cross my arms, squeezing at the pity that fills my chest. I can't afford to feel sympathy. "Well, I'm not going to handfast with you, so don't worry about that. What did you mean it's his fault we wound up here?"

His voice becomes cautious. "He's got a way of making things go his way."

"What does that mean?"

"Nothing." He jerks his head. "Come on, I'll walk you back."

"You go back. I'm good here."

"You waiting for that Chinese kid? My dad's got plans to get rid of him."

Fear weakens my knees, though this is no surprise. We have to fly the Nest tonight. "Get rid of him? How?"

He crooks his index finger and beckons to me. "Be a little nicer to me and maybe I'll tell you."

Any reply I can think of will only make him mad, and I want him to get lost. I give a prim huff and turn away. Then I freeze. Bridie and Kingfisher aren't among the dancing couples.

I hurry across the grass, craning my neck as I search the

common area. They're gone. I turn back to the playground. Mikey Boy stares at me as if awaiting my return. If I go back to the Wren caravan, he'll follow me and get in the way. Kai and Lennon will help me, but what if we have a run-in with his crew? He'll have no trouble stalling and even stopping us.

Just standing here is wasting valuable time. Lennon will be back soon. When he sees I'm gone, he'll come after me.

I run to the fire pit and weave in and out of the dancing couples who are too drunk to pay me any mind. I duck behind the musicians and look around. No sign of Mikey Boy. My sigh of relief is short and burns in my chest. I wipe my damp palms on my legs and dart down the dark road in the direction of our caravan.

Lennon

Jack Sparrow screams and flails his arms like a cartoon character while being chased through a jungle by an angry mob. Kids lounge around the room laughing and talking over the already blasting television speakers. I lean against the window, pressing my ear to the screen so I can hear any noise coming from outside.

Kai nudges me. "Hey, Lennon, look." He holds out his phone.

I pull away from the window, ready to leave. "What?"

"I got a message."

I'm about to say, 'so what?' when it hits me. "Your phone works?"

"I guess." Kai taps the message icon. "It's from Jose. Guy at my school. It says, 'Dude, where you been? Is this why you're MIA?' There's a video link." His eyes narrow. "This better not be a Rick Roll."

He taps the link. A video appears, titled, 'Neighbor Kicks Out His Wife and Kids.' It's grainy, shaky and dark, but I can see it's the Sparrows being chased around and yelled at by some angry, middle-aged bald guy. Must be Bridie's husband - what's his name? Bill?

"What the fuck?" Kai rewinds the video a few frames. We watch as Kai turns his back to go into the garage. Bill slaps Bridie across the face. She clamps her hand over her mouth in an obvious attempt to keep from crying out. When Kai and Penny come back into frame, she ducks her head to hide her distress. "That. Fucker." Kai whispers.

A few moments later, Bill shoves Bridie and she has to hold back her kids from attacking him. Man, I wish he were here right now. I'd give him a shove he'd remember.

The video ends. Kai stares at the screen like he's been punched in the gut. "Aw, man. It's got over a thousand views."

I wince. "That sucks." Bill deserves the bad publicity, but not Penny and her family. Unless it works in their favor. "Hey, you know, it's probably no coincidence that that video's got a bunch of views and suddenly your phone starts working."

Kai's mouth twists in a satisfied sneer. "Yeah. Maybe Bill's got in trouble with the cops." Then his eyes light up. "Hey, I can call my grandparents. I'm gonna do it right now." He grimaces at the TV. "It's too loud in here. I'll go to the loo."

"Tell me when the timer goes off."

"Yeah, yeah. We got more than ten minutes to go."

I wait by the window for what feels like a lot longer than that. I'm about to go pound on the bathroom door when Kai makes his way into the room, still holding the phone to his ear. He waves. I nod back and head for the front door. Mikey Boy's crew are still in the kitchen, horsing around, throwing dirty napkins at each other, but where's Mr. Silver Gloves? A bad feeling in my chest makes me push past them to head out the door. I run to the playground. My stomach drops when I reach the empty slide.

"Penny," I call out in a loud whisper. Only the swings answer, squeaking and creaking as they sway in the wind. My heart starts pounding. Could Mikey Boy have come out here and done something to her? I look over at the common area. Bridie and Kingfisher are both gone. Maybe Penny's behind the trailer trying to get my attention. I breathe a little easier. That sounds right. Unless… damn. Did she go after Bridie and Kingfisher on her own? Why would she do that? She has to be somewhere nearby. Hopefully, we won't waste more time passing each other in the dark. I sprint back to the Wren trailer.

I smell him before I see him. Mikey Boy is sitting on the steps, sucking in some weed. Smoke sputters from his lips as he laughs. "You looking for your girlfriend?"

I clench my fists to keep from grabbing him in a chokehold. "Where is she?"

"Out back, looking for you, I guess." He grins. "Don't do anything I wouldn't do."

"Fuck off."

I run around the back of the RV. Nearby trees cast a deep gloom over the metal hull. I stop and listen. Wind rustles through the leaves, making the branches creak. A chill shudders through me. Something tells me not to say Penny's name. From the open windows, the score of *Dead Man's Chest* blares in cacophony with Bon Jovi's *Wanted Dead or Alive* coming from the Rock On crowd. Is Penny in the trailer? No. Somehow I can tell, as if I can sense her presence.

I take a deep breath, focusing my *chi*, stilling my body to sharpen my hearing. Other sounds come to the forefront, different, distinct voices, none of them Penny's. Should I bother questioning that loser again or go back to the playground? Then I hear another sound – footsteps, so faint I shouldn't be able to hear them, wouldn't be able to if I wasn't concentrating.

The Silent Step.

I spin around in time to see Tony bearing down on me. With Swift Steps, I skid backwards, leaving Tony grasping at air. As I turn to run, two black-clad men drop from the trees, landing on either side of me. They grab hold of me, twisting my arms in a painful lock that will dislocate my shoulders if I try breaking away.

Memories of being captured by Payroll's men send a rush of fear adrenaline through me. No, I won't be a victim. Not ever again. I have to get free. I can't let Penny down. Despite myself, I struggle. Hot, sharp pain shoots from my elbows to my shoulders. I grit my teeth to keep from crying out.

Tony approaches. His pale face glows in the dark. His mouth looks like a slash of disappointment. Why does he always have to get in the way?

"Little Brother."

The words make me want to spit.

"You have a choice." Tony speaks in his usual calm, cold, infuriating way. "You can walk out of here with us, or, if you continue to struggle, I'll use *dim mak* and we'll carry you out."

I don't want my pressure points frozen, but I'm not about to walk away like a lamb to the slaughter. I swallow and manage to speak, calm and cold as my cousin. "Let me go."

"Only if I have your word you'll come with us."

It's so tempting to agree, but even on the Wayward Way, I can't go back on my word. "Why should I go with you? You'll just turn me over to that murderer."

Tony sucks in his breath. "Little Brother…"

"No. Not Little Brother, not Paul, not Dragon Son. I'm none of those things. I reject you. I reject my clan. You murdered my parents." I aim all my anger and frustration at him, even though a voice in the back of my head says, *Don't. He's innocent.*

Tony looks as if he's been slapped across the face. Anger flares in his eyes. "You don't know what you're saying."

"I know your parents did Head Elder's dirty work. I know my ticket to Hong Kong was one way and he was going to keep me prisoner while he rules the clan. Screw him and screw you. Screw you all. I'm not doing what you want. Murderers."

Paul, don't do this. We're brothers. We swore an oath.

Pain jabs at my chest that has nothing to do with the two men holding me. Tony is my brother. This is the exact opposite of what Dad wanted for us, but Tony is blinded by his loyalty to the clan. And can I blame him for not wanting to believe his parents are capable of murder?

I'm sorry. I know it's not your fault.

Something flickers in Tony's eyes. Hope. I feel like a shit, but I have to exploit it. I need to stall for time. I take a deep breath as if trying to calm down. "How did you find me?"

"The head Gypsy, Kingfisher, told me you were here. He said someone paid him to take you in. He wouldn't say who, but I already know. John Walks Long. I traced you to the Beggar Clan before you disappeared again. The Beggar Chief denies it, but I know. Kingfisher said you were making trouble and he wants you out of here. He said his son would lure you to the back of this trailer during the party."

So that's why that loser was hanging around outside. And I walked right into it. I sag as if disgusted with myself. The guards loosen their grip as I drop. I start to twist and their hands become iron clamps.

Tony's expression becomes resigned. "Hold him still. I don't want to hurt him."

I gulp in air to calm my pounding heart. Do I need to raise my left arm? Didn't Jade Dragon fill me with power? Despite my denials, I'm still the Dragon Son. I can focus that power. This won't be like last time. I'm not helpless anymore.

Tony raises his hand, his index and middle fingers poised to jab my pressure points.

I concentrate on Jade Dragon's energy flowing through me. It's enough, more than enough. Too much. I have to focus, channel the power to push, but not destroy. I open my mouth and breathe out the word, "Kaah."

Tony flies backwards, slams into a tree and drops to the ground.

The men let go of me and run to him. They kneel beside him and carefully turn him over. He doesn't move.

My limbs weaken as the thrum of energy drains out of me. My stomach twists enough to make me want to double over. What have I done? Have I killed my brother?

Ancestor, help me. Don't let him be dead.

No answer, not even a gust of wind.

My legs shake as I force myself to walk to where my brother lies. The men glare up at me. The sick feeling in my throat makes me unable to speak. As my mouth works around words I can't say, Tony sits up.

I grab hold of a tree branch to keep from falling to my knees.

Tony shakes his head and flexes his arms as if testing their strength. Then he looks up at me with that thousand-mile stare. "You've mastered the Dragon Shout."

I nod. Then I lick my dry lips. "You okay?"

Tony stands without the aid of his men.

Energy returns to my limbs as I back away. I won't use the Dragon Shout again, can't risk hurting my brother. I'd rather run.

Tony makes no move to pursue me. Instead, he speaks in a quiet voice. "My mother has cancer."

I blink. "What?"

"My mother has pancreatic cancer. It's inoperable."

Is this a trick? No, Tony wouldn't lie about something like that.

"While we were in Hong Kong, she went to see a doctor about abdominal pain. It's been troubling her for a long time, but she kept ignoring it. She got the diagnosis right before we came home. She waited too long. It's inoperable. She's dying."

I rub my brow. "Why are you telling me this?"

"You said she killed your mother. Why would she do that if she knew she was dying of cancer?"

I shake my head. It doesn't matter. There has to be a reason.

"I know you think you saw my mother kill your mother. But have you asked yourself why?"

"A million times."

"Do you have an answer?"

"What about my father? Do you really think your father had nothing to do with his death?"

Tony's expression goes bleak. "No. I think he did." He takes a breath. "Paul, I loved your parents. If I thought my mother had harmed your mother, I wouldn't turn a blind eye. I know my mother never liked your mother, but why would she kill her?"

I whisper, "I know what I saw."

"You have to come home. You can run, but I won't stop, either. Why don't we end this now?"

I look over my shoulder. The longer I stand here, the worse it could be for Penny. If I go to her, Tony will definitely catch up, but I can't abandon her. I take a deep breath.

"If you leave this place without me and give me your word you won't have me followed, I'll meet you at Auntie Cat's place in a couple of hours. I give you my word as a *Xia*."

We stare each other in the eye. Tony nods once. I nod back. Then I turn and sprint toward the playground. If Penny's still not there, then she must have gone after her mother and King-fisher on her own. I hope I'm not too late, because if I am, I'll hate myself and Tony forever.

Penny

The caravan is dark, except for a single light shining through the back bedroom window. My teeth grit painfully. Does Bridie really expect me to sleep there after she and Kingfisher rut? Sanitizing the sheets in boiling water and bleach won't wash away the facts. My eyes narrow. Fact is, I won't be sleeping there or anywhere in this Nest ever again. I creep up to the front door and give the handle a cautious twist. Locked. As if that will stop me. I pull the spare key from my pocket.

The click of the lock is loud enough to make my mouth go dry. Maybe I should go back and try finding Lennon and Kai, but it could be too late by then. Once the deed is done, Bridie will stay and try to make the best of it, the same as she had with Bill. Sweat pools in my armpits despite the cold. A strong gust of wind shakes the caravan. I open the door quickly, using the sound to cover the creak of the hinges. The wind blows stronger and almost rips the door from my hand. I hold on tight and manage to close it softly.

A shiver runs through me as I stand in the dark kitchen, my hands clasped to my chest. My heart pounds in my ears, making it hard to hear. I take a deep breath to slow my pulse.

Voices murmur through a crack in the bedroom door. I walk softly toward the back, biting my lip as the floor creaks beneath me.

"I… I don't think this is a good idea." Bridie sounds slurred and tremulous.

"You backing out?" Kingfisher's bullying tone makes my hands clench into fists.

"I'm still married and… and…"

"And what? You don't like having a roof over your head? You don't like food on the table for your kids?"

"I have to be able to look at my kids."

"You want to look at them starve? You want to watch them be arrested by the cops when that fool Bleater you married peaches on you? You can keep that from happening. All you have to do is be nice."

"You make me sound like a trull."

"Oh, you ain't no trull, Bridie. A trull gives it up to a bunch of men. You're just giving it up to me. If you're nice tonight, I won't kick you out for nonpayment of rent this week. You let me move this trailer next to my place, and you and your kids won't want for nothing."

"What about Doreen?"

"I told you. Me and Doreen are through. Can't help it if she don't want to face facts."

"But her children – your children…"

"I'd be more worried about your own kids if I were you."

I inch along the dark hallway. Through the open door, I can see Kingfisher's broad back looming over my mother. Bridie sits on the edge of the bed, clutching her fringed shawl to her neck, her pale hand a stark contrast to her reddened cheeks. Slowly, her hand slides to her lap. The shawl slithers off her shoulders. Despair glimmers in her eyes as her lids close.

"That's my girl. You are one rum piece, you know that?" As he speaks, he tugs his shirttails out of his trousers.

I push open the door and launch forward, ramming into him with my shoulder as hard as I can.

Kingfisher gives a startled, "Oof," though he barely budges.

As he swings around, I leap backward, slamming into the wall to avoid him. The caravan shakes with the impact. Kingfisher teeters as he punches the air. Then he draws back his fist. I raise my forearms.

Bridie jumps to her feet and squeezes between us, spreading her arms to shield me. "What are you doing? How dare you hit my daughter?"

Kingfisher takes a step back, his chest heaving. "The girl jumped me. I didn't know who it was."

Bridie speaks over her shoulder in a sharp tone. "I told you to stay at the party. What are you doing here?"

I'll take my mother's anger over that horrid, submissive pose any day. "Stopping you from making the biggest mistake of your life." Bridie sighs. Her breath smells of stale beer. I grimace. "You're drunk."

Bridie's gaze sharpens. "I am your mother. Don't talk that way to me."

"If you're my mother, then act like it. My mother wouldn't let a rakehell turn her into a trollop."

Color drains from Bridie's cheeks. She looks away.

Kingfisher reaches around Bridie. "This is adult business, girl. Get out." He tries grabbing my arm.

Bridie pushes his hand away. "Don't touch my daughter."

"Tell her to get the hell out of here."

"No." Bridie's posture straightens. Her shoulders square. "I changed my mind. You should leave."

Joy sings through my body. All the planning and sneaking around has worked. I knew she wouldn't go through with it if I caught her in the act. I can't keep myself from gloating at Kingfisher's sour expression.

His eyes go piggy small. He shrugs. "This is my trailer. You change your mind, you pack your bags and hit the road. Now."

Bridie convulses. Her knees seem to give out as she sinks to the mattress.

My grin fades. Kingfisher is good at manipulation, but he hasn't reckoned on my determination. I sit beside Bridie and wrap my arm around her. "Mum, I'd rather live in the car than spend another night here. You're strong. We're strong. We'll figure something out. We always do. Please."

The Upright Man sneers, "Don't come crawling back here."

I glare up at him. "We won't."

"I mean it. You drive out that gate, you ain't coming back in."

Bridie covers her eyes. Her lips quiver.

I gently rub her forearm as I speak in a soothing tone. "Mum, think of Gerry and Matthew. What would they want you to do?"

"They'd want me to fight." A sigh wavers through her. "But I got so tired of fighting, of struggling, and this is where it got me. If Matthew saw me now, if he knew..." A tear rolls down her cheek. "If only he hadn't died. If only he and Gerry were still here."

"They're not, but they'd want us to carry on and be strong. We don't need Bill, we don't need," I thrust my chin toward Kingfisher. "We have each other. We'll figure something out."

"But we're skint. We don't even have enough to buy food."

"We do have money, remember? That money we got this morning. It's enough to get us out of here."

"Where will we go?"

Kingfisher sneers, "There's nowhere for you to go but here."

Tears fill her eyes again. Time to bring out the big guns. I squeeze her shoulder hard and sharpen my tone. "Mum, if we stay, I'll be forced to handfast with Mikey Boy."

Her spine stiffens. "What?" She glares at Kingfisher. "That wasn't part of our agreement."

He shrugs. "Girl's sixteen. Can't have her running around loose. I figured I'd let my boy find out if she's a virgin. Don't worry. If she is, I'll make 'em marry proper."

Fire sparks in Bridie's reddened eyes. She jumps to her feet, fists pressed into her hips. "Not my daughter." She takes a deep breath and shouts the words. "Not. My. Daughter. You bastard. Sod off. I'm done with you. To think I almost..." She shudders. "Sod off."

Kingfisher doesn't budge. "It's time the girl left and you and I finish our business."

"We have no business. Get out."

He still doesn't move.

"Then we'll leave. Come on, Penny." Bridie puts her arm around my shoulders. I can feel her tremble.

Kingfisher shifts so he blocks the door. "You ain't going nowhere. Not until we finish our business."

I step in front of my mother. "Stay away from her." My heart pounds so hard, I can barely hear. As soon as he gets close enough, I'll fake a knee to his groin, while he blocks that, I'll gouge his eyes and...

The front door swings open, slamming against the wall. My heart lifts. Lennon!

Kingfisher turns. Past his bulk, I see Kai running down the hall, followed by someone else, an adult... a woman.

"What the hell are you doing?" Doreen. I would recognize that shrill voice anywhere.

Kingfisher glares at her. "Get lost, woman. This is none of your business."

"I'm making it my business."

Kai squeezes past Kingfisher and spreads his arms to shield our mother and me.

"Where's Lennon?" I whisper.

"Don't know. He went to the playground to switch places with you, but you didn't come back, so I went out looking for you guys and ran into Doreen."

What happened to Lennon? Maybe Kingfisher set some of his men on him. The thought makes my chest hurt. I don't want to abandon him, but I can't leave my family.

Doreen shoves her way into the bedroom and stands before us, hands on her hips. She jerks her head toward Kingfisher. "He played you for a hob. I made up my mind to be square and stop him, but it seems your girl got here first."

Bridie looks down. Her voice falters. "Doreen, I'm so sorry. I don't have any money and Kingfisher, he… he…"

"He threw you under the bridge."

Kingfisher grabs hold of her arm. "Stow it, Doreen."

She shakes him off. "To hell with you. She has the right to know."

Bridie looks at them with suspicion. "What do you mean? Know what?"

Doreen jabs a finger at Kingfisher. "He told your Bleater husband that you're a Strowler and that you planned to drain his bank account before leaving him high and dry. He paid a caterer to take pictures of you and the Beggar Chief together and send them to your husband."

Bridie gasps. My mouth drops open. There are few crimes worse than betraying a fellow Strowler.

Kingfisher takes a step toward Doreen. Then the anger in his face shifts to indifference. He shrugs. "She's lying. She's jealous because I want to dump her for you."

"No, she's not," I jump in. "Mikey Boy told me it's your fault we're here."

Bridie rises to her feet. "You did this to us? You're the Upright Man. You're supposed to protect us. How could you?"

Kingfisher rubs his chin. His chest rises and falls as he

maintains his casual pose. "You ought to thank me. I saved you from a life of misery with that Bleater."

Bridie lays her hands on my and Kai's shoulders and gently pushes us aside. Then she steps forward to face Kingfisher, her every word ground with bitterness. "You threw me under the bridge and lured me here. You demanded money from me. Then you threaten to kick us out if I don't rut with you. And now you want me to thank you." She tilts her head, her green eyes blazing, as she draws back her hand.

He catches hold of her wrist and twists it, hard. She grimaces, but doesn't cry out.

Kai leaps forward, his fists raised. Kingfisher swings his free arm and slams him into Doreen. They crash into the closet door before tumbling to the floor. Blood spills from Kai's nose. Bridie cries out and tries to go to him, but Kingfisher holds on tight.

I ready my knee to smash into his bollocks, but as if reading my mind, he turns sideways, dragging Bridie along with him. This time, she whimpers in pain.

Confidence returns to Kingfisher's face. "I'll twist her arm out of its socket if you don't all calm down." He waits while Kai picks himself up and helps Doreen to her feet. "You three get lost." He nods toward Bridie. "Me and her got business to finish."

No one moves.

Kingfisher wrenches Bridie's arm again. Tears come to her eyes and she bites her lip as her face contorts with the effort to not cry out.

I grind my teeth, determined not to tremble or seem weak. There has to be something to fight him with. Some kind of threat. "You rape my mother, I'll tell my Uncle Oisin. He'll kill you."

"You tell anyone anything, I'll kill your mother and you brats. Now, stow it."

"No."

I brace myself, waiting for another threat or for him to strike with his free hand, but he just stands there staring at me. Then a look comes into his eyes, like panic. Breath hisses in his throat, but he can't seem to talk.

Lennon steps around him. He looks at me apologetically. "Sorry I'm late."

He's all right. Relief floods the fear coursing through my body. My knees quiver, but I manage to stay upright. Where the hell has he been? Part of me wants to jump into his arms and the other part wants to shove him into the wall. Instead, I take a deep breath to slow my pounding heart. "What did you do to him?

"I froze his pressure points. He won't be able to move for a couple of hours." While he speaks, he jabs Kingfisher's hand at a spot between his thumb and index finger.

Kingfisher's hand flops and Bridie snatches her wrist away. As she clutches it to her chest, rubbing the reddened flesh, his fingers contract as he tries grasping for her. Lennon's jabs the spot again, rendering the hand motionless.

"*Dim mak*," whispers Bridie.

Dim mak. I know the term. Matthew had the same skill, though I'd never seen him use it. It's a Two Dragon Clan skill, but one shared by lots of other Asian clans.

Lennon acts like he didn't hear her. "We better get out of here while we can."

Bridie rushes to Kai side and examines his nose. "Is it broken?"

Kai presses his sleeve to his nostrils to staunch the bleeding and replies with a muffled, "I don't think so."

"We'll get some ice on it just to be sure." She starts to head out of the bedroom.

"Wait." Kai lowers his arm. Blood trickles down to his chin as he speaks. "I've got news. Good news. Our phones are working again. I called my grandparents and they're sending us money. We can get out of here."

Bridie's face freezes. I hold my breath. If she refuses, I'll ask Lennon to stun her so we can carry her out. Then she glances at Kingfisher. "Good. Very good, but I don't want to discuss our future in front of him."

"Can he still hear?" asks Doreen.

Lennon nods. "He can hear, see and breathe. All the stuff that keeps him alive still works, but he can't talk or move."

A toxic smile spreads across her face. "Good." She marches over and stands before him. "While you were busy with your party, I packed up my and the girls' things and loaded the car. I'm taking the dog so you can't breed her no more. We're getting out and we're going where you'll never find us. I'd say I gave you the best years of my life, but they were bad years and so were you."

I breathe out a sigh of relief when she mentions the dog. Then she turns to Bridie and her next words tighten my throat again. "Have you got a mirror?"

Bridie's face stiffens. Then her eyes narrow. "I've got two we can use."

"Good." Doreen smirks at Kingfisher. "Take care of your boy first."

Kingfisher's breath wheezes in his throat. His eyes are maddened with helpless rage.

Bridie turns to Kai. "Let's get some ice for that nose and then you can tell us everything."

A chill prickles my skin. "Mum…"

Her look silences me. As much as I don't like what's about to happen, I'll take a vengeful Bridie over a submissive one any day.

Lennon whispers to me, "A mirror?"

I grab hold of his arm and tug him into the hall. I wait until everyone passes before I speak. "Never mind about that. Where were you?"

He ducks his head. "I'm really sorry. If I got here sooner, he wouldn't have been able to hurt Bridie and Kai."

"What happened? Did you run into Mikey Boy or something?"

He looks me in the eye, in a way that makes my heart sink. "My family caught up with me. I have to go."

Penny

"What are they doing?" whispers Lennon.

"Blood curse." I don't bother lowering my voice.

Neither Bridie nor Doreen pay me any mind. They're standing at the kitchen counter, Bridie with the square, silver compact mirror from her purse and Doreen holding the mirror from Bridie's face powder. They use red lipstick to write Kingfisher's name on each surface. Then each takes a knife and pricks her finger. A drop of blood falls on each mirror.

When they've finished, Bridie tosses her knife in the sink, but Doreen keeps hold of hers. We follow them back to the bedroom.

Kingfisher's breath hisses through his nose as they enter. Then they hold up the mirrors so he can see them. His eyes bulge and his chest heaves as he reddens with the effort to move.

"Mum," I say loud enough to make them pause. "What about the darkening of the soul?"

Bridie keeps her eyes on Kingfisher. "I'll risk darkening my soul if it means saving my children from this monster."

Doreen slices Kingfisher's thumb. Then she squeezes until a drop of blood falls on each mirror.

"Cool," whispers a wide-eyed Kai.

I spin on my heel and head back to the kitchen. Then I lean against the counter and close my eyes. "Kingfisher, may kings respect you…" The words fall into the sink and go down the drain. I can't bless him.

Lennon leans beside me with owlish eyes. I sigh. "You take a mirror, write someone's name on it and smear it with your mingled blood. If the mirror breaks, he'll die within seven days. After that, whoever cast the curse will die soon after."

He sucks in his breath. "That's some serious shit. Do you believe it?"

I don't want to answer, almost as if saying so will make it real.

"All he has to do is stay away from us," says Bridie as she and Doreen return to the kitchen. "If he tries anything, I break the mirror. Simple as that."

"And die." I choke on the words.

"Worth it," Bridie says as she pats my cheek. Then she reaches into a cupboard and pulls out a box of cling wrap. She and Doreen use almost the whole roll to pad the mirrors against breaking.

"All right then." Doreen gives a curt nod.

"Walk in peace," Bridie says. The other woman doesn't reply as she heads out the door. "Ah well." She turns to us. "We best get cracking."

"Don't say that word," I mutter. She ignores me.

Packing up is similar to when we were kicked out by Bill, except this time we're loomed over by Kingfisher as we shove our belongings into suitcases and plastic bags, his enraged eyes tracking our movements. I "accidentally" step on his feet a few times. Kai intentionally punches him and would've done more damage if Lennon hadn't pulled him off.

Lennon. He stays with us, helping us pack while keeping a close eye on Kingfisher. I can't tell if what happened with his family is good or bad, and he's not saying. His glasses are gone and that hunted look in his eyes has been replaced by a solemn, faraway gaze.

It's so unfair. I want to feel happy and triumphant, and laugh in Kingfisher's face. Instead, my heart squeezes every time Lennon and I brush shoulders. What if I never see him again? How can I say goodbye without telling him how I feel? How do I feel? Do I love him?

I stop in my tracks as my face grows hot. No, I don't love Lennon. I can't. It hurts too much.

"Bedroom's clear," Bridie announces as she comes down the hall carrying a final bag.

"Bathroom's done, too," says Kai.

"Anything left?"

"Just one thing." I open a cabinet and carefully lift out my sewing machine. Wherever we're going, hopefully I can start designing clothes again. I need something to keep me busy, so I won't think about what might have been.

Lennon gives me a gentle smile before taking the sewing machine from my hands and heading outside. The perfect boy and I'm losing him right now. My nose tingles. I rub it hard to keep my eyes from filling with tears.

Bridie picks up her phone, which was charging on the kitchen counter. She turns it on and stares at the screen. Then she holds the phone to her ear, frowning as she listens.

"What is it?" I ask.

"A message from your step…" She clears her throat. "From Bill. He's in trouble with the police because of that video. He's begging us to come back, no strings attached."

"I don't want to go back." I say the words so fast they run together.

"I don't, either." Her thumb slides across the screen. Then

she smiles. "Matthew's parents wired us some money. More than enough to find a decent place to stay for the next few nights."

I'm still a little surprised by that. Maybe they know Kai won't accept their charity if it doesn't include his mother.

Bridie wraps the mirror again, this time with a kitchen towel, before placing it gingerly into a side pocket inside her purse. We exchange looks. "There's no curse until the mirror breaks, so stop fearing for my soul."

"What if it breaks accidentally?"

"It won't. I'll make sure of it."

"You'll have to carry that thing for the rest of your life."

"Or his." She takes a final glance down the other end of the caravan. Kingfisher casts a wide shadow on the hall wall. She shudders. "Let's get out of here."

The place feels like a tomb. We'd come so close to being buried alive. I try to think of some final insult to hurl at the man who tried digging our grave. Is he worth the effort? No. In fact, leaving without a word and closing the door behind him feels incredibly satisfying.

I climb into the backseat with Lennon, except not really because there are several plastic bags full of clothes between us. I can't hold his hand or lean my shoulder against his, or whisper in his ear. As we drive through the Nest, the party is still in full swing. Mac in the Box must have joined in the fun since no one challenges us when Kai gets out and opens the gate.

Once the car pulls onto the main road, Bridie lets out a huge sigh and whispers, "Thank God." She gives her head a brisk shake. "All right, I'll get some gas and we'll find a decent place to spend the night."

"Can you drop me off at a light rail station?" asks Lennon.

The pulse in my throat starts to throb. I swallow hard to make it stop.

Bridie glances at him in the rearview mirror. "Lennon, you're welcome to come with us, wherever we go. More than welcome."

He glances down for a moment, almost as if he was seriously considering her words. But when he looks up, his eyes are resolute. "Thanks, but I can't. I have to go back to my family. It's time."

"I understand," she murmurs sympathetically. I want to scream: No, you don't. "Why don't I take you there?"

"No. I have to go back on my own."

"You're sure?"

"Yeah."

My chest hurts. It feels as if all the oxygen has been sucked out of the car. I crack open my window. The cold air feels good on my hot cheeks. Then Lennon reaches across the plastic bags for my hand. For a moment, I want to snatch it away and punish him for leaving me. If I do that, I'll only be hurting myself, though clasping his hand and squeezing it hard has its own sweet pain.

When we reach a stoplight, Bridie turns to Kai. "It's good of your grandparents to send us that money. I don't like taking charity, but this can't be helped. Besides, I suppose they might feel a bit guilty."

"Why?" he asks. "Because they were never nice to you?"

"No." The word holds a trace of bitterness. She pauses as the light turns green and the car accelerates. "I mean because they encouraged me to marry Bill and move to San Francisco. They told me we should make a fresh start in a new place." She gives a soft snort. "They can't be blamed. Who knew it would turn out like this? And now we're off to make a new start."

"Can we go back to London?" asks Kai.

"Possibly. We'll see."

I should be overjoyed. Instead, I want to cry.

She pulls into a gas station on Third Street. While she fills the tank, I walk with Lennon across the street to the light rail platform. We head for the far end, to a bench surrounded by Plexiglas walls, and huddle into the corner. My throat squeezes too tight for me to talk. Our foreheads touch. I close my eyes and open my lips with a soft gasp. Our kisses make me press against him as our arms wind around each other. It feels so good and hurts so much. How can I feel this way, knowing I'll never see him again?

The rails began to rattle. The train is a block away, stopped at the light.

I clutch his shoulders, my fingers digging into his jacket. "Can't you at least tell me your real name?"

His whisper is so soft, I almost don't catch it. "Paul." Then he sucks in his breath. "But that's not me anymore. I'm Lennon."

"Paul." It doesn't sound like him. "You're right. You're Lennon."

His small smile quickly disappears.

The train starts moving. I speak quickly. "Which clan?"

He shakes his head. "It's better if you don't know. I'm in a lot of trouble. I don't know if I'll survive."

"Let me help you."

"You have. Letting me stay with you, giving me hope." He clasps my hand and holds on tight, his brown eyes so sad. "I hope I see you again someday."

The train pulls into the station. The doors slide open.

Tears fill my eyes. "I don't know where I'm going to be."

"Me, neither."

He stands. Kisses my cheek. Releases my hand. Backs away until he has to step aboard the train. The doors close. He stares at me through the window as the train rumbles out of the station.

He's gone.

I draw my knees to my chest and bite my trembling lip.

Kai runs across the platform, his face lit with a smile. "I got a message from my grandparents. They're buying us plane tickets. We're going back to London."

I blink. The tears slide down my cheeks. I finally got what I wanted. "Good."

Lennon

I wipe my eyes on my sleeve. It feels like a hole has been dug in my chest. This is almost as bad as losing Mom and Dad. I'd finally found someone to trust – and I could have trusted her. I could have told her everything. That might have made me feel better, but what about her? Penny and her family have enough problems. They don't need the Two Dragon Clan breathing down their necks. So, I stay silent, I say goodbye, and I lose my best friend forever. I guess I should feel good about that, but I feel like shit.

I have to pull myself together. I can't face Tony looking like a crybaby. I wipe my face again and move into another car where no one has seen me look so weak.

I planned to switch from the K to the N at the ballpark, but when the train stops at the station, a throng of baseball fans climbs aboard, with tons more waiting on the platform. They're acting all cocky and rowdy, so the Giants must've won. Are they in the playoffs? I usually pay attention to stuff like that, but now, I don't have a clue. It's a weird feeling, to not care, to not want to listen to the loud chatter of the people pressing close around me. I want earphones so I can drown them out.

I wait until the train reaches the Civic Center station to switch to the N. It's still crowded, but the passengers are less noisy, allowing me some space for my thoughts.

Pay your obligation to the girl and return to your family.

I don't think I can ever pay my obligation to Penny. If it weren't for my parents, I would have said fuck all and stayed with her family. I feel like part of my heart is still sitting in the car with them.

Power without wisdom is useless and you are not wise.

I'm not going to become wise in the next ten minutes. Mastering the Dragon Shout has given me some leverage, but I can't take on the whole clan. So what can I do? I lean my head against the cold glass window, letting it roll with the motion as the train heads out of downtown and into the Sunset district. I've been drained of so much energy – internal and external – I want to go somewhere and sleep for a month. My eyelids droop. I blink hard, because if they close, I'll see a girl with green eyes and a brave smile who dances like a fairy.

A shaky breath rattles my chest as the N reaches the stop at Ninth and Irving. I push myself down the steps and off the train. As it trundles away, I take the cardboard cup sleeve out of my pocket and stare at Penny's phone number. I want to keep it so bad, it hurts. You know what will hurt worse? Someone in my family finding it and tracking her down. As I head down the street, I toss the sleeve into a trashcan.

It feels like I'm throwing away my heart.

When I reach Auntie Cat's place, the front door is unlocked. I step inside soundlessly and stand in the entryway with my arms folded. The hall light is on, but it's so quiet, I wonder if anyone is home. Going to the right will lead to the bedrooms and the kitchen. Going to the left leads to the front room. I turn that way, but can't seem to want to make myself move.

Soft footsteps sound behind me. I turn. Auntie Cat's steps falter. We stare at each other for a moment. She's wearing jeans and a dark pullover sweater, and her hair is tugged back off her pale face. I'm pretty sure she's older than Bridie, but she seems younger. She's never married or had kids, and sure as hell didn't sign up for the mess I brought on her, which makes me feel even worse.

"You're back." Her mouth stretches as if she's trying to smile, but can't.

I take off my shoes, hoping she sees this as more than politeness, that I intend to stay. I place my Vans on the shelf beside the door, next to a pair of trainers that look way too big to belong to her.

"Are you hungry?" she asks.

I shake my head. The pizza sits like a lump in my stomach.

"Your brother is waiting for you."

"He's not my brother." I speak louder than I intended. Then I wince, knowing Tony must have heard.

"He thinks of you as his brother. This has been a very hard time for him," She sucks in her breath, "For all of us."

I feel like such a little shit. All I've thought about is my pain and loss. I've barely considered how other people must feel. I clear my throat, but my words still come out raspy. "Dad was your brother and Mom was your friend. I'm really sorry about…" There's so much to be sorry about, I don't know where to begin. "About everything."

The chill thaws from her eyes and she gives a little nod.

I reach out to her using the Silent Speech. *Tony said his mom has cancer. Is that true?*

Yes. Pancreatic cancer. It's inoperable. She's dying.

Karma is a bitch and so is cancer. Auntie Sylvia will pay for her crime with lots of pain and suffering. I try feeling satisfied, but can't. Tony and Aaron will suffer as well, and Mom still won't have any justice.

Whatever you think of Sylvia, don't take it out on your cousins.

I don't blame them. But I still want Tony and Aaron to acknowledge their mother's guilt. I speak aloud. "Can I stay with you?"

Auntie Cat's hands go to her hips. "If I can trust you not to run away again."

"I won't, as long as no one tries forcing me to go back to Hong Kong."

"As long as I have custody of you, I won't let that happen, I promise."

Some of the tightness eases from my chest. "I'll see him now."

In the front room, Tony stands like a sentinel, staring out the bay window. Has he been standing there every day since I left, knowing this is the one place I'd eventually turn up? My stomach drops. I owe him some kind of apology, but I don't have words for it.

I stop in the middle of the floor as he turns. We stare at each other. Tony doesn't blink. Neither do I. It feels weird. Almost like we're equals. Are we? Do I really think he has nothing more to teach me? Suddenly, I wish I could drop to my knees, bow my head and humbly ask Big Brother for forgiveness.

Instead, I perch on the edge of the sofa. "You okay?"

After a moment, Tony sits in the armchair, rigid as a soldier. There's no taking the chill from those eyes. "Where have you been all this time?"

I can refuse to answer or lie, but I don't want to. I'm tired of being a fake, both as Lennon and as Paul. It's time my relatives know who I am and what I'm capable of. Auntie Cat lingers by the door. "Auntie, sit down, okay?"

After a moment's hesitation, she sits beside me. Neither she nor Tony look at each other. I can feel the tension between them. Our family is divided and it's all because of me. I suck in air. No, it's the murderers who are responsible, not me.

"Most of the time, I was in the Haight."

Tony shakes his head. "We checked all the shelters. You weren't in any of them."

"I wasn't in a shelter. I hooked up with a gang of kids. I begged and stole."

Now Tony and Auntie Cat look at each other, exchanging surprised glances. I roll my eyes. "How do you think I survived? Would you be happier if I said I ate out of garbage cans? Cuz I did that, too."

Tony stands and glares down at me. "Who did you steal from?"

I stand and meet that glare. "I posed as a hooker and robbed guys who wanted blowjobs."

Auntie Cat gasps.

Tony blinks. His lips thin into a tight line before he speaks. "You're lying. Trying to shock us."

"Nope. It's the truth."

"Does the Beggar Chief know this?"

Now I blink.

"John Walks Long claims he'd taken in a street kid named Lennon who fit your description. He refused to tell me where you went."

I swallow hard. I've been taught that honorable men don't lie. Now I know they twist the truth. Still, it's strange how easily the words come. "The Beggar Chief knew me as Lennon."

"Did he know you as the Dragon Son?"

"I'm not the Dragon Son. I'm Lennon, a beggar and a thief who walks the Wayward Way."

Auntie Cat jumps up and steps between us. She addresses Tony. "There's no point in this. He's been through a lot. You can talk to him another time. He's promised to stay with me. Let's leave it at that."

Tony doesn't budge. "You are the Dragon Son and you will walk the Glory Road as a true *Xia*."

Neither do I. "Tell Head Elder this. I want to know why he ordered your parents to kill my mother and father. And I want him and them to face the justice of the clan. Until then, I am Lennon, not Paul. There will be no Dragon Son."

I'm pretty sure he's going to punch me and I'm going to let him. My way of apology. But then he turns and strides out of the room. Moments later, the front door slams shut.

If we turn aside from righteousness or forget kindliness, may Heaven and Earth destroy us.

Auntie Cat grabs hold of my shoulders. "I know you're hurt, but if you continue on like this, your brother won't forgive you."

My eyes fill with tears. I take a sharp breath to force them back. I don't need righteousness or kindness. I need justice, and if this is what it takes, then, "Good."

The story continues in Folly: Dragons of the Crossroads Book 2. When Penny and Lennon reunite, they spurn the laws of the Crossroads to form a perilous alliance. Their search for answers will take them on painful journeys and their quest for justice will pit them against family and clan. Forbidden romance provides the perfect cover for their actions, but can they resist the folly of falling in love?

To find out more about Dragons of the Crossroads and to purchase more books in the series, please go to loriwriter.com.

Acknowledgements

I want to thank Jennifer Gagliardi and Meej Jupin for their support and encouragement throughout the years. Thanks also to my friends and family for all the love. Thank you to L.J. Redding for proofreading this manuscript.

I want to acknowledge the following sources for research and inspiration for FAKE and the world of the Crossroads. My heartfelt gratitude and appreciation to them all.

- Wuxia, the literary genre of Chinese martial arts, including novels, movies, TV shows, and games. The Beggar Clan is a creation of wuxia and can be found in all its forms.
- *The Water Margin* by Shi Nai'an
- *The Return of the Condor Heroes* by Jin Yong
- *Gypsy Boy* and *Gypsy Boy On the Run* by Mikey Walsh
- *The Gypsies* by Jan Yoors

Strowler speech is based on Thieves' Cant. My main source is the website of Stephen Hart: pascalbonenfant.com.

The following song lyrics and oaths in this book are attributed to these sources which are all in the public domain.

- Chapter 3, song lyrics, "Raggle Taggle Gypsy"

- Chapter 3, song lyrics, "Black is the Color"
- Chapter 4, Oath of Fraternity, from *The Romance of the Three Kingdoms* by Luo Guanzhong
- Chapter 19, song lyrics, "A Begging I Will Go"
- Chapter 19, song lyrics, "A Beggar I'll Be"
- Chapter 19, The Oath of the Canting Crew, from *The Life of Bampfylde Moore Carew* by Robert Goadby

About the Author

Lori Saltis left her heart in San Francisco. She goes to visit it whenever she can afford the bridge toll. She's been an indie author since 2016. She's very passionate about the themes of alienation and found family. Her favorite genre is fantasy because who doesn't want to believe they'll look up in the sky one day and see a dragon?

To find out more about the world of the Crossroads, check out her website loriwriter.com.